THE CRYING GAME

As bombs descend on their home, fifteen-year-old Trixie and her young brother, Teddy, are fighting a more private battle against their violent father. Fleeing Portsmouth, towards the safety of a relative's home in Gosport, Trixie's luck finally seems about to change as fate introduces her to Jem, a handsome young market trader who takes her under his wing and into his heart. When Trixie's uncle sends Teddy away under strange circumstances, she finds some comfort in Jem's unfaltering adoration. But Trixie's heart never strays from her beloved little brother who seems lost for ever. Until Teddy's found, her own happiness remains a world away.

THE CRYING GAME

THE CRYING GAME

by

June Hampson

Magna Large Print Books
Long Preston, North Yorkshire,
BD23 4ND, England.

British Library Cataloguing in Publication Data.

Hampson, June
    The crying game.

        A catalogue record of this book is
        available from the British Library

        ISBN   978-0-7505-3850-3

First published in Great Britain in 2013 by Orion Books
an imprint of The Orion Publishing Group Ltd.

Copyright © June Hampson 2013

Cover illustration © Nik Keevil by arrangement with
Arcangel Images

The moral right of June Hampson to be identified as the author of this
work has been asserted by her in accordance with the Copyright,
Designs and Patents Act, 1988

Published in Large Print 2014 by arrangement with
Orion Publishing Group

Magna Large Print is an imprint of Library Magna Books Ltd.

Printed and bound in Great Britain by
T.J. (International) Ltd., Cornwall, PL28 8RW

1860932

For Bertie, for his unconditional love

Everyone chases at happiness, not noticing that happiness is right at their heels.
– Bertolt Brecht

Oh God! That one might read the book of fate.
– King Henry IV Part II
William Shakespeare

Chapter One

'Shut that noise!'

Trixie's father's thunderous voice accompanied the well-aimed kick at her heavily pregnant mother sprawled helplessly on the floor, petrifying Trixie.

At the same time, 'Leave 'er alone!' Teddy screamed, heaving his skinny arm backwards and throwing with all his might.

The chopper seemed to embed itself in the side of Dad's head then drop like a stone to the floor. Dad buckled at the knees, a look of great surprise on his face, and then he concertinaed down to lie face up over the axe, as though hiding the terrible instrument of his death.

Silence filled the sparsely furnished scullery. Even Mum, huddled on the floor near the fireplace, where she'd been trying to shield herself from Dad's heavy leather workboots, stopped her dreadful screaming. Her unblinking eyes took in the still form and the blood oozing from Dad's head. A glassy look filled her watery blue eyes as though she'd suddenly become unseeing. Outside, on the street, footsteps and voices could be heard. The siren had wailed, announcing the moment for people to make their way to Portsmouth's air-raid shelters and safety from the bombs.

Trixie looked across the room at her brother, now sheltering behind the upturned ragged sofa

11

and making hideous sounds as he cried and hic-cupped into the torn sleeve of his jumper while muttering, 'I didn't mean to 'urt him, just to stop him.'

Trixie cautiously stepped towards the figure on the floor and looked down, half expecting her father to open his eyes, maybe even to leap up and clout her one. Her heart was beating fast. His blood had trickled across the floor, its brightness at odds with the dull pattern on the worn lino. He was quite still.

He looked peaceful. The red kerchief that all the boatmen wore gave her father's handsome face, tanned by the open air, a rakish look. Although sweat stained, its colour was brighter than the blood.

A sudden spark bursting noisily from the apple-wood fire burning in the grate made Trixie jump and its noise brought her back to reality.

Teddy had killed their dad.

She knelt down and listened to his heart through his thick navy blue crew-necked jersey, but all she could hear was her own thumping against her chest. Another spark crackled loudly from the firewood as it jumped to the lino. Trixie stood up and put her foot over the burning splinter, her haste causing her sandal to kick against a tin mug with drops of weak tea inside. A piece of potato nestled next to a lump of carrot trodden into the rag rug. She could still smell the remains of the meatless stew that was to have been their supper even though the saucepan lay empty and upturned on the floor where Dad had thrown it.

She looked over at Teddy. Her brother had

stopped sniffling. They had to get their father's body out of the house. To leave him here would cause all kinds of problems.

'Is he dead?' Teddy's voice was shaking.

Trixie felt all the air leave her body as she looked down again at the man who had made their lives a misery. Never again, drunk or sober, would their father ever beat any of them. A feeling of thankfulness stole over her.

'Yes,' she whispered, 'he's dead.'

'What'll we do? The police'll take me away!' Teddy was rocking his body backwards and forwards and staring at her as though she had all the answers. Trixie looked at her mother, slumped against the wall, thin hands clutching her swollen belly, supporting its heaviness. Her eyes in her wax-like face were blank.

Her mother needed help. The beating she'd received had stunned her.

And ten-year-old Teddy was out of his mind with shock at what he'd accomplished with one thoughtless action.

Trixie felt her brain flood with adrenalin. It was up to her to protect her mother and brother.

'Grab Dad's legs, Teddy. We'll drag 'im downstairs to the winkle barrow and get 'im out of 'ere.'

With her heart beating so loudly she was sure her brother could hear it, Trixie bent forward and slid her arms beneath the big man's shoulders and heaved. The smell of damp cloth and beer rose strongly to greet her. The bile rose inside her as her fine blonde hair fell forward to mingle stickily with the bloody wound at the side of her father's head.

Trixie, fifteen years old, was faced with disposing of her father's body so that her brother wouldn't be taken away for murdering him. She shook her head to dislodge her hair from her father's congealing blood and screwed her eyes tightly shut, willing herself not to lose her courage to protect those she loved.

When she opened her eyes she saw the scullery with its dresser and a few precious blue and white plates still sitting on its shelves. She saw the overturned table and mismatched cutlery spread across the lino and she saw Teddy hadn't moved except to continue rocking backwards and forwards.

Anger suddenly swept through her. 'I can't do this all on my own. *You've got to help me,*' she cried. Teddy looked at her, tears welling in his eyes. He's just a kid, she thought; he's just a kid.

Somewhere near, in Pompey's city, a bomb exploded. Trixie jumped. The building quivered and dust shook itself in the room then began settling like snow. Red and orange flared against the blackout curtains. The shadeless bulb hanging from the centre of the ceiling swung crazily, moving in a dance of its own creation.

Teddy too was scared by the closeness of the explosion. The boy's face was as white as parchment, his eyes wide as he thoughtlessly babbled, 'I didn't mean to kill 'im. Don't let them take me away. I didn't mean to kill 'im.' Trixie sprang forward and delivered a sharp slap that echoed round the scullery. Teddy's hand went to his face and it was as if the force of her smack had wakened him from a dream. Trixie, satisfied he had regained his senses, snapped, 'Thank God the All Clear hasn't sounded. When he's found, people will think he got caught in the raid. With a bit of luck we'll be out of the city and on our way by then.' She watched and sighed as Teddy scratched his dirty blond head; the nits were biting again. No matter, she thought, how many times their mother washed the buggers out, they came back to haunt Teddy. Tears had flooded the little boy's eyes. She gathered him to her thin body and felt him relax against her. 'I know you didn't want to hurt him,' she murmured. 'You just wanted to stop 'im beltin' ten bales of shit out of our mum.'

A soft moan from their mother caused Trixie to look towards the hearth where she was huddled.

'Chucking the axe at Dad's head wasn't the right way to stop the bugger, though,' Trixie said. Pushing him away, she knelt and picked up the faded patchwork quilt from the floor and went over to stand looking down at her mother. Already bruises of blue and welts of blood red were appearing on the thin woman's face and neck. 'Got to go out, Mum,' Trixie said softly, bending and tucking the quilt snugly around her. 'I won't be long.' She kissed the woman's damp forehead hung about with wispy bits of fair hair. Trixie could see her mother wouldn't move while she was gone, might even welcome the peace after the aftermath of the row. 'You,' Trixie looked towards Teddy and her voice became firmer. 'Help me.'

The noise from falling bombs hadn't let up as Teddy tried grabbing hold of his father's feet. Together, this time, they managed to manoeuvre the weighty form down the scullery steps and pull him into the yard. Tipping the hand cart Trixie

15

was able to hoist the body on to its flat bed. She quickly covered her father with a tarpaulin sheet.

The smell of cordite and the bright flashes from the bombing cut through the mist from the sea and the haze of bomb dust. Trixie stood with her fingers on the handles of the winkle cart.

God, how she'd feared this bully of a man, she thought, but fearing him didn't mean it was right to throw him away like a discarded fish and chip newspaper. But what else could she do? She *must* keep the family together. Teddy mustn't be taken from them.

Suddenly the buildings about her rippled with the aftershock of yet another bomb dropped by the German Luftwaffe. It barely missed the target of the Portsmouth Dockyard that supported the Royal Navy with dry docks big enough for the world's largest and most powerful battleships. Thousands of men and women worked there, at the base, and in the victualling and armament yards overlooking the murky waters of the Solent. Teddy's voice cut into her thoughts.

'I didn't mean. I thought he was goin' to kill her.'

'Shut up, Teddy.' Her voice was weary. She stared at the snail-like smears of blood trailing down the stone steps. 'When we get back we'll clear up. Leave the place looking as though nothing happened. But now you get the barrow outside the yard and into the street and don't let anyone see you. Make sure you put the blackout curtain back against the door while I take a last look at Mum.'

Trixie ran back up the steps to the scullery.

Broken crockery littered the floor and underfoot the sticky mess of food caused her sandals to cling limpet-like to the lino. The meal had been meatless, because her father had drunk away the money for food and rent. The letter from the landlord, giving them notice to quit for rent arrears, lay on the floor where it had fluttered from her father's hands after he had read its fateful news. Trixie picked it up and slipped it in her pocket. The ensuing row between her parents had ended with her trying to hide behind the battered sofa, her mother broken and bloody on the floor and Teddy throwing the axe he'd been using to split tomorrow's firewood at his father's head.

Trixie didn't think she'd ever forget the look of surprise on her father's face as the weapon found its mark. He'd crumpled to the floor like a stone down a well. It had all happened so quickly.

Trixie went over to her mother; it was as she'd thought: eyes closed now, the woman was sleeping.

She turned and made for the stairs. Disposing of her father's body was the next thing to do. And then they must leave this place, their home opposite the Portsmouth ferry where her father worked as a boatman on the small, squat tugs that plied passenger trade between Portsmouth and Gosport. Albert True would be missed. Despite his heavy drinking he never missed a day's work and like most bullies, he was an affable man in public.

Teddy wouldn't be able to cope with the questions that would be levelled at him about his father's disappearance. To lie would be anathema and sooner or later everyone would know he had

17

killed his own father. Teddy would be taken away, put into care, possibly never to see his mother or her again. He wouldn't survive, neither mentally nor physically.

She switched off the electric light. They would find another place to live. Night flittings during the war were commonplace with bombs destroying homes. Thank God their school was closed. One of the classrooms had been hit during a night-time raid. There were no casualties but it did mean that both she and Teddy wouldn't be missed until the school reopened and possibly not even then. They would have a new address, a new school for Teddy and new lives for the three of them and the coming baby. And freedom from Dad's fists. Trixie closed the door behind her. She must make the new beginning happen.

'Ain't you frightened of the bombs?'

Trixie looked down at her brother. Despite the blackout she could see the tear streaks on his face. His big blue eyes were opened wide and he lifted a grubby hand to scratch at his head. His other hand was clenched tightly on the handle of the cart that was solidly built with wooden wheels that trundled noisily over the cobbles of the Hard.

To make money they helped their mother when the tide was out, picking winkles from the rocks that fringed the jetty and pontoon where the ferry-boats landed. Cockles, too, could be teased from the sand and mud at the shoreline. After their mother had washed and cooked the delicacies, leaving the scullery smelling freshly of the sea, Trixie and her brother would sit on the bollards near the gates of the Dockyard and wait for passers-by to approach the barrow. Cockles or winkles placed between slices of fresh bread and marge was a delicious meal and soon all the fruits of the sea would be sold.

'Not much point. I reckon if one of Hitler's bombs 'as got my name on it, it'll find me, won't it?'

He gave her a nod. 'Where we takin' 'im?'

'I reckon the railway embankment is far enough, don't you?'

The boy nodded again.

'I want to get back to Mum as quickly as we can,' Trixie said. 'I think she's in a bad way this time.' Trixie feared for the unborn child. Her mother lacked energy. Trixie remembered when Teddy had been born her mother was always happy and busy.

For a while, apart from flares lighting up the skies and the steady thwump of far-off bombs finding targets, the ominous silence was punctuated only by the barrow's creaking wheels as they pushed their heavy burden along the narrow streets. Without the usual busy crush of people, the Hard had an eerie, misty presence.

'The air-raid shelters in Queen Street will be filled with people hoping to save their lives,' said Trixie. 'We've got to get this done before the All Clear sounds.'

Across the playing fields flickering searchlights lit the skies as bombs fell from the growl of planes.

'Here, I think.' Trixie pulled the barrow to a halt and put her hand on top of the tarpaulin to stop the body from sliding. Bushes and privet hedges at the base of the embankment made a shelter for the cart. Trixie looked about her. The railway line loomed above. There seemed to be no one on the road.

Teddy's voice sounded reedy in the darkness. 'Shall I hold the barrow still and wait for you to tip it so he slides off gently?'

'Don't think it matters to him one way or the other,' she said, 'whether he falls carefully.' But she was moved by Teddy's thoughtfulness all the same.

Together they watched as the heavy form slid, then fell to the earth to lie lumpen as a log. Trixie picked up the tarpaulin, folded it and set it back on the upright barrow.

Teddy was staring at his father's body. 'We can't just leave him. Shouldn't we cover him or say a prayer, or something?'

Trixie narrowed her eyes. 'We can't tuck him up like he's sleeping. It's got to look like he crawled in there and died.' She let out a huge sigh. After all the unhappiness this man had caused them, Teddy's kind heart pricked at her conscience. 'You can pray if you want.' Her voice was snippy. 'He's leaving Mum with her mind half gone and I've been thrashed so many times to within an inch of me life I couldn't care less.' Teddy snuggled against her. Her heart melted. 'Go on then, you say what you want and I'll sing along with you. But we daren't linger. When the siren goes there'll be people everywhere. We need to hurry back to Mum.'

After they had both recited the Lord's Prayer, Teddy started singing, '*There is a green hill far away*.' Trixie's eyes filled with tears. It was the only hymn he knew all the way through. She joined in, careful not to let her strong voice ring out in the darkness. Then, as the last notes died away she said, 'That was a nice thing for you to want to do. You're a good boy.' She put her hand beneath his chin, tipped it up and looked down at him. 'I want you to run home now as fast as you can. I think we've left Mum for long enough. I'll bring the barrow back.'

Teddy looked down at the still form on the ground. 'We gonna just leave him?'

Trixie nodded. 'Best thing,' she said. 'Scoot.'

He lingered, looking at the body. 'I didn't mean to hurt him.'

'I know. But Mum needs us now,' she said. 'Buzz off.'

When she was sure he was gone she bent down and, though hating to touch him, rifled through her father's pockets. She didn't want Teddy seeing her search her father for money, money that he might have left on his body from his foray into the pub. Besides, she needed to be alone, to think over all that had happened and to be sure the next steps she took were the right ones, not just for herself but for Teddy and her mother.

The hymn they'd sung ran around her brain. Forever now, she knew, when she heard that music she would remember the reason she and Teddy had sung it. As a child, when she had helped her mother around the house, the two of them had sung happily in their pure, clear voices. But as the years had flown and the bitterness had grown her mother's voice had become silenced by the hate

21

and drink that fuelled her father's temper.

Not so Trixie; she had often found herself humming or singing a piece of music whenever she felt unhappy. At first she didn't realise she did it. Singing softly in times of loneliness, or after her father had hit her and she'd escaped to another part of the house to be away from his pounding fists. The music lifted her thoughts, stopped the tears and helped her forget the pain of an empty stomach or the weight of her father's hands on her body. In her head the songs and their stories of love, sadness and happiness gave her hope to cling to as she envisaged herself as the heroine of the songs. She could be a costermonger, laughingly telling the world about her bunch of coconuts; she could be a serviceman talking about his love, the Rose of Picardy. The music gave Trixie the chance to escape from her miserable surroundings and be anyone she chose for the duration of the song. But she wasn't singing now as she searched her dead father's pockets.

Her collection of money from her father amounted to very little. 'Damn,' she said quietly. They needed as much cash as she could find and she prayed she might discover more in the house.

Standing she looked down at the man who seemed to bear no relation to the smiling person in the photographs she had seen in the worn shoebox her mother kept solely for all important documents.

One snap Trixie clearly remembered was of the handsome moustached man looking proudly down into her mother's eyes. His hand was on her shoulder and his face was full of love and longing. How had it happened that the love her father so clearly felt then for her mother, had been replaced by disgust and violence?

And how could a man of his breadth and stature justify knocking his children about so that some days she and Teddy had bunked off school for fear their bruises and welts would be seen by their peers or the teachers and commented on?

Trixie tried to hold back her tears. Whatever pain this man had inflicted upon them, he was still her father.

'I'm sorry, Dad,' she said. 'I wish things could have been different.' The sound of her voice brought her thoughts back into focus.

The barrow. She must get the cart back to the house so they could start loading it with their belongings. At any moment the All Clear could sound and it wouldn't look good, her being discovered with her father's dead body.

After slipping the coins into her pocket she hoisted up the handles of the cart and began pushing it back towards the Hard.

The All Clear sounded its mournful cry as she was within sight of home.

Immediately Portsmouth's streets became a hive of activity again with doors opening blinds rolling up from shop windows, people running – some laughing, some serious. Most were praying as they emerged from the shelter, hoping to find their homes still intact. No one glanced her way or took any notice of the schoolgirl pushing an empty barrow, until she reached the pub.

'Hello, Trixie, love. Bit late for you to be out selling, ain't it?'

Trixie's heart began thumping faster. 'Not selling winkles, Rosa. Our Teddy left the barrer out.' There it was, the first lie. To Rosa, the barmaid from Nelson's, the public house where her dad regularly drank his ale. The blonde was dusting off the windowsills with a bedraggled ostrich-feather duster. Trixie noticed one of the lines painted in eyebrow pencil up the back of her shapely legs was crooked.

'Can't leave valuables about outside, love. That cart could walk during the night.' Rosa's ample figure swayed as the duster danced in tune to the wireless and the melodic voice of Bing Crosby singing 'Swinging on a Star'. Always a cheerful body, Rosa stopped dusting and said, 'Didn't see your dad tonight.' A waft of heavy flowery perfume floated towards Trixie as Rosa continued, 'He was in earlier. Him and Mickey Payne was 'aving quite a disagreement about them new buzz bombs raining down in Britain.'

'Dunno nothin' about that.' Trixie shrugged her shoulders. She didn't want to get caught up in a conversation that could force her to tell more lies. She began moving the barrow forward to show her part in the conversation was over.

'Nice man, your dad,' called Rosa thoughtfully.

'Night,' Trixie called. When she reached their yard door she used the front of the barrow as a battering ram and pushed it through, over the step, and into the yard. The stone steps were wet, the blood washed away. She could smell carbolic soap. Teddy had been working hard.

Up in the scullery, Teddy was washing the floor where his father's body had lain. He looked up at her. She nodded at him, then turned towards their mother, who hadn't moved.

'I thought it best to wait for you to come back before getting stuff together.'

'You did well, Teddy.' Trixie's voice was soft.

She knelt down beside the woman and picked up her cold hand, warming it with her own. 'I'm going to wash the blood off your face, Mum.'

Teddy had come up behind her and now thrust an enamel bowl of warm water towards her. Trixie took it from him.

'I put the kettle on the fire, figuring we'd need hot water,' he said.

'She'll need a good strong cup of tea and I wouldn't mind one meself.' Trixie smiled, then turned back towards her mother before slipping the clean piece of rag that Teddy had found into the water. She gently raised her mother's chin and with the gaunt face towards her, dabbed at the dried blood with the cloth.

'It'll be all right, Mum,' she said as the woman winced. Bess True was a bag of bones. She opened her eyes and stared at Trixie.

'He's gone then?' Her voice was weak.

Trixie nodded. 'He can't hurt us any more.' Bess closed her eyes again but not before Trixie had seen the relief in them. She went on gently wiping at her mother's cut skin and the water in the bowl quickly became red. Bess was like a child, unmoving now and allowing Trixie to do her will, screwing up her eyes in pain only when the warm flannel rubbed against a particularly tender part of her skin. 'Listen, Mum,' said Trixie, staring into her mother's bloodshot eyes until the woman focused upon her again. 'Where does Auntie Joan live?'

Bess took a while to digest the question.

'Gosport,' she said.

'I know it's Gosport. But where?'

'Prefabs. She got one of them new-fangled pre-fabs near Haslar.' The talking seemed to exhaust her. Bess closed her eyes again.

'Teddy, help me get her off the floor and on to the sofa.'

'Clayhall.' The woman's bony fingers gripped Trixie's hand.

The body of their mother was as light as a feather as they gently lifted her and laid her on the sofa.

Teddy noticed the blood first. 'She's bleeding; is it the baby?'

Tixie saw the damp, dark stain on her mother's clothing. 'Mum, you want me to look at you down there?'

Bess shook her head. 'I'm all right. I can't feel any pain. I'm just tired, that's all.'

Trixie wasn't going to argue with her. The sooner she got the three of them away from Portsmouth and to the safety of her mother's sister's house, the better. Once more Trixie tucked the patchwork quilt around her.

'How we going to get anywhere with Mum like that?' asked Teddy. Worry spilled from his eyes. 'Shouldn't we get a doctor?'

'No!' For such a frail woman their mother's voice was strident. Agitated, Bess tried to sit up. 'No. No doctor. What if they take me away from you? I'm all right. I just need to rest. Get me a cloth an' I'll see to meself down there, later on.'

'She's right,' said Trixie to Teddy, then to her mother. 'Don't upset yourself, Mum. Anyway I doubt if we could find a doctor who'd come out for a pregnant woman, not after the air raid and the damage the bombs leave behind.' Trixie was thoughtful. 'We'll use the cart,' she said. 'Pile it with whatever we need and tuck Mum up on it, nice and warm. We can walk to Gosport around the harbour.'

'Why do that when we live opposite the ferry and just the other side of the water there's a bus station and a bus that'll take us to Clayhall?' Teddy was frowning.

'With Dad working on the boats we can't go anywhere near them. His mates will know we've crossed the harbour. When his body's found and they come looking here for us, the next place they'll go asking questions is his workplace. The bobbies'll be all over Gosport like ants on a piece of cake if they know we travelled there. Anyway, we don't have the money to squander on boat and bus fares when we need to eat.' Trixie took the coins out of her pocket. 'This is all we've got unless we can find some more while we're packing up our goods.'

'There's nothing in my purse,' Bess murmured.

'Well, if we get to Auntie Joan's, she'll take us in, won't she?'

Bess shrugged her thin shoulders at Trixie's question. 'Years ago, we was close. She got married. I got married. Your dad wouldn't let me go near her or her husband. I only know Joan's at Clayhall 'cos I met an old friend of hers.'

27

'Well, she's our only chance,' said Trixie. 'Teddy, go and find some cardboard boxes. I know there's a couple down in the shed.' She waved a hand towards the steps. 'Then come back and we'll start gathering our stuff together.' None of them possessed many clothes.

'Can I take my drawing stuff?' Teddy's voice was small.

Trixie smiled at her mother but Bess had dozed off again. She turned to Teddy. 'Of course you can.' His face lit up.

Teddy spent hours down on the Hard near the Dockyard gate sketching the boats and gulls that flew screeching overhead. Any spare paper suitable to draw on he carefully saved along with his charcoal and assorted bits of pencils that he kept in a lozenge tin. Trixie reckoned he was talented.

'All this is my fault and—'

'For God's sake, Teddy,' she said. 'It was an accident.' She put both her hands on his shoulders and looked into his eyes. 'An accident,' she repeated, enunciating the words. But even as she said them she knew Teddy would never be able to put his father's death to the back of his mind and get on with his life. Teddy would always brood about this night. Always.

'We'll make a fresh start,' said Trixie. 'And look after each other. But leave no trace.'

'I've been cleaning this place as best I can,' Teddy said. 'But I don't want ever to touch that thing again.' He pointed to the axe and began shivering. 'I keep seeing it hit Dad.' Teddy's mouth began quivering and Trixie put her arms around him. Was Teddy's fear of the chopper something that would forever haunt him? Surely not, Trixie prayed. What a burden for a ten-year-old to carry.

'I'll see to it.' Her voice was soft. 'Don't forget that pot of tea; we could do with it,' she said, briskly changing the subject. 'Then you make a start by gathering the bedding. We'll need to make Mum comfortable on the barrow and I think a couple of pillows won't come amiss. Saucepans: we'll need at least two. One to boil up something to eat when we stop for a rest and one to boil water for tea.' She moved towards the cupboard and opened it, looking at the remnants of vegetables and food. 'I'll see what we can take with us to make a meal.' She poked at a few of the opened packets and sighed. 'Nobody'll take any notice of us pushing a packed barrow after tonight's air raid.'

Uninterested in what she'd found in the food cupboard her eyes roved along the top of the mantelpiece. She picked up the small oval mirror and glanced in it. Her face was grey, her eyes wild and her hair a dirty and unkempt blonde. She ran her fingers over the scar on her forehead, another keepsake from her father. Disgusted, she put the mirror down. Surely Auntie Joan would have a mirror? Did she, Trixie, really want to worry about keeping the looking glass safe? If it broke it would mean seven years' bad luck and Trixie reckoned they'd already had enough trouble to last a lifetime.

Teddy held out a saucerless cup of tea towards her.

'Bless you,' she said. Trixie took it from him and turned back to her mother. 'I want you to

29

take a few sips of this; it'll do you good. Then I'd like you to go back to sleep while me and Teddy get everything ready for our flit.' Supporting her mother's shoulders, she held the cup to her lips and her mother drank. When the cup was less than half full her mother waved it away and sank back into the depths of the sofa.

'That was a lifesaver,' said Bess. Trixie gratefully finished the tea, then gave the cup to Teddy and settled her mother, satisfied when the older woman's eyes closed and sleep overtook her.

From outside in the street came the sounds of ambulances. Voices too were heard. Would this awful war ever end? wondered Trixie. And how long would it be before her father's body was discovered?

'C'mon, Teddy,' she said softly, feeling like crying but knowing her tears would serve no purpose at all, especially as her mother and Teddy were depending on her to be the strong one. 'We've no time to waste. It's a fair distance to walk to Gosport.'

Chapter Two

'I can't walk any further.'

'Stop moaning, Teddy,' said Trixie. Her brother had been dragging his feet for about a mile now. His pace had become slower and slower and she felt sorry for the little mite. 'I promise when we get to Portchester we'll stop for a while.' The palms of her hands were covered in blisters from the splintered wood of the barrow's handles. And the cart seemed to be getting heavier and more unwieldy with each turn of its wheels.

Bess was asleep – hopefully, Trixie thought, oblivious to the ruts in the road.

The sun was rising now, peeping above the ruins of Portchester Castle, giving the sea and fields a golden glow to accompany the birdsong that heralded the morning.

Portsmouth had taken a beating the previous night from Hitler's bombs and as Trixie looked back a grey haze hung over the remains of the buildings. Smoking rubble and craters the width of the streets had almost barred their exit from the city. People had been wandering, wrapped in blankets, dazed expressions on their faces as they searched for loved ones in the transformed streets.

Trixie had been terrified walking at night through the war-torn roads but she was even more scared of meeting anyone they or their father knew and having to explain why they were flitting from the city.

Portsdown Hill looked fresh and green and was dotted with clumps of early summer flowers that loved the chalky soil. The shore of the Solent framed the other side of the road and was fringed with muddy seaweed and small wooden boats, some rotting at their moorings, some painted in bright seaside colours of blue and white.

'What did they use that place for?' Teddy pointed towards the distant grey stone battlements of the castle.

'Long ago the Romans built a chain of coastal

forts to stop the German Saxons from invading. At one time civilians lived within its walls but now it's a ruin. We can rest a while inside the walled area where it'll be quiet. Mum needs to take a few steps from that cart before she gets stiff with lying there and we could all do with a brew of tea.'

A faint smile crept over Teddy's dirty face. The going was slow now, Trixie having reduced her pace to match Teddy's. He scratched his head. 'I'm hungry.'

Trixie thought about last night's dinner of stew thrown to the floor. Then, no one had eaten. They were all hungry. 'By the time we get there the market'll be up and running. I'll buy some bread.' She'd scoured the cupboards for food before they'd left but all she'd been able to find was an opened tin of dried egg powder, a couple of potatoes, a box of porridge oats and a tin of Spam. An unopened quarter of Brooke Bond tea and a tin of condensed milk had been a bonus. Trixie had filled three empty bottles with tap water so they wouldn't have to look for a standpipe.

'We're all hungry,' she said wearily. 'But when we get to the castle grounds we can put blankets on the grass, make a fire and get some tea going. If you put the potatoes in the fire they'll cook and we'll open the tin of Spam.'

Trixie looked at her mother; it worried her that she was sleeping so much. And the bleeding? How serious was that? Her mother needed a doctor but Teddy was practically dead on his feet with weariness and hunger and even Trixie needed to rest. Surely a while spent eating and having a refreshing cup of tea would do them all good?

'I brought cups and plates,' Teddy said importantly. 'Can I be in charge of the fire? Then without waiting for a reply he asked, 'Anyway, how d'you know so much about the castle and the market?'

'One of my teachers was telling us about it and the church – St Mary's I think it's called – that's in the grounds.'

'I see,' said Teddy. Trixie steadied the cart so they could push it more easily over the cobbles of Castle Street. Portchester, the village, was waking up. Men on bicycles were riding to work, women were taking in milk from their doorsteps and snatches of music were coming from open kitchen windows, proof of a new day dawning but already overhead the skies told of rain to be expected. Trixie's heart plummeted; pushing the barrow in a downpour would be difficult. She looked down at Teddy and saw his face was wet with tears. She knew he'd been worrying about the events of yesterday.

'Teddy.' He looked up at her, his eyes red rimmed. 'It was an accident. You, me, and Mum have to stay together and look after each other. I keep repeating it because it's true.' She licked her lips to ease their dryness. 'You know of course we can never speak of last night to another living soul?' She waited for his reply and was satisfied when he nodded. 'And now promise me that you'll try to put it out of your mind?' Again he nodded. Trixie smiled at him. Deep in her heart she knew she had to take her own advice.

The entrance to the castle grounds loomed ahead. 'This is where we'll spend a few hours getting a bit of rest and something to eat.' Trixie tried to jolly her voice up. And if you're in charge of the fire you'd better clear off and find some sticks.' Happier at being given a job to do Teddy gave her a big toothy grin and wandered towards the shore and began picking up driftwood.

'You're a good girl.'

Trixie looked at her mother. 'So, you're awake? How do you feel?'

'Better.' Her mother tried to free herself of the blankets cocooned around her. Trixie was pleased to see a bit of colour in her mother's face. 'The sound of you singing softly, and the trundling of this barrow lulled me to sleep. But I'm awake now and want to stretch me legs.'

'Wait till I prop this blessed cart against the wall before you start wriggling, else it'll all go over.' Trixie positioned the barrow against the stones jutting from the broken wall, steadying the cart. She gently lowered the handles to the ground. When she considered it was firm enough and not likely to tip, she held out her hands to her mother, who stood shakily. 'Don't you go falling; hold on to the cart or the wall.'

Trixie pulled the bedding from the barrow and shook out a blue blanket. It was stained with blood. She stuffed it back on the cart, too late – her mother had caught her looking at the offending article.

'You're not all right, Mum,' Trixie said.

'No. Well, there's not a lot we can do about it until I get to our Joan's.' Her mother's voice was small and fearful. 'You just give me a few more cloths and I'll clean meself up before Teddy

34

comes back. Stop worrying, girl. I'm not in any pain and a nice cuppa will see me all right.'

'Sit here.' Trixie, feeling happier that her mother was so cheerful, shook out another blanket and set it in a patch of warming sun. She helped her mother practically fall on the softness of the long grass. 'Where's that boy?' Trixie made a show of looking for Teddy, who was already walking towards them with arms full of wood.

'Reckon he thinks he's lighting a bonfire,' said Bess, 'size of that lot he's collected.' She and Trixie laughed, the awkwardness of talking about the baby and her mother's loss of blood put aside for a moment.

'About Joan's man... It's not my idea to go to them.' Bess's worried eyes stared into Trixie's and she put out a thin hand to clutch at Trixie's arm. 'She's my only relative but her and Sid aren't what you might call a happy couple. He can be a bit, you know.' Her voice faded.

'He can't be any worse than Dad, can he?'

Bess shook her head. 'Men can be bad in different ways. I'm just saying.' Her voice petered out. Amazingly, Teddy's fire had caught within the confines of the four bricks he'd set out as protection against it spreading. He was now busily searching for the bottles of water. Bess and Trixie smiled at each other conspiratorially. Trixie knew all the time the boy was occupied he wasn't dwelling on what had happened to their father.

'I know you don't want to go to them,' said Trixie. 'But we don't have anywhere else to run to, so the choice is mine.'

'Maybe,' said Bess. Trixie watched her as she

35

called to Teddy. 'That's a good fire.' He was carefully watching the pan of water so it wouldn't overturn. He grinned proudly.

Later, when a cup of hot sweet tea had put new life into her, Trixie decided to visit the market.

'I really don't want to leave you, Mum,' she said, hovering.

'Now don't be silly. I can send our Teddy after you if I need anything. And the one thing we can do with is something in our bellies so we can get on the road again. Them potatoes'll be cooked by the time you get back. I'm not keen on the porridge and Teddy don't like Spam but if you can get a nice bit of crusty bread it'll solve all our problems. Though come later on we'll probably be so hungry we'll be glad of anything!' Bess grinned at her so Trixie felt happier and set off with the thought of food on her mind.

Although it was early, farmers had brought their produce to sell and the stalls were set up with foodstuffs, old clothes, fancy goods and second-hand furniture. There was an air of expectancy on the light wind and customers jostled each other as they examined the goods for sale.

Trixie wandered around the colourful stalls inhaling the scents and the sounds of the traders' cheeky banter as they lured in unsuspecting customers to buy their wares.

At the bakery stall, Trixie carefully counted out her precious coins for a cottage loaf that she knew was her mother's favourite. She stared at the meagre amount of money remaining. Thank God, with a little bit of luck, they might make Clayhall and her aunt's home before nightfall,

36

even with a stop to eat the Spam or porridge.

And then Trixie drew a sudden gasp as she rounded a corner and saw the sheer beauty of the goods on sale at a stall.

Patchwork pillows in rich velvets, cotton patchwork skirts, quilts made of satin remnants that shone and glittered in the sunlight. One gorgeous skirt was stretched out on the top of a pile of pillows. Trixie wanted to finger the soft silk. She could never hope to own such a lovely article of clothing. At the back of the stall a bedspread hung, its vibrant soft material a pattern of shapes that must have taken ages to sew. Hanging from every available space around the stall were items for sale that took Trixie's breath away. And sitting on a wooden stool was a young woman with dark swinging hair, and dressed in what was obviously her own creation of colourful clothing.

'Did you make all these?' Trixie's words tumbled from her lips. Her fingers hovered over a velvet drawstring bag.

The young woman gave her a lazy smile that didn't reach her eyes. 'I did.'

'They are so beautiful.'

'Thank you.' The girl raised a slim hand and raked it through her shining hair. 'It's all cobbled together from remnants and jumble sale materials.'

Trixie admired the young woman's beautiful stock but knew she could never hope to make anything even half as pretty, just as she could never have the self-assurance of this stunning girl. Trixie was as different from this person as chalk is to cheese.

'But it's all so breathtakingly beautiful.'

'I'm glad you like it. I only hope I sell plenty today.'

The young woman stared at her with eyes of a startling blue surrounded by long dark lashes. Trixie was suddenly aware of the state of herself. How scruffy she must look after trudging through the Portsmouth streets pushing a heavy barrow. She felt ashamed that she couldn't afford to look through the goods for sale because she didn't have any money to buy even the cheapest article on the stall. And what was she doing wasting time even looking when she should be getting back to Teddy and her mother, who were waiting to eat?

'I hope you do; in fact I'm sure you'll sell everything,' she whispered in a guilty voice. Trixie turned away quickly after giving the young woman another smile.

She was so wrapped up in her thoughts that the voice startled her.

'Fresh strawberries.'

The young man held out a small wicker basket filled to the brim with luscious red fruits. His hands were rough and worn and his clothing serviceable for a market trader.

'I don't have money for fruit,' said Trixie. She made to walk away, knowing she mustn't stay longer.

The lad laughed, showing white, even teeth. He was tall and strong-looking with dark curly hair and an infectious grin. He was, Trixie supposed, quite a few years older than her.

'Taste one.' He took a fruit, and holding it by its stem, leaned across the table. 'Eat,' he commanded. Trixie did as she was told and as her teeth bit into the flesh the strawberry burst in her mouth, its sweetness filling her with happiness. 'Isn't that the best thing you've eaten all day?' He threw the stem to the earth.

Trixie nearly confessed it was the only thing she'd eaten all day.

'I still can't afford to buy any,' she said. 'But it tasted heavenly.'

'I grows 'em,' he said proudly.

'I don't have money for fruit,' Trixie pressed. She thought suddenly how her mother would love one of the bright sweet-tasting berries. And Teddy? Trixie didn't think Teddy had ever tasted fresh strawberries.

The young man looked her up and down. 'I can't turn a pretty girl away just because she can't afford my wares. Take them and enjoy.' He pushed the punnet into her hands.

His kindness was too much for Trixie and she burst into tears.

'It's only a punnet of strawberries,' he said. His brown eyes were wide with worry. 'Oh, Gawd, what have I done?' And then he was round to her side of the stall and his arms were about her. 'I'm sorry,' he said. 'I didn't mean to upset you.'

Trixie sniffed in the warm scent of soap and vegetables from his jacket and immediately began to feel better. And then a tall man with a blue raincape who had come, it seemed, from nowhere said, 'Everything all right here?'

Trixie opened her eyes to see a policeman standing next to the young man. Immediately she panicked. Had something happened to her mother? She must get back to the castle grounds immediately.

Her heart was beating fast as the young man said, 'Whatcher, Burt. Sure, everything's all right.' With great gentleness he pushed Trixie away from him so she could confirm his words and she nodded vigorously.

'Mornin', young Jem. Gonna rain later.' Obviously satisfied with the scene before him, the policeman went on talking about the weather. 'The gardens need the water.' His eyes took in Trixie, who wanted nothing more than to run away.

'I hope to be sold out and on me way home before the downpour comes.' The young man called Jem looked up to the heavens.

'And I hope to have got rid of a couple of gypsies who've set a fire going inside the castle walls.'

Trixie couldn't help herself. 'We're not gypsies!' She squeezed the strawberries so hard one popped from the punnet and lay at her feet. For a moment she stared at it lying on the grass, then bent and picked it up and put it back in the box. She could feel the policeman's eyes on her and it discomfited her.

'Oh, so you're another of 'em, are you? How many more of you are trotting around this market looking for something to steal?'

'Wait a minute, Burt.' Jem put his hand on the policeman's arm. 'She says she's not a gypsy.'

'We, we got bombed out in Portsmouth.' The lie rolled off Trixie's tongue like a knife slicing through warm butter. 'We're takin' a rest before we move on to me auntie's.'

40

'Where does she live?' The policeman frowned.
'At Gosport.'

'This is a long way around. Wouldn't it have been easier to have crossed by the ferry?'

'Sure. If we'd had the money.' Trixie stared into the tall man's eyes. She was angry. Why did she have to explain herself? If she was dressed as well as Miss Glamour-puss with her lovely patchwork materials no one would have considered her a gypsy.

'I can vouch for her – well, the fact she's no money,' said Jem. 'Would she refuse to buy my delicious strawberries if she had money?'

The policeman looked at Trixie and smiled. The problem defused. 'Well,' he said, 'just make sure you don't spend the night there else the sergeant'll have my guts for garters.'

'No need to worry about that, Burt. I'm taking the lot of 'em on to Gosport in my van when the market packs up.' Jem swung his arm to the back of his stall where a green Morris van was parked.

'Just you make sure you do, young Jem. Can't abide gypsies,' he muttered, walking away from the stall. Then he stopped, turned back and said, 'Heard the news? The big invasion of Europe has begun. Caen is under attack and throughout the night RAF bombers have been pounding German forces along the coast.' The policeman's eyes were glittering. He didn't stop for an answer, just walked on.

'I heard this morning on the wireless,' called Jem. 'Cheerio, mate.'

Trixie stared at Jem. 'You can't do that,' she said. 'Offer to take us to Gosport.'

'Why not? I live there, and when my fruit's gone the van'll be empty. Where does this aunt of yours live?' Jem turned away to sell some strawberries to a customer, giving Trixie time to think how good it would be not to have to push the cart the rest of the way to Gosport. Why, with a bit of luck they might even escape the rain. And certainly this man would get them to their destination a lot faster than her and Teddy pushing that heavy barrow. It would mean that her mother could see a doctor sooner. She began to relax.

'Prefabs. I don't rightly know the number but there can't be many of them new prefabs in Gosport at Clayhall. What about your petrol though? I'm sure you don't want to waste it on us.'

'Don't you worry about my petrol allowance. I don't do unnecessary journeys. Anyway, Clayhall's even better because that's where me small holding is. I know where the prefabs are,' he said. Again he had to break off to serve a woman with a small child who was grizzling until she filled its mouth with a large strawberry. Trixie knew she must get back to her family and leave this kind man to his work. Teddy would be so pleased about not walking.

Jem again pointed behind him to the van. 'It's big enough to take four of us – there aren't any more of you are there?' Trixie laughed and shook her head. 'This market closes down around midday,' Jem added. 'You just be here then and we'll get loaded up. As long as we're back before it gets dark,' he said. 'The blackout regulations about covering the lights with cardboard is pretty dangerous so I don't like travelling much at dusk but it don't apply in this instance.'

'I don't know what to say; you're very kind,' Trixie said. 'But we've got a barrow.'

She thought for a moment when Jem went quiet that he would say he couldn't take them after all. But she realised he was only thinking as he insisted, 'That's all right. I've got a tow-rope so we can tie the barrow behind the van.' She looked into his cheerful brown eyes and grinned. 'If I was you,' he said, 'I'd get a bit of rest before twelve.'

Her heart rose. How lovely it would be to eat the bread and have another cup of tea and rest a while. It would be so nice not to have to walk to Gosport. And Aunt Joan would be able to get the doctor to her mother. However, Trixie was still worried.

'But suppose that policeman comes and finds us asleep?'

'Burt's bark is worse than his bite. He patrols the market to scare off thieves and pickpockets. Now he knows you aren't going to set up a gypsy encampment he won't bother you any more; I'll see to that.' He stared into her eyes. 'Trust me,' Jem said. And somehow Trixie knew she could trust him.

Clutching the box of precious strawberries and the loaf of bread she turned to go. As she looked over towards the stall filled with the amazing patchwork articles she saw the girl staring at her. And the look in the girl's dark blue eyes was enough to make Trixie's blood freeze.

Chapter Three

'I never realised when you said you'd be travelling to Gosport you'd end up being just across the road from me,' said Jem. He pointed through the open window of the van towards some fields. At the top end, almost hidden by trees, was a house. The fields next to the house contained strawberry plants and Trixie could see the red fruit that had ripened during the day's sunshine. 'The land and that house, and the house we live in, which is further down Clayhall Road, belongs to me grandad and in time will come to me.'

'That house looks charming, hidden away like that.'

Jem broke in, 'My grandad built it for his wife. He wanted to give her the best of everything but unfortunately she died before they could move in, so it's lain empty for years.'

'He's never wanted to rent it out?'

'Couldn't bear anyone else to live there. There's well water, fenced gardens in an orchard, and it was one of the first houses hereabouts to have electricity put in. We live together, him and me, over there.' He pointed to a large, rambling house facing the road. 'This smallholding is his life.'

'If I loved someone and lost them I'd want to shut myself away in a place like that,' she said. She was thinking that the small house looked as though it would cocoon anyone against the harshness of life.

'You're young and beautiful. Too pretty to be thinking dark thoughts like that,' said Jem.

Oh, dear, thought Trixie, as a blush warmed the back of her neck. If only Jem knew what had happened to her these past days, she was sure he'd not have such a rosy view of her life. Trixie glanced at her mother fast asleep in Teddy's arms.

'They're so tired. But I'll have to wake them soon. Is it much further? And what about your mum and dad? Where are they?'

'My parents went everywhere together. One night while my dad was fishing off Haslar sea wall a squall blew up and the boat overturned. I'm lucky I've got my grandad. I want to pay him back for bringing me up. And to the question about how far away are the prefabs, there they are.'

The squat grey buildings were laid out in a herringbone shape. With paths between them, some had the makings of pretty gardens with bright bursts of flowers and others were strewn about with crisp wrappers and old bicycle frames.

'I've never seen houses like them before.' Trixie was amazed.

'They've not been built to last, so I've heard, but they have modern appliances in them, cookers, boilers, fridges and such. They even have inside toilets and a separate bathroom and hot and cold running water. Like little palaces, some are. What number do you want?'

'Ah, I'm not sure of the number but Joan and Sid O'Hara are their names.'

For a moment there was silence, a drawn-in

45

breath from Jem, then he clicked his tongue dis-approvingly.

'I've got a feeling you've not had much to do with these so-called relatives of yours.' Trixie heard the clipped tone in his voice. 'That'd be number nineteen you'll be looking for.' She looked at his face; his mouth had set itself in a hard, thin line.

'I take it you know them? What are they like?' Trixie saw the dark shadow flit across his face.

Her head was in turmoil. Obviously Jem, who until now she'd thought completely trustworthy, didn't like them. But why?

He pulled the van to a halt outside number nineteen, an end prefab with a parking place and a tangled garden and scruffy curtains that dipped on their wires.

'They expecting you?'

Trixie shook her head. She glanced at her mother and Teddy still fast asleep. 'I think I'll go up to the door on my own,' she said. Though it was the last thing she wanted to do.

What she was going to do if Joan O'Hara refused them shelter, she had no idea. Jem slipped out of the driver's side and came round to help her out.

'I'm going to stay here until you come and tell me everything is going to be all right,' he said. Was it her imagination or did she see worry in his eyes?

'Thank you,' she whispered. A rustle of clothing and movement showed Bess to be awake.

'I think I'd better be the one to go.' Her mother's voice was small.

'I thought you were still asleep,' said Trixie. She thought how tired her mother looked.

'My sister will be more amenable to us staying if she hears our tale of woe from me.' Holding a blanket around her and with help from Jem, Bess stepped down from the van and walked unsteadily to the broken gate. Trixie watched anxiously as her mother made her way to the front door.

It seemed an eternity before the door opened and Bess was standing opposite an older version of herself. Trixie couldn't hear what was being said but after a while, the two women embraced. Bess then turned towards the van, her face a smile from ear to ear.

'Teddy, Teddy, wake up.' Trixie gently shook the boy's shoulder and he opened his eyes and began scratching his head.

'Wassamatter?'

Trixie laughed at him. 'We've got to get this van unpacked, sleepyhead,' she said. 'And I wish you'd leave them things in your head alone, stirring them up the way you do. If we stay here and there's some soap and water I'm going to give your head a good scrub.'

Trixie saw Jem looking about the roadside and the fenced garden and said, 'There's no room here for your barrow. What say I take it home with me? I can leave it in one of the sheds and if you need it, well, you know where it is.'

'Would you mind?' Trixie looked into his brown eyes. 'You've been so good to us.' She thought he was proving to be a true friend.

It didn't take long with Jem, her and Teddy running backwards and forwards to unpack the van with their meagre belongings and as Trixie watched Jem wave to her from the open window of the van as he drove out of sight, she felt quite bereft.

Once properly inside the compact property, Joan introduced herself then said, 'We must get the doctor to your mum; she needs to rest. Now, we've two bedrooms. Me and my hubby share one, your mum can have the other one and you two can sleep in the big living room.' Trixie nodded. She heard the first spatters of rain on the windows and was grateful they weren't still trudging the streets. She also knew the prefab was a new invention and it was the first time she'd been inside one.

Prefabricated housing had been built especially to ease the lack of accommodation due to the bombing raids. Already this small house had an air of neglect and a smell of mustiness about it. Bess had a saying, 'Cleanliness is next to godliness.' Trixie realised Joan had a very different approach to life.

Joan pushed some strands of hair beneath her hairnet and said, 'When Sid gets home he'll make some noises about you being here but don't you worry about it. It's my name on the rent book, see? Anyway, when I tell him the real reason you ran away, he'll understand.'

Trixie looked at her mother, who was now sitting in an easy chair in front of the fire. Bess blushed and looked away. Teddy closed his eyes, his face white with fear.

'Mum,' began Trixie, 'I thought we'd promised each other we'd keep Dad's death a secret?'

But Trixie was interrupted by Joan, who snapped, 'We may not have seen each other for years but we are sisters and your secrets are safe with me. Living with my Sid has taught me there is a lot of sadness in this world. Let's not worry about your dad now but have a nice cup of tea.'

Trixie turned away. It was Teddy she felt the most pity for. He shrugged his shoulders, obviously hurt at the way things had turned out. He rushed past her, throwing open the front door and running out into the rain, accidentally knocking against a large carton standing in the hallway that fell onto its side, exposing packets of Player's Weights cigarettes.

'They belong to Sid,' Joan said sharply, jumping up and putting the packets back inside the carton. 'He doesn't like his stuff messed with.'

It was obvious to Trixie that Joan was more worried about the cigarettes than Teddy.

Joan, when she'd finished replacing the cigarettes, slipped into Trixie's hand a piece of paper that she took from underneath the clock on the mantelpiece.

'Your mum needs a doctor. Explain everything. Here's the coppers for the phone call; get going – don't just stand there. The phone box is down near the bus stop.'

Relief flooded through Trixie that at last her mother would have medical attention. It gave her feet wings as she ran back out into the rain.

The room was warm, overrun with potted plants that crept and curled around dark wooden beams, their shiny green leaves giving an exotic appearance to the parquet flooring and oak walls. Jem was glad to be home amongst the brightly coloured rag rugs and throws covering the worn furniture, which made for a cosy lived-in feeling in the house.

He pulled out a ladder-back chair and sat down at the table, sniffing the air appreciatively. Two places had been set for a meal. 'You cooking my favourite, Gramps?'

'Cooking? It's been cooked this past hour, you young whippersnapper! If it ain't eaten soon I shall 'ave to throw it in the pig's slops.'

Jem laughed, pushed away the knife and fork and undid his money-bag from his waist, then set it on the table where it landed with a healthy clunk. 'You'd never do that to me, Gramps, not throw me favourite liver and bacon to the pigs. Give me five minutes more and I'll have today's takings counted.'

Jem looked towards the kitchen door just as his grandfather entered the room. His cardigan had a button left over at the bottom. His wiry frame and grey steel wool hair showed a strong man shrunken with age who had all his faculties about him.

'Don't tell me I shall 'ave to start dressing you,' Jem said.

Gramps frowned, looked down at the offending button and said, 'I ain't out to impress anyone.' He took a large red leather ledger from the wall shelf and set it down on the table. Jem looked at him and grinned.

'Did well with the strawberries today,' he said. 'Portchester can be a little goldmine on a Wednesday morning.'

Soon he'd made piles of silver and copper coins. Then he began making notes in the ledger before he slipped a float of cash back in his leather purse. Gramps counted the piles of money, put them in a tin box, then entered the amounts in the book. While this was happening Jem had gone to the butler sink and was washing his hands. He'd taken off his jacket and rolled his shirtsleeves up high, showing strong, muscled arms browned by the sun. He then went over to the oven and came back to the table with two covered plates held with a teacloth to stop his hands getting burned. Gramps swept the ledger and tin box to one side.

For a while the two men ate heartily and in silence. Jem was aware of the clock ticking and his grandfather's laboured chewing, due in part because he'd never looked after his teeth. Jem was well used to the noise and smiled to himself. Nothing Gramps ever did upset him because the sun rose and set for him when his grandfather was present.

When the last of the fragrant mashed potatoes had been swallowed, Jem pushed the plate away, clattered his knife and fork on his plate and said, 'That was good; it filled the right spot.' The old man fairly purred with happiness. 'Met a girl today,' Jem added.

'Thought you might meet someone before long.' Gramps chewed steadily. Jem saw he wasn't surprised by his words.

'Much too young at present but I reckon she's worth waiting for.'

'Let's hope she feels the same about you, then.'

Jem thought about Trixie's green eyes and blonde hair and how it had glistened in the sunlight despite not having seen a wash for some time. She was skinny but he could tell her figure would fill out with the right kind of food inside her. One thing he had taken to was the complete honesty in her eyes as she'd stared at him. Honesty and kindness – a pleasing combination, he thought. And she had the voice of an angel. She'd started humming Priscilla Lane's 'It Had To Be You' as he'd driven the road from Portchester to Fareham and within minutes the van was filled with the sound of them all singing, so infectious was her voice.

'I don't reckon she's had a boyfriend so I'll be waiting a while.' A grunt came from Gramps as he pushed his plate to the centre of the table. 'While I'm waiting for her to grow up,' continued Jem, 'I also need to wait and find out what's causing her grief.'

The old man stared at him. 'Got a few problems, 'as she?'

'Not that she's said anything,' Jem said. He opened the top button of his twill trousers, for the meal had been filling.

He watched the old man sitting next to him, fumbling for his clay pipe. When he'd located it, where it always was, in his top pocket, his grandad got up from the table with a series of grunts and groans that signalled his age and went over to the wireless, fiddling with the knobs. Tommy Handley's cheery voice filled the room.

Jem thought about the early start he was needing tomorrow. He had to rise sooner than usual if he was to pick some of today's ripened strawberries before he left for Gosport market in the morning. Then his mind wandered to Trixie and how she'd suddenly come into his life, and he thought about Eva and how her face had darkened when he'd told her he was going to take the strange little family to Clayhall. Eva was a good friend and a grand homemaker, but there was no spark between them. Not like the one that had suddenly jumped into a flame when that scruffy girl, Trixie, had appeared at his stall.

Then guilt overtook him. He wished he'd confided to Trixie about Sid O'Hara and his un-savoury reputation.

Eva Brooks put away her solitary china cup and saucer that she'd just washed up and folded the tea towel over the back of the kitchen chair. She sniffed the air appreciatively; the polish she'd used on the wooden furniture smelled of beeswax and its clean smell soothed her jangled nerves.

The letter from her sister sat on the top shelf near the oven. Myra wasn't, for the foreseeable future, coming back to live in the prefab. She and little Johnnie were happy living with Dennis in London and Eva was welcome to stay at the prefab for as long as she liked, if she paid the rent.

Eva sighed. That was the problem, paying the rent.

This morning she'd been up early to cycle to Portchester. The wooden box on wheels fixed to the back of her bike had contained her patchwork offerings for sale and by the time she'd reached the market place she'd felt as though she'd already done a day's work before she earned enough money to pay for her market pitch. Today, she'd been lucky. The double quilt had been sold. That meant for this week and next she had the rent money.

Eva walked from the kitchen into the living room. Evidence of her craft was everywhere. Second-hand furniture shone with country newness as her quilts and throws brightened the room. The curtains she was especially proud of, with their pelmets and ties in a single colour complementing the red background. The windows of the living room ran the length of the wall. It looked rich and inviting. And all the materials had come from jumble sales she'd scoured to find just the right colours.

She walked through to the bedroom and began getting changed into a tight black skirt and a blue short-sleeved jumper that she'd knitted herself. She looked at the alarm clock. She had fifteen minutes before her shift started at the Fighting Cocks, the pub on the corner, near the road. If she wanted to keep a roof over her head she had to work. Much as she loved being creative with a sewing machine or a needle and thread, it didn't bring in enough money to pay the bills. And now, with Myra out of the picture, she'd have to work even harder.

Eva slipped the jumper over her shapely body, then started on her face. She didn't like a lot of make-up, which was just as well now there wasn't any in the shops to buy. She knew her dark hair and her pale skin gave her a glamorous look, a bit like the film star Dorothy Lamour. Eva put her fingernail into the lipstick tube and scraped out a sliver of dark red.

As she patted the bright colour into place on her full lips she thought of the girl who had been brought to the prefabs by Jem. Her heart plummeted. She'd seen the way he had looked at her. Of course, the girl was too young for him but as she'd left the market Jem's eyes had followed her until she'd gone from his sight. Probably not from his mind, thought Eva. Eva was in love with the smallholder. Had been ever since he'd given her a lift home one day from Fareham market. And she didn't want a scruffy fly-by-night girl spoiling her chances with him.

Eva pushed open the door of the Fighting Cocks and strode into the noise, the cigarette smoke and the smell of stale beer, and lifted the wooden counter hatch to take her place behind the bar.

'Hello,' she said, to no one in particular and got a few grunts in reply.

The wireless was on and Tommy Dorsey's band was playing 'In The Mood.' Eva reached across and turned the volume up.

After taking off her coat she hung it up in the hallway then came back into the bar to say hello to Old Tom, who was, as usual, propping up the counter. Later, a band was coming in to play a few tunes that would liven the place up. When there was live music in the bar it brought in more customers and it was at times like that that Eva wished Jack, her boss, would hire an extra pair of hands.

Tom picked up his Guinness and swallowed.

'Well, Tom,' Eva said. 'So the Allied troops have stormed ashore in Normandy. What do you think about that, then?'

Chapter Four

It had stopped raining but the air was damp and wet weeds brushed against her legs, making her shiver. Around every dark corner Trixie imagined monsters were ready to pounce. God, she thought, how frightened her little brother must be, alone in the dark, in this strange place. Trixie had been up all night searching for Teddy, terrified that harm had come to him. She was cold, wet and hated her aunt for being so uncaring in worrying more about packets of cigarettes than the fate of Teddy. She wasn't pleased with her mother, either, for telling her aunt about Teddy and their father's death.

And then a noise alerted her to a brick shed at the back of the small parade of shops. Already, earlier in the evening, she'd searched there but discovered nothing.

Secreted into the corner was Teddy, eyes wide and terrified. She climbed in beside him and gathered him into her arms. His hiding place smelled fusty and stank of cat's urine. 'I've been so worried,' she said, kneeling beside him in the gloom. A cat jumped onto a nearby dustbin and the sudden noise made both of them leap with fear. The sun was struggling to rise in the dullness of the morning. 'I must have walked this estate a hundred times,' she said, leaning her head against his.

'You'll get nits,' he said doggedly.

'I don't give a bugger about that,' she said. 'The main thing is that you're safe.' He was also cold and teary. 'C'mon,' she said. 'Let's get back to Auntie Joan's.'

Teddy didn't move. 'I did come back to the pre-fab,' he said. 'But there was this man in the living room shouting. I could tell he was drunk. He was yelling at Auntie Joan. I was frightened so I left again and came back here. He was just like Dad.'

Trixie gave a long sigh. She'd been scared to death by Sid's shouting but in a way she could understand what all the fuss was about. Sid had come home to find the prefab full of his wife's relatives and he didn't have a say in the matter.

'He's quietened down now.' She wasn't going to tell him about the bad language that was far worse than any her father had used or the insults that had dripped from the small man's tongue. Most of the jeers seemed to be about where the money was coming from to feed a pack of leeches, as he had called them.

'Is Mum all right?' Teddy asked.

'Amazingly, I think she slept through the lot of his ranting. I left the prefab when Joan tipped me the wink to get out. I didn't want to leave her but it looked as though she'd sorted Uncle Sid out before when he was in a fighting mood.'

'What did the doctor say?'

Trixie put her hand on his shoulder. 'We didn't get a doctor. He was "indisposed". The midwife what arrived gave Mum an injection of something that sent her to sleep. Then she said Mum's got to rest.'

'What about, you know, all that blood?' Teddy's eyes were big and dark.

'That's why she's got to rest, to slow it all down, so the baby ain't born too soon. The woman didn't even ask about all the bruising on Mum's body from Dad's boots. But it was like she understood. She left some cream.'

Her brother nodded. Then he gave a huge sigh. It was as though she'd answered one weighty question but he had many more worrying him.

'I'm really scared.' He stared at her. 'Mum's told Auntie Joan about me and Dad. We came to Gosport to get away and now she's told on me. What if the police come here?'

Sooner or later, Trixie thought, Teddy was bound to ask this.

'Mum needed to find us a place to sleep, not that you or I have done much sleepin' yet. She trusts her sister and I think we should trust Mum's judgement. Mum's sick, Teddy, a lot more ill than we realise. Whatever happens we've got to stick it out and stay together.' Trixie pulled his skinny body even tighter towards her own.

'I'm hungry,' he said in a small voice.

Trixie laughed and smoothed back the hair from his forehead. 'Let's get you back, then. Sid's gone so there's no one there except us and Joan. I can make us some porridge.'

Obviously heartened by the mention of food, Teddy began to wriggle away from the corner in which he'd hidden himself.

Sid's words played on Trixie's mind. Where was

the money coming from to keep them? She couldn't expect Joan and Sid to feed them all for nothing, could she? Legally she was old enough to leave school and go to work. Further education was now out of the question. She must get a job.

'Let's walk round the front of these shops, Teddy.' She'd spied a newsagent's, a greengrocer's, a Co-operative and a baker's shop while she'd been searching for Teddy during the night. The shops were clustered together amongst the prefabs, almost like an island. 'They won't be open yet but sometimes there's cards up in the windows selling stuff and advertising jobs.'

Grabbing his hand she walked him round to the front. Despite the darkness she could see the windows held no postcards offering employment.

'Later, I'll go in and ask,' she said, not at all defeated.

Teddy pulled on her hand. 'You'd better get yourself cleaned up,' he said. She looked at her reflection in the window.

'Jesus, I look a sight, don't I?'

Teddy laughed. 'Well, I wouldn't give you a job in my shop; you'd frighten away the customers!'

Trixie gave him a mock clip around the ear. 'Cheeky bugger,' she said.

When they reached the prefab both her mother and Joan were waiting at the open front door. Teddy ran into Bess's arms. Half crying, half laughing, Teddy was led into the warm kitchen where the kettle was on the stove.

'Teddy, you don't have to worry,' said Joan. She pressed a hairgrip back into her wispy hair. 'Now there's no secrets between us, we'll all look after each other, Sid reckons.'

Teddy's head shot back. 'So he knows as well now, does he?'

'He's my husband, boy, we don't have no secrets from each other.'

Teddy began to cry. Trixie could see it was all too much for him, especially after being out all night in the rain. He broke down, sobbing. 'I didn't mean to hurt my dad.'

Trixie pulled him into the safety of her arms and Joan half-heartedly tried to make up for upsetting Teddy by saying, 'You can trust Sid. My Sid won't say a dicky-bird to anyone, least of all the coppers. He hates coppers, my Sid does.'

Trixie propelled Teddy into the bathroom. She reckoned he'd had enough of wailing women and needed a bit of tender care. 'Bed for you, love. Don't take any notice of what's going on out there.' She thought of her first impression of her uncle and the way, last night, his eyes had raked her body when Joan had asked her to go into the kitchen and stick the kettle on for tea. He'd followed her, standing between the gas stove and the sink, leaning so close she could feel his breath on her neck. Without asking him to move it was impossible for her to fill the kettle with water.

'Excuse me, Uncle Sid,' she'd said.

'What's it worth?' he'd replied, standing so close to her she could smell the sweat on him. The lower part of his body had rubbed against her and she'd moved back in alarm. Just then, Joan had pushed open the door.

'Bess wants a glass of water,' she'd said sharply, planting her form firmly between them and glaring at Sid, who stepped back, raising his hands in the air, saying, 'Just showing her where we keeps the kitchen stuff, love.'

Joan took the kettle from Trixie's hand and plonked it on the draining board. Taking an up-turned tumbler she half filled it with water.

'Take this to your mother, love,' she said. Trixie, glad to escape, scurried back into the living room. Trust Sid? Trixie wouldn't trust Sid as far as she could throw him. He'd frightened her with his closeness. Uncles didn't all behave like that, did they? But she couldn't let Teddy know how she felt about the man, could she? Teddy was scared enough after what had happened in his short life as it was and needed kindness and looking after.

'First I'm going to run you a bath to warm you up, then when you've got clean clothes on and have had something to eat you can pop into Mum's bed and sleep.'

Trixie looked at the dirty ring around the bath. 'Well, my love, it won't take me five minutes to clean that, will it?' She gave her brother a half smile to cheer him up, but inside she was thinking, whatever have I done, bringing us to this dreadful place with these awful people?

Bess sat with the patchwork quilt around her and stared into the fire. She put her hands on her stomach, but the unborn child had stopped moving weeks ago. She knew she was going to go through the motions of bearing the child, but that it would never breathe. She thought it had probably died when she had been about four months gone and the kick from her husband had

61

done more damage than she'd realised.

She should have left him years ago; she knew that. Then the terrible accident of Teddy throwing the axe to save her would never have happened. But where does a woman go when she has no income of her own and two children to look after and has so little confidence left that all she can do is hope and pray that her husband comes home from the pub with a smile on his face and money to give her to feed her family for the next day?

Bess could hear Joan in the kitchen. She was rattling cups and making tea. But Bess had seen the whisky bottle at the back of the cupboard. A nip here and a sip there that helped Joan through the day. Was it any of her business if her sister needed a crutch to help her cope with Sid and his schemes? They weren't so different from each other after all, were they, her and Joan?

Ten years is a long time to hold a grudge. Sid said he'd never forgive her for squealing on him for the kiss he'd tried to steal from her. A bit of fun, he'd called it. Only Bess didn't think it was fun to be squashed against the wall by her soon-to-be brother-in-law, on his wedding day. That he had his hands beneath her skirt even more disgusted her and it was only the thump on Sid's nose from her own husband that had stopped his little game. That and the promise to Sid that if he ever touched her again she'd make sure Joan knew about it. But Sid had got his own back: Joan and she had lost touch – until now. But that was all in the past, wasn't it? Bess hoped so. Oh, she did hope so.

'I got no biscuits.' Joan set the two mugs of

strong tea on the glass coffee table. She tugged at the strings to her wrap-around pinny. Bess saw the grey mixed with the blonde in her hair, saw the tired skin loose on her once-pretty face.

'That don't matter,' said Bess. Joan had aged. No longer the blonde curly-haired girl with the cheek of the devil. She watched as her sister settled herself in the opposite armchair. 'You've been very kind taking us in,' she said. Bess thought of Teddy and Trixie asleep, worn out, in the other room.

'It's what sisters are for, isn't it?'

Bess thought she could smell the sweetness of alcohol waft towards her on Joan's breath. She put out a hand and felt for Joan's arm.

'I guess neither of us ever expected the lives we got.'

Joan sat back in her chair and Bess's hand fell away. 'I don't ask what he gets up to when he leaves this prefab and I don't care. He's not all bad, you know. Sid, I mean,' Joan said.

'No, I can see that. He wouldn't let us stay here, otherwise.' Bess saw the tears rise in Joan's eyes.

'Like I said when you first arrived, it's my name on the rent book.'

'Wake up, wake up, Trixie.' Teddy was pulling the blanket from Trixie's neck. She opened her eyes and looked in his terrified face as he cried. 'It's them new weapons, them doodlebugs coming to get us.'

'Don't be silly, Teddy, it's not even properly dark yet.' Even as the words left her mouth she knew she was talking rubbish, for it was well known the buzz bombs came over in daylight as well as the

63

dark. They fell on schools, on crowded streets and the south coast seemed to be a desired target.

Trixie rolled out of the warmth. 'Where's Mum?' Her voice was sharp.

'She's with Auntie Joan,' came Teddy's reply.

'We must get to a shelter.' Trixie was throwing on her clothes.

'There isn't one.'

Trixie left her skirt unbuttoned and stared at him. 'What do you mean, there's no shelter?'

'Auntie Joan says we just have to be brave as the nearest shelter is near the beach and it's too far away now that the siren has already sounded.'

Trixie felt as though her whole body had turned to jelly. For a few seconds she stared at Teddy until he scratched at his head and then she gave him a smile. 'Still biting? Them buggers?' She'd given his hair a good washing when he'd had a bath earlier but what she needed was a nit comb and it had been left behind in Portsmouth.

Then she heard it. The noise of the engine above them suddenly stopped. 'Under the bed, Teddy.' She pushed him to the lino and slid beneath the bed, dragging Teddy after her. The silence as she waited, punctuated only by their breathing, was terrifying. And then it came. The bang that sent tremors through the earth, jolting the little oblong house about as though it was made of toy bricks. 'Oh, my God,' whispered Trixie. Everything about them shook. A book fell from the bedside chair. A cup rolled along the floor. And then there was silence.

Trixie pushed Teddy away from her and crawled out from under the bed. As she banged open the living room door she saw Joan and Bess tightly enfolded in each other's arms. Bess had her eyes shut but Joan looked at Trixie and said, 'Put the kettle on again, lovey. We could do with a cuppa before the next one comes over.'

The bombs fell all the rest of that day and well into the evening. It amazed Trixie that they could get used to the crashes and bangs as they went about their everyday business of living. At eleven o'clock that night Sid returned and the sunny atmosphere that had prevailed in the prefab despite the ever-present fear from the falling bombs was immediately replaced by a different kind of fear.

Trixie and Teddy, who had been playing a game of draughts and giggling and laughing suddenly felt self-conscious. So much so that the game fizzled out and they both lost interest. Joan grew quiet around Sid and seemed to watch every word she said for fear of offending him. Bess sat quietly reading.

'They reckon we're getting upwards of one hundred and fifty doodlebug bombs thrown at us every day along with all the other bombs,' said Joan.

'You don't want to believe everything you hear,' said Sid. 'Do you, Trixie?'

Trixie looked up from the table where she'd been watching Teddy sketch a picture of the Dockyard Gates and the boats moored alongside. She wondered why Sid had singled her out for a reply.

'S'pose not,' she replied, aware of Joan staring

at her.

'Come outside and help me carry in a present for my Joanie.' Trixie looked at Sid and shuddered at the weasel of a man. She thought that when he'd been younger he might have been really good looking, but now his features were hard and he acted as though the world owed him a living. Not that Trixie knew exactly what it was he did to earn a living. The cartons of cigarettes had gone from the hall. Trixie was aware that that particular brand was difficult to get so Sid obviously had some kind of scam going there. She'd heard about the black market where goods could be bought and sold without using coupons and wondered if he was involved in any way with that illegal operation. Sid smiled at her. Trixie looked away. 'I've got a surprise for her,' he said. His voice sounded oily.

The last thing on earth Trixie wanted to do was to go outside in the dark with Sid. Yet how could she refuse? If she spoke outright and said she was frightened of him then Joan would be offended.

'Can't Teddy go?'

'I'm busy,' the boy said. He was drawing a boat. Trixie looked at Sid, who had a smug look on his face.

'What is it?' Joan was curious now. She was also annoyed that she was being made to wait for her treat. Trixie sighed and rose from the chair she'd been sitting on.

'It's in the shed,' Sid said. With her uncle close on her heels she walked out through the kitchen and unlocked the back door. The latch wasn't secured so Trixie pushed open the shed door to be greeted by the smell of scorched linen. Sid squirmed up against her and then twisted her around to face him.

'Gettorf!' Trixie hissed. In the narrow confines of the dark shed she realised there was nowhere she could run to. Sid stood in front of the door and leaned across to draw it closed. Her body felt the whole hard length of him even though she leaned as far away as possible. A small round tube-like object was pressed into her hands.

'That's for you to give my Joanie. But what are you giving me?'

She could feel a cottony substance around the tube. His arms snaked around her body, drawing her close.

'Leave me alone.' There was a sob in her voice. She didn't like this man clawing at her and holding her against her will.

'You can stop that crying. Remember you owe me for letting your mother get well again in my house. Remember, it's my good food she's eating and I don't see any money coming in from you for bed and keep.'

Trixie bit her tongue. So he was going to blackmail her, was he?

'You can't use my aunt's kindness as a lever for me keeping quiet about you touching me every time we're alone!'

And then his hand was kneading her breast. His awful dirty-nailed bony hand was touching her. Trixie swivelled the tube until her hand held what she thought was the base of it, then she jammed it into where she hoped his groin was.

'OHH!' His hands dropped and he slumped

against her, but as she moved out of his way he fell against the push-along lawnmower. She heard him swear, just as the small shed was illuminated with light and Teddy said, 'Auntie says I'm to help as you're taking a long time!' Still holding the tube, Trixie fell out onto the garden path. She clutched at Teddy and the pair of them tumbled to the paving stones. Teddy must have thought it was some kind of game for he said, as he laughed, 'Why is Uncle Sid hopping about like he's doing a war dance?'

Trixie knew it would cause trouble if the truth about Sid trying to touch her came out. She decided to say nothing. The last thing she needed was for her mother to be thrown out onto the street if she tried to explain what had really happened in the shed. She got to her feet, pulling Teddy with her and saying, 'Yes, he does look funny, doesn't he?'

In the mirror hanging on the kitchen wall, breathing deeply, she glanced at herself. She patted down her hair and smoothed a dirty mark from her cheek. You'll do, she thought. Through the open back door she could hear Sid gasping with pain. A smile tipped her lips as she shut the door, and the sounds, out.

In the living room the wireless was on. Spike Jones was singing his parody of 'You Always Hurt the One You Love.' Trixie handed Joan the package.

'Sid said to give you this.' Just then the back door banged open. Sid had arrived. 'Took us a long time to find where he'd hidden this, auntie. Didn't it, Uncle Sid?' Trixie grinned at him, defy-

68

ing him to say anything detrimental.

Trixie saw Sid was glaring at her but Joan was too busy unravelling the piece of cotton from the hard metal tubing to notice anything was amiss.

'It smells burnt,' Joan said.

'I rescued it from a burning building,' said Sid.

'Isn't that called stealing? Or perhaps, looting?' Trixie asked.

The blackened cotton fell to the carpet and Joan unscrewed the container and tipped the tube so that a rolled up drawing slid out.

'Whatever is it?' Joan looked at Sid and smiled at him with such tenderness that Trixie felt sick. Joan smoothed out the painting. It was a watercolour of an old-fashioned sailing ship. 'That's pretty,' she said, without any real emotion.

'Let me look?' Teddy stood by Joan and gazed at the thing with wonder. 'It's so lovely,' he said with reverence. For a moment there was silence. 'It's the *Victory*, Lord Nelson's flagship.' Teddy touched the drawing tenderly.

Then, Sid asked, 'You really do like it, Joan?'

'I love it,' she lied. 'I wonder if it's worth anything?'

Sid was still looking at Trixie. She knew he wouldn't say anything about trapping her in the shed. And she hoped and prayed he'd keep his promise to tell no one about their father and what had happened to him.

But she now knew it wasn't an accident that he had opened the door to the bathroom when she was in there. She would have to try to keep away from Sid. She was tired and longed for bed and the library book she had nearly finished reading.

Then for some reason she thought of Jem and how kind he'd been to them. She thought of the way his eyes crinkled at the corners when he smiled and how tall he was. He was a whole head and shoulders taller than her and had an infuriating dark brown curl that fell on his forehead even though he pushed it back time and time again.

She decided thinking about Jem was a great deal nicer than worrying about Uncle Sid. To help her forget she began to hum along with the music on the wireless.

Chapter Five

Trixie was singing softly as she thumbed through the books on the shelves. The proper library had been destroyed in a huge explosion that had also claimed the Town Hall and the council chambers. Deep holes, broken masonry and purple fireweed were trying hard to disguise the wrecked buildings that gave the High Street a battered look.

A temporary building, similar to a Nissen hut, now housed the makeshift library. Trixie loved the smell of books. The shiny new pages felt like silk between her fingers and the thicker, well-worn pages that were like cardboard and smelled of must were just as exciting to touch as they were for her to read. She smiled at a small child rifling through the pages of a Rupert Bear book. His mother was busily engaged looking through the Romance section.

'Hello,' a voice whispered. She turned to see Jem. He looked pleased to see her and held two books in his large hands. One was a gardening book. 'What are you after?' The lock of hair was across his forehead and he brushed it back.

She shrugged. 'Anything that takes my fancy.' Trixie wouldn't have thought that Jem was the sort of man to read books. With his athletic build she thought of him as being more of an outdoors person. 'Though I shouldn't be reading, I should be working,' she confessed. 'I need a job.'

'What sort of job?' His eyes were enquiring. He leaned towards her and she could smell shampoo from his freshly washed hair. 'More to the point, are you really serious about needing some work, any work?'

Trixie nodded. 'I can't stay at Joan and Sid's without paying my way, or rather, our way. Mum's in no condition to work and Teddy's too young. I've asked about but there's nothing going. With most of the men away at war their jobs have already been taken over by women. And many women have found they can still do a full day's work for one boss and fit in a part-time job with another, then enjoy two wage packets.'

Jem looked as if he agreed with her. 'I happen to know of someone who needs a bit of help. Immediate start,' he added.

Trixie mulled over his words. Her fingers travelled the length of the shelf, then she picked up a novel that her eyes had alighted on while they had been talking. 'This one, I think. I've been wanting to read *The Good Earth* by Pearl Buck.'

'Won the Pulitzer Prize, didn't it?'

Trixie nodded. She was surprised he knew that. She was beginning to realise there was a lot more to Jem than she'd first thought. 'What's this job, then?'

'It's only part time,' he said. 'But we suffered in the bombing a few days ago. Lost a greenhouse and salad stuff growing in one of our fields. Grandad can't tend the store and make good the damage to the smallholding and I need to be at the markets, so we talked about getting someone in to open up the shop. What do you think?'

'I've never served in a shop before.' It didn't sound as if it would be difficult.

'Grandad'll see you right for a couple of days. Stay and show you the ropes, like. Only I can't be in two places at once and we make more money selling fresh veg and fruit at the markets.'

'Where is the shop?'

'Round the corner from you, in the parade.' Trixie remembered the closed greengrocer's. 'You'd be doing me a favour.'

Trixie thought back to how kind he'd been to them and the shop was indeed just around the corner. She put out her hand.

'Do we shake on it?' She put her book on the counter ready for the librarian to stamp. Jem shook her hand, laughed and set his two books beside hers.

'Did you come into town on the bus?' he asked her. The librarian barely glanced at Trixie but gave Jem a big smile. Trixie realised the deal was done and dusted.

'I walked.'

'Then I shall give you a lift back,' he insisted. As

they walked out of the hut and into the sunlight, she felt Jem's hand on her shoulder. Trixie felt like singing.

The two men were huddled over glasses of beer in the Black Bear on Gosport's High Street. The air was thick with smoke and beer fumes and from the wireless at the back of the bar Rudy Vallee was singing 'As Time Goes By.' A darts game was in progress filling the pub with noise. A plate of cheese sandwiches sat forlornly on the bar top, the bread's edges curling.

'So you'll bring him down to the slipway at ten o'clock? Should be dark enough by then.' The man lifted the glass to his lips and drank.

'I said so, didn't I?' Sid drank down the dregs of his pint and looked expectantly at the man beside him, who glared but nevertheless got up and forced his way through the crowds to the bar.

Sid picked at the grime beneath his fingernails. His missus should never have taken in her sister and her kids. For one thing he couldn't abide kids and now the sister was about to drop another one. It was all right for Joan, them being her kin, but he liked it better when there was just the two of them about the place. Why, the silly cow had even cut down on her drinking so she could play the bountiful sister.

He looked at the blackout curtains that covered the taped glass. The Black Bear was a decent enough place to drink in. The manager asked no questions and kept a good pint. Sid did a lot of his deals sitting at this table. And beneath the bar, for regulars only, were packets of fags that he'd provided, for a decent fee of course. Sid liked a dabble on the black market.

Sid also liked the Fighting Cocks up the road from the prefabs. It was on his doorstep, and that was where he drank for leisure and pleasure. The Black Bear was his place of work.

The man returned and set the drinks down on the table. He wore a suit that was shiny and had seen better days and he needed a shave.

'Won't the boy be missed?' he asked.

'Not the way I'm going to work it, he won't. Anyway it's my job to see to that part of it, just like the other times. There's parents what needs kids an' there's kids what needs parents. And there's kids what's needed to work. My job is to satisfy them all by bringin' them together. It ain't your job to wonder where I gets the kids from. Your work is to transport the little buggers.'

The man pushed back the brim of his flat cap before he sat down, exposing thinning grey hair. 'Ain't the first, is he?'

'And won't be the last,' grinned Sid. He took a gulp of the liquid and raised his glass as a salute to Josie the barmaid. Josie, dark and voluptuous, waved back at him. Sid knew he'd lost a lot of his good looks. Beer, fags and hard living had taken a toll on him. Funny thing was, he thought, he still managed to get the women running after him. Charm, he reckoned; that's what it was, charm. If only that little bitch, Trixie, would give in, he could show her the time of her life. 'Pity,' said Sid, still thinking about Trixie, 'our man on the island ain't in the market for girls. Got a nice piece of prime tail just come on the market.'

'I'll pay what I owes then I want to get in an order to last me through the weekend which I'll put on tick. Is that okay?'

Trixie looked at Gramps in confusion. His eyes were twinkling when he said, 'Isn't that what you always do, Mrs Kowalski?'

The shop was large and airy and had been swept clean by Trixie herself just that morning before she'd put boxes of vegetables outside to lure customers in.

Immediately she'd entered the store with its tinned goods on the shelves and potatoes tumbling from sacks she'd loved the earthy smell of the place. At the rear of the shop was a small kitchen, a table, a solitary chair and a toilet near the back door. There was a drawer till on the counter where Gramps had placed a bag with two fresh cream doughnuts that he'd bought from the bakers, for elevenses, he'd said.

The large woman grinned at Trixie then pushed away a small red-haired girl who was attempting to climb up the front of her coat. 'Sweets, you promised, Mum,' chanted the girl.

'This isn't the sweet shop,' said Mrs Kowalski, tugging herself free.

Then her arm was yanked back by another red-haired girl, who stated, 'We don't want a cauliflower.'

'Tommy likes cauliflower, I like cauliflower, so you'll eat what you're given,' Mrs Kowalski said as she brushed herself off. Her bottle-green coat was grubby and worn. Her eyes, almost the same colour as her coat, were sharp yet kind. She

75

pushed a strand of dark hair back beneath her headscarf. Behind her lounged an assortment of more red-haired children. All had freckles and very white skin.

'Sorry about this. It's the school holidays.' The stout woman watched as Gramps put two large punnets of strawberries on the counter top along with all the tins and brown paper bags full of vegetables he'd been setting down as part of the woman's shopping.

'Order almost done, Mrs Kowalski.' All the time the children had been climbing over her, Gramps had gone about piling the counter with goods.

'Beats me how you remember what I need every week when I can't remember it myself.'

'You've been a good customer so I like to give good service,' the old man said. 'Trixie, weigh out five pounds of onions, while I sort out the coupons.'

Trixie went about her task, remembering all she'd been told by the old man about using the scales.

'That your new girl, then?' Mrs Kowalski stated the obvious.

'Yes, and she's shaping up nicely,' said Gramps. Trixie put the onions on the counter. She thought there were rather a lot of them.

As though reading her mind the woman said, 'Onions is good for growing children.' Trixie smiled at her and the woman treated her to a big grin in return.

'Go on, Trixie, you add up her bill and I'll check it. Mrs Kowalski'll sign for it. That's right, isn't it?' He started packing stuff into the woman's bags. It wasn't long before the woman had left with her tribe of children following her. Trixie was reminded of the old woman who lived in a shoe.

'Is it always like this, Gramps?'

'You mean people buying on tick?'

Trixie nodded.

'There's no money on this estate. Those people with jobs are in hock up to their necks and do what Mrs Kowalski does, pay and then tick up again. Other people on the estate beg, steal or borrow. One thing about that woman,' he nodded to the open doorway, 'she'll come to you when you're in trouble and no questions asked. Good woman is Mrs Kowalski. Rough and ready and a heart of gold.'

Trixie pointed to the sign pinned to the wall that said, *Please don't ask for credit as a refusal often offends*. She said, 'You don't stick to that then?'

'No,' said the old man. 'I've known Mrs Kowalski before she called herself Kowalski. Got a bloke that worships the ground she walks on and Dmitri would be with her now but for the government and its silly rules about Polish men.'

'Isn't Dmitri a Russian name?' Trixie had been learning about the origin of names last term and had really enjoyed the class, so much so that she'd come top in an end-of-term examination.

'Fancy you knowing that,' said the old man, reaching down a tin of peas from the shelf and transferring it to a box of goods that he was putting together for another order.

'We did it at school,' she replied. 'I bet he was born on October twenty-sixth. That's his name day and it means *devoted to*.'

'Well, well,' said Gramps. 'I know nowt about that except that Marie said he was named after some long-dead ancestor. Anyway, his name might be Russian but he's a Pole and as nice a bloke as you could wish to meet. But you're right about the devoted part. That bloke's devoted to Marie.'

Trixie decided if Gramps said Dmitri was a good man then he was. She wondered if she'd get to meet him. Gramps interrupted her thoughts with a sharp note to his voice.

'But there's one couple on the estate you're never to give credit to and that's your uncle and aunt.' Trixie knew she was frowning. 'Sorry, love, but someone's got to tell you, your uncle is a bad person.'

'What d'you mean?' Although she'd been with the couple only a short time Trixie now knew Sid was not to be trusted, but she wondered what Gramps had to say about him.

'I'm not speaking ill of your family but I will tell you to watch out for yourself. Aye,' he looked at her fondly, 'and that little brother of yours.' Trixie waited but no more words seemed to be coming forth. That was another thing she liked about the old man: he seemed to take people as he found them. He'd help out genuine cases of hardship but wouldn't be taken for a fool. She decided she liked Gramps.

Trixie spent the morning absorbing all Gramps was telling and showing her about the shop and how to run it. He was very particular about keeping it clean and presenting the vegetables and fruit in a way that would appeal to the customers. Everything came fresh every morning from the

78

smallholding. Anything left over from the day before was sold off cheaply.

'Never tell the customers the goods are fresh when they aren't,' he said. 'I like to keep my customers happy and I need them to trust me.'

She was pleased when he praised her skills at adding up the customer's bills. Trixie was determined to show him she could be trusted to be left alone in the shop. She knew he was longing to get back to the smallholding to begin repairing the damage the bombs had done.

'I reckon you're doing fine. Think you'll like working here?'

'So far, so good,' said Trixie. It was time for a cuppa and the doughnuts and she had to swallow quickly so she wouldn't speak with her mouth full.

'Tomorrow I'll show you what we do about the food coupons in the ration books. Not all the stuff I sell is rationed but some is.' He pointed to the tinned fruit. 'But tomorrow is good enough to go into the intricacies of that. For now though, if you'll give it a bit of a tidy in here,' he waved his hands to where potatoes had rolled to the floor and carrots had mysteriously got mixed in with the lettuces. 'Them kids is little buggers. High spirited,' he added.

Trixie set about picking up vegetables and while she did so began to hum. Gradually her humming turned into a song and pretty soon Gramps was joining in with her.

'Anyone ever tell you, you got a fine little voice there,' the old man said when the impromptu song was ended.

'Only me mum,' Trixie laughed. 'Anyway

enough about me, where's Jem?'

'He's at Gosport market today, gave young Eva a lift in. You met her yet?'

Trixie shook her head. 'Don't think so.'

'Dark-haired girl, very pretty, makes the patchwork stuff.' So her name's Eva, is it? Trixie thought. She remembered how the girl had glared at her. 'What you asking about Jem for? You got your eye on him?'

Trixie's heart pounded against her chest. 'I'm too young to be thinking about boys, Gramps. Besides, I got me mum and Teddy to take care of. This is me first job, you know. I was at school.' She saw Gramps' face fall. 'Oh, don't worry, I'm old enough to be working,' she said. Then she laughed. 'What I mean is I've got too much on me plate to worry about lads. Besides, I got Teddy acting all funny.' Too late she realised she'd said too much.

'What d'you mean "acting funny"? I think it's time I put the kettle on again and made use of the lull in customers coming in,' said Gramps, bustling out to the kitchen. 'You goin' to explain yourself?'

'It will be better when Teddy gets back to school,' she said. 'He's especially good at drawing and painting and school brings out the best in him, but just lately it's like he's all closed down inside and scared all the time.' Trixie wasn't going to be lured into talking about their father and his death but she did say, 'Me mum's a lot better. She's even got some colour in her cheeks.'

She saw that Gramps was watching her with a sad look upon his face.

80

When it was time for her to go home Gramps gave her a bag full of vegetables and fruit. 'You take this home; your mum could probably do with some fresh vegetables inside her. Good for her, they are.' Then he looked thoughtful. 'Tell you what, girly, why don't you come round to our place for a bite of tea tonight. Jem'll love to show you the greenhouses and fields. I'm making pork chops.'

Trixie's eyes widened. She couldn't remember when she'd last had a real juicy chop to herself.

Gramps grinned and said conspiratorially, 'Me and the butcher does a food swap, beneficial for the both of us, see?' He obviously saw the horrified look on Trixie's face so he added, 'It's not black marketeering or anything like that.' He tapped the side of his nose. 'Just a little exchange between the two of us friends.' Trixie nodded. That was all right by her then.

'If you're sure? I'd love to come for me tea.'

'Course I'm sure. Wouldn't be askin' if I wasn't. Though maybe you got somethin' better you needs to do at home?'

Trixie thought of her mother sitting quietly reading, Teddy busily drawing, Joan taking trips into her bedroom for a few mouthfuls of whisky that she thought no one knew about and Sid, who might be in the prefab, in which case he'd be leering at her.

'I'd love to come for me tea,' Trixie said determinedly. 'But do you think I'd be cheeky if I asked if our Teddy could come as well?'

Gramps put his hands on his hips, threw back his head and gave out a loud guffaw of laughter.

'Course the lad can come. Tell you what, girly, you're not backwards in coming forwards, are you? The both of you come over whenever you like and as soon as possible.'

No one except her mother mentioned Gramps' kindness. But they ate the contents of the bag just the same.

'I'm making cottage pie for tea tonight. Would you like to come round, just as a thank you for giving me a lift to the market?'

Eva watched Jem's face. His strong hands were on the steering wheel of the van. He shook his head without looking at her.

'While the evenings are light, I need to get as much done on the smallholding as I can. Them damn doodlebugs played havoc with the greenstuffs.' Her heart fell. He turned and looked at her, seeing her distress. 'Oh, Eva, I'm not turning you down, not really. It's just that Gramps and I need to get back on our feet again. He'll be expecting me.' He took a hand from the wheel and laid it over her fingers, which were folded in her lap. 'He's taken on a young girl to train up in the shop so there's wages to be found for her. You do understand, don't you?'

Mollified, she nodded. It would be another night indoors finishing the tea cosies she'd started making. She wasn't working in the Fighting Cocks either so it would be cottage pie for one. She nodded, liking his hand entwined with hers.

'Of course I understand. Another time when we both aren't so pressured by work?' She moved a little closer to him; they were now shoulder to shoulder in the confines of the front bench seat.

'Another time,' Jem said, removing his hand.

'It's a big place, ain't it?' Teddy's eyes were wide as they crossed Clayhall Road, mindful of the traffic, and stood in front of the smallholding set back from the main road.

'It's long and rambling and looks like it's been here for ever.' Trixie laughed and pushed him to keep on walking. Various creepers covered the walls with flowers she didn't know the names of. Their heavenly scent filled the summer evening and she breathed deeply. It seemed the front door of the house was around the back and as they passed outbuildings, she saw their cart, safely housed in a wooden shed. There were small greenhouses, all filled with greenery and plants. Cats lay sunning themselves, sleeping and warily watching the visitors.

Towards the rear of the smallholding, almost hidden by trees, was the house Jem had told her about. It didn't look desolate, what she could see of it. With its red brick walls and slate roof and the same flowery creepers adding colour it looked restful, a refuge. Gramps, she thought, must have loved his wife very much to have built her such a beautiful haven.

'So you found us then?' The old man had a tea towel tucked into the waist of his trousers and was in the process of lifting a large orange cat out of the house and over the doorstep. 'He's a bugger, this one,' he nodded at the cat. 'First scent of meat and he's sitting on the table like I invited him to dinner.' Gramps set the cat carefully down, whereupon a flicked tail was its grumbling response. 'Come on in,' he said to them.

Immediately Trixie walked into the cool slate-floored kitchen she felt at peace with her surroundings. The large scrubbed table was set for four and a heavenly smell of food cooking enveloped her. Teddy looked up at her and she squeezed his shoulder to let him know it was all right if he bent down to play with a white cat that was sitting beneath a chair.

'You like cats?' she asked Gramps.

'These are old buildings. Cats keep the vermin down.' Gramps went on stirring at a pot on the stove. 'Jem's the one for animals.' He looked at Teddy and the cat. 'Give me half an hour for the meal to be on the table. I reckon me and the lad can get in a game of draughts before then. What do you say, boy?'

Teddy jumped up. 'You won't beat me,' he said. He gave his head a scratch but stopped when he saw Trixie glaring at him.

'Betcha I will,' the old man laughed. 'Set 'em up.' He pointed to a box on a board near two armchairs and Teddy scrabbled over towards it. 'Jem's in the greenhouse next to the old apple tree. Why don't you go out to him?'

She heard Jem before she saw him. He was setting panes of glass in a greenhouse frame. He was humming to himself. The smell of putty was sweet yet earthy. On the bench in front of him was a glass cutter and several sheets of glass that had obviously been used before, but which he was now cutting to fit the smaller frames. At his feet broken glass crackled. All around on the benches and on the earth lay ruined lettuces and the mush of cucumbers. Wasps and flies were having a party, she thought, buzzing about over the mess.

'I'm not disturbing you, am I?' Trixie asked. She could tell by the sudden smile on his lips that he was pleased to see her.

'Not at all,' he said. 'I'm making do and mending. Replacing what was shattered in the bomb blast. Luckily the housing was still intact. Unluckily we had some cucumbers growing in here, almost ready for selling. Anyway,' he wiped his hand across his forehead but the curl sprang back, 'you won't want me to bore you with my work. Let me wash my hands.' He dunked his hands in a bucket of water and wiped them on an old piece of towelling. 'I'll take you around our spread.'

He ushered her away from the buzzing, flying insects and led her down a wide path between vegetable plots, all the while explaining what was growing and when the plants would be suitable for harvesting. Trixie was amazed to see there were hardly any weeds anywhere. The soil was rich and brown and she could tell from his tone of voice that he was extremely proud of all the work that he and Gramps put into the growing vegetables.

When the small house came into view, Jem opened the white painted gate and ushered her inside. He told her the names of the apple trees that surrounded its garden and showed her the rows of fruit bushes, some with berries almost ready for picking. He produced a wooden tray of seedlings from inside a smaller greenhouse at the rear of the little house, telling her when they were bigger they would be planted out and could provide stock to harvest for market. He told her the growing season was almost at an end but that was why the greenhouses were so important, as they helped to extend the seasons. His fingers hovered lovingly over the small green leaves. He pointed out the fields where the strawberries grew and where the raspberry canes stood and explained about the casual labour they hired for picking fruit.

'I guess this is a full-time job,' she said. The setting sun was still warm and the sky was suffused with colour. For a while Trixie was able to forget all about her father, Uncle Sid and how poorly her mother was.

'It's my livelihood,' Jem said. 'I can't imagine not working on the land.'

He looked down at her and Trixie felt a shiver of excitement run through her. She loved the way he spoke tenderly of the growing plants, touching the fruit carefully. She wondered how it would feel if he ran his fingers across her skin as lovingly as he touched the plants. Some girls at school had confessed about going 'all the way' with boys. And though Trixie was not sure what 'all the way' amounted to she thought there had to be an element of tenderness from the boys because of the dreamy looks that came into the girls' eyes while talking about it. A sudden wave of warmth flooded her body as she went on watching Jem and the way he lifted a bunch of berries from behind some leaves, bringing them into the last of the sunlight.

He smiled at her and she almost fell into the depths of his brown eyes.

And then the moment was shattered.

'Gramps says the meal's ready!' Teddy yelled with full force.

Jem put his hand on her shoulder to turn her in the direction of the kitchen and immediately she felt his hand jerk away from her skin as though she was red hot to the touch. She looked at him and saw his face was colouring up. He was blushing!

'I won't break, you know,' Trixie said. Then she realised why his body had tensed up. *He liked her.* But he was scared of giving the wrong impression because she was so much younger than him. Trixie had never been involved with a boy before. Most of the boys in her class were scared of her father. People had witnessed her and Teddy's bruises and steered clear of becoming friends with her. But Jem was different. She smiled at him. Her stomach rumbled with hunger. She thought about the pork chop. 'Come on,' she said. 'I'm starving.'

After the meal, Trixie sat back on her chair and said, 'I'm so full I think I might burst.' Teddy and Jem laughed. Trixie saw Gramps look contentedly at the four empty plates.

He began clearing the table and she got up to help him. Never before had she sat down at a table to eat where conversation flowed so easily and laughter helped the food go down. There was an obvious loving chemistry between Gramps and Jem that had been missing from her own family meals. Trixie felt suddenly sad that all her mother and Teddy had ever experienced of family life had been hardship and fear.

'You sit down, old man; we'll do the washing up, won't we?' Jem looked at Teddy, who nodded enthusiastically and got off his chair and Trixie took the tea towel from Gramps' hand.

'You deserve a rest after that grand meal,' she said.

'You go and find that smelly old pipe,' said Jem, filling the sink with water. Trixie watched Gramps light up contentedly and sit in an easy chair near a large, shiny-leaved house plant.

The three of them did the washing up, then, as it was still early Jem suggested they play Snakes and Ladders.

Trixie didn't know when she'd last laughed so much. 'I seemed to be sliding down a lot of snakes without going up many ladders,' she groaned.

'Bad loser, bad loser,' chanted Jem. But he was a loser as well and so was Teddy. Gramps had a smile from ear to ear as the winner.

Later, as Jem saw them safely across the road and waited by the railings while they walked together down the pathway between the prefabs, Teddy said, 'I liked being with them; did you?' He slipped his hand in Trixie's.

'It was a magical night,' she replied and turned to wave to Jem.

Before number nineteen came into view Trixie felt sad she hadn't let Jem see them all the way home.

She didn't want Sid asking questions.

Eva drew the curtains to shut out the darkness. She could hear footsteps and laughter and strained her neck, peeking to see who was walking along the prefabs' pathway.

Her heart began thumping wildly when she saw the boy, Teddy, skipping along holding his sister's hand. And then she saw the girl's smiling face as she turned and waved to a lone figure standing by the railings. Jem waved back, looking happier than she'd seen him in ages.

Now it made sense why he'd refused her offer of a meal tonight. He'd been with the girl and her brother. Eva let the curtain drop, feeling lonelier than ever.

'All I'm saying is that it's a farm on the Isle of Wight. The owner's got no children and needs a lad he can train up. Maybe even leave the farm to when he passes on.'

'I don't want to go!' Teddy stood with his legs apart, perfectly balanced and openly defying Sid. Then he made a bolt for freedom. He got as far as the prefab's living room door before Sid pulled him back and thrust him face down onto the sofa. The hairy material against his cheek and mouth smelled of a thousand farts and made him feel sick.

'This is the chance of a lifetime,' said Sid. 'We can't go on living like we do now, with your sister and me being the only breadwinners. You'll be able to go to school over there. Study drawin' as you like it so much.'

Bess, witnessing Teddy's refusal to cooperate, looked worried sick. She asked, 'Will he be able to come home?'

'Of course he'll come home,' Sid snarled. 'It's not bleedin' Timbuktu he's going to, is it?'

'I wanted to keep the family together,' said Bess in a tiny voice. Sid released his hold and Teddy scrambled up and looked at his mother.

'Think of the good fresh air he'll be breathing,' persuaded Sid, 'the fine food he'll be eating. Good meat, fresh eggs and butter. Think of the future he'll have.'

'I don't know,' said Bess.

Teddy said, 'If I'm to be some sort of farmhand will I get paid for it?'

'Of course,' said Sid. 'You can either take your wages weekly or let 'em mount up to a sizeable sum. The choice will be yours. And,' he paused for effect, 'I don't want you sending any money home. With you gone we'll be able to manage nicely now Trixie's working.'

Teddy looked at Trixie for help but her face was closed.

'Will this farmer have to know about, about...' He didn't want to say the words.

'Why would he need to know anything?' Sid made a show of looking surprised. 'I'll tell you one thing. You'll be a hell of a lot safer on the Isle of Wight than you will here with the bleedin' coppers patrolling the estate regularly for yobbos who get out of hand. Portsmouth, bein' a small island, have got their coppers 'and in glove with Gosport's lot.'

Teddy had seen the police on their bicycles and in their cars going about the prefabs. Only the other night there had been a barney that started in the Fighting Cocks and ended near the parade of shops where a window had got broken and a Black Maria had carted off half a dozen drunken blokes. There were a few undesirable characters

90

living in the prefabs. Including his uncle.

'What about if I miss Mum and Trixie so much that I can't stand it? Will I be able to come home?'

'Of course,' said Sid, all smiles. 'Your mother's already asked that question.'

'And if the coppers come looking for me you won't tell them where I am?'

'You can depend on it,' said Sid.

Chapter Six

Teddy was sad that Trixie hadn't been allowed by Sid to come and wave him off at the ferry. But she'd have cried and he wouldn't like to have seen her big green eyes full of tears and him the cause of it all.

His aunt had said, 'You're a big boy, nearly eleven. In the old days, up north, you'd have been working down the pits by now, eyes full of coal dust and skin as black as the ace of spades. Think how lucky you are; you're going to live and work on a farm and start at a new school.'

He'd looked towards his mum, who'd sighed and said, 'You'll be safe on the island. I can't bear to think of the authorities knocking on this door and taking you away.'

That was the last thing Teddy wanted. He'd heard about the homes for young criminals. That's what he was now, a criminal. A boy who'd killed his father. At first he'd wondered if his mother and Trixie had simply wanted to be rid of him for all the trouble he'd caused.

'Don't be silly,' Trixie had snapped when he'd plucked up the courage to ask. 'No one *wants* to send their children away. And I shall miss you dreadfully. Kids younger than you are being sent to the country to escape the bombing. You just look upon this as you bein' an evacuee. We don't want you locked up in no prison-like place. If it wasn't for having to look after Mum, I'd come with you.'

He'd looked into her moist eyes and knew she was telling him the truth.

'One day I'll come back,' he said.

Trixie had put her arms around him and held him for a long time. He realised she was crying.

'I know you will,' she'd whispered.

He'd seen the big Isle of Wight steamers pass by the pontoon. They made the ferry boats look like little beetles. He wondered where the big boat was going to tie up so he could board it. It seemed funny he was the only one waiting to travel to the island.

It was dark with only the lights on the jetty and lamps on boats signalling their presence on the water. The air smelled heavily of oil and seaweed and a breeze was ruffling the feathers of the sleeping gulls.

He'd decided to make a go of working for the farmer. The past and the terror it held had been on his mind more than he'd like to admit. In his mind's eye he could see his father's body lying in the pool of blood. The images came into his head as soon as he woke in the mornings and stayed with him throughout the day. Then they stopped him sleeping properly at night. Teddy wished with all his heart that they would go away.

A thin drizzle had started up. Sid's voice cut into his thoughts. 'This side of the pontoon, lad. The boat's here.'

Teddy strained his eyes in the darkness. A man in a Guernsey sweater and Wellington boots with the tops turned over was tying a small boat up to a bollard. Surely he couldn't be going all the way to the island in this little boat?

'Jump in, lad.'

'I thought it would be a bigger boat.' He looked to his uncle for reassurance. Sid was shaking hands with the man who was now on the jetty.

'On one of those big boats a lad alone would stick out like a sore thumb. People might start asking questions, then they'd remember you. If or when your dad's body is found, people might wonder why you were alone.' Sid was all smiling teeth at him. 'A summer's night, a small boat and no one around. No, it's better this way, Teddy. Get in.'

Teddy hesitated. Waves lapped against the wooden pontoon that was now slippery with the rain and he could hear the splish, splosh of fish jumping in the muddy waters. He steadied himself by holding on to the side of the wheelhouse as he stepped aboard. He was scared. But surely everything would be all right; his uncle had assured him of that, hadn't he?

The man in the warm jumper picked up his holdall that contained clothes, his beloved drawing materials and bits and pieces that his mother and Trixie had decided he might need.

'I ain't supposed to be moored here. Get down

in the cabin and make yourself comfortable. By the time you've had a little kip, we'll be there.' The man passed him the holdall as he climbed back aboard the boat. Teddy could smell cigarette smoke on him. The man started up the engine.

Teddy stood on the boat's deck and watched his uncle unravel the rope from the bollard and throw it into the boat. Teddy waved as the vessel made a wide half circle in the murky water and then pointed itself towards the island.

He realised he was crying.

'It's been a month and we've heard nothing,' said Trixie. She folded the tea towel now she'd finished wiping the dinner plates and glanced at the piece of paper with the Isle of Wight address on it that Bess had handed to her.

'You got his whereabouts there. If you want to make him look like a mother's boy, write again. If you want to give the lad a bit of independence, leave him to write to you.' Sid wiped his hand across the back of his mouth and then burped.

'Suppose you're right,' said Bess. Trixie knew she wouldn't let on to Sid that she couldn't read. Bess took the paper back from Trixie and stuffed it in her cardigan pocket.

'I've got a surprise for you, Trixie girl.' Sid put his fingers beneath her chin and tipped her face towards him. Disgusted, she wriggled away. Sid moved closer, seemingly undeterred. 'My mate what manages the Fighting Cocks needs a girl to help out in the evenings. I said you'd be willing to think about it.'

'I think you'll find I'm not old enough to work

in a bar.'

'Ah, now, as so many of the local women are working in the armaments yards and doing blokes' work, he'll shut his eyes to that. Anyway, with a little bit of paint and powder you'll pass for eighteen.'

'I've already got a job.' She wasn't going to give up working in the greengrocer's for she'd come to like the regular customers and loved having a laugh with them. Gramps, too, made her laugh and talked to her like she was a grown-up, listening to the suggestions and ideas she had about improving the shop. Money was tight but happiness wasn't.

'That's only part time and so is this. Just a few evenings here and there.'

His voice had that wheedling quality that she so hated.

'I thought you said we were managing nicely since Teddy's no longer here.'

'That's true, Trixie, love.' Sid put his hand on her mother's shoulder. 'But your mum's going to need no end of bits and pieces for the new baby.'

Bess looked at her and blushed. It was emotional blackmail, for Bess would never say outright that she needed anything for herself or the baby. Trixie gave a deep sigh. She knew she'd have to do what her uncle wanted, if only to keep the peace.

'What on earth are you doing in here?' Jem stared at the heavily made-up girl behind the bar.

'Serving you,' said Trixie. He couldn't take his eyes off her. Either there was no mirror in the prefab or she really did want to look like a tart. A group of men were sitting in the corner playing dominoes, a couple of elderly blokes were playing shove halfpenny and there were a few younger lads and their girls all primped up and leaning against the jukebox tapping their feet to 'Mairzy Doats' by the Merry Macs. He knew the younger element were in the Fighting Cocks because there was going to be a group playing there later on. No one else was staring at Trixie. Was he really the only person who cared whether she made a laughing stock of herself?

She had on a tight white sweater that looked too small for her and a red scarf tied around her neck, a skirt that clung to her hips like a second skin and high heels that made her bottom wriggle every time she took a step in the smoke-laden bar. He gulped. If he'd ever thought Trixie was still a child he'd been mistaken.

'You don't look nice with all that make-up plastered over your face. It makes you look cheap.' He pursed his lips and stared over her shoulder at the bottles on the shelves behind her. Very few contained the liqueurs promised on the labels. Coloured water had been exchanged for the alcohol – the war years had made it difficult to come by.

'Thank you,' Trixie said. She put her hands on her hips and pouted at him like an out-of-work actress. He realised with dismay that she had been sampling the drinks. She didn't appear drunk, simply that her inhibitions were lost. 'A girl likes to hear compliments. Anyway, Eva says I look great. It was her as helped me put the make-up on.'

'I ... I'm sorry. I didn't mean to sound so blunt.'

He didn't want to hurt her feelings; it was simply that he cared about her and didn't want any harm to come to her. Girls who wore too much make-up were often thought of by men as 'easy'. At the end of the bar, Eva gave him a little wave to attract his attention. She was serving a customer and laughing while she pulled a pint.

'I want to look older.'

'You look cheap.'

Trixie sniffed. 'But do I look older?' Her hair was shining like gold. She'd tied it back somehow and it made her eyes look larger. He wondered why it upset him so much that Trixie was working in the pub and trying to make herself look older than she was.

'Well?' Trixie pressed.

'Yes,' he growled.

'Right, do you want serving or not?' She was agitated, tapping her fingers on the bar top. Damn! He'd upset her now.

'A pint of Brickwoods,' he said. Trixie began pulling on the pump. It was obvious it hadn't taken her long to learn how to serve a smooth pint and to memorise the types of drinks – not that customers wanted fancy cocktails in the Fighting Cocks. She gave him the glass of foaming beer and took the money. 'But why work here?'

Clayhall estate wasn't exactly the best part of Gosport and sometimes the rougher element came in the pub looking for trouble, wanting a fight. What if she got caught up in a brawl? She might get hurt.

'What's wrong with this place? You're in here.' Trixie, after putting the money in the till, had resumed her stance of hands on hips, looking as though she was ready to fight *him*!

'There's nothing wrong with the Fighting Cocks, it's–'

'It's that men might be staring at me and you don't like it.' He stared at her, took a large mouthful of beer and then choked on it. 'Ha! So I'm right,' she said.

He knew he looked ashamed of himself. Trixie might be young but she'd just worked out exactly what was on his mind. He took another pull on his pint but this time afterwards he said quietly, 'Look, we seem to have got off on the wrong foot and I apologise. It's all my fault because I'm a bloke and I know how other blokes' minds work when they see a piece of tail the other side of the bar, painted to the nines. They ask to see you home and then...' His voice tailed off as Trixie broke in with, 'Well, you don't have to worry about me. Me and Eva are walking back together.' Jem blessed Eva for her foresight. He took another drink as she said, 'I don't like your description of me but I'll take the apology. So I forgive you,' she said. 'Still it's better in here where there's a wooden counter between me and a pair of groping hands. Not like at home in the prefab where Sid's always waiting to catch hold of me. I make sure I always keep the bathroom door firmly locked so that Sid doesn't "accidentally" come in while I'm bathing and I try to never be alone with him.' Her voice was slightly slurred by drink and he guessed that had she been completely sober she'd never have let that information slip.

'Are you saying what I think you're saying?' Jem

had heard that Sid couldn't keep his hands to himself, but this girl was Sid's niece, for Christ's sake!

'Don't worry, he hasn't caught me, yet,' she said. She gave a cheeky grin, but Jem could sense her underlying worry. She stopped talking to him to draw Old Sam a whisky from the optic and to take the payment for it.

When she returned he said, 'I want you to promise you'll come to me if there's anything you can't handle.' Trixie stared at him. He needed to make her understand he would do anything and everything in his power to keep her safe. 'Well?' He knew he was demanding a lot of her. 'Well?' he repeated.

Trixie stared at him. 'I promise,' she said. 'But I'll need to keep on my toes now my brother's left home. So perhaps it's just as well that Sid's got me working here.'

'Gramps told me young Teddy's gone away. He didn't say where.'

'I didn't tell him, that's why,' Trixie said. 'But I'm worried because he's been gone some time and he's not written. It's not like him to forget all about us.'

'Got an address?'

Trixie nodded.

'You can always go and see him.'

Then Eva sauntered up to Trixie and said, 'You've got a lemonade bought by Dennis and it's at the end of the bar.'

Jem looked along the bar and saw a man with Brylcreemed hair eyeing up Trixie. Jem knew him as a married man with an eye for the ladies. Trixie mouthed, 'Thank you,' at him while Eva's eyes swept over the sea of customers. Jem saw those eyes linger on the dirty glasses on the tables. 'Them ashtrays want cleaning out. You'd better go and see to it and bring the glasses in for washing.' Jem had the feeling Eva liked ordering Trixie about.

Trixie shrugged and walked down the length of the bar to the drink sat on the shelf at the back. She picked it up, took a swallow and shuddered. Jem had an idea that the drink didn't just contain lemonade. His heart fell. The last thing Trixie needed was to be introduced to alcohol at her age. He watched as she looked beneath the counter and found a cloth. She used her shoulder to hoist up the wooden hatch near him. Eva lowered it after Trixie passed through and into the crowd on the other side of the bar.

A customer claimed Eva's attention. Jem finished his drink and went out, slamming the door and feeling extremely unhappy.

Teddy sat on the stained blue silk chair. Henry sat opposite him.

'Ever done anything like this before?' Henry's foot was swinging back and forth, back and forth. The room stank of neglect and dampness.

Teddy didn't want to answer him. Henry was new to the game and Teddy didn't want him crying all over him. He couldn't help Henry any more than he could help himself. 'I hate the men; they're nothing but dirty bastards,' he growled and looked away from the boy, who was younger than him. Barely a couple of months had passed since he'd stepped off that little boat, a boy full of hope for the new life he was going to. Those weeks had changed him. He'd learned to shut his eyes and mouth to what went on around him. He'd learned that he didn't have an opinion about anything. And he'd learned to accept without question everything he was told to do, say, or be.

To agree to his fate was less trouble and less painful.

The room was squalid with bare boards. Once upon a time, Teddy guessed the velvet curtains had been luxurious. Now they fell from ceiling to floor like red rags. Teddy knew that the house had taken a small hit during the early part of the war and the original owners had moved out to the mainland. The once-stylish Victorian house in Ryde was now used as a residence for the children, all boys. And it was where the men came to visit them.

In that house the men would choose their 'friend', take them upstairs to another room with a bed and begin seducing the boy.

Teddy had lost count of the men. That first time had been the worst. The unknowing, the fear, the distaste and of course the pain of the act. Nothing anyone could have said would have prepared Teddy for that first hateful performance.

And now? Now Teddy knew he was trapped, that it was impossible to escape from the house or from the men. Guards and iron bars saw to that.

His life before with a sister and mother who loved him was as if it had never been. He was a boy to be fucked by any stranger who had a fancy

101

for him and the price in his pocket.

Teddy had sprouted a little blond fluff on his chin and his fair hair was in long strings around his head, but he knew his shapely mouth that curved upwards and his small slim body made him a desirable target and there was not a thing he could do about it.

He also knew all the rubbish Sid had spouted about him working on a farm had been lies. He'd been sold.

Henry was crying.

'Just think about something else,' said Teddy. 'Anything to take your mind off what they do to you.' Henry's eyes opened even wider. It was the little boy's first time.

Unless it was absolutely necessary Henry wouldn't be drugged first. The men didn't want the boys to be like zombies. But Teddy knew that before dawn came Henry would have been used so many times he would be an object, not a person. Eventually, when the boy was allowed to sleep, he'd wish he were dead.

After Henry's initiation the boy could join the other lads down on Ryde Pier.

Teddy remembered the first morning he'd become a member of the parade. The man, his guard, his restrainer, had pointed to the iron railings near the pavement where the road winds into the town.

'That's called the Meatrack. You'll be on show there for the punters to take their pick. Don't get any stupid ideas about trying to run for it. We got guards everywhere. Too much trouble from you and you're expendable. End of the war and kids

102

go missing all the time.'

Teddy hadn't really known what the man was on about. But when he'd been brought back to the house and met the other boys he was told, 'The authorities close their eyes for a backhander and a taste of the boys they fancies.'

Teddy could see the tears in Henry's eyes. 'I'll give you a tip.' Hope sprang across the boy's face. 'Try to make out you like it. That way they're kinder to you.' Teddy scratched his head – the nits were biting again. He'd never thought that vermin in his hair would be the least of his worries.

He thought of Trixie and remembered how happy they'd all been that night of the meal at Jem's place. Perhaps he had no right to be content after what he'd done to their dad. Perhaps this was fate's way of punishing him, this terrible life he had now.

Trixie jumped at the sound of her name being called. She rolled off the lumpy sofa and ran into her mother's bedroom, switching on the electric light. Overhead the drone of planes signalled another raid. When had she become so used to raids that she could sleep through them? Automatically she looked at the windows to make sure there was no light shining out into the night.

Her mother was sitting up in bed looking unhealthily flushed.

Another pain gripped the woman and Trixie saw her clenched fingers dig into the bedclothes as she tried to fight it. The sheet was red with blood.

'Joan,' Trixie shouted. 'It's the baby.' To her

mum she said, 'Don't worry, it'll be all right.'

When Joan didn't immediately appear she ran into her bedroom. Joan was sprawled across the bed and a half-empty whisky bottle was on the floor. In Joan's hand was a small photograph in a wooden frame on the pillow that had made an indent in her cheek. Trixie gently removed the photo in case it hurt her. She stared at it. Joan and Sid smiled back at her. The young Sid was handsome, with a cheeky grin and he was looking fondly at Joan. Trixie could see he'd been quite a catch in his younger days. She put the photo on the bedside table and pulled the counterpane up over Joan's naked shoulders. Alcohol fumes filling the room suggested that Joan was out of it and Trixie'd get no help from her. Trixie ran back to her mother. Bess sat holding her stomach. 'Help me,' she croaked. 'The contractions are really close.'

A huge clattering sound filled the air as the aftershock of a bomb falling nearby shook the prefab. Dust swirled like snow. Trixie held on to the doorframe.

'What a time to start having a baby,' she grinned at her mother. Dirt and bits of loose plaster were still falling from the ceiling. 'Can you stand?'

'I'll try.' Her mother gripped the metal bedstead and hoisted herself upright. Trixie grabbed the bloodstained sheets and blankets from the bed and threw them in the corner of the room. From a trunk near the window she pulled out clean bedding. Voices and footsteps sounded outside, then faded away.

Bess was doubled over with pain as another

contraction took her.

'Hold my hand.' Her mother's voice was fearful. 'It's coming too quickly.'

'I want you back in a clean bed, ready for the birth.' Nevertheless Trixie held on to her mother's hand, which felt papery and hot.

'You're a good girl,' her mother gasped and doubled over as far as the bulge would allow. 'I'm having a baby and we could be blown to smithereens any minute.'

'I've got to get the midwife,' Trixie cried. 'Grab the iron bedhead. Grip that to help you with the pain.' She threw clean bedding on the mattress and smoothed out the sheets. She didn't bother about the pillows but chucked them in the corner of the room.

'Get your soiled nightie off; I'll find you another. Then get in there. I must go.' Trixie put out her hand to help her mother.

'Don't leave me. There's no time for a midwife. You were there when I had Teddy; you can help me with this one. You can do it, Trixie.'

Trixie remembered. She had been a tiny girl, five or six perhaps? And the midwife blessed her for being a run-around, staggering in with piles of old towels that her mum had put by for such an emergency. Trixie would never forget the tenderness she had felt for Teddy as he had slid from between her mother's legs, all long and slithery. That tiny baby had looked at her and she knew she would love him, without question, for ever. Afterwards, Teddy, as soon as he could toddle, had followed her everywhere.

Despite dishing out the orders, Trixie could see

her mother was very scared as she fell into the clean bed. Trixie sat down on the edge and held her mother's hand, smoothing back the hair from her forehead as Bessie sweated and cried with pain. Could she help her mother give birth? Well, there was no guarantee she'd be able to find the midwife. Because of the bombing, she could be anywhere and Trixie didn't want to leave her mother on her own while she searched.

Then a hooter cut through the night. Despite the bombs already falling it was a warning of further enemy action.

'Jesus,' cried her mother, gasping for air, 'bloody buzz bombs as well.' As though on cue the ominous sound of the buzz bomb grew louder and louder as it came closer and closer. A scream rent the air as Bessie then began breathing heavily and grunting. She lay on her back, her knees fallen apart. Another long scream and out slid a long, thin child covered in a pale waxy substance. Almost at the same time the buzz bomb went silent. Trixie held her breath and placed her hands on the bed, propping herself above her mother and the baby to protect them as best she could. A loud bang cut through the silence and the prefab began to shake once more. In the kitchen crockery fell to the floor, adding to the noise.

'A boy, it's a little boy.' But as soon as Trixie shouted she knew it was a dead child.

Trixie ran into the kitchen, stepping carefully over broken glass and shattered cups. She foraged in a drawer for the scissors so she could cut the baby's cord.

Back in the bedroom, her mother said to her,

'The kiddie's been dead a while.' She lay pale and gaunt amongst the birth detritus, not moving, just looking at the ceiling.

Trixie wiped the child, and was about to hand it to her mother when her mother turned her face away.

'Not sure you should do that, Mum. You might regret it.' How would Bess reconcile herself later to refusing to cuddle the baby? To not wanting to acknowledge the dead child's existence?

Bess shook her head. 'That baby's brought me nothing but unhappiness,' she said. 'Take it away.'

Trixie carried the tiny, naked form to the chest of drawers and slid out a small drawer on its runners. She emptied the drawer, placing the baby inside on a towel. Her eyes were full of tears as she stared at the unwanted child. She stood for a few moments saying the Lord's Prayer inside her head.

Then she went back to cleaning up Bess.

'Put this beneath you.' The big bath towel helped soak up the flow of blood from her mother but did nothing to stem it. Trixie had just covered her up when the front door banged open and Sid came in. He walked through to the bedroom and stood in the doorway, staring at Bess. He was hung over, scruffier than ever and stank of booze.

'Fucking bombs,' he said.

Trixie ignored him, turned to the window and pulled back the curtain a smidgeon. She could see searchlights criss-crossing the sky. She let the curtain fall but the beams were changing the dark colour of the blackout cloth to orange and yellow as the sky was checked for enemy planes.

'She needs a doctor,' Trixie said, attending to

Bess, then wrapping the afterbirth in a newspaper and taking it into the living room and throwing it in the fire that fed the back boiler.

'Where's my Joan?' Sid, unsteady on his feet, had followed Trixie and didn't seem perturbed about the scene around him.

'Drunk. Useless.'

'Watch your mouth, girl.'

'Get a doctor!' she screamed at him.

'Who wants a doctor?'

The green-coated woman filled the open door-way. Two red-haired boys peered into the living room from behind her ample form. Trixie almost wanted to hug Mrs Kowalski. 'It's me mum; she's had the baby, it's dead and I can't stop her bleeding.' All her words tumbled over one another as she tried to make the woman understand her fear.

'Kenny and Paulie, run for Dr Dillinger. He'll ask no questions and give her the best attention,' she said, turning back to Trixie. 'Get out of the way, you useless man,' she said, pushing Sid into the other bedroom where Joan lay asleep.

Sid, about to protest, seemed to shrivel up. He kicked the bedroom door shut behind him. Obviously deciding to leave Marie Kowalski to it.

Trixie felt she had to air her disapproval about the kids running the war-torn streets. 'But there are bombs falling outside! Your children.'

'My Kenny and Paulie got the same chance out there as we 'ave in here.' She looked at the closed door of Joan's bedroom, then turned away. 'Besides I wouldn't send that bugger Sid on an errand I knows he couldn't handle.' Mrs Kowalski now stood over Bess who was lying quite still with her eyes closed. Then she saw the dead baby in the drawer and picked up the embroidered runner from the dressing-table and covered the child. 'Poor little mite,' she murmured. 'Didn't stand a chance. Your mother must have had a hell of a time.' She went very quiet, standing there. Then she steered Trixie out of the bedroom and pulled the door to behind them. 'Get the kettle on, girl; we could do with a cuppa. Looks like you already attended to the worst part of the birth. You done good.'

In the kitchen Trixie lit the gas and shook the kettle to see how much water it held. Marie was picking up the broken crockery.

'I heard the commotion as I was coming up the path from the Fighting Cocks. They've had a group there tonight singing and my two eldest wanted to listen. The manager said they could as long as they was with me because they aren't old enough to be in a pub on their own.'

'I'm really pleased to see you,' Trixie said. 'Mum wouldn't let me leave her.'

'I should think not,' said the woman. 'I just don't want you to think I'm interfering.' Marie tucked a stray lock of hair behind her ear.

'She's going to die, isn't she?' Trixie was filled with emotion. 'There's so much blood, see, and it can't be right.'

Mrs Kowalski put her arms around Trixie, who thought she smelled of freshly cooked cakes. 'Don't you go courting bad luck before it comes.' Marie had now taken over the chore of tea making and had pressed Trixie down on one of the kitchen chairs. 'I'm not making tea for your

109

mum; let her sleep – it'll do her more good. And as for them other two drunken sots...' She shook her head in disgust.

Trixie heard the front door, that she'd left on the latch, fly open and hit the hall wall. Footsteps sounded outside on the flagstones. Then silence. It had to be Sid, for Joan was practically comatose. He'd gone out again. Trixie breathed a big sigh of relief.

Mrs Kowalski looked at her. 'Nasty piece of work, him. We're better off without the bugger.' She filled the teapot with boiling water, set the kettle back on top of the cooker then left the kitchen. Two minutes later she returned with two bottles of whisky. 'Bit of luck. I went in the bedroom to see if Madam was awake but she's still out for the count. Did you know Sid has a couple of boxes of whisky in there? Trixie shook her head. 'This'll do to pay the doctor with. Partial to his drink is Dr Dillinger. Have you met him?'

Trixie shook her head. She was feeling more secure now the big woman seemed to have taken charge. And that's when she noticed the silence. 'Another raid over,' Trixie said.

The two stared at each other. Mrs Kowalski smiled and Trixie knew in that instant that she had a friend. She slid off the chair and stirred the pot before she poured out the tea.

'That's it, good and strong.' Mrs Kowalski nodded towards the teapot. 'I was telling you about Dr Dillinger. He got struck off. Trouble over an abortion, but all the petitions in the world didn't do any good with reinstating him. There's many of us would sooner have his opinion than one from them new young doctors fresh from university.'

The banging at the front door shattered the silence and Trixie got up to let in the wildest-looking man she had ever seen.

Chapter Seven

'Where's the patient? The man strode past Trixie, his black cape flapping about his body, giving him the appearance of a large bat.

'In here.' Mrs Kowalski stood outside the bedroom door with her teacup in her hand. 'Fancy a brew?' she asked.

'Drop of the hard stuff would be better, Marie.' He pushed the bedroom door open and went in. Marie turned to her boys and said, 'You two go on home. Don't let the little ones eat all the bread but make a few sarnies for yourselves. I'll be home as soon as I can.' She gave them each a kiss on their foreheads that, strangely, thought Trixie, neither seemed to mind.

Trixie thought Dr Dillinger was the scruffiest man she'd ever seen. Uncle Sid was bad enough but Dr Dillinger was worse. He also stank of booze.

Marie Kowalski went back into the kitchen and reappeared with a cup in her hand. Trixie saw it contained alcohol.

'Don't worry, girly. He knows what he's doing. You look at his hands.'

In the bedroom Dr Dillinger had pushed aside her mother's nightdress and was listening to her heart. Trixie looked at the doctor's hands and saw they were scrubbed pink with cleanliness, their nails short and white. Trixie looked at Marie and smiled. Marie smiled back.

'The pair of you can help while I clean her up,' he announced, opening his Gladstone bag and taking out wrapped dressings that he put on the side table. He drank from the mug that Marie passed him. 'That's a nice drop of stuff,' he said, his eyes taking in Bess.

Afterwards, when Bess was comfortable, he took a final swig of the whisky and said, 'Thanks, Marie. There isn't a drop more, is there?' He looked at Trixie and said, 'Come outside. I want to talk to you.' Trixie looked at her mother making barely a mound beneath the bedclothes. Dr Dillinger said, 'I've pumped her full of stuff to make her sleep and I'm leaving medicine for you to give her.'

In the living room he added, 'She knows she's not got long. She wants to see Teddy. That your brother?' Trixie nodded. 'Be a good idea to let her see him as soon as possible. She's also begged me to take the baby away. You all right with that? Only some families prefer to bury their little ones, you know, have a service to say goodbye?'

Trixie nodded. Her head was spinning. Her mother blamed the child, was ignoring the boy's existence, wanting her first son close to her. How could she find Teddy?

'There's something else.' He stepped back and fingered his moustache. The sweet smell of whisky

112

was heavy about him. His dark eyes narrowed as he said, 'I heard you were drinking spirits at the Fighting Cocks. I'm no spoilsport but if you want to end up like your aunt or me, go ahead.'

Trixie opened her mouth to say something but closed it again when he interrupted her.

'No, I'm not telling you how I know but there's not much I miss,' he said. 'You can't learn by my example, but I allowed drink, or rather my own weakness for it, to take away the only job I ever wanted.' He shook his head. 'Of course, you know I'm not supposed to practise but I've got a lot of people who still have a bit of respect for an old drunk who only ever wanted to cure the sick. Don't you be like me, weak, girl; be strong enough to live your life to the full.'

Trixie thought of her father, drunk, laying into them. And her aunt, finding solace in a bottle. It wasn't what Trixie wanted. Trixie had fallen over on the way home that night. Arm in arm with Eva, she'd stumbled in the high heels, resolving that she'd never borrow Joan's shoes again. She hadn't hurt herself, only her dignity. It had never occurred to her that she was actually drunk. Even being sick through the night she'd thought she was ill. In the morning she'd felt like death warmed up. Later she realised that Eva must have been putting the odd shot of gin into her lemonade. Trixie had hated not feeling in control of herself.

The next evening that she worked with Eva, she'd taken the girl to one side and said, 'If you ever spike my drinks again, I will push your teeth down your throat.' Then she'd asked the manager if she could have the money instead for all the drinks that the customers bought her and was overjoyed when Jack agreed. Now, Trixie put bottle-tops at the back of the counter and Jack happily paid her threepence for each one.

Trixie fiddled with the sleeve of her cardigan. It had taken her a while to realise that Eva was being nasty to her because of the attention Jem was giving her. She wasn't sure yet how she would deal with the situation but in the meantime she had to work with the young woman, so she decided to ignore Eva's nastiness.

'Thank you for the excellent advice,' she said to the doctor. 'In fact thank you for all you've done. I've seen too much of what drink can do and I promise you that I'm a teetotaller from now on.' Then suddenly she burst into tears. 'I don't want my mum to die,' she wailed.

'I'm sure you don't,' he said. 'But the poor woman has had one kicking too many. She's going to a far more peaceful country, but if I were you I'd find Teddy as soon as possible.'

He went back into the bedroom and when he came out again he had a bundle in his hands. Trixie saw the bottles of whisky peeping from his bag. Marie kissed him on the cheek and then the door opened and he was gone.

Marie said, 'He's a good man but, like us all, deals with his unhappiness in his own way.'

Just then Joan came out of her bedroom, her hair like a bird's nest. She was shrugging herself into an old dressing-gown of Sid's. 'What's all the noise about?' She looked at Marie as though she was quite used to seeing her standing in her house.

'Just woke up from our drunken sleep, have

114

we?' Marie curled her lip in disgust. 'Well, it's too late to do anything for your sister. She had her baby and she's on her way out of this life. And all this has been happening while you've been sampling the delights of Sid's ill-gotten whisky.'

Joan pushed past her and went into the other bedroom, where she stood over the sleeping Bess. She tucked in the counterpane round her sister, then came out of the room, closing the door.

'Is this true, Trixie?'

Trixie began telling her of the doctor's visit and ended with, 'If you ever loved Bess, you have to tell me how to find Teddy. For I don't believe he's at that address.'

Joan said, 'I don't know where he is any more than you do. I promise you.'

'Believe her and you're daft,' Marie spat.

'I do,' Trixie said. 'Sid only tells her what he wants her to know. But,' she stared at Marie, 'if all we have is that address then we must begin looking there. It's a start.'

The moment the women stepped into the kitchen Trixie heard a key in the door and knew her uncle was home again.

Marie took one look at him and said, 'I'm going home to salvage what's left of this night. If you need anything, girly, you know where I am.' She glared at Sid and swept out.

Joan ran up to Sid, crying, 'My sister's going to die and she wants to see Teddy.'

Sid took off his coat, taking a while to hang it on the back of the door.

'We must make sure we get hold of him, then.'

'I don't believe he's at that address. If he is he

115

would have answered our letters.' Trixie stared at Sid.

'There's only one way to find out,' Sid said, staring right back at her. 'Go to the island. And now if you don't mind I intend to get some shut-eye.' And he slunk into the bedroom closing the door behind him.

Nice one, Siddy, he told himself. Young Trixie's got no way to get to the island. He took off his clothes, lit himself a cigarette, then lay on the bed. He inhaled deeply. His eyes roved around the room, taking in the scuffed furniture and the clothing hanging on nails banged in the walls and on the back of the door and then he breathed in the smell of his wife on the pillow beside him. No one would find out about the deal he had going with the lads in London. He was safe enough. Hadn't he been delivering children and stealing babies all through the war years and never once had he been suspected of anything.

The older children, unless a specific order for one was demanded, went to homes where they'd be used for sex. It was amazing, he thought, how many children were left walking dazedly about the streets after a bomb blast, and each of them in need of a helping hand. He smiled to himself. He gave them a helping hand all right. Straight down to Beattie's place in North Street if the kids were local. And she kept them hidden until they were removed to addresses he didn't even want to think about. If he went walkabout and picked up a kiddie from some place back of beyond, a quick phone call, and the child was taken from him. All he was ever left with was a bundle of notes and that's the way he liked it.

Babies were a nuisance but he got paid a hell of a lot more.

Sometimes it was underage girls giving birth, the parents too ashamed to keep the kiddie in the family. Couples unable to give birth to a kid of their own were very generous to his London friends in return for a newborn baby. He was a delivery man; he laughed at his own joke. He took the newborn and delivered it to its new parents.

Sometimes the poor cow giving birth didn't even know she'd had her child stolen from her. 'It's stillborn' was a very handy phrase. He stubbed out his fag on the overflowing saucer near the bed and his eyes fell on the box of whisky. He got off the bed and looked inside. Thieving bitch! She'd been at his drink! Surely the drunken sot hadn't downed that much? Ah, well, plenty more where that came from.

Jesus! What if Trixie got that stupid moony-eyed lump of a bloke called Jem to take her to the Isle of Wight?

He thought about her for a moment or two and felt his cock harden. She was turning into a curvy young thing. She reckoned she was helping the family financially by working at her two jobs. Well, it certainly saved him from having to cough up the cash to put food on the table. He laughed. He couldn't abide kids and young people. Not until young girls got to a fuckable age, at any rate. And she was gagging for it.

He sat down and drummed his fingers on the bed frame.

The chances of them finding Teddy were slim. Sid grinned. Meanwhile, if Jem offered to drive Trixie to the island, the least he could do would be to offer to get him some black market petrol, and none of that dyed red stuff either. He'd make sure it had been poured through a gas mask filter to remove the dye.

Sid got into bed. He was safe enough. If he wasn't, he'd do another flit.

'I think we'd best go to the Isle of Wight in my van,' Jem said. Secretly he was pleased Trixie had come to him for help. Her cheeks were rosy; thank God she'd stopped plastering her face with all that heavy make-up, and she'd just seen off a large slice of Gramps' apple pie. But she was wistful. He was worried about her, especially as she hated living in the prefab with Sid and Joan. But he could offer her no help as she wouldn't leave her mother while she was so ill, and he admired her for that.

'You'll come with me?'

She turned and he saw her large green eyes filled with tears. All he wanted to do was protect her. It wasn't fair she had such a big burden on her young shoulders.

The waves were making a large V shape behind the boat as it neared the port at Ryde. A disembodied voice over the tannoy system warned drivers to return to their cars. Trixie had enjoyed the short trip but was now filled with apprehension. She took the slip of paper with Teddy's address on it out of her skirt pocket and stared at it. Whatever would she say to him when they saw

118

Teddy? Would he be cross that they'd come to the island looking for him? She handed the piece of paper to Jem.

'Sandown's on the south-east part of the island and as the island isn't very big we should be able to find Warrington easily enough. The farm isn't far from the bay,' he said.

Jem drove the van down the pier, past several boys lounging near the railings, and turned towards the town. Out in the countryside the fields were still very green without signs of the early frost they'd experienced on the mainland.

'That's why people come here to live,' said Jem. 'The weather is just that bit better than ours on the south coast.'

'It's certainly pretty here,' Trixie replied, admiring a postcard-like village as they drove through. But after they'd been driving for some time, she said, 'Are you sure we're going in the right direction?'

'As far as I can tell,' said Jem. 'This is the road to Sandown and we need to go down as far as the beach, then turn off.'

The sands stretched as far as Trixie could see. On the seafront there was a pier and back from the pier a fairground. 'It's a great place to bring a family for a holiday,' she said. The van trundled away from the amusements, through the town and towards Warrington.

When the next village came into sight, Jem said, 'I'm going to stop at the next pub I see. We can't have missed the farm, but the area seems to be getting built up again.'

In the Quill and Pen, the barmaid shook her

head. 'I've lived here all my life. This is King Arthur's Road but there ain't no Mayflower Farm, and never was.' It had taken ages for Jem to get her attention. There was some kind of discussion going on and the locals were all talking at once.

'What's going on?' he asked.

The barmaid turned to him. 'Ain't you read no papers lately?'

Jem frowned and shook his head. The barmaid leaned close and said, 'That damn Hitler. It's come to light that there's now proof that in Majdenek concentration camp in Poland more than a million people have been gassed then cremated. Then the buggers used the ashes as fertiliser.' The barmaid looked like she might cry. She turned away to serve a customer.

Jem stared after her. He was stunned.

Trixie looked downcast. 'Bloody war,' she said finally.

Jem took a sip of his pint and was quiet for a long time before saying, 'I reckon this address is false and maybe that's why there's no telephone number on this.' He twisted the scrap of paper in his fingers. Trixie could see he could barely conceal his anger. 'The place doesn't exist. It's some big con your uncle thought up.'

'No, he wouldn't do that. Teddy's his nephew.'

'You don't know the man. He's a mean bastard.' Trixie realised Jem was probably right. She didn't know what Sid was capable of but she did know he wasn't a nice man to be around. Jem finished his drink and Trixie, with a heavy heart, swallowed the last of her orangeade. As she followed him to the van she wondered how she was going to tell her mother that Teddy wouldn't be coming home to see her after all. Trixie felt sure the only reason Bess was still with them was because she wanted to see Teddy and then die happy knowing he was all right. 'I'm driving to the local post office,' Jem announced. 'I certainly didn't disbelieve the barmaid but the postmaster will be able to check the address. If it really doesn't exist then I'll take you home. I suggest when petrol rationing ends,' he gave her shoulder a squeeze, 'we come over and drive around, scouring the island.'

Trixie nodded. 'You're a kind man,' she said. 'I'll have to hope he senses something's wrong and that he's needed and comes home of his own accord, won't I?' And she turned to Jem and allowed him to put his arms around her while she cried into his jacket. Trixie thought that, perhaps, it wasn't such a bad thing that she hadn't found her brother. If she couldn't find him then the police, if the business of their father came to light, wouldn't be able to, either.

Back at the end of Ryde Pier Teddy had recognised Jem's van leaving the ferry. He practically bent himself double hiding behind Mick's large figure.

'Oi! What's the matter with you?' Mick stepped aside and the shaken Teddy watched the van trundling up the road. It had shocked him seeing his sister sitting beside Jem.

'Hiding from someone I don't want to see,' Teddy confessed. In any other circumstances he'd have stopped the traffic to get at Trixie. But how could he be anywhere near her after what he'd become?

Big Mel was looking at him. The burly minder of the Meatrack boys never for one moment allowed any of the five boys under his care to think they could escape. Teddy gave him a wave. He'd long ago learned that being nice to Melvin meant that Melvin allowed him special privileges like a trip to the tea kiosk or to go unsupervised to the public toilets, where the deeds of the Meatrack boys were played out. Carl, the other minder, was on duty there to make sure none of his wards thought they could make a run for it.

Teddy knew if he attempted to escape he'd be hounded until he was caught and then set up as an example to the other boys. Henry had tried escaping not long ago. Castration had been the penalty, or so word had got round the boys. How much truth was in this story was anybody's guess, thought Teddy. But the story and Henry's disappearance had had the desired effect of stopping the lads from talking about escape.

No matter how many times Teddy washed and scrubbed himself he couldn't get the stink of the men off him. No, the shame of what he'd become meant he could never face Trixie or his mother again. Hadn't he brought enough shame to his family already by killing his father? Then he thought for a moment. Why should Trixie be looking for him? Whatever reason had sent Trixie looking for him, he told himself, she was better sorting it out without his help.

A tear slid down his cheek as he watched a large man with greasy hair trying to catch his eye. He sighed and went to greet his new friend.

Chapter Eight

The bar was packed. Trixie pulled a pint of beer and set it on the counter. She looked for another pint glass and found the shelf was empty. She sighed; the shortage of glass meant that the pub had to rely on collecting the empty glasses as quickly as possible. Tonight there was plenty of beer on tap at the Fighting Cocks, Trixie thought – wasn't that just the way of things? But then tonight there was a band playing. Trixie was so looking forward to singing along with the music, especially as she'd heard the band was excellent. The boys were setting up their equipment at the end of the room.

'I'll go,' offered Eva. You could have knocked Trixie down with a glass cloth. It wasn't like Eva to make her life easier. But she had been showing Trixie a kinder side of her nature recently.

'Won't be a moment,' Trixie mouthed to her customer, a lad with long hair who'd followed the band in.

Not only did Eva come back with a tray full of glasses, but she proceeded to wash them up. Trixie finished serving the lad.

'Seen Jem lately?' Eva asked. Trixie smiled. Eva wanted something she was sure of that. Trixie shook her head.

'Me mum's too ill for me to leave the prefab, except for work.' She stared at Eva, who looked pretty pleased with herself.

'He's taking me to the pictures on Friday.'

'*Double Indemnity*'s on at the Forum,' said Trixie. 'Fred MacMurray and Barbara Stanwyck, isn't it?' She felt a little bit miffed but didn't want to let on. Why hadn't Jem asked her if she'd like to go to the cinema? But then Jem knew she wouldn't leave her mother. 'You'll have to tell me all about it,' she said.

'Oh, I shall do that all right,' Eva said, with a toss of her long dark hair.

'I bet you will, an' all,' Trixie said under her breath.

The band began testing their gear and then everything seemed to happen at once as the music burst forth and Trixie felt so happy she thought she might explode with the enjoyment of it all. The bar seemed to be transformed to a place where everyone began tapping their feet as the music to 'Till Then' burst forth.

Trixie couldn't help but sing along.

'I didn't know you could hold a tune,' said Eva. 'You got a smashing voice.'

Trixie stared at the dark-haired girl. She'd really meant the compliment. Trixie blushed and watched as the three young men then struck the first chords of 'Twilight Time'. Then a girl stood up wearing a tight white jumper and a knee-length black skirt. Her hair was in a fashionable page-boy bob and she took centre stage to much applause. 'I'll Get By' came next and was one of Trixie's favourite songs so she hummed along with the girl, happy for once to be out of the prefab, even if it was just for work. Half way through the song the poor girl had a coughing fit and Trixie ploughed through the sweating crowds with a glass of water. The girl took it gratefully and said quietly, 'I thought I was getting over this bout of flu; obviously not.' Then to the customers, using the microphone she said, 'Sorry about that, folks.' Trixie could see the people liked the girl and her singing.

The group was called The Tropics. When Trixie asked Eva why they'd named themselves that, Eva said, 'Because they're really hot.'

Trixie loved the special musical arrangements the four-piece band gave to the songs normally played by big bands. And the girl, blonde and beautiful, was a perfect foil to the group, especially as the songs she sang were excellent for her sultry alto voice. Trixie also thought a good deal of their success was because they were young.

'They're really good,' she mouthed to Eva.

Just then Jack wove his way through the punters and managed to lean over the bar while setting down six dirty pint gasses he'd collected on the way.

'Take some drinks over to the band, Trixie. Pull up a big jug of beer for the lads and make a large gin and tonic for Kathy; that's her tipple. They'll be spittin' feathers if they don't wet their whistles soon.' He took out a handkerchief and wiped his forehead with it. The room was stifling now. 'I've also told them you're going to take the mic tonight.'

'What?'

'Take the mic.'

'Do you mean sing?' Trixie put a large jug beneath the beer pump. She'd heard it was a tradition for someone from the pub, usually a customer, to have a go at singing with the band. Sometimes, she'd been told, it was a right laugh.

'Well, I didn't mean scrub the floor.'

'I can't sing in front of people.'

'Of course you can. It's no different from singing like you do around the pub, except that you're doing it into a microphone.'

Trixie was stunned. How could he do this to her? She'd never sung in front of anyone before. Well, not a proper audience. She was scared stiff.

'If it's that easy, you do it!' She pulled down on the beer pump and beer sloshed everywhere except in the jug.

'Watch out! That's me profits!' Jack laughed. He repositioned the jug and poured the beer into the receptacle. 'I did, once,' he smiled for her alone. 'Everyone reckoned I had a voice like someone was treadin' on a cat's tail!'

Trixie began to laugh. She turned to the optic and double clicked for a large gin in a stemmed glass. Why shouldn't she sing? Yes, why not?

'All right then,' she said, flicking the top off a small bottle of tonic water. 'But if they laugh at me it'll be your fault!'

'They won't laugh.' Jack was very serious.

Trixie asked Eva to find her a tray.

The smoke in the bar stung Trixie's eyes but as she watched her pile of bottle tops growing she knew they would later amount to a tidy sum that she could use to buy something special for her mum. Suddenly she felt released from the sadness that permanently enveloped her and she realised she was quite looking forward to singing. Yes, she was. Even Eva was humming, caught up in the band's music.

In a moment of quiet Trixie asked Eva when Jem had asked her to the pictures.

'We've been working together down Gosport market today. He offered me a lift in. It's much easier sitting in a van than it is riding my bike. As we passed the cinema I mentioned I liked Fred MacMurray and he said he did as well. I said we ought to go and see it together then. But the only night he had free is tomorrow.'

Eva was quite animated. Trixie thought how much prettier she was when she wasn't scowling. Indeed when she talked about Jem, her face seemed to light up like a Christmas tree. Trixie realised that Eva cared a great deal about him and it was she who'd initiated the cinema visit.

'There's nothing between me and him, you know,' she said to Eva. 'I've got too much on my plate to think about blokes.' She felt a little disloyal telling Eva that, especially as she knew if she was just a couple of years older everything could be quite different between her and Jem. The plain fact was, Jem cared for her but there wasn't the same spark there from her perspective. Not like all that romantic love you saw in the films. Sure, she liked him, but it was the same way anyone would love someone who cared about them, wasn't it?

Eva stopped what she was doing and looked at her.

'I thought you were making a play for him.'

Trixie shook her head. Eva smiled at her. Trixie suddenly felt that everything had changed

127

between them.

And then the music stopped and restarted with a drum roll.

Kathy had taken the mic. 'Now, everyone, it's our newcomer slot and tonight's star solo singer is...' She paused while the customers shouted and whistled for sheer joy. Kathy put her hands up to quieten the audience then said, 'The pride of the Fighting Cocks: Trixie!'

Trixie honestly didn't have time to feel scared.

'What you gonna sing?' the lad at the guitar asked.

Trixie passed the tray of drinks, now complete with glasses in which to pour the beer, to Kathy and said, '"I'll Get By As Long As I Have You". D'you know it?'

'Course they do,' smiled Kathy. 'It's one of mine. Good luck, Trixie.'

Music started and Trixie opened her mouth.

When she stopped singing there was silence.

And then the pub erupted.

Bess's body made barely an outline in the bed. Her skin and the white sheets were almost the same colour. She was propped up by pillows and Trixie sat on the edge of the bed, trying to spoon some soup into her mouth.

'That man's gone again, I see.' Marie was a regular visitor to the prefab and her red-haired children often knocked to ask if any errands were needed. She hoisted herself onto a chair near the bed.

'Sid's been gone a month or so,' said Joan. 'Got business in Southampton.'

'So he says.' Marie never tried to hide her dislike of Sid. 'I heard you sang in the pub, Trixie.'

'She's a lovely singer,' said Bess.

'You know, I was scared stiff when they suggested it but when it came to singing, I just did it,' said Trixie. 'Once I'd started it was like it wasn't me there singing in front of those people, it was whoever had written the song and all the meanings of the words came from deep inside me, making me want to share the song with all the pub.' She suddenly stopped talking and looked at Marie to see if the woman thought she'd lost her mind.

Marie smiled at her. Trixie knew she understood exactly what she was trying to convey.

'It was like it was something I was born to do, if that doesn't sound like I'm trying to be big-headed.'

'You couldn't be big-headed if you tried,' said Joan.

'She came out of me, singing,' said Bess.

Trixie knew she was blushing. She looked at the dish of food and saw that Bess had eaten a fair bit. 'Anyway, how are you getting on?' she asked Marie. 'Have you heard from Dmitri?'

Marie looked sad. 'No, not since I had that letter from him saying he'd reached Wroclaw, his home town, and that his family's glass business was in deep difficulties.'

Trixie knew nothing of Marie's life and hadn't liked to ask her. She wiped Bess's chin and settled her, leaving her to sleep. The other women quietly left the bedroom and congregated in the kitchen.

'Put the kettle on, Joan,' said Trixie. 'I'll get this washing up out of the way.' She started collecting dirty dishes and piling them in the enamel bowl. 'So what's he like, your Dmitri?'

'Sexy,' said Marie and they all laughed.

'That's why she's got so many kids and no money,' said Joan.

'He's got hair the colour of fire and a little beard that tickles when he kisses me.'

'How did you meet him?' Trixie asked.

'The second time? Or the first?' Marie laughed.

Trixie was stunned but she let Marie carry on. 'The second time was at a dance at the Connaught Hall. He was working at Haslar Hospital after leaving Diddington Camp where they'd taken him after he was injured, fighting with the rest of our lads in France. But I'd had a fling with him a few years before when he was on a training course at St George's barracks.'

'And you fell in love?' Trixie thought it was so romantic.

'Well, the very first date resulted in my eldest kiddie. I didn't tell Dmitri I was pregnant because I didn't want him to feel trapped. When the course ended and he left Gosport, I didn't think I'd see him again.'

Marie went all dreamy eyed. 'He'd been trying to find me. Not that I knew it, then. But I couldn't get him out of my head. Fine big strapping man.' She paused. 'We met again when he was sent back to Gosport. We got no end of Polish blokes in England who are helping us during the war. Dmitri then got news that he should return to Poland. The Poles are fighting gallantly at present to save Warsaw. It's being reduced to ashes. His mum can't look after the factory and there's a sister whose husband got shot by the Germans. Two brothers, one older than Dmitri, the other only twelve years old, had been taken to Majdenek.'

There was silence in the room. Trixie knew all about the prison camp and the atrocities being discovered there. Marie continued, 'Anyway, he sends me money when he can and I know he'll come back here as soon as he's able. He wants me to go to Poland when the war is over but that's not what I want. Nor him; deep down he wants to return and stay here in England.'

'Oh, Marie, I never knew.'

'You thought I was an unmarried slut, didn't you?' Marie was laughing but Trixie was surprised Marie had said that. 'I'm not stupid; I hear what I'm called on the estate.'

'Are you married to him?' Joan asked.

'No. But I comfort him as much as I can, when I can. Trouble is I only got to touch his trousers and I fall for another kiddie.'

Marie convulsed into laughter again and this time Joan and Trixie laughed with her. Joan stopped giggling long enough to go into her bedroom and come out with a bottle of whisky.

'What about a little snifter in our tea, eh, girls?'

'Not for me,' said Trixie.

'More for me then,' said Joan.

Trixie dozed, curled up on an old cane chair, at her mother's bedside. The laboured breathing had lulled her to sleep and now she had woken. It was ten past three in the morning and only the usual creaking night noises marred the prefab's silence. Trixie smiled, her mother had been chirpy tonight, happy that the women around her had included her in their banter. It had been a long while since she'd seen her so bright.

Trixie pulled the old shawl around her shoulders. It was cold in the bedroom. A shiver passed through her. Whatever had woken her? The silence, yes, that was it: there was no sound of her mother's breath. Trixie felt for her mother's hand. Its chill and papery touch told her Bess had passed away.

Trixie gulped back tears. It wasn't the time to cry for herself. Her mother was free from pain and she should be happy for her. Happy that her last evening on earth had been spent in the company of women who loved her. But how much more contented her mother would have been if Teddy had been there as well. Trixie knew it was silly to dwell on Teddy's disappearance. She got off the chair and stood over her mother.

All the lines of heartache seemed to have been wiped away from her face. A hint of a smile raised the corner of her soft mouth and her eyes were closed. It looked as though she was in the throes of a happy dream.

Trixie bent and kissed her mother's cool forehead. 'I love you, Mum,' she said. Then she walked out of the room and went into Joan, who was sleeping perilously close to the edge of the bed.

Trixie shook her aunt's shoulder. 'She's gone,' was all she said as the woman opened her eyes.

There was no need for explanations or discussion and Trixie felt so tired she was happy when Joan said, 'Go back to bed.' Joan swung her legs from the mattress and tied herself into her pink candlewick dressing-gown. 'I'm making tea, then I'll take over sitting with her.' A waft of violet perfume was released by her exertions.

Trixie rubbed her eyes. A wave of tiredness swallowed her.

She slept like a log. It was, she thought, when she woke later, as though all the waiting was over and she had, at last, been able to relax.

Dr Dillinger was called out to sign the death certificate. He smelled of stale whisky but the way he walked, talked and explained exactly what they must do next, showed him to be as sober as a judge.

Trixie and Joan started preparing for the funeral. The next day, when Joan had gone to the funeral directors in Stoke Road, Sid came home, breezing into the prefab without a care in the world. He had on a new suit and new shoes. Trixie thought he was definitely in the money this time.

Trixie was ready for him. 'Where's my brother?'

'Where's Joan?' was his answer.

'Gone to the funeral parlour; me mum died.'

Not an eyelid flickered as he digested the news. Then he said, 'You know he's on a farm on the Isle of Wight.' Trixie was amazed that such a barefaced lie could emerge from his mouth.

'That farm doesn't exist. Jem and I looked for it.'

'Might have known he'd be there as well, dear Jem.'

'Where's Teddy?' It was too late now for her mother to see her son, but Trixie wanted Teddy back home with her. She bitterly regretted leaving Portsmouth and knew it was all her fault that things had turned out the way they had. If only

133

she'd not taken charge of the family.

'If your brother's gone missing it's nothing to do with me. Perhaps he ran away because the police frightened him; who knows?' Sid had taken off his jacket and thrown it over the back of the chair. She smelled the sweat of him and stepped away but he followed her movements as though they were in a dance.

She could see the bulge rising in his trousers, straining against the material. He instinctively cupped his hand to his cock. He groaned. Now Sid was very close to her. His breath smelled of dead things and it made her stomach heave. She saw his raw need and she was terrified of him. She turned away, pushing him aside, but he grabbed her, pulling her back.

'Oh, no you don't,' he said. 'I reckon you owe me.'

'What for?' What on earth did he mean? She worked at two jobs and almost all her money came to the prefab to keep food on the table. She knew from Joan that Sid contributed very little.

'Living in my house.'

'It's not your house; it's Joan's name on the rent book and I pay my way.' Trixie was shaking. Where she was getting the courage from to answer him back like this she didn't know. 'And when there's nothing in the cupboard to eat, I watch your wife guzzling whisky.'

'So you begrudge Joan a drink, do you?' He hit her then. Slapped the side of her head so hard that she staggered and fell. Trixie tried to get up but he hit her again and it felt as though everything in her head had become unfastened.

A cry escaped her lips. And then he kicked her so she fell onto her back and he was on top of her, lashing out with his feet so the furniture was not in the way.

Dizzy, she felt his hands hold her lower body. He used one hand to unbutton his flies and then heat swept into her genitals as he thrust his cock inside her, hurting her, and uncaring as he thrust his penis deeper and deeper.

'Leave me alone!' Trixie knew she was screaming but Sid put his hand over her mouth. She heard the sound of ripping material and realised it was her clothes that the crazed man was pulling off her.

'Ahhhh.' He groaned.

And then it was over.

His body shuddered. Sid got up, pulling on his trousers and doing up his fly buttons. Trixie lay on the filthy carpet, too scared to move in case he hit her again, too frightened to cry. When he was dressed, he looked down at her, then took his wallet out of his back pocket.

The bank notes floated down and settled on her as he said, 'They're talking about bringing in a free National Health service to help people who can't afford doctors. They'll never bring in a free funeral service. Use this to bury your mother, for your sexual services certainly aren't worth paying for.'

He slammed the door on his way out.

Trixie lay on the floor for a long time before she went into the bathroom and sat in a bath as hot as she could take it. Even then she got out, went into the kitchen and searched for a wire pot scourer to scrub at her flesh until it bled.

And all the while the voice inside her head was singing so that she would not go mad.

Marie stepped carefully over the broken paving stone. The council never seemed to do repairs these days, she thought. Perhaps, once the war was over, if it ever ended, they'd get their act together and repair the broken fences, smashed streetlights and rebuild on the bomb sites.

It was dark, gone eleven, but she didn't think Trixie would be in bed yet. Not with the funeral from this morning fresh in her mind.

There weren't many people at the graveside to see Bess off. Marie had watched as Trixie had allowed the tears to roll unchecked down her face. It wouldn't be so bad if Trixie could depend on her aunt for a bit of support while she was grieving but the silly woman had crept inside the whisky bottle again and was no use to anyone, including herself. Even that bastard of a man, Sid, hadn't been at the funeral. Marie wouldn't trust him as far as she could throw him.

She thought about her own brood safely in bed with the older ones looking after them. Life was hard with Dmitri gone but Marie knew he would come back when he could and that gave her strength to start each new day. She considered herself a very fortunate woman. Which was why it wouldn't hurt her to befriend young Trixie. She'd be a pretty poor specimen of womanhood if she turned her back on the brave girl, wouldn't she?

Marie knocked on the prefab door, not expecting an answer straight away. When the door opened Marie could see Trixie had been crying.

'I won't bother you, if you're all right, but I just want to make sure.'

Trixie burst into fresh tears and threw herself in Marie's arms, almost bowling her over.

'Let's get inside, in the warm. Whatever's the matter, love?'

Trixie raised her blotchy face, 'Oh, I'm so glad you've come.' She took Marie's hand and led her into the kitchen. 'Joan's asleep,' she said. 'Losing Bess hit her hard and she's asleep.'

'With a few hard nips of drink inside her, no doubt,' said Marie. 'But they were sisters, after all.' Marie sat down on one of the kitchen chairs and watched as Trixie put the kettle on. Then Marie saw the marks on the girl's wrists and as she looked at Trixie's legs saw more bruises. At the funeral the girl had been wearing thick black stockings and was muffled up to keep the cold out. Now she was home, she'd changed into a skirt and jumper with a blue checked pinny over the top.

'Whatever are those marks on your legs?'

Trixie looked at her and she saw the tears well in her eyes.

'It's Sid, ain't it?' Marie jumped off the chair and grabbed hold of Trixie. She held the girl still while she peered at her neck, her face and then pulled her jumper away so she could see the mauve and red of the bruised shoulders. 'Where is the bugger?'

'He's gone,' said Trixie. 'He went as soon as he'd raped me.' Marie heard the word fall from Trixie's lips with great difficulty, like she, herself, couldn't believe what had happened. 'That's why he wasn't at the funeral.'

'We have to get some help for you. Maybe go round to Jem or see his grandad. You can't be left alone here, he could come back and do it again.' Marie pushed Trixie onto a chair and began spooning tea in the teapot.

'I'll be ready for him, if he tries anything. But I don't want anyone to know.'

'Why ever not? It's not your fault. We'll get the police.'

'No!'

Marie shook her head. The girl didn't want anyone to know what that bastard had put her through. She stared at Trixie, who was looking at her, hoping she'd agree to keep the secret. Marie knew what she should do; the girl needed all the help she could get. But Trixie wanted her to keep it a secret. And Marie wanted to be a friend to the girl. She nodded her head.

'Your secret's safe with me,' she said. 'But what about Joan? Are you going to tell her what her pig of a husband has done?'

Trixie gave her a horrified look. 'I can't hurt her. She's right on the edge now about Mum's death.'

'You'll have to be careful who you let know about things, then.'

Trixie shook her head. 'No one else, just you and me.'

'Fair enough, girly. But do you realise how strong you're going to have to be both mentally and physically to get on with the day-to-day round of jobs while all you can think of is that pig of a bloke forcing himself on you?'

She could see Trixie considering her words. At present the girl was a bunch of nerves. Could she

138

put the rape to the back of her mind and go on with life as though nothing had happened? If she wanted it kept a secret, she had to do so. Trixie's answer was a long time coming.

'Yes.'

'Then you're a bloody marvel, Trixie,' Marie said.

Chapter Nine

When Trixie woke in the morning it was to the ammonia smell of wet nappies. And she realised if she was to get away from this press of warm bodies it would have to be now, while they slept.

She remembered Marie's words of last night: 'I'm not leaving you here on your own tonight. That bugger could just as easily return knowing you'll be at your lowest ebb because of the funeral. With me you'll be safe.'

'I don't want to leave Joan,' she'd protested.

'Joan won't wake until tomorrow and when she does all she'll want is another drink. Stop thinking about her; think about yourself for once.'

And now Trixie looked at Marie's broad back covered by a flower-patterned flannelette nightie and decided to make a run for it before the children woke up and she was deafened by their good-natured chatter.

As she untangled herself from the sheet the memory of the rape returned. And the effort she'd needed to convince Marie not to tell Jem. How could she face Jem, knowing he cared for her and that Sid had put his dirty hands all over her body? And the last thing she needed was the police involved.

For sure, if they questioned Sid, he would tell them all about Teddy and his part in their father's murder. She hadn't been able to find Teddy, but the police had a wider net.

'Trying to get away from warm, sweaty little bodies, are you?' Marie laughed a big laugh that wobbled the bed.

'I didn't mean to wake you.'

'Can't sleep long with this lot draped everywhere. Sadie.' Her voice echoed in the sparsely furnished bedroom and two pairs of children's eyes opened to stare at Trixie.

A girl of about ten in a pink nightie pushed open the door and, rubbing her eyes, said, 'I've already got the kettle on, Mum.' She wandered out to shout at the boys who Trixie supposed slept in the second bedroom because their noise had reached a sort of plateau. She'd already guessed from the pink nighties that this was the girls' bedroom.

'That'll be Jacob and Harry, always at each other first thing in the mornings.'

'Thanks,' Trixie said to Marie, who was now struggling into a pair of stays. 'I *was* scared at home with just Joan for company. But I feel so much better now.'

'That's all right, love. I just want you to make sure you call me if anything worries you; promise?'

'I promise,' said Trixie. She got out of bed and went to the window. Looking out, she was surprised to see Jem's van drive past.

Jem knew he was lucky to get a last-minute cancellation on the ferry to the Isle of Wight. He wouldn't have long to search for the boy because the booking was for the night return ferry. But it suited him fine. He wanted to search in some places that he was pretty sure Trixie didn't know existed.

He wished he had a photograph of Teddy to show to people but Trixie had told him they had no family portraits. Money didn't run to frivolities like photographs. He could believe her. When he'd seen the stuff she'd brought from Portsmouth on the handcart he had been saddened. It wasn't much more than rubbish.

He'd been at the funeral. Not that there'd been many mourners. He'd watched her break her heart as the coffin sank out of sight. Thank Christ that kind woman Marie had been there to hold her. But she needed her brother and if he could he'd do everything in his power to find the lad.

He wandered around the boat until the speaker system called the drivers to their cars. Once off the boat he encountered grey drizzle. But he knew where he was going and it was to the centre of the island, to Newport. Through the shopping centre he drove carefully, until on the outskirts of the town he came to the long, twisting road he wanted.

At Godshill Street he knocked on the door of number twenty-three, a Victorian house with paint peeling from the door and window frames with cracked putty.

'Hello, Greta,' he said to the woman with impossibly red hair who'd answered the door.

'Jesus,' she said, 'I haven't seen you since schooldays. How did you know where I was?'

'I didn't until I asked about,' he replied. She was just the same as she'd been at school: large, smiling, and heavily made-up. She'd shown him into the front room, where the smell of polish was overpowering, and he sat down on a chair with an antimacassar on its back. For a moment he just sat and looked at her, and she at him. Both were sharing a memory. And then she laughed, a hearty sound that came from deep inside her. Greta Fellowes was the first girl he had ever touched. He'd been thirteen years old and she'd gone with him for a walk in Skinny Woods in Gosport and from her he'd learned how to make a woman happy. She was two years older than him and he'd smiled across the school dinner table at her, watching her round, full breasts jiggle against her white blouse and he had wondered what it would be like to put both his hands round one.

That after-lunch walk he had found out about the mysteries of girls' brassieres and white knickers that could be pulled aside far enough to insert a hard part of him into a soft, moist space he never before knew existed on a girl.

He got up from the chair, bent down and kissed her on the cheek.

'I don't think I ever thanked you, Greta,' he said. Then, 'Phil Broadbent told me you had a few girls working for you now.'

'That, I do. Though I still take in the odd client myself.'

Over a cup of tea that was so strong it stained the cup, Jem asked her whether she'd heard of anyone taking on a boy.

'He's pretty, small for his age, very quiet.'

The woman thought hard and long. 'I haven't heard of any lad fitting that description and I know all the brothels round about. Of course I only use girls – women, not young girls,' she added. 'I hate hearing about the youngsters picked up from the amusement arcades, tea shops, and the lads they catch straight off the boats.' She sat back in her chair and stared hard at him. 'Did you look for him there? Ryde Pier?'

He realised how confused he must have appeared, for she continued, 'Bottom of the pier? The Meatrack?' He shook his head. 'You can take your pick of the boys there. Big Mel is the one to see; he's their minder.'

'I'll take a look before I leave the island,' he said. He told her of a few places he had in mind to search and Greta gave him a couple of addresses. 'You've been really helpful,' he said. 'If I'm going to ask about in all these places, I'd better get going.'

'Just you remember you never spoke to me about any of this,' she pressed. 'I don't want anyone coming to my door with a flick knife for either me or my girls.'

Jem held her close. 'My lips are sealed,' he said. As she followed him to the front door, he stopped and said, 'You always were the best, Greta.'

He spent the rest of the day searching for Teddy and coming to the conclusion that it was quite possible he wasn't on the island at all.

At the end of the pier in the Tea Shack Jem bought himself a cup of tea and stood outside watching the lads larking about. The boys looked well fed and clean; there were four of them, the youngest about six, the eldest about ten. During the time Jem watched only one man approached the boys, accompanied by a middle-aged man. They went to the lavatory. After a while, the boy returned alone.

It was dusk, and the drizzle had started up again after a break earlier in the day. Jem was tired. He decided he'd be glad to get home and have a decent meal after eating snack food all day. His car was waiting in the lane of vehicles due to drive on board the boat.

He approached the eldest lad and was about to speak when the boy said, 'You pays Mel and he gives the say so for me to go with you.' Jem realised the boy thought he was a punter.

'I only want to ask you a few questions,' he said.

'Same price as for a fuck,' the boy said. Jem was amazed at the lad's cold-blooded reply to his question.

'No, I want to ask if you know of a blond lad: name's Teddy?'

The boy shook his head. 'Any one of us would do just as well, surely?'

Jem looked at him. Poor little sod, he thought. This really was a way of life for him.

Just then a man approached, the one who had accompanied the lad and man to the lavatory, and said, 'Can I help? You want one of my boys or not?'

'No, I'm looking for a special boy,' he said. Then he wandered away. He realised whoever

144

really ran this had the business sewn up.

Teddy watched the boat leave its moorings. His eyes roved the sea, taking in the lights on the water from the small craft and the way the water glittered.

'You're a good lad for telling me about that bloke, Teddy,' Mel said. 'You could have come out from that cubicle in the gents' and gone home with him and we'd never have seen you again.'

'I told you, he used to knock me about. I'd rather take me chances with you.'

Mel nodded. 'I like a lad I can trust.' He shoved some money into Teddy's hands. 'Go over to the shack and get some chips for everyone.'

Teddy walked away, leaving the big man looking after him. He felt guilty that he'd lied about Jem but it seemed the easiest thing to do. He'd spotted the van coming into the parking area set aside for the vehicles. The one thing he didn't want was Jem catching him taking punters to the gents'. How that would hurt his sister when all she'd ever tried to do was keep him safe. Of course, it would be wonderful to go home and see Trixie. But where was home? Certainly not the prefab where Sid would take one look at him and try another way to get rid of him. Maybe even tell the police about him. No, it was better that Jem didn't find him.

As he carried the chips and cups of tea back on a battered tin tray he made a decision. He'd had enough of this God-awful life and even if they killed him or chopped off his privates for trying, he was going to escape.

145

'Don't fall over any of those wires, Trixie: we got The Tropics setting up their equipment again.'

Eva grinned at Trixie, who took off her coat and hung it out in the passageway. She had on a new tartan pinafore dress with a black jumper beneath it. She had an idea she was going to get very warm before the evening was over and she'd felt queasy as she'd got dressed this evening, but put it down to the corned beef she'd eaten at dinner.

Trixie was happy. The lad on the drums waved to her. She smiled back at him. He was a lovely-looking blond lad with blue eyes and a smile that lit up the room. Eddie knew how to play as well. His one fault was that he tended not to take life too seriously. Since singing with the group Trixie had become friendly with them. Eddie was always asking her to step up to the mic and sing but she refused. Kathy was their lead singer and although there were times when her voice wasn't so stable, Trixie thought she'd be hurt to hear another girl singing her songs with her band. Trixie was content to stand behind the bar humming along with the music, enjoying the atmosphere and chatting to her new friends whenever possible.

Mo played the piano. His real name was Maurice and he lived in Queen's Road in Gosport and had been a bit of a tearaway before he discovered how much he loved playing the piano.

George played the guitar and sang a bit and made up for Eddie's lack of seriousness. Quiet and softly spoken, he could always be found reading a book when he wasn't playing his beloved guitar.

Eddie also played the guitar and it was great to

146

see and hear the two lads in motion together. Eddie was the one who took chances with his music, but he was also the one who followed George when they moved in time to the music.

Kathy Kline sang like an angel. Or rather, thought Trixie, like Billie Holiday. She had that similar gut-twisting sound in her voice that made you believe every note she sang. Trixie chatted a lot with Kathy and knew that she and George had been going out with each other since school-days. George wanted them to get married but Kathy wanted to make a name for herself first. She had been in ill health a lot with sore throats and she'd ignored the doctor's advice to take things easy. Trixie could see she'd lost quite a bit of weight since she'd first met her.

The group had been performing around Gosport and coming to the Fighting Cocks for so long that whenever they played there the pub could be sure of good takings.

I reckon we'll see a lot of these small bands appearing now the big bands are finding the pinch of money.' Jack, the manager, had come up behind Trixie, picked up a glass and poured himself a rum from the optic. He downed it in one.

'I suppose you know that this lot with their electric guitars have copied The Tympany Five?'

'That's Louis Jordan's group, ain't it?'

'I'm surprised you keep up with the music scene, Jack,' said Trixie.

'I know he left Chuck Webb's band to do it,' he said. He gave a mock bow to show how clever he was and Trixie laughed.

Jack slipped his arm around Trixie's shoulders. 'I

147

wish we could have them playing here more often. I'm fed up with the regulars who make half a pint last all night. The group brings in youngsters who drink me out of Babychams and snowballs,' he said.

Almost as if on cue, Old Harry, who came in every evening said, 'Give us half a pint of Brickwoods, Eva. I see that band is setting up. I'm not stayin' to listen to that so-called Race music; I'm off when I've supped up.'

Trixie began to laugh and had to put her hand over her mouth. Jack whispered in her ear, 'See, what did I tell you?'

Eva grinned at Trixie. 'Daft old sod,' she said, after she'd served Harry. 'You want to come round to my place after?' Eva was wearing a dress made of soft blue material with tiny buttons up the front and a sweetheart neckline. Trixie thought she looked lovely with her dark hair, shiny and swinging and a yellow flower pinned to one side.

Trixie and Eva had got really friendly. Trixie guessed it was because Eva no longer felt threatened by her now she had been taken out by Jem a few times.

'Why not?' Trixie answered. She liked being in Eva's cosy prefab with Eva showing her how she'd made a certain cushion cover or sewn a new blouse.

Trixie wasn't one for sewing because she'd discovered the Provident Cheque Club. She could now have a cheque for five or ten pounds that was an absolute fortune to her and pay it back weekly. So she loved going shopping and buying clothes, something she'd never been able to do before.

She also loved working in the pub and in the shop. The people she served she had a chat and laugh with. But when she closed the front door and went into the silence with only Joan for company, who was frequently drunk or in bed, she missed Teddy. Never would she stop thinking it was all her fault her brother was missing.

Sid came back infrequently and rarely stayed long. He never gave her money for housekeeping, neither did he give any money to Joan. Trixie's money kept the prefab afloat.

'I've never known it as busy as this,' yelled Eva above the noise. She looked back at her pile of bottle tops and pointed at Trixie's pile. Both girls would have a nice sum of money to take home with them tonight.

It was early in the morning when at last Jack closed down the Fighting Cocks.

The two girls walked along the path between the prefabs singing and arm in arm.

'Wait while I find the key,' said Eva.

'Hurry, I'm dying for the toilet,' said Trixie.

When the door was opened they tumbled inside. Trixie looked around the pristine place. She'd scrubbed Joan's place from top to bottom but Eva's house was special. It was colourful and cosy. She heard Eva in the kitchen filling the kettle and followed her in, leaving her coat on a chair. She went into the bathroom that smelled of soap; Eva always smelled of lemon soap. Back in the kitchen, Eva had taken a cake from a tin and put it on the table. She began cutting a slice for Trixie, saying, 'I made this, this morning. It's got cherries in it.'

Just then, Trixie leapt up from the chair she'd collapsed in and disappeared back into the toilet. A while later, she came out.

'Jesus, you look awful. All pale and pasty-faced,' said Eva.

For a while nothing could be heard except the loud ticking of Eva's cuckoo clock.

'I think I'm going home,' she said.

When Trixie left Eva's prefab there were still plenty of people about, singing and laughing. She didn't really want to go home but she did want to think about the changes in her body she'd ignored until they'd decided to show themselves. The swollen breasts, the sickness, her tiredness. Hadn't she witnessed it all before with her mother?

Stumbling along in the darkness, she reached number nineteen and paused. The prefab was dark too and that meant that Joan was asleep after a drink or two. Trixie's heart was beating fast. She needed to talk to someone and wondered why, just for a moment, she'd not confided in Eva. No, Eva was not the right person. Sure, she was now a friend, and it wouldn't be long before the whole estate knew of her condition, but she wanted Marie. Marie would know what to do. Would she still be up? There was only one way to find out.

The lights came on immediately Trixie knocked on the door.

'Thought you'd still be in the pub. What's the matter, girly?'

Trixie fell into her arms. 'I'm going to have a baby,' she said into Marie's clean white long-sleeved nightie.

Then she felt herself being pulled inside to the

150

kitchen and the sound of the kettle being set upon the gas.

'I gather it's not that nice Jem's.'

Trixie shook her head. 'I don't know what to do.'

'Well, you aren't the first and you won't be the last girl to have a kiddie without the benefit of a wedding ring – I'm a testimonial to that.' She sat down heavily on a chair and took hold of Trixie's hand. 'How far along are you?'

'The night of the rape.'

Marie sighed. 'That changes things a bit, being as that was quite a few months ago. If you was less than three months I'd have dragged you along to Ida Blair's at Mayfield Road; she'd take care of you. But she won't do a thing if the girl tells her she's over the three months mark. If it don't work, it can make the baby deformed or worse. Look, love, I'm sorry if you think I doubted how long you've been pregnant but I had to ask; you understand, don't you?'

'It's Sid's.'

Marie got up and poured water in the teapot. The liquid hissed and bubbled as it hit the earthenware vessel.

'What about you? You thought of keeping it?' Marie stared at her. 'I never once contemplated not giving birth to any of my brood and now I got so many I can't keep track of 'em. But I'll tell you straight, each one brought its love with it.'

'Of course I'll keep it.' Trixie had thought no such thing until that moment but the more she thought about it the more she became attuned to the idea.

'There is one thing.' Marie started sorting out

151

the tea, getting cups from cupboards and pouring milk and sugar into them. 'If it gets out it
belongs to your uncle your name'll be mud.
You'll be ostracised. No one'll speak to you.'

'But it isn't my fault.'

'And so sayeth girls for evermore but that's the
way it is.'

'Then I'll tell no one.'

'Right,' said Marie. 'Then a new baby is just
what we want for a new beginning after this
bleedin' war game.'

'War game?' Trixie gave her a watery smile. 'If
you ask me a woman's lot is more like a crying
game.'

Chapter Ten

Jem walked up to the front door of number nineteen and banged his fist hard upon the peeling
paint. He sighed. Other prefab dwellers had been
thrilled to be housed in such luxurious little
houses and did all they could to keep their homes
looking fresh and smart. Sid did nothing but let
the place fall around him.

In Jem's other hand he held a bunch of flowers,
early daffodils, tightly budded. He waited awhile
then knocked again, even harder this time. Sometimes when Joan was asleep she didn't wake when
someone came to the prefab. He was just about to
leave when the door opened and a tousle-headed
Trixie stared at him with eyes as round and big as

saucers with dark circles beneath.

'Sorry, were you in bed? Eva told me you weren't well.'

Jem had decided he quite liked being with Eva. She could never take Trixie's place in his affections but he enjoyed going to the cinema with her and once or twice she'd cooked him superb meals. He had to be honest with himself. He got lonely staying at home in the evenings after work. Eva, when she wasn't making stuff to sell for her stall, hated her own company. Going for a drive and a half a shandy to a pub out in the countryside gave the pair of them companionship and the chance to chat and laugh over the day's happenings.

Trixie allowed him to enter. The place was in a mess, as though no one had bothered to clean up. Newspapers lay on the living-room floor alongside cups that had dregs of tea in them and plates with remains of food were perched on the arms of the sofa. Trixie looked dreadful.

'I've been working and I can't seem to look after this place as well as I used to.' She was wearing a padded dressing-gown that was stained down the front. Her blonde hair was in strings around her thin face.

'I've brought you some flowers and I want to tell you all about my good news,' he said. 'Though by the state of you somebody else's good fortune won't do much to cheer you up.' He cleared away a pile of un-ironed clothes and sat down on an armchair.

He wanted to put her to bed and look after her until she was well again. Instead he asked, 'What's the matter?'

153

She shook her head. 'You tell me your good news before I have to run to the bathroom and be sick again. And thank you for the flowers; they're lovely.' She took them and laid them on the top in the kitchen.

'You know what would do you some good?'

She shook her head.

'To get some fresh air,' he said. God help him, if he had to stay in the staleness of this prefab much longer, he'd be throwing up as well.

'We could walk along the sea wall,' she said. He could see even thinking about it had brought some colour to her cheeks. 'I'll get dressed.'

Within moments she'd come back from the bedroom wearing a pair of slacks and a blouse. It wasn't particularly cold outside so he didn't press her to put on a coat; all the same he was glad to see her pull on a cardigan. After she'd tied her hair back off her face they shut the door behind them and walked along the pathway towards the top end of the houses, where a path led out on to Fort Road. He planned on walking along the shore near Fort Gilkicker.

She tucked an arm through his. 'Come on, what's your news?'

He took a deep breath. 'I've been offered a loan, a big one, by the bank and I've decided to buy some land at Titchfield to grow strawberries.'

He saw her eyes flicker. 'How will you run two places?' They'd reached the small path that was overgrown with brambles. Newly budded bushes barred their way. He pulled the sharp branches back so she could walk through unscathed. He took a deep breath of the freshness and he could smell the salty tang of the sea beyond.

He was ready for her question. 'I'll go and live there; there's a good house on site and when I've got the fields up and running, I'm going to put a manager in there and come back to Grandad.'

'Will he be able to cope while you're away?'

'He's sprightly for his age. He'll have no money worries and I'd like it if you moved in with him. I don't mean to degrade Joan and all that but the smallholding is a lot bigger and in better nick than the prefab and Grandad would look after you.'

He saw a frown cross her face. 'Who would look after Joan?' she asked. 'I know she's not ready for her grave just yet but she's taken it bad about Bess. I can't just run out and leave her.'

They crossed the road. The fort was in view now. Disused and overgrown on the outside with weeds it was close to the beach yet surrounded by barbed wire.

'We have to stick to the path here. To stray could mean being blown up. The army planted bombs along the shoreline in case we're invaded by the Germans. They'll remove them later, when the war's over but they won't be in a hurry to do it. This is all government property round here.'

'Who would look after Joan?' repeated Trixie. She looked up at him.

'Grandad doesn't want her at the smallholding. Says she's more of a hindrance than a help and Sid could come looking for her at any time. He only wants you, Trixie.'

Neither of them spoke for a while. Jem looked out to sea. An Isle of Wight boat was cutting through the water.

'I've not stopped looking for your brother,' he said. 'I've been to the island a couple of times.'

'Really?' He nodded. 'I don't believe he was ever there.'

Trixie knew Jem had gone looking for Teddy because he cared so much for her he didn't like to see her unhappy.

'That bloody Sid,' said Trixie. 'Whatever he touches turns bad.' She put up a hand to push her hair back where it had slipped from its tie.

'Let's sit down for a moment,' he said. He moved up to make space for her on the stone wall and she sat down beside him. He watched the waves breaking on the beach, the pebbles sliding back and forth, the sea reflected blue from the sky.

'It's so nice and peaceful here,' she said. 'You wouldn't think there was a war on.' Tears, of their own accord, started streaming down her face.

'You're not well,' he said. 'Tell me what's the matter?' He pulled her towards him.

'I'm having a baby,' she said. 'Sid raped me.'

It took a long time for her words to sink in. Here was he wanting to look after her and all the while that bastard had been waiting for his chance to take advantage of her. He pulled her in even closer.

'You're sure? About the baby, I mean?' His voice was choked with emotion.

She nodded.

He couldn't think of what to say for a moment, then, 'Where is the bastard?'

'We don't know. You know as well as I do, he comes and goes.'

'If I could get at him, you know I'd kill him?'

'And what good would that do when you're carving out a better life for yourself?'

She was right. All the same he *would* kill him. This girl next to him was the one he wanted to spend the rest of his life with. He also realised she couldn't possibly move into the smallholding to look after Gramps. She needed someone to look after her!

'We could get married.' As soon as he said the words he knew how silly they sounded. She was little more than a child herself. 'Would you live with me? I could look after you.' Yes, that was it. They could live together. But she was twisting away from him.

'What about the baby?'

Yes, the baby. 'I could pretend it's mine.'

She sighed. 'You'd be ostracised. Would a bank give you another loan when it comes to light you're living with a young girl? And there's a baby involved? The world'll change when eventually the war's over, but businessmen will still be expected to show an example. No,' she said, 'I'll manage somehow. But nothing will give me greater pleasure than to see you buy strawberry fields and smallholdings so that eventually you really make your mark in Gosport.'

He felt his own tears rise. So the choice was his. Do what his grandfather and he had always hoped for – grow vegetables and fruit that sold in the shops and those new big stores that were springing up to feed the south of England. Or take in the girl he loved and scrape a living be- cause public opinion wasn't as far advanced yet as it should be? He looked into her eyes.

'I know what you're thinking,' she said. 'Only you don't have a choice because I'm making it for you. Make your sons with someone else to carry on your smallholdings. I'll manage.'

Now Trixie had told the secret about her baby to Jem she knew it was time to tell Joan. Her heart plummeted.

She made a pot of tea and set out cups. Then she went into Joan's bedroom. It was in an appalling state. Clothes were slung over the back of the chair and underwear hung from the corner of the dressing-table mirror. The air was heavy and stank of body odour and whisky. Trixie didn't often venture into Joan's room, feeling privacy was necessary, but now she determined she'd at least get Joan out of the room and come in and give it a good clean and get the windows opened to let in fresh air.

Joan's face was grey, her breathing erratic and Trixie realised how old she looked. But Joan wasn't old. She'd just let herself become old living with Sid.

Trixie shook Joan's shoulder and the woman opened her eyes. Trixie gave her time to focus then she said, 'I need to talk to you.'

Joan struggled to a sitting position. 'What's the matter?'

'It might be better if you come out in the kitchen. I've made a pot of tea.'

Trixie handed Joan her stained blue silk dressing-gown.

'If you're going to start moaning about my drinking...'

'It isn't that.' Trixie walked out of the room, pausing just long enough to make sure that Joan was out of bed and following her.

When Joan was sitting at the table with a sandwich in front of her, Trixie said, 'You're not going to like this, but I'll come straight to the point. I'm going to have a baby and Sid is the father.' She got as far as that before the force of Joan's hand sent her spinning away from the kitchen chair she was sat on.

'You little liar. My Sid wouldn't touch you.'

Trixie's hand went to her face. Joan was standing over her, her dressing-gown open and showing the outline of her scrawny body. Her hand was flashing forward again, but this time Trixie was quicker and grabbed hold of it, forcing Joan to sit back down on the chair.

'I know what you're thinking, but I didn't sleep with the fuckin' bastard. He forced me.'

Joan stared at her dumbly. 'He wouldn't.'

'You can make yourself believe that if you want, but you know he would if given the opportunity. You know exactly what that man's like. That's why you watch him when he's around me.'

'What d'yer mean?' Now Joan had cooled down she was curious. Her temper was simmering. Trixie could tell by the tiny muscles dancing in her neck and her mouth, that was now a hard, thin line, that her rage could erupt again at any moment.

'You were out, we were alone and I didn't stand a chance.' Suddenly all the hateful memories came rushing back and Trixie crumbled. 'I didn't stand a chance,' she whispered again. 'I couldn't say nothing at the time because I didn't want you to be hurt and I certainly couldn't bear anyone else knowing what had happened. The bastard knew I wouldn't go to the coppers because it might stir up things about me dad.'

Her outburst over, Trixie sat back on her chair, put both her hands over her face and wept. After a while she stopped crying, took a deep breath and looked at Joan, who was sitting as still as a statue. 'I wouldn't have told you now if I wasn't having a kiddie.'

Joan got up from the chair and Trixie froze. Was she going to hit her again?

To her surprise Joan put her arms around her. Trixie could hear the older woman's heart beating.

'I believe you,' she said. 'Sorry I lashed out, but no woman wants to hear something like this.' Joan then went to the kitchen tap, where she sluiced her face in cold water. 'Sid's always had an eye for the women. I used to think I was lucky he married me because I'm nothing to look at and never was. But he had a gift for chatting up the women and the looks to go with it.' She was quiet for a few moments, drying her face with the tea towel. 'How far gone are you?'

'Happened the day you went to sort out Mum's funeral.'

'Poor little girl,' Joan said. Then her voice hardened. 'What are you going to do?'

'Keep the baby.'

'Are you sure?'

'Sid doesn't know I'm expecting. I'll never let on it belongs to him because I want no part of him interfering in my life. It's not the baby's fault. I'll manage.'

'You don't have to manage; you'll always have a home here.'

'Are you sure about this? I was certain you'd turn me out.'

'Well, you're wrong. And what's more I think it's about time I stopped moping about. Your mum's gone; I can't do anything about that. Sid comes and goes now because he thinks I'll put up with anything. He's got a shock coming. The next time he shows his face, I'll tell him in no uncertain tones to sling his hook.'

'You don't have to do that on my account.'

'The bloke is pulling the pair of us down to the gutter. It's time it stopped. Now, where's that tea?'

Teddy knew he had to escape. But he made good money for his bosses and knew it wouldn't be easy. He stood at the end of Ryde Pier watching the families walking along, going back to the boat after a day out on the island, holding hands, enjoying themselves. He put up a hand and scratched his head. No matter how often he washed his hair he couldn't get rid of the nits. Sometimes they seemed to go away for a while, then they'd return with a vengeance.

He'd seen Jem a few times now in his van coming off the ferry or returning. He knew he couldn't go on hiding for ever; one day he was going to get caught out and there'd be a confrontation.

He couldn't go back to Trixie and his mum. He wondered about the baby. Perhaps he had a little brother, or a sister. He'd thought a lot about letting Jem find him so he could be taken home. But wherever Teddy went he made bad things happen. Trixie and his mum deserved to live in peace, without him.

He began humming 'Cruising Down the River' as he wandered over to the tea van. He could smell the onions and sausages, though God knew how much meat was in the sausages. The war took care of shortages. He smiled at Big Mel lounging against a metal railing, cleaning his nails with a flick knife.

Teddy thought about the window in the toilet cubicle he had broken and how carefully he'd hidden the glass behind the water tank where he'd left a cricket bat that some young kid had dropped near the railings. Teddy and the boys had played a good game of cricket with it before it disappeared. That window and hiding the bat had taken him a few days to do without being caught. It was easy enough, as he was trusted, to linger a few minutes in the gents' when the punter had finished with him. He'd come out of the toilets all smiles so as not to arouse suspicion. He wasn't stupid either. No one knew of his plans. He'd figured if he kept his secret to himself he'd have no one to blame if it went wrong. But it *mustn't* go wrong.

Sailor came waltzing along the promenade. A skinny bloke with the beginnings of a paunch who made Teddy feel sick every time he touched him. He was called Sailor because he had a penchant for wearing an American sailor's hat.

Teddy had never seen him without it.

Sailor winked at him. He'd already paid Big Mel.

'How's my special boy, then?'

Teddy gave him a smile and walked across the wooden boards to meet him, giving him a handshake. Sailor's hands always felt damp and limp. He always wore some sort of violet perfume that stayed on Teddy's body for hours afterwards.

'I'm fine, Sailor.' They walked across to the gents'. Teddy went in first and Sailor followed. Teddy put the bolt on the door. 'Don't want to be disturbed, do we?'

'Give us a kiss, lovely boy,' begged Sailor.

Teddy leaned over the cistern and took out the bat, then hit him. He hit him again, not to hurt him but to incapacitate him so he fell silently to the floor. Teddy pulled the man to a sitting position, thinking how fortunate it was that the biggest part of Sailor was his belly. If anyone looked under the door all they'd see was feet.

Teddy searched in his pockets and took out the few notes and coins he found. Then he hoisted himself onto the toilet seat, careful not to tread on and dislodge his sitting friend. He was through the window in no time and when his feet touched the railings at the back of the toilets he knew he only had to walk a short way along their flat surface before he could swing down and mix himself in with the people returning from the pier. No one would know he was gone until they reckoned that Sailor was taking his time.

At ten to ten he was walking through the town, money in his pocket and a smile on his face. At half past ten he was out in the country on the top of the cliff with the roll of the sea in his ears and the brisk wind raking his blond hair.

He turned onto the narrow road, where the bushes either side were full of spring buds and sprouting leaves and at eleven fifteen he failed to see or hear the car that ran him down.

Chapter Eleven

It was a huge celebration, VE Day. Victory over Europe, the war was over. Mussolini had been captured and the German armies had given up.

Suddenly, after all the years of worry, England took to the streets with parties, dancing and celebrations. Flags hung from buildings and fireworks exploded and people began to relax and sleep easy in their beds.

Trixie was run off her feet at the pub but being busy kept her mind from other matters. Until Eva said, 'You can't keep it a secret much longer, you know.' She handed her a tea towel so Trixie could help her polish the glasses.

Trixie said, 'I'm not telling Jack until the baby becomes really obvious, because if he sacks me I don't know how I'll manage.'

'The customers'll start talking if anyone finds out it's your uncle's kiddie and Jack'll lose takings. That's when he'll want you to leave, not before. You're too good a barmaid for him to let you go until it really becomes necessary.'

Trixie looked at Eva, then around the for once, near-empty bar. It was lunchtime and there were few customers in. Now she'd stopped feeling sick she felt as though the child inside her really mattered.

'I don't know how you can love that coming baby so much. Just thinking about Sid makes me feel sick.'

'I don't think about the child having Sid as a father. It's mine, this baby, mine.' She lovingly smoothed her hands over her extended stomach.

'I'm going to be an auntie. Don't you forget that,' Eva said.

How could Trixie forget? Eva had spent ages making tiny white nightgowns and a soft coloured quilted pram set. She'd also taken to making sure Trixie ate well after seeing her gorging herself on a meat pie from the shop.

'You've got to eat proper food with lots of vitamins in to keep your strength up and milky foods to make sure the baby has strong bones, teeth and nails.' Then she appeared at number nineteen with plates covered in clean tea towels to make sure Trixie did as she was told.

Marie, too, was playing her part. She made Trixie walk with her into Alverstoke and down Haslar Road into Gosport town.

'Exercise is good for you.'

'Don't you think I get enough exercise being on my feet all day?' retorted Trixie.

'This is a different kind of exercise. Fresh air is good for you. Breathing in dirty old vegetables in the shop and smelly fag smoke from the bar isn't good at all. This way you gets your lungs cleared.'

And it seemed to be working, for Trixie was blooming. Her hair shone and her eyes were clear and sparkling.

165

But she wasn't as happy as she could have been.

Every day she wondered where Teddy was and if he was all right. She couldn't get it out of her head that if she hadn't made them all leave Portsmouth, Teddy would still be with her.

'Jem's grandad won't turn me away from the shop, thank goodness,' Trixie said. As the glasses had been set back on the shelves she'd gone out to the bar area and was furiously polishing the tops of the tables.

'That's a blessing.' As soon as Trixie's cloth left the empty table, Eva set down a freshly washed ashtray. 'Jem's been writing to me,' said Eva.

After Jem had borrowed the bank's money he'd bought agricultural land at Titchfield and rented a small house for himself, in the village. He'd told Trixie in a letter that it was easier to live near the strawberry fields, working from early in the morning, clearing the ground, to late at night, than to travel back to Gosport every day. He'd done a deal on some caravans from a holiday firm that had gone bankrupt and set about using them as temporary buildings for workers. He had a good solicitor who used the loopholes legally so that everything Jem touched turned to gold for his business. Trixie read and reread his letters. The sentences that told her she was never out of his thoughts gave her the courage to keep going each day.

'Thought he might.' Trixie was glad because Eva loved the bloke. She'd never told Eva that Jem had asked her to move in to the smallholding, here at Clayhall. All that was in the past. She'd never go back on her word and change her mind about

166

letting him ruin his life because he loved her.

The distance between them didn't stop Trixie missing Jem. And all the letters he could possibly write to her didn't make up for that awful feeling that a part of her was gone. How easy it would be for her to ask him to come back so they could live together. He would, she knew that. He would leave Titchfield and come back to Gosport like a shot. Then his money-making venture would be ruined, his reputation would be in tatters and he would say it didn't matter because at last she belonged to him. Then would come the resentment. Even if he didn't actually say anything he might blame her for ruining his life. And Trixie realised she loved him too much for that. How much better that he keep in touch with her, but write to Eva as well. And who knows, Eva might very well turn out to be the woman he would marry, who would give him sons to carry on with the business. A voice shook her out of her thoughts.

'Did you talk to Joan?'

'I did, Eva. Had to wait and catch her when she was sober. I asked her if she'd think about getting a part-time job when I can't work any more.'

'What did she say?'

'Amazingly she agreed. I told her Jack said she could collect glasses when we had the band here or on busy nights. I thought she might like being where there's a bit of life. She promised she'd ease up on the bottle.'

'I'll see that when it happens.' Eva was now flicking the duster over the bottles at the back of the bar.

'Seriously, she's been a lot better. She's been

cleaning up the prefab, too.' Miracles do happen, thought Trixie with a smile.

It was July when Sid arrived back at the prefab, stepping in, out of the rain as though he hadn't been away. He was amazed at how clean the place was. He walked into the bedroom after throwing his wet coat on the back of a chair, expecting to find Joan in her usual place in the bed and the room smelling of whisky fumes.

'No Joan and no whisky,' he muttered. The corner where the box of whisky had stood was empty. There was food in the fridge and a basket full of fresh washing waiting to be ironed.

He'd come back to Gosport because throughout London a watch was being kept on black marketeers. Markets and vans were being searched for food and coupon-free clothing. Sid had been selling poultry at way above the legal prices because he could get away with customers buying it under the counter.

He was also meeting a bloke from Portsmouth who could provide Sid with some very nice nylons, chocolate and perfume that had come over from the continent. But actually Sid was killing two birds with one stone.

Little Daphne Morton was sixteen and about to drop her sprog at any moment. She didn't want the kid any more than her parents wanted to be saddled with it. Her parents had forked out for a private nurse who would remove the baby quickly to the care of Sid. Now Daphne was near to full term and Sid was phoning regularly. Sid had a nice couple out in the country at Midhurst who couldn't have children, so Daphne was going to provide that very nice couple who'd paid good money up front with a little boy or girl. Sooner than pay for lodgings Sid reckoned Joan owed him bed and board.

He went back into the living room put on his coat and went down to the Black Bear to see his mates.

Joan knew immediately her husband was home even though there was nothing in the prefab to suggest he'd been there.

She was about to tell Trixie that Sid was back when she realised how upset the girl would be if she knew. They'd bumped into one another as Joan walked up the flagstoned path and Trixie was waving goodbye to Eva.

Joan eased off her court shoes and plumped herself down on the sofa. She was angry; Sid had been gone so long this time she was hoping this time he would stay away. Well, one thing was for sure, he'd never touch her sister's kid again. The bastard knew how to wound her, then he went and twisted the knife in the sodding wound, didn't he? Well, she'd spent time trying to booze him out of her thoughts and now she'd realised how useless that was, she was determined to make a new life for herself.

She watched Trixie shrug her cumbersome body out of her coat. It was funny how Trixie's baby had hardly made any difference to her neat figure until all of a sudden she'd sprouted a mound the size of a mountain. Presently she heard the sound of the kettle on the go. Looking down at her aching feet,

169

Joan saw the new skirt she'd bought just yesterday to go with her new cream jumper. What did it matter that she'd got them from the clubman? They were the first new clothes she'd had in ages. And if she had to buy them on tick, so what? She thought of the new Royale blue and white high pram in the shed covered safely with an old blanket. She'd be paying off for that for ages but she wanted Trixie to have the best. Trixie had been mad when she'd discovered the pram. 'It'll bring bad luck buying something like that before the baby's born, you mark my words.'

'Well I'm payin' for it, not you, so it'll be my bleedin' bad luck,' she'd yelled back.

She'd seen the tears in Trixie's eyes and knew the girl was as pleased as punch.

The whisky was gone. It had been sold to her neighbours at cut price because Joan no longer wanted alcohol in the house. In fact, she thought, it was quite nice being able to think clearly without her brain befuddled with spirits.

Just when she was getting herself back on her feet, that bastard Sid came back to spoil things.

'Did you tell Sid about the baby, Trixie?'

Trixie turned and faced Joan. 'He doesn't know he's going to be a father,' she said. Joan knew that Trixie's fear of the man caused thoughts of him to be on her mind all the time. She wondered again if she should voice her own thoughts about Sid being in the prefab. She decided against it. Trixie didn't look well and she wouldn't get any rest if she thought Sid was on the prowl, especially as he had keys to number nineteen.

'I never had a clue he was the father, until you

confided in me. I'm only too sorry things got as bad as they did. He used you, like he used me up, Trixie. He took my youth and gave nothing in return. I can see it now, though I couldn't see it then. I'm telling him I want me front door key back because I want the bugger out of our lives. You all right, love?'

'I'm holding on to the back of this chair until this twinge in my hip goes away.'

'You been carting them boxes of mixers up from the cellar again? Jack told you weeks ago to leave them to him but you won't be told, will you?'

Trixie could be a little cow at times, thinking she could carry on working just the same as she did before she was expecting, thought Joan. Then she forgot about Trixie as the girl glared at her and flounced into the kitchen.

Would she be able to turn Sid out? And forget him? Sid had been her life. The only man she'd ever loved. But he was a dirty bugger to have touched Trixie. And she couldn't forgive him for that.

So little Trixie was heavy with a belly full of arms and legs, was she? And talk on the estate was that Jem was the father. Sid smiled to himself as he put his key in the lock, turned it and went into the prefab. Joan was nowhere to be found. Something strange going on, he thought. Not like Joan to be out at night.

In the spare bedroom Trixie looked as though she was asleep. He never expected her to be home or in bed. He stood looking at her, realising she'd

171

grown into a lovely young woman. Pity she'd gone and got herself up the spout. No decent fellow would want to marry her now she was damaged goods. He crept to the door.

'Get out!' So she hadn't been asleep after all.

He turned and looked at her again.

'I'm going.' Stuck up little cow, he thought. 'You look like you've seen a ghost. And it's only me, your favourite uncle.' He hoped she'd notice his new clothes and expensive shoes and realise he did better when he was living away from bloody Clayhall and if she'd played her cards properly she could have been his bit on the side. Joan was getting saggy now.

'What have you come back for?'

He wasn't going to tell her the real reason he was back in Gosport, was he? So he said, 'Where's Joan?'

'She's got a job in the Fighting Cocks.'

Jesus, he thought. That's a bloody turn up for the books. His wife must have got her shit together to hold down a bleeding job. He looked at his watch. She wouldn't be back yet awhile, not working in a pub.

Just then Trixie gave a cry and clutched the sheets.

'What's the matter?'

She looked as though she was in agony, with her eyes all screwed up like that. He remembered about the baby. How far gone was she?

'I think I'm having the baby. I been having pains all day.' Another bout of suffering seemed to grip her. When she spoke her words came through clenched teeth. 'Will you go and get Marie for me

172

and phone for Doctor Di–'

The poor little cow didn't get any further for what must have been a terrific wave of pain enveloped her and she began screaming.

Wasn't he supposed to do something about putting pans of water on the gas and foraging out clean sheets and bedding? What did he know about women's stuff? Swiftly he returned to the bed and put his hands over her mouth. God, she had lungs on her, this girl. And after all she was only giving birth to a sprog same as millions of women did every day.

'Yeah,' he said. 'I'll get anyone you want but try to keep the noise down.'

It was then the idea came to him.

He'd arranged to keep in close touch with Daphne Morton's nurse, who'd let him know when it was possible to collect the child.

Well, why shouldn't he double his money?

With so many people on the books waiting for newborns, he could add Trixie's baby to his list of kids for sale.

He'd have to be quick. And make a phone call. The nearest phone box was near the bus stop. It wouldn't take long to get his favourite nurse here to remove the child. Then it would be taken to a wet nurse who would look after it until it was sold. Which would be quicker than the blink of an eye. He'd tell Trixie it had been stillborn. Of course he'd have to give Trixie something to make sure she was so sleepy she was out of it when she gave birth. It would be easy enough to give her a jab of something that wouldn't hurt the kiddie. He was doing her a favour. What did she want to

173

be saddled with a baby for at her age? Everyone could benefit from this, him most of all.

'I'm going to get your mate and phone for the doctor,' he said. Without looking at her he swiftly left the prefab. On his way out he wondered how long it would be before Joan came home. Then he realised if she was working at the Fighting Cocks she'd be late, very late if there was a function going on. He was pretty sure he'd seen a band advertised. He needed to keep Trixie on her own until she'd given birth because it would be easier for him to get rid of the child. But even more importantly, would Trixie give birth before Joan came back? He'd find it difficult to persuade Joan that the child was being taken away by a nurse for its own good. Unless he could get the nurse to say the child was ill, jaundiced, perhaps? What a god-send the nurse was at her parents' house today at Lee-on-the-Solent. With a bit of luck she could be here in half an hour or so in her car. But wait, he didn't need to worry about that unless he encountered problems. As to problems... What was he worrying about? He could talk the hind legs off a donkey and get out of problems easier than a warm knife slips through butter, couldn't he? But was he about to get hold of Marie and the doctor?

Of course not.

Trixie was screaming. Where was that bastard, Sid? If the pain didn't stop soon she was going to cut this child out of herself with a knife; she swore she would. And then the pain started up again like two bands of steel reaching around her lower regions and squeezing her to death. The power of it made her head swim. But wait, was that the front door? She tried to call out but her mouth wouldn't work properly. She needed a drink. She was dry with all the screaming, yet she was wet with sweat. Another pain. This one wanted to drag her insides out. Arhggg! A thought fluttered into her mind. Suppose that wasn't Sid she'd heard? Suppose she had to deliver this child with no one here to help her? Don't think about it. Don't think about it. It was Sid! He was speaking. Now he was wiping a cold, wet cloth across her forehead and it was so good. Arhggg!

'C'mon, you can do this, Trixie, there's a good girl. Just let me give you this to help ease the pain.'

She wanted to push down inside her. Wanted to push. Jesus Christ. Was that a cry?

'Good girl. Oh, fuck! Fuck!'

She lay back and felt the swimming sensation take her body, her head, her brain.

She opened her eyes. There was movement, a woman, in a blue dress with a black belt and silver buckle. 'Are you a nurse?'

Kind hands were tucking a sheet over her shoulders. She felt sore and tired.

'Would you like a cup of tea, Trixie?' Trixie was unable to answer and she felt her eyes close.

The argument woke her. Joan's voice was like a knife sawing through metal.

'You had no right to let Dr Dillinger take the baby.'

'No one objected when he took Bess's boy.'

'Bess refused to see the child or have anything to do with the poor little scrap. Trixie's been

175

making plans for this baby. She needed to see it so she can put all her suffering behind her. It's a way of helping her to heal.'

Trixie tried to think. Why did she need to heal? Jesus, she had a headache that eclipsed all her other aches. The baby? Of course, she had a baby! Her body enthused with excitement, she pushed herself up on one elbow and called, or tried to call, for her voice was like gravel and her mouth so dry that hardly any sound came out.

'Joan!'

Joan came into the bedroom. 'Hello, you're awake then? A nice cup of tea is what you need.' Tea? Why was everyone trying to make her drink tea?

Joan's face was white, her eyes full of sadness.

'Where's my little one, then? I want to hold him. Or is it a girl?'

Joan collapsed upon the side of the bed and took Trixie's hand in hers.

'Don't you remember, my love?'

'Remember what?'

Trixie saw Joan give a deep sigh. 'The child's gone. Stillborn. Dr Dillinger took his little body away, like he took your mum's little one.'

'What are you on about? Dr Dillinger's been no-where near me. The nurse? You mean the nurse took my child?'

Joan shook her head. 'The doctor was here. Sid helped you and though it sticks in my gut to say this, it's a good job he was here or you'd have been completely on your own. He got the doctor in and a nurse. Don't you remember anything?'

Little bits and pieces flew into Trixie's brain.

Yes, she vaguely remembered being asked if she wanted tea. She also remembered hearing her baby cry, didn't she? Why couldn't she remember clearly? Was childbirth always like this?'

And then a huge wave of desolation washed over her as she at last took in Joan's words. Her baby was gone.

Chapter Twelve

Teddy opened his eyes and saw the hazy outline of a man bending over him. The man was wearing a panama hat. Teddy struggled to sit up. He couldn't move one of his legs. When he focused on it he saw a cage-like object covered by the bedspread holding the covers off his knee. He felt no pain.

'No, no, young man, you must stay quite still.' Along with the hat the man had on a light-coloured linen suit. Wavy fair hair peeked from below the hat's brim. Teddy was in bed. Why was the man dressed for outdoors when he was in-doors?

Teddy felt as weak as a kitten. He turned his head and saw a tall metal frame by the side of the bed that looked like a hospital bed and a bottle of clear liquid hanging from the frame. He was being drip fed into his upper arm. He was in hospital.

'Nurse,' called the man in the hat. A nurse with swishing skirts approached the bed and looked down at him. She was small and pretty.

'Ah, you're awake. Tell me your name,' she

asked. Teddy opened his mouth and croaked, 'Teddy.' Then he stopped speaking and thought very quickly. If he didn't tell these people his real name or his date of birth he could be anyone he wanted. Since he'd been brought to the island he felt as though he'd become as old as the chalk hills. The police would be looking for Teddy True, a kid who'd be twelve next birthday. He could have a new beginning with a new name.

'Edward,' he whispered, 'Edward Somersby.' Somersby was his mother's maiden name.

'Where's your parents, Teddy or Edward?' asked the man in the hat, who had a kind face and a twinkle in his eye.

The nurse looked at the man and said, 'There doesn't seem to be any concussion.' Then she turned again to Teddy. 'Can you tell me where your parents live?'

'Wiped out by one of Hitler's bombs,' said Teddy. He hated to lie to these two nice people but a new identity needed a few untruths because the truth was unpalatable.

'You poor boy,' said the man. 'Where do you live? You must live somewhere, have someone to care for you?'

'No.' Teddy frowned. He answered, 'I've been living best I can.' He couldn't tell anyone about Trixie or his mother, could he?

'How–' began the nurse.

'No,' the man interrupted. 'I think that's enough questions answered for now. The main thing is for this young man to get well again.'

The nurse looked at the gentleman and Teddy realised he was a *gentleman*, the sort of man one

178

didn't argue with because his presence spoke volumes.

'We need an address to send him home.' The nurse looked agitated. She was speaking softly and Teddy thought it was because both she and the man didn't want him to hear what they were deciding should be the outcome of his hospital stay. The man seemed to listen, then he smiled and spoke.

'Teddy Somersby, it was my car ran you down on the narrow road above the sands. I came around the corner and couldn't miss you.' The man looked as though he might cry. 'I don't make a habit of running into young people.'

'It's all right,' said Teddy. To be honest, he thought, he'd rather be in hospital than back at the end of Ryde pier.

'You might think it's all right and very kind of you to say so, except you're not all right. Your right knee has been smashed to smithereens and the kind medical team at this hospital have had a hell of a job putting it all back together.'

'It doesn't hurt,' said Teddy.

'Of course not; you're topped up to the eyeballs with painkillers. Now are you going to tell me what you were doing walking down a lane on this island?'

Teddy thought quickly. 'Our house got bombed while I was at school. I came to the Isle of Wight to find my uncle. Dad once said he had a brother who lived in Ryde. I found out he'd since moved back to London, address unknown.'

Teddy hated this web of lies that seemed to be growing by the minute. But no way was he going

179

to tell the truth. The war had split families and his story was believable. The man stared at him and for a moment Teddy felt as though he was being scrutinised.

'You're going to need care. Not hospital care. Too many patients and not enough beds means this hospital needs to remove you to a place where you can recuperate. Unfortunately the war has filled those places with people far worse off than you.' Teddy didn't speak. Where could he go? Surely they wouldn't just kick him out if he couldn't walk or look after himself? He suddenly felt very alone. He turned his head away before a tear could roll down his face and be seen.

'I'll have a word with the doctors here and if you agree I'll take you to my house. I have a housekeeper who cooks and I can make sure you'll be well looked after. I feel it's the least I can do after putting you in this predicament in the first place.'

There seemed little point in Teddy arguing with the man, because he thought it was a brilliant idea. No more Ryde pier. No more Big Mel. No more paying 'friends'.

'How do you feel about it?'

'I'm not sure,' Teddy said. 'You'd be willing to do this for me?'

'I'm well aware if we involve the police I could be charged with dangerous driving. I'd prefer that not to happen.'

'I don't want the police.' Teddy realised he'd spoken just a little too quickly.

The man stared at him. After a while he said, 'My name's Rafe Jennings.'

Teddy felt by the way he said those words that

perhaps he ought to have known the name.

The empty feeling inside her seemed to swallow Trixie whole. She looked at the clock. It was five in the morning and she couldn't sleep. Joan slowly pushed open the bedroom door and came in and sat on the edge of the bed.

'I'm so sorry,' she said.

Trixie turned her head away. 'I'm not much good at keeping people close to me, am I? First, Teddy, then Mum, now my baby.'

'None of it is your fault,' said Joan. She had wire curlers in her hair and traces of Pond's cream on her face. 'It's just rotten bad luck.' She stood up. 'I think if I change your sheets it might make you feel cooler. You could hobble to the bathroom and have a bit of a wash while I do it.' She gave Trixie a small but warm smile.

Trixie got out of bed. Her head was still swimming but she managed to make the bathroom and sat down on the stool while listening to Joan bustling about in the bedroom. She got up and ran the tap for a bath. She wondered where Teddy was. There wasn't a day went by that she didn't want him back safe with her. The depressed feeling that came over when she opened her eyes in the mornings was staying longer with her throughout the day. She blamed herself for her brother's disappearance. If only.

'Joan?'

Her aunt knocked on the bathroom door.

'Don't bother with all that. I need a hand climbing into the bath.' And then all the breath seemed to be squeezed from her body and she

181

was gasping for air. She could feel her heart beating wildly as everything closed in on her and she fell into Joan's arms.

Joan allowed Trixie to lean on her while she stepped into the bubbles.

'You're not well enough to go gadding about so soon after having a baby. Lucky I was here to catch you. I hope that water's not too hot.'

Trixie looked at Joan and managed to get her breathing under control enough to smile. She liked the way her aunt good-naturedly bossed her about. 'I want you to do something for me in the morning.' She knew she was gabbling and breathing hard. Her aunt nodded. 'Will you get in touch with Jem for me?'

'Course I will. But only if you promise to take things easy.'

Trixie nodded. 'Where's Sid?'

'Ah, now that's a difficult question to answer. Who knows where he gets to. He said he'd register the death for you. You feeling better now?'

Trixie felt her eyes fill with tears. 'I'd forgotten all about that,' she said. 'I'd have liked to have seen my baby,' she said.

'No, you wouldn't. Better to wonder than to know the truth,' Joan snapped. She flounced out of the bathroom and Trixie heard her pummelling a pillow. It was one way of trying to get rid of the hurt and anger she felt about Sid.

Trixie put her fingers to her eyes. She was crying! She had no idea when the tears had started but they were flowing thick and fast now. She took a deep breath and grabbed at the clean white towel on the cork-topped seat and dabbed at her eyes. Still the tears flowed.

'Joan,' she called.

Her aunt bustled in. 'You want a lift out, sweetheart? You got a lovely clean bed to pop into and I was lucky enough to get hold of a couple of bananas today. Martin wotsit from Queen's Road in Gosport managed to get a hand from off a banana boat in Southampton Docks. Ask no questions and he'll tell you no lies but I happen to know his son works on the cargo ships there. I ain't seen a banana in ages, almost forgotten what they look like.' Trixie allowed herself to be rubbed down with a brisk towelling. It was almost as though Joan was attending to a small child. 'I'm going to mash one of them and put it between two slices of bread and marge. That'll be a lovely bite to eat for you.'

At last Trixie managed to get a word in. 'I can't stop crying, Joan.'

Joan stopped in the process of putting Trixie's nightdress over her head and pushed her away then stared at her. After a while she said, 'Let's get you into bed.'

Trixie couldn't eat the dainty sandwiches Joan had prepared. She managed a few mouthfuls of tea while Joan prattled on, 'You'll feel better after a good sleep.' She produced a *Woman's Own* magazine from her bag sitting on the living room floor and said, 'I was lucky to get this. What with the paper shortage magazines fly off the shelves in the shop like they got wings.'

Trixie got back into bed and opened up the magazine. She read through the first page then realised she'd taken in not one printed word. She read the page again, it was like the writing was completely new to her. Trixie picked up her handkerchief and wiped her eyes because she was crying again. Then she found a short story in the magazine and started to read. She got to the fourth line and knew it was happening again. She couldn't take in the words of the story. She switched off the bedside lamp and went to sleep.

Joan was shaking her shoulder. Trixie opened her eyes and was amazed to see Joan dressed for going out and a cup of tea on the table beside the bed.

'I can't stay here with you, love. I need to earn some money. I've left a dinner under a plate on the kitchen table.'

'What's the time?' Trixie's voice felt thick and slurry.

'Half past six in the evening.'

Trixie scrambled up. 'I can't have slept nearly twelve hours.'

Joan nodded and Trixie caught a whiff of lily of the valley perfume.

'You sure you'll be all right if I leave you?'

Trixie nodded. What did Joan think she was, stupid or something?

The front door banged and Trixie was left alone. She got out of bed and, taking her tea with her went into the living room to put the wireless on. It was almost time for the serial Paul Temple to start. The familiar music introduced the detective programme. Trixie made herself comfortable and sat back in the armchair to listen to Paul and his wife's adventures. The voices of the main characters washed over her.

Fifteen minutes later Trixie rose from the chair and stood very still. She thought of Paul and what an exciting life the writer of the programme made him live. Why, he'd just escaped from ... from? Trixie couldn't remember. She'd just listened to an episode of a favourite programme and now she couldn't remember a thing about it. And Paul's wife? What was her name? A feeling of weightlessness had enveloped her. It was like she wasn't really there. Sing. That's what I can do, she thought.

'*I'll get by as long as I have you, as long as ... as.*' What came next?

This is silly, she thought. Never in her life before had she forgotten a song's lyrics. Trixie held on to the arm of the chair and carefully lowered herself back down. She breathed slowly in and out and after a while the feeling passed. What's going on? she thought. Am I ill? Am I going mad?

As soon as she thought of madness, Trixie knew that was nearer to the point than being physically ill. She wiped away the fresh tears that were running from her eyes. Then she saw Joan's library book on the sideboard and rose carefully to go and get it. Sitting back down again she started to read.

The book, F. Scott Fitzgerald's *The Great Gatsby* was a favourite novel Joan was forever quoting from.

Trixie opened at page one and began to read. Then she threw the book across the room, where it clattered against the wall and slid down with several pages floating after it. Trixie was still unable to read and take in the words. She was going mad.

Trixie was frightened. She would be alone until Joan came home around eleven or so. She couldn't stop crying and she was turning into a madwoman. She pulled her legs up and sat in the chair hardly moving until a knock on the front door roused her and she went to let her visitor in.

His arms enfolded her.

'I only got back today and Grandad told me you'd lost the baby.'

'Sounds like I took the child out and lost him the way one loses a coin or a pen, doesn't it?'

He looked at her and frowned. 'I still want you to be with me,' he said.

'I've got some living to do, Jem, before I settle down,' she said. 'But first of all I need to get well again.' Did she look or act as though she was losing her mind? Had Jem noticed she wasn't quite right?

'I'm sorry,' Jem said. 'About the baby, I mean.'

'Perhaps it's for the best. I don't think I could make a good mother. I don't even know where my brother is. It's like people don't want to be around me for very long.' Again he stared at her. She pulled her dressing-gown belt tighter around her waist and stared at him. That feeling of weightlessness had returned and although she could see and hear Jem talking she wasn't able to take in all he was saying.

'Will you take me back to the island?' she asked suddenly.

'No need,' he replied. 'I didn't want to worry you with the details but I've been over there several times.' He shook his head. 'There's no sign of him. I even searched places that are not healthy

186

to be in.' She didn't understand him. 'Brothels and places where children are sometimes soliciting.'

'Teddy wouldn't do that; he's a good boy.'

'Of course he is, but he'll do what he's told to do if someone is cruel enough to make him.'

Trixie nodded. Of course, Teddy would do as he was told if he was hungry enough.

'It's possible the lad doesn't want to be found, Trixie. It's been a while now, hasn't it?'

'Yes.' She didn't want to think of Teddy any more. Her head hurt and although that funny feeling had passed she was so tired that she wanted to sleep and sleep. But instead she asked, 'You didn't tell me if everything is working well with you and your plans.'

He looked pleased that she'd remembered. 'I've engineered the takeover of a smallholding near the New Forest, Cadnum actually, and I've got a family to live in the house and run the place.' Trixie knew it was another step up the ladder he so wanted to climb to success.

'I'm really pleased for you,' she said.

'And you? Do you need money, Trixie?'

'No, Joan has decided to turn over a new leaf. She's cut way down on her drinking. And since she's been working she's a different person.'

'I'm sorry to bring this up, but what about Sid?'

'You mean, where's Sid? It's like trying to catch hold of an eel, he's that slippery. Last I heard was yesterday he went to register the baby's death but he didn't come home last night and the longer he stays away the better it will be for Joan and me.'

'You know I'll kill him.'

'You can stop that kind of talk,' she said. 'We've been through this before.'

'All right,' he said sullenly. 'Do you want me to do anything for you? Make tea? Get you something to eat?' She looked at his kind face and wished she was the kind of woman who could say, sod everything, I want to be looked after by you. But although Jem was a kind and loving person, did she really want to spend the rest of her life with him? And the honest answer was, no. She wasn't ready for that kind of commitment, even though she knew she was turning down an offer most women would think she was mad for doing. She got up. What was she thinking about? Jem was a good friend; the least she could do was make him tea.

Without any warning her legs buckled like jelly beneath her. She crumpled downwards but before she hit the ground, Jem had caught her.

'Trixie, I'm here.'

She couldn't speak, there was no air in her lungs. Jem's voice seemed to be coming from a long way off. Everything around her was unreal, as though she was watching it happen to someone else. But Jem's arms were around her and she felt protected, held safe. And then she was lifted and put down in the chair.

'Rest until I get back. Don't move,' he warned. 'I'm going for Dr Dillinger.' He was gone almost before she could thank him.

The door slammed.

Trixie held her head between her hands. Thoughts ran through her brain but she couldn't put them in any order and all the time the tears fell unheeded. She was going mad. She knew she was. She closed her eyes, lay back in the chair and felt darkness take her.

So many people were talking that the noise woke her.

'Can't I go to sleep without you lot wittering on!' She was angry, crying, light-headed and had to concentrate carefully on who was in the room with her.

Jem bent down on his haunches near her knees and said, 'The doctor's here. I've also got Joan here as well.'

Dr Dillinger was staring at her. He looked as though he'd just been pulled from the rag bag. Trixie wanted to giggle. The doctor said, 'Trixie, I need you in the bedroom so I can examine you.' He turned to Joan. 'You come too.'

Moments later she was lying on her bed and the doctor was examining her. Lifting her wrist, he took her pulse, then he felt her neck for the pulse spot there. His watery eyes betrayed nothing. When he'd finished he asked, 'Want to tell me what's bothering you?'

'I can't stop crying,' she said. When she saw the understanding look on his bewhiskered face she spat out exactly what was wrong with her, ending with, 'Am I going mental?'

He was about to speak when Trixie was over-taken by a bout of coughing. Then, when she tried to breathe, she couldn't get any air into her lungs. The doctor tilted back her head and lifted her chin. Prying open her mouth he breathed air into it and all the while he was pinching shut her nose. A couple of good strong breaths then he placed the heel of his hand on her chest, laced the fingers of each hand together and pumped hard on her ribcage. When he completed the pumping motion he went back to the breathing technique. Trixie gulped in air and yelled, 'Get off me!'

The doctor laughed and said, 'So, we're back in the land of the living, are we?'

Joan was dancing up and down and Trixie could see she was worried sick.

'Pop into bed,' he commanded. Then, 'You can come in, now,' he called to Jem. Trixie climbed into the bed and wiped her eyes on the sleeve of her nightie.

'You should be at work,' Trixie said to Joan.

'Jack's given me time off,' was her reply.

Jem sat down on a straight-backed chair and spread his legs wide. The doctor sat on the edge of the bed and frowned.

'You're heading for a breakdown if you don't get some proper rest.'

'Am I going mad?'

'No, it's not madness. More like a panic attack.'

'Will it go away?'

'Not if you carry on like you are doing. You're working two jobs, you've just lost a full-term baby and I gather you've had family worries for a long time, even before your mother died.'

Trixie looked at Joan. She hoped she hadn't told him about Teddy. Joan shook her head and Trixie relaxed.

'If I was practising I'd try and get you into Knowle Mental Hospital, near Fareham.' Trixie's heart started pounding; she began to speak but he cut her off. 'They've got psychiatric doctors there trained to help. I don't believe this is a case of what is sometimes referred to as "baby blues", a depression that can occur after the birth of a baby and descends like a black cloud. It's more than that, girly. I'd tell you to go on holiday but most of my patients can't afford holidays and I don't suppose, Trixie, that you're any different. A complete change of scene to a stress-free environment and good food will certainly help to get you back to normal. But then,' he smiled, showing discoloured teeth, 'what's normal?'

'Going to Knowle'll make everyone think I'm mad.' Trixie was indignant.

'Oh, dear,' he said. 'Why is there such a stigma attached to that place when there's no need for it? When will people realise that the mind can become poorly, just as bunions can grow and a skin complaint can flare up?' He looked at her and shook his head.

'Doctor?' Trixie finally plucked up the courage to ask. 'Why did you take my baby away so soon after I'd given birth? I would have liked–'

The doctor interrupted, 'I haven't seen you since I was called out to your mother.'

Joan said, 'Sid said you were here.'

Dr Dillinger turned to Joan, 'I can assure you, madam, I would prefer a mother to see her child. Unfinished business can cause problems later. Might even, as now, contribute to ill health in the mother.'

Trixie cried. 'But you *were* with me.'

'Hallucinations can be part of breakdown symptoms.'

Jem sat down on the other side of the bed and

took Trixie's hand. 'I can't bear to see you like this, shhh! I'm going to do something about it. Will you let me help you to get better?'

Trixie looked at him through wet eyes. 'Please?'

Jem turned to Dr Dillinger and after searching his pockets for his wallet took out several notes. The doctor looked pleased and said, 'I'm going to give her some medication to help her sleep and leave some for you to make sure she takes it for the next few days.'

Joan said, 'I'll look after her.'

Trixie felt the needle enter the vein in her arm. 'Lie back and count to ten,' said the doctor.

Is all this a dream as well? wondered Trixie. Was it a hallucination that Dr Dillinger took her baby away? And then sleep claimed her.

Chapter Thirteen

Rafe Jennings looked at his charge over the top of his morning paper. The boy was stuffing toast into his mouth as though it was going out of fashion, on ration maybe, not that Rafe worried about that. When one had money one had power and one had bread and butter to make more toast. Then, with the paper as a shield, he gave a huge grin.

The boy was a delight. Blond hair ... he shuddered. God, how long had it taken him to get rid of the parasites that invaded the boy's hair? He'd had to give almost daily washings with a medication that stank to high heaven. But what else could he do? He didn't want the nits deciding they'd like to live with him as well. Rafe remembered the day the boy had asked gruffly, 'Are they gone?'

'Yes,' confirmed Rafe, his fingers skating through the boy's soft hair.

'Wow! I've had nits all me life!' Then he ran round the room whooping like an Indian. At the memory Rafe smiled again. Then he lowered the paper. One day the boy seemed like a child and the next he acted so adult that Rafe was shocked.

'Would you like some more tea, Teddy?'

'Can I have another glass of milk?' The request was shyly given.

'Of course, help yourself.'

Teddy looked at him gratefully before pouring milk into his glass from the bone china jug. Rafe didn't think Teddy had been able to drink milk freely before.

The boy had filled out living with him; he almost looked a different person. Now the lad spent ages in the shower and bathroom fastidiously grooming himself, not that Rafe disliked that. On the contrary, it heartened him to think he'd brought a boy devoted to cleanliness into his house. He remembered his own mother saying to him, 'Cleanliness is next to Godliness'. Rafe put down the paper after folding it neatly and said, 'I've arranged to go to Southsea on the mainland today. Some of my sketches are going into an exhibition there. I'm not leaving until ten, how would you feel about coming with me?'

He saw the boy's eyes light up. Then he asked, 'Where we leaving from?'

'Cowes,' Rafe said. 'I need to have lunch with

my agent first.' He wondered why the boy asked the same question every time he suggested going to the mainland. The boy showed a willingness to come along whenever he asked him to accompany him on trips, unless Ryde was the exit venue. Obviously Ryde held bad memories for Teddy. Perhaps one day the lad might trust him enough to explain.

'I like ol' Pearson,' Teddy said, leaning back in his chair and patting his stomach, contentedly full of food. 'The only thing I don't like is that awful comb-over he has. Does he really think five strands of hair covers his whole head? I like it best when we walk out of the King's Head and the wind catches it, making the strands of hair stick straight up.'

'Yes, well, perhaps that's a little disrespectful, to talk about the man who makes money for me in that way.'

'Go on, you laugh too! When you think he's not looking. You called him a sad old queen.'

Rafe couldn't help himself – he began to laugh. This boy had brought so much fun into his life. Rafe, prior to Teddy's arrival, had thought of himself, too, as a sad old queen.

Teddy had made him feel young and had imbued him with a passion that enabled him to paint again. He couldn't believe he had almost killed this boy who sat sketching alongside him on the shores of Reeth Bay for hours without complaint. How lucky was he to have as his protégé a boy who could actually share in his love of art? Not only share, but had a talent that was immeasurable.

Rafe had never had children. He had been

involved in a marriage arranged by his father to Lady Lucinda Wheely's daughter, Janice. He'd been nineteen and thought he could hide his true sexual feelings. After a scandal that, luckily for him, his father hushed up, Janice had taken a trip to Rome and never returned. Rafe had willingly gone to Paris for a year and realised more than a few ambitions with his love life.

With Teddy living in his house by the sea, Rafe was aware how important it was to have someone to care about. He hadn't wanted it to happen, but Teddy had become the son he'd never thought he wanted. In less than a year his life had changed completely – for the better. Would he have made advances to Teddy if he'd been older? He thought not. Rafe prayed, though he knew it was wrong of him, that Teddy would never consider going back to his family. The boy had been mistaken if he thought Rafe had been taken in by the story of the parents being killed during the war. No, there was a secret that Teddy held close to his heart. And if the boy didn't want to share the secret then Rafe hoped he would consider his house a home until he grew up.

'You'll need your crutch,' Rafe said. 'There's quite a bit of walking involved.'

'No, I'll take one of your walking sticks.'

The boy's knee had never properly healed. A slight limp remained and caused him to become tired quickly.

'I'll take the stick with the bone handle because I know it's your favourite.'

Rafe smiled.

'I can't believe I'm going on an aeroplane.' Trixie couldn't stop smiling.

'I thought we might as well take advantage of flying to Athens. It's somewhere I've always wanted to go.'

Trixie held on tightly to Jem's arm. She felt very sophisticated wearing a long lightweight coat, high-heeled lace-up shoes and a hat just tipped over one eye. The tented terminal was huge and although she knew there was only one runway at present it was rumoured that within the next year or so another two runways would be built.

She looked about her as she began to climb the steps to the aircraft. Fields as far as she could see. The wind was blowing steadily and she had to hold on to her hat to stop it flying away.

'Do you reckon it'll take on, this air flight business?' Her voice was almost swept away by the wind.

'I don't see why not. Anyway, it would have been a shame to waste this area.' He shook his arm expansively to encompass the few brick buildings. 'It was already being used for military planes.'

It had taken Jem a while to sort out all the details for the holiday. He'd been like an excited child arranging cover for the smallholdings and help for Gramps in the shop.

And now Trixie was being helped inside the plane and shown to her seat by a very pretty young woman with a clipboard.

'Take your coat off and stow it beneath the seat in front,' whispered Jem. He was already struggling out of his heavy jacket.

'Hold on to this for me.' Trixie pushed her

handbag into his arms as soon as he'd rolled up his coat and stowed it away.

'Did you bring–'

'My medication? Yes, and I'm going to take a sleeping tablet the moment we've taken off. I know the flight will take a few hours and the doctor suggested I sleep as much as I can.'

Jem give her a lingering smile. When he'd suggested a holiday abroad she had agreed. Not straight away, because she didn't want him spending so much money on her. But he pressed her to agree, and she finally decided she would go with him. But only if he promised to look upon the money spent as a loan that she would repay when she was working again.

She looked out of the small window and sighed. She was excited and that was a sign she was getting better. The tears, at times, still fell unheeded and it was difficult for her to get out of bed in the mornings; she would much rather stay curled up like a hedgehog and let the day pass without her being involved in it. Her ability to read and take in words had resumed but her inquisitive nature had been overtaken by lethargy. Every day she thanked God for Joan, who'd become a tower of strength, and Marie and Eva who tried unfailingly to cheer her. But her saviour was Jem.

His businesses were taking off. Managers lived on the smallholdings he had purchased with loans from the bank, eager to help get the country back on its feet again after the war. And Jem was happy that his profits were not only paying back his debts but enabling him and his grandad to pay employees to make their lives easier.

Jem and Joan made sure Trixie helped herself back on the road to recovery by eating well, taking long walks and plenty of rest. She smiled at him, took her handbag and foraged for a bottle containing small white tablets. The air hostess brought her a glass of water and Trixie swallowed the tablet. As soon as it was gone she said, 'I trust you to look after me if the plane crashes.'

Jem tucked his hand in hers. 'Why would it crash? Air travel is the way to the future. I've dreamed my whole life of being able to travel. To do it with you by my side is an absolute bonus. Go to sleep.'

So she watched the other passengers being shown to their seats while talking and laughing. Everyone seemed to be wearing their Sunday best clothes. And she slept.

'C'mon sleeping beauty.' Trixie awoke to Jem lightly shaking her shoulder. 'Here, drink this.' He handed her a glass of water and she took it, gulping greedily. 'Sorry,' he said, 'you've missed the meals. I thought it better to let you sleep.'

She passed him back the empty glass. 'I take it we're nearly there.'

'The pilot's circling the plane to land.'

She put her hand to her neck and began rubbing it. 'I didn't even have time to feel frightened,' she said. 'Gosh, my neck is stiff.'

Trixie felt her stomach rise when the plane landed at Athens. She felt elated, still tired but excited at being soon to tread on foreign soil for the first time ever. It was something she could hardly believe. Fancy *her* in Greece! What would Greek people be like? Would they speak any

198

English? Because she certainly didn't speak Greek. Jem had taken charge of getting foreign money for the journey and had spent weeks poring over maps and books borrowed from the library so they would at least know a little about the places they planned to visit. Trixie was apprehensive too; where would they sleep tonight?

Trixie had never been on holiday in her life before. This was so much better than being sent to Knowle Hospital with its tag of the Loony Bin. How could she fail to become a whole person again with Jem looking after her?

When at last Jem and Trixie were standing outside Hellinikon Airport with their baggage, alone in a foreign country, she worried about the way the heat was making her clothes stick to her. Trixie was flustered but extremely proud at the way Jem seemed to know how to collect their luggage and show their passports. She was sure she'd never have accomplished it on her own. Jem made her feel safe and cherished. And now she was very proud of the way Jem spoke to the men who surrounded him, speaking Greek, offering rooms.

'This one, I think,' he said to her. And he shook the hand of a swarthy man in his shirtsleeves who was leaning on a car that was so old she was sure she had seen one just like it, but in better condition, in the old gangster films she loved to watch at the pictures. Soon all the luggage was stowed in the boot and with more handshaking the man got in the car followed by her and Jem.

Sitting in the rackety car that stank of petrol, Trixie sat back and watched the city unfurl before her with its shops and houses every bit as war torn as the cities back home. But there the resemblance to England ended. Doric columns almost hid tiny archways of cobbled stone. Old women dressed in black sat in shaded doorways. There was a feeling inside her that told her she was going to love Greece.

The house was in viewing distance of the Acropolis. A courtyard opened up to show bright red flowers growing in tin containers. The cobbles were shiny and wet where they'd obviously just been washed and the coolness of the tree-shaded yard made Trixie sigh with relief to be out of the sun that seemed to shine brighter than any sun pouring over Gosport.

A dark-haired woman led them up the wooden stairs to a top room containing two iron beds and an old-fashioned hand basin set in the corner. She proudly showed them how the cold water ran from the tap. Then she turned a key and opened the balcony door and said in broken English, 'Come, look.'

Trixie stood on the vine-covered balcony, and gasped. The ruins of the Acropolis were lit up. 'Come and look at this,' she begged Jem. 'It was worth coming all this way just to see this.'

The woman left the room, only to appear moments later with a bottle of wine. There was no label on it but she was telling Jem that they had made the wine themselves, a family venture. Along with the wine she'd brought bread and cheese, a white crumbly goat's cheese that Trixie liked the taste of, cutlery, plates and glasses. She had a great deal of energy, thought Trixie, who was herself feeling tired again. What she really wanted to do was sit on that balcony with a nice cup of tea, but Jem had already told her that the Greeks drank coffee boiled up in a very small saucepan and served in tiny cups. It was very strong, he'd said. She looked at the wine and decided a glass or two wouldn't hurt.

And then they were alone. And Trixie realised she was expected to sleep in the same room as Jem. She opened her mouth to speak but he beat her to it.

'It's just for tonight. It's late and I couldn't make her understand we wanted two rooms; she kept showing me the two beds.' He looked very dejected.

'Don't worry, I won't tell anyone back home if you don't,' she said. She pulled the bread apart and sat out on a small, very uncomfortable blue-painted chair that was hardly wide enough to fit her bottom. 'The bread's delicious,' she said. 'Come and sit down and look at this view.'

Jem handed her a small glass of red wine and as she drank, she shuddered but decided she could get to like it very much. There was a wonderful smell of honeysuckle and she closed her eyes momentarily.

'Go and get into bed.' Jem was taking the glass from her and she saw she'd allowed it to slip to one side and the contents to spill as she'd nodded off.

She grinned at him and lay down on the bed nearest the wall. Both beds had pictures of angels above them. She wondered if there was an angel looking over Teddy while he slept and another angel, a smaller one, looking after her lost child. Silently the tears fell. Trixie slept.

The next morning Trixie was already awake, sitting on the balcony with the warm sun on her face, watching the bustle of life below her, when a gentle knock on the door announced the presence of their landlady with a breakfast tray. She entered and set the tray down on a small table covered with a crocheted cloth. She smiled and said, '*Kalimera.*'

'Morning, Helena,' Trixie called.

Jem was shaving at the washbasin and raised a hand in greeting. The woman turned to leave but Jem hastily wiped his face and caught up with her in the doorway. Trixie could see by his arm movements that he was asking directions. She was perturbed when his face clouded over and the conversation became serious.

When the woman had gone Jem took the tray out on to the balcony and set it on the table. Trixie looked hungrily at the toast, honey and coffee.

'What was that all about?' she asked.

'I wanted to do some sightseeing. Just asking directions.'

Trixie buttered a piece of toast. 'No, a bit more than that, I think.'

'Okay, I'd have had to explain anyway. I've always dreamed of being here in Athens. Pity I didn't read the news before we came. There's trouble brewing.'

'What do you mean?'

'Helena advises that we stay close to crowded places that appear full of ordinary people about their everyday business. She says it's obvious we are visitors to the country but to take no chances.

An internal Greek quarrel has broken out, causing what could be an outbreak of civil war.'

Trixie, toast in hand, stared at him. She heard his words and didn't doubt the woman's sincerity in telling them to be aware of their surroundings, but as she saw the blue of the sky and the white marble and stone of the Acropolis in the distance and the chatter of children playing below in the courtyard filled with tangy lemon trees, she found it difficult to imagine the seriousness of the conversation between Jem and Helena.

'What does it mean for you and me?' she asked.

'It means that we are going to cut short our stay here and travel on.'

Trixie sighed. 'It's meant so much to you to be here. Why are they unable to agree?'

'It means more for me to be alone with you,' he said, taking her hand. 'Helena says Greece remains divided about whether to go communist or to remain a Western-oriented country.' He was silent for a moment, then said, 'However, we can visit the Acropolis and the Plaka in the old neighbourhood; they're both near and there's a flea market between Monastiraki and the ancient Agora. Helena reckoned you might like to browse around the stalls. But then I think we'd better leave Athens to sort out her own problems.'

'We're going home already?' That would be a shame, she thought. We've only just got here.

He looked at her with such longing. 'No, you goose. I'm not taking you home until I've proved to you that I can take care of you. Then maybe, just maybe, you'll change your mind about your feelings for me. I've brought you away to make you better and we're not going home until this damned depression takes a nosedive.' He took the remaining piece of toast from her fingers and popped it into his mouth.

'We'll go on to the islands,' he said.

Chapter Fourteen

Jem settled the suitcases and bags in the luggage room, tipped the guard and went up on deck to join Trixie. She'd clipped her blonde hair back to keep the wind from blowing it into her eyes. She was wearing a long skirt and a white blouse that left her arms bare. Sitting on the slatted bench seat with her head thrown back to absorb the sun's rays, she looked more rested than he'd seen her in a while. His heart bounced rapidly as he realised just how much the young woman had crawled beneath his skin. Two years ago he'd not known her. Now, not only did he love her to distraction but he wanted her to feel the same way about him. If it meant waiting for ever for her to realise she cared, so be it; he'd wait.

First, he had to make her whole again. Already he'd noticed a difference. Her tears were less frequent, her mood swings not so violent and slowly her sense of humour was returning. She hadn't told him half of what had probably brought about the breakdown and he'd already decided he wouldn't push her. When she was ready, she'd talk. Until then, he'd wait.

He was glad he'd taken Dr Dillinger's advice and got Trixie away from Gosport. A complete change of scenery and a rest was what the doctor had suggested and Jem was glad he'd not only been able to afford to bring Trixie to Greece but that his greatest wish to visit the place had been granted.

As he got nearer he realised she was singing softly to herself. The wind was taking her voice across the blue, blue sea. He smiled; she had a lovely voice, deep and melodic.

'Look at the scenery,' she said, waving an arm away from the busy, noisy dockland area of Piraeus with its greasy haulage ships and men and passengers scurrying with boxes and bags, to the far seas where peaceful white-cliffed islands peaked from the sea. The air around the docks smelled of wet sawdust and oil but he knew the moment the boat left Athens and headed out to sea the enticing scents of herbs and flowers would be blown from the scenic islands to entice the passengers.

He realised how much unlike the string-haired waif she was when he'd met her that day at Portchester. She was a young woman now. She'd had a child that, had it lived, he'd have willingly brought up as his own. At present she was frail, but he'd already witnessed her inner strength. He smiled at her. The sea, reflected in her eyes, made them as green as emeralds.

'It'll take us hours and hours to get there.' He sat down beside her. The sun was warm, already making him feel drowsy. 'There will be stops on the way and we'll have to sleep as best we can in the cabin. So I hope the sound of the engine and the swaying of the boat doesn't make you feel sick.'

'If I am sick, will you hold my hair off my face?' She was joking but he answered with all sincerity.

'You know I will.'

He'd bought bread and wine and oranges from a street seller but was happy to see strong coffee could be purchased on the boat. Unhappily there was little else that could be bought to eat or drink. He closed his eyes and listened to the other passengers as they toured the ferry or sat about reading or chatting. There were no other English voices.

Jem awoke to Trixie gently rubbing his shoulder.

'You'll get cold if you stay here any longer.' Her face was pink with the sun and wind.

'Where's the day gone?' It was dusk on deck and out at sea were pinpricks of light showing other vessels on the horizon. The air smelled of salt and strangely, he thought, oranges. 'You must have slept as well.'

She nodded. She'd covered herself with the second-hand black-fringed shawl he'd bought her at the flea market. Momentarily he thought of the labyrinthine streets of the Plaka and the bustle of the market. He rose, rubbing the back of one leg and sighed. 'Come on,' he said. 'Shall we go in and get some coffee?'

Trixie nodded. He pulled her up to his side.

'Smells just like the Fighting Cocks.' Trixie laughed as they entered the cabin. The smoke from cigarettes was thick. He saw a corner seat that was empty and it looked like they could both stretch out on it. He guided her towards it.

206

Already people were sleeping, arms and heads on tables, and a child lay swaddled in coats on the floor. Trixie stepped around him while an anxious mother watched, then smiled from her seat surrounded by parcels and bags. He bought coffee in small cups from the moustached attendant and took them back to the table.

The coffee was thick and bitter but warming.

'How do you feel?' Trixie asked. 'That was good,' she added, putting down her cup.

'I suppose it's the sea air but I'm still tired,' he said. 'More to the point, how are you?'

'I've done a lot of thinking,' she said, pushing strands of hair behind her ear.

'That sounds ominous.'

'I don't know if I'd have come through all this if it hadn't been for you, Jem.'

Her eyes were staring almost into his soul. 'You think you're getting better?'

'Yes, slowly. There's so much I don't understand or have answers for, especially about my baby and my brother's disappearance. I reckon worrying about him was one of the factors helping to tip me over the edge. My mum used to say I was highly strung. I guess a string snapped.'

'You can say whatever you want to me; you know that, don't you?' He felt she was ready to unburden herself some more and he felt honoured that she'd decided it was to him.

He let her talk. He guessed she felt safe. She began by telling him of how her father had hit her mother and of the bombing stifling her mother's screams. And of Teddy throwing the axe that had killed their father. She told him of the winkle barrow carrying her father's body and how she and her brother had sung for him a funeral song while the stars glittered and the searchlights flickered. He listened carefully as she told him of their hunger on the walk from Portsmouth to Portchester, where she'd visited the market to buy bread and found him, a guardian angel selling strawberries.

When she finished, she was crying. He wrapped his arms around her and let her cry until she slept. Carefully he rearranged her sleeping body on the scruffy padded seat so she wouldn't wake with a crick in her neck, then covered her with the knitted shawl. Then, when he was sure she wouldn't wake and be alarmed he'd gone, he got up, returned the cups to the bar and went outside into the fresh air.

The boat's motors were running more slowly than during the day and the clacking noise soothed his troubled mind. Despite the breeze the air was sultry and he stood watching the dark sea that was like velvet with sequins where ships' lights pierced the blackness.

No wonder she'd broken beneath the strain of the terrors Trixie had endured. He was surprised she'd had the strength to hold on to her mind as long as she had. Dr Dillinger would have found a way to hospitalise her, had he thought she couldn't come through her illness. The doctor also understood that mental illness still held a stigma, even in this day and age. One that Trixie didn't need to be tagged with for the rest of her life. Wise man, that doctor, Jem thought.

He thought of the American film star Frances Farmer, hospitalised, who had reputedly had electric shock treatment and later an operation on her brain – a lobotomy, he thought it was called – to help lift her depression and stabilise her. Apparently it had completely changed her personality. Thank God Dr Dillinger had believed that Trixie, more than anything had needed love and care to help regain peace of mind. Jem sighed. If he'd had to carry the burden of what Trixie had been through, he wouldn't have been able to survive. The girl was a bloody marvel.

He'd promised Trixie he'd never speak of what she'd told him. He would keep his promise. But when they got back to England he'd do everything in his power to help find her brother. Sid O'Hara was to blame for a lot of Trixie's misery. It was about time that rat of a bloke was sorted out.

Trixie watched the island growing larger as the boat chugged nearer towards it. She could see a castle, its ruins spreading along a stone esplanade. There were shops and houses behind the boat moorings and a road that led to a sort of large stone building that seemed to be where they were heading. Smaller boats lined the quayside, their flags, denoting countries of origin, blowing in the breeze. Trixie had watched the sun come up. Rays of gold and red turned the horizon to a fire-like glow that made her feel privileged to see it.

'Morning.'

She turned and grinned. He needed a shave. She knew she didn't look up to much herself. There was a fly-specked mirror in the toilet that showed her she needed a wash and brush up. She'd vigorously cleaned her teeth and decided to leave everything else until she could have clean water and a clean sink. Jem held two cups of the strong coffee. At first the coffee had tasted bitter and she hadn't really liked it much. Now, she decided, it not only tasted like nectar but it gave her energy. She took a cup from him and sipped at it then said, 'We'll be docking soon. What's going to happen then and where the hell are we?'

'The island is called Kos and I've wanted to visit it ever since I read about the place when I was at school. We'll be safe here and I'm hoping there'll be people to greet us at the quayside touting, like before, for visitors to stay in their accommodation.'

'It's certainly an adventure you've brought me on.' She put her cup on the floor beneath the seat. She looked at his cup of coffee, barely touched. 'I'll take them back in a moment.'

'Good idea. I'll see to the bags.'

'It's exciting, isn't it, not knowing where we'll end up tonight?' She saw him looking at her with that funny little smile he had.

'You reckon?'

'I reckon,' she said.

Trixie held her breath as the boat docked and cars and lorries and people all rushed together to exit the boat. No one seemed to want to wait or queue.

On the quay funny little three-wheeled trucks were parked and many men and women held placards with the names of places on. There was a smell about the place that at first Trixie couldn't put her finger on. Then she realised it was the scent of herbs blown down from the mountains on the warm, dry air. There was shouting and laughter as quickly the boat emptied of its cargo and passengers. Trixie thought it was better to stand by the luggage on the quayside and wait for Jem, than to get caught up in the swirling mass of humanity. She watched the clear water and the tiny fish swimming like slivers of silver.

'Come on.' Jem grabbed a suitcase and hauled it into the back of a cart and a large man in braces took her hand and helped her up onto the grubby seat cushions. A sad-looking donkey stood and waited while Jem climbed on.

The cart rattled noisily and slowly along the cobbled road away from the heart of the busy town, out into the relative peace of the country-side. Fields were either side of the road that had now changed to a dirt track, wide and dusty. Trixie was content to let Jem talk hesitantly in broken Greek to the man who told him his name was Alexio. Trixie saw his arms and hands were strong and burned brown with hard work in the sun.

The track led up into the hills and every so often they passed small white-painted stone houses. Donkeys grazed beneath trees and chickens ran squawking amongst the undergrowth. They passed through a small village, little more than a few houses, a sort of café that the man said was a taverna and a couple of shops. A large tree was in the middle of the village square and old men sat, drinking wine and a white liquid, at tables on rickety chairs playing what appeared to be some kind of game. Trixie felt it all seemed slow and inviting, especially when children waved and she waved back while they giggled and laughed. All about her were scenes the like of which she'd never experienced in England. No wonder Jem had longed to visit the island, she thought.

After what seemed an eternity Alexio made the donkey stop and Trixie saw steps, painted white and leading upwards on the hillside. Across the road was a large, rambling house. A dog barked and Alexio shouted. A woman appeared from the door of the house, closely followed by a yellow cat that twined itself around her feet.

'Thelma,' Alexio said, getting down from the front of the cart. Jem jumped down and went to shake the woman's hand, then came back to help Trixie, who went over to greet the woman. Middle-aged and grey-haired, she was smiling and immediately Trixie felt at ease with her.

Alexio had already started up the steps carrying the two suitcases and Jem followed with the smaller bags. Thelma touched Trixie on the arm and bade her follow her towards the house. Inside the kitchen area it was dark and cool and on the large table were loaves of bread cooling on trays. Thelma waved towards the huge fireplace with the biggest oven Trixie had ever seen. The kitchen smelled of baking. Thelma took a tea cloth and wrapped a loaf in it and then pressed it into Trixie's hands. Milk was poured into a jug from a small urn standing in a stone-floored cupboard. Then rich yellow butter was cut from a larger pat and that too was wrapped in a cloth and handed to her. Finally a bottle of white wine was tucked beneath her arm and she was pointed towards the steps that Jem had climbed.

The house was small and cool inside. The furniture was polished, yet scuffed with age. The bed, a double, was covered by a crocheted cloth and sagged in the middle. Yet to Trixie it looked so comfortable she wanted to climb in it straight away. There was a pump for water emptying into a stone sink. A small scrubbed table and two mismatched chairs and a dresser filled with crockery all jostled together in the kitchen. A door led from the kitchen into an overgrown garden. A vine-covered trellis gave shade and two chairs were set beneath. The view from the garden took Trixie's breath away: pine trees, fields and the yellow sand of a lonely beach.

Alexio shook Jem's hand yet again then left them to it.

On the kitchen table was a bunch of bright flowers in a jam jar. Trixie began to cry.

'Look at those flowers,' she said, the tears streaming down her face. 'Aren't they lovely?'

He anxiously scanned her face. 'Are you crying because you're touched Thelma left the flowers to welcome her new guests?'

Trixie sniffed. 'Of course; I'd be mad to cry otherwise, wouldn't I?'

Jem began laughing and then put his arms around her and whirled her around. When he let her go, he said, 'Nice you've got your sense of humour back. I hope you don't mind being out here rather than staying in a hotel in Kos town. I intend to make sure you get plenty of sun, good food and I was going to say, do what I can to help you get better, but already you're doing fine, aren't you?'

'Of course.' Trixie traced her fingers down his

213

dear face. In that instant she realised he *was* very dear to her. 'You're a good man,' she said. Then, 'What's that?'

On the draining board was a large bottle of clear liquid. There was no label.

'Another gift from our landlords?' Jem removed the cork and sniffed.

Already the aniseed smell filled the space between them. 'I think it's ouzo,' he said, searching in a cupboard for glasses. Jem poured a little into the glasses and then set them down. He let his tongue drift to one glass, saying, 'Aniseed. I think it's supposed to be taken with water.'

The pump groaned and creaked as the water gushed into a jug and splashed back at him. Trixie began to laugh. 'I see there's definitely a knack to using that, and you haven't got it.' He handed her a glass and told her to top it up as she wished. It was bitter yet refreshing.

'A toast to us,' he said. His hair flopped over his forehead and he pushed it back.

'To us,' Trixie agreed. She drank almost half the glass straight back and he shook his head as he watched her, then smiled.

'Now,' he said. 'How would you feel about lying in the sun for a while? We'll leave unpacking our stuff until later. I need to get hold of some kind of transport because we're out in the sticks here. If you need anything while I'm gone I'm sure Thelma will help.'

'You are coming back?'

'Silly goose. We need provisions other than the ones our hosts have provided. You can come with me if you're worried but I thought after the uncomfortable night we spent on the boat that a sleep in the sun would be more to your liking.'

'I'll stay,' Trixie said. She pushed away the panic that had risen. But she couldn't help imploring, 'Don't be away too long.'

When he'd gone Trixie sat down on a chair beneath the vine and presently she put her feet up on the other chair. With the heat of the sun marbling the table through the leaves and the noise of drowsy bees making her feel protected, Trixie slept.

It was the chugging of an engine that woke her. It stopped and Jem came loping round the side of the house carrying bags overflowing with groceries. His face was animated.

'I've got hold of a motorbike,' he sang out. 'It's old but it goes and so tomorrow I'll take you sightseeing. I've read up on this place and there's loads to see. Have you been all right while I've been gone?'

'I've slept,' she said. 'How come I can sleep all day and sleep all night as well?'

'It's probably your body telling you what it needs.' He took an apple out of a bag and handed it to her. 'I'm going to cook us some food.'

'Jem, it's nice being looked after,' Trixie said.

'I wish you'd let me do it full time and for always,' he said softly. He looked towards the open door. 'I expect you noticed there was only one bed?'

'You can have it,' she said. 'I'll make up somewhere to sleep on the sofa.'

'No.' He looked cross. 'You have the bed.'

'We can always string up a blanket so we can

215

have some privacy from each other. A bit like Clark Gable and Claudette Colbert in *It Happened One Night*.'

He began to laugh. 'I would never force myself on you,' he said.

Trixie believed him.

As she lay in bed that night with the door open to expel the heat, the scent of jasmine and herbs filled the room. Trixie listened to the night noises. They were interspersed with ragged snores from Jem. When she looked over towards the sofa she saw his slim body tucked well into its depth but one of his long legs hung over the arm of the piece of furniture and the other drooped disconsolately along the floor.

Above the sofa, on the wall, was a religious picture of a saint in flowing robes holding a child safe. The look on the little one's face showed he was where he wanted to be.

A shaft of moonlight showed Jem's face with that infuriating yet lovable lock of hair spread about his forehead. A feeling grew in her breast. She realised what he was to her. That somehow they would always be together and yet apart from one another. She felt such compassion. He would never leave her and she couldn't at this moment be without him.

A sort of loneliness engulfed her. She put her hand to her cheek and felt it was wet with tears. Trixie slid from the bed and tiptoed towards him, peeled away the thin blanket that was his only covering and nuzzled her body into the tiny space left on the sofa. His arm fell around her and she was cocooned with him in the softness and warmth. In the stillness of the dark she could hear his heart beating and it made her feel safe.

The words of a song came to her: 'I'll Get By As Long As I Have You'. She finished the first verse and word for word in her head sang the chorus. It was there! Complete! Every single word and she could remember them all!

Her face was close to his and she turned and searched for his lips. A soft kiss and her breath mingled with Jem's. My saviour, she thought. I love you.

She slept.

Jem didn't move. The scent of Trixie's hair and the musk from her sleeping body inflamed him. He wanted to crush her to him but he knew he mustn't rush her or scare her. That gentle kiss she'd given him so freely was the promise of love to come. Hope for the future filled him with happiness.

Chapter Fifteen

Three weeks later, back in Gosport, Trixie had never felt so well and she knew it was all down to Jem's care. He'd taken her away to Greece, away from the stresses and strains of her life in Gosport that had begun to drive her crazy. There, she had let herself think that dreaded word. Crazy. The balance of her mind had been truly disturbed by all that had happened before the holiday. For years she'd tried to hold herself together dealing with her father's death, then Teddy's disappearance, then her rape and finally her mother's and her child's deaths. And the weight of all that unhappiness had finally crushed her.

But Jem, the best friend anyone could ever have, had stepped in and made her whole again. He'd made her feel safe. Secure in that tiny whitewashed house, he'd cooked for her, read to her while she lay on a lounger in the shade and made it easier for her to think about the past and come to terms with it.

The holiday had given her a taste of what living with Jem might be like. There was no doubt he cared deeply for her. And Trixie was aware of her love for him. But whenever she thought of the actual, physical function of making love, all she could imagine was Sid's groping hands and probing fingers and her mind seemed to close down.

She knew there was still a long way to go before she could imagine being sexually involved with Jem, or indeed, anyone. It had felt natural to snuggle against him in bed and kiss him that night while he'd slept. The feelings she'd had for him had overwhelmed her, telling her she wasn't completely dead inside.

Jem had taken her away to Greece, not just a holiday but an experience that would live with her for ever. Who would have thought that she would have flown in an aeroplane? Walked on the Acropolis? Swum the Aegean Sea? And been made whole again. And it was all down to Jem.

The pub was practically empty and Marie had

popped in to chat. She was wearing a cheeky little red hat that looked like an upturned flowerpot but it reflected colour to her cheeks. She gazed around the bar, hesitating before she perched herself on a high stool. It was well known Jack didn't like his barmaids standing around talking, but he'd gone into town to the bank. Joan was washing glasses and frowning as water splashed on her new white blouse that she'd bought off the catalogue. And Eva was polishing the shelf at the back of the bar; her face was set and miserable.

Trixie knew it was because of the holiday. Eva had persuaded herself that Jem was beginning to think she was more than just a friend. For him to take Trixie away had obviously wounded her deeply.

'That two-roomed house in Greece was special,' Trixie said in answer to Marie's question about where they'd stayed. 'Jem reckoned one day perhaps he'll buy one just like it.'

'Won't be the same. And if you went back sightseeing, it wouldn't be like visiting those places the first time around,' Marie said.

Of course not, thought Trixie. Always first impressions were the ones that came to mind, especially if they were magical. Trixie remembered the look on Jem's face when he stood beneath the plane tree in Kos town – Hippocrates' tree, reputedly the place where the great man taught his students about medicine. The sun had shone through leaves dappling the cobbles.

'I thought Kos was wonderful,' she said. Joan had asked how they got around the island and whether there was public transport. 'Then to ride that motorbike back to our little house where he looked after me...' She lowered her voice, not wanting to rub Eva's nose in the fact that Jem, despite Eva's love for him, didn't return the affection. Trixie didn't want to hurt Eva; she'd become very fond of her.

'I've watched the roses come back to your cheeks, and you've put on a little weight that makes you look terrific,' Eva said grudgingly. She got off the stool and moved it along to attack another part of the shelf.

'So I'm fat now, am I?'

'I didn't say fat.' She knew how to wind Eva up and it worked every time.

She looked at her tanned arms and remembered how lovely it had been lying on the deserted beach with just Jem for company and she marvelled that they'd not argued once but always had something different to talk to each other about. She thought about the sofa, the kiss and felt a blush rise.

After that first night when she slept on the sofa with Jem it seemed so much easier for them to share the bed. And Jem had held her each night, waiting until she slept before he too, succumbed to slumber.

'I need to be close to you,' she'd said to Jem. 'But I couldn't bear it if you touched me. Sid hurt me. I'd never been near a lad before and he frightened me.'

'I understand,' Jem said.

'If I ever do it with anyone I'd like it to be you.' She didn't tell him that there were times when she didn't understand her feelings towards him. Sometimes she wanted to be close to him in every possible way and then she'd be terrified he'd touch her. But those thoughts were for herself and Jem and certainly not to be shared with her mates.

She was happy, rested and eager now to work in the shop and bar. For too long she'd left Joan to work and bring in the money needed to keep the prefab afloat.

Eva stepped down from the stool and foraged beneath the bar counter. She came to Trixie and held out a small tissue-wrapped gift.

'I know I can be a cow,' she said, pressing the package into Trixie's hands. 'It's not your fault that Jem loves you and I hate it that I can't help myself wishing it was me.' A red flush had appeared on her heart-shaped face. 'Anyway, I made this for you.'

Trixie smoothed open the paper to find a purse made of tiny patchwork squares. It was intricately worked and must have taken Eva hours to make. Impulsively Trixie put her arms around the girl.

'Thank you,' she said. Her voice was gruff with emotion. She knew it was Eva's way of telling her that her friendship meant more than bad feelings about spending time with Jem in Greece.

'Let's 'ave a look,' begged Marie. Trixie saw her eyes open wide at the dainty gift. 'That's beautiful,' she said.

Joan fingered the material. 'I wish I had a talent like you,' she said to Eva. Eva stood straighter and Trixie realised she was so lucky to have the friendship of these women. But there was always that black mist on the horizon, forever creeping closer, making her remember Teddy. What had happened to him? Where was he?

'C'mon,' Eva said. Trixie knew compliments didn't sit well with Eva. 'We've got to get this bar sorted out for tonight.'

'The band's arriving about eight and it should be a good gig.' Joan took a notice from the side of the till and perused it thoughtfully. 'Jack's advertised it in the papers and got mates of his in the victual trade to put up posters in their premises, so wear sensible shoes. I reckon we'll be on our feet all night.'

'He could do with getting the punters in – trade's dropped off a bit lately.' Trixie was thoughtful. She looked around the near-deserted bar; it was common sense to see two barmaids and a pot lady were overstaffing.

'Is it The Tropics?' Marie asked. 'I might bring my lad down; they're a brilliant band.'

'Sure is,' Eva said. 'I phoned to book them and Kathy said they couldn't play until tonight. Poor girl's had trouble with her throat again.'

'She hasn't been well for ages, has she? Lovely voice though,' Joan said thoughtfully. 'Like an angel.'

Jack returned just before Eva was about to call time and Trixie saw him looking anxiously for Joan.

'I don't pay her to toddle off when she wants to,' he said.

Eva caught Trixie's eye and winked. 'I think he's got a soft spot for her,' she mouthed.

Just then Joan came in from the garden where she'd collected glasses left outside the previous evening. 'It's cold out there,' she said.

Jack blushed, then left the bar, hastily going upstairs.

Eva laughed. 'He can't speak to her without falling to bits and when she's not around he tries to disguise his feelings by being tetchy with her.'

'Well I never,' said Trixie.

Joan said, 'What's the matter?' Trixie and Eva laughed all the harder.

'Think you got an admirer,' said Trixie.

Joan said, 'Don't be stupid. I'm married.'

'Jack's worth a hundred of Sid,' Eva said.

'Sid would find some way of hurting Jack if he thought there was any funny business going on.'

'And is there?'

'What?' Joan's eyes crinkled up at the corners.

'Funny business?'

Joan sighed and walked back out into the garden, slamming the door behind her.

'Has he been around?'

'Sid?' Eva shook her head.

'Not shown his face around the prefabs for ages, thank goodness.'

Yes, thought Trixie, thank goodness. When on unguarded moments she caught herself thinking about him she began to shiver with pent-up emotion. When he'd attacked her he'd not only made her pregnant, he'd made her fearful of all men's advances. Even imagining a possible sexual scene with Jem filled her with panic, though she knew deep in her heart he would never hurt her.

Jem moved the empty coffee cup to the side of the pile of invoices. He'd checked them all and was ready to write cheques to pay his creditors.

'Want a refill?' His grandfather's hand reached for the cup. 'And how we doing this month?'

Jem looked up into his grandfather's face. Bits of toilet paper clung to his grizzled chin where he'd cut himself shaving.

'Been tryin' to cut your throat and missed, have you?' Jem smiled at the old man. 'You don't need to end it all yet. We're doing fine.' He paused for a moment then said, 'Remember the sleepless nights we both had wondering if we should borrow against this place to open up the other small-holdings?' He didn't wait for an answer but carried on. 'The next year is going to be good for us. We could move from here, if you wanted. Buy something a bit more luxurious.'

He didn't get any further for his grandfather broke in with, 'And why would I want to do that? All my memories are here. You might be all right taking chances; your life is ahead of you. My life is with my memories of your gran and that's rooted here in Clayhall. No, I'll go on living here and as long as I have a bit of help with the shop, I'll stay.' Jem knew his grandfather liked Trixie helping him out in the store but they'd long since stopped selling produce from the roadside stall. Selling to stores meant bigger profits.

'I wanted to ask you a question, lad. You don't have to answer if you don't want to, but I'd like to know why you took young Trixie away.'

Jem sighed. 'It was going to come up sooner or later, I suppose. One reason was purely selfish. You know how I've longed to travel to Greece, and taking her with me gave me a companion. But I could also see she was in a bad place,

Gramps. She could have been taken to Knowle Hospital for the depression to run its course. A breakdown from which she might have taken a long time to recover. The doctor suggested a change of scenery. I trust that drunken ol' bugger and,' he paused again and stared at Gramps, 'I knew the day that girl came into my life that I loved her and she'd be the only girl for me, ever.'

Gramps opened his mouth to speak but Jem shushed him. 'You knew Gran was yours the moment you first met, didn't you?'

The old man nodded.

'So, too, I know Trixie has to belong to me even if I have to wait my whole life.'

'But aeroplanes? Foreign countries? Been cheaper to have taken her to Margate for the weekend!'

Jem laughed, 'You mean ol' bugger! That girl's never been anywhere except across the ferry. Now she has. And she's experienced air travel. And the most important thing of all is that the sun has recharged her batteries and she's well again.'

'Does she feel the same way about you?'

Jem drummed his fingers on the table. 'She's too young to know what she feels. I can wait.'

'An' while you're waiting you gonna become a bleedin' monk?'

Jem narrowed his eyes at his grandfather. 'I have to take the chance that maybe she'll never love me. In which case I want her to be happy. But there's plenty of women in this world, in Gosport even, who like men. They like their company. And some are content with gifts and no strings attached. I'll tell no woman a lie. But the moment that girl tells me she loves me, I'll follow her to the ends of the earth.'

Gramps sniffed. He pulled at a piece of stuck-on paper on his chin and it came away, free and clear. 'I like your reasoning. But you must have spent a pretty packet on the holiday.'

'Yes, and I'd do it again, if needs be. You got no worries there, ol' man. I told you we're going to do well over the next months. The corner shops are on their way out. We're going to sell to the large stores that are springing up. And I've recruited family men who can live on site; they aren't so flighty as young blokes–'

Gramps broke in, 'You're lucky with the blokes running the other smallholdings. Honourable men are hard to find in this day and age.' The old man walked slowly to the sink and rinsed his cup. He lit the gas beneath the kettle for more coffee. 'What about Trixie?'

'What about Trixie?' He'd just been pouring his heart out to his grandfather and it was like he hadn't listened to a word he'd said.

'She's of marriageable age. Have you thought about asking her?'

'Just come straight to the point, why don't you,' said Jem. 'She's got problems. That rape and losing her kiddie hasn't done her any favours.' He would keep Trixie's secrets about Teddy and their father because to him, a promise was a promise. 'She needs time. She needs, as she says herself, to live her life before she settles down. The girl's not been set a good example of home life and she's scared of commitment. But it doesn't worry me. I can wait, like I said. I can wait.'

'Does she love you?'

'She trusts me. I can love enough for the both of us if needs be,' Jem said. He ran his fingers through his hair and then looked at his grandfather. 'Anyway, old man, weren't you supposed to be making coffee?'

He thought about the past weekend when he'd spent time on the Isle of Wight looking for Teddy. He was beginning to think the boy had vanished off the face of the earth. He needed to get hold of Sid. He'd pretty soon give up a few secrets if he had Jem's hands around his neck, he thought. But Sid hadn't been seen around the prefabs for quite a while and, looking at Joan and Trixie and the life they were making for themselves without that bastard about, perhaps it was better if he stayed away.

Jack hauled up a crate of brown ale from the cellar and set it down on the floor behind the bar. Then he went down the wooden steps and brought up some bottles of spirits and left them on the back of the bar. His girls would set the bottles on the shelves and the spirits in the optics when they came in tonight. He stared at the slices of lemon covered with a paper serviette. That would be Eva's doing, he thought. Getting the place ready for the band's arrival and the change in customers, young ones tonight, who'd be asking for fancy drinks. He thought about 'his girls', as he liked to call them. Hard workers, the three of them. Young Trixie had turned up trumps. The punters loved her. And that's what counted in the pub game. He smiled as he thought about Joan.

She was a winner in every sense of the word. Look how she'd been as near to a bloody alcoholic as one could get and now refused a drink but worked with the stuff around her. That bloody Sid had never treated her right, never.

Years ago Sid would stand with his elbows on the counter moaning that she wouldn't give him kiddies. Said he'd always wanted a kiddie of his own but the woman was barren. Knocked her about for it, too, the bastard. Joan was just what this place needed. A cheerful little body who took an interest in everything that was going on in the place. And since she'd started work and taken an interest in herself she was quite an eyeful. He wouldn't kick her out of bed, no siree – that's if he could entice her into it!

Sid turned over in bed and eyed the big red-head asleep beside him. Jesus, but she was a goer. Cooked a tasty breakfast as well, which was what he'd be getting when he woke her up. Her arms were white and plump, one slung across his body as though she owned him. He thought back to last night. Just thinking about her big arse made his dick quiver. If he treated this one nicely he could stay here a bit longer, get his feet under her table. What was her name? Melanie? Something like that. He wasn't sure. Better just call her 'love'. And with Harry Barnes looking to him to drive away the lorry-load of meat off Southampton Docks so he could distribute it round the markets, he was in clover. He yawned. God, but his dick was straining against her skin.

'Good morning, love,' he whispered in her ear.

'I've got something for you.'

Eric Blomberg sat in the corner of the bar nursing
a half-pint of Brickwoods Best. Wherever there
was a local brew he liked to try it. He took a sip
and looked about him. He had a good view of
everything going on in the crowded bar, especially
the four young people setting up their loud-
speakers and taking sound tests for the instru-
ments. The boys were lithe and pretty, especially
the one constantly messing about and giving the
others earache. He'd already ascertained his name
was Eddie. The girl was a no-no. She moved like
an old woman. It didn't matter to him whether she
sang well or not. He wondered if he should leave
straight away. Eric looked at his watch. Even if he
drove like the devil he'd be too late for the show at
Guildford.

He stood up, took off his wool coat and settled
down. The bar was warm, outside it was enough
to freeze the bollocks off a brass monkey. The
forecast was snow.

The snooty dark-haired barmaid was delivering
a tray of beer and soft drinks to the lads, who
looked like they were nearly ready to start playing.
Their singer was leaning across the bar chatting
with the young pretty blonde. Her and the dark-
haired girl had been staring at him earlier. Surprised to see an old bloke dressed in expensive
clothes in the backstreet pub, he guessed. That
blonde barmaid had a look of Doris Day about
her. Ah, he thought, now there was a singer who
wasn't afraid to tackle anything from big band
material to solo spots. He shuddered, remem-

bering how her voice moved him when she sang 'Sentimental Journey'. The singer was making her way back to the boys and the mic. There was definitely something wrong with her. Even if the lads were knockouts the girl didn't look as though she could take the strain of the bus travel. Not that he'd be overly worried about a new band and the mistakes they'd make at gigs. Max, his road manager, would look after them. But the band deserved a stable singer. Eric looked at his watch again. He might as well, now he was here, sit back and listen to The Tropics.

'What did you agree to this for, Jack?'

Trixie shook the fistful of music at him. 'Near You', 'I Wonder Who's Kissing Her Now', 'How Are Things In Glocca Morra?' The pages rattled.

He sighed and said, 'I 'ad to agree. Didn't think you'd mind helping me out. The punters love you an' you can see that poor girl ain't got the breath she used to have. If she stops singing an' there's no bit of fluff to carry on singing, my customers'll leave.'

'At least you could have asked me before they started playing.' Trixie's anger was melting. Where was the harm in singing a couple of songs to help this bloke out? After all, he'd been good enough to give both her and her aunt a job.

'I'll do it on one condition.'

He looked at her gratefully, 'What?'

'I need a cup of tea. My throat's as dry as the bottom of a budgie's birdcage.'

She saw Jack shuffle off to the kitchen. He wasn't such a bad old stick, she thought. She started humming the first song and watching where the notes on the sheet music rose and fell.

Later she opened the door and crept in to stand beside Eva. The bar was packed and the main door was open, despite the freezing cold, to let in some air to clear the fug of cigarette smoke and beer fumes.

'She's got cancer.' Eva's whisper knocked Trixie for six. 'George is cut up about it as there ain't nothing else they can do.'

It was impossible for Trixie to speak. The tears had welled up in her eyes and her throat felt as though someone was strangling her. She heard the clapping then and felt Eva shove her through the wooden hatch and into the crowd. Through the mass of bodies she saw Kathy's face, white and strained and the girl smiled at her and mouthed, thank you.

George took her hand and said to the crowd, 'Trixie's going to sing, "How Are Things In Glocca Morra?"'

The piano started up and Trixie found her own level with the first few bars. The words of the song were haunting. The news about Kathy's illness cut into Trixie's heart and she sang the melody as if by singing she could make everything better. What a dreadful thing to have happened to Kathy with her whole life ahead of her. One moment she had everything and a voice to die for and now ... to be waiting to die. When the boys stopped playing there was silence. Trixie realised the audience was staring at her as though transfixed, then they began clapping. And whistling, and shouting. She'd sung okay; they'd liked it.

Kathy came over and said, 'Thanks, you don't know what it means for me to have a break. You sang that song beautifully.'

Trixie nodded. The tears at the back of her eyes had won in their attempt to spill over. As she headed towards the back room, people were patting her on the shoulders and back and calling out, 'well done'. She looked over the back to where the strange man had been sitting. He'd already left.

Chapter Sixteen

'Move out the way, Grandad. I can't brush potato dirt away when you're standing on it.' Trixie leant the broom against the counter and stood with her hands on her hips. 'Why don't you make us both a nice cup of tea?'

'Bloody lives on tea, you do,' he grumbled. All the same he walked out using his stick and it wasn't long before Trixie heard the sound of water flowing into the kettle. He was getting old now, she thought. Rarely did he move without the stick. She loved the old man and he knew it. He hoped one day she'd move in with Jem. But one day was a long way away for Trixie. She went on sweeping up, then brushed the dirt and bits into a dustpan, finally throwing the rubbish into a bin.

Trixie was just about to open the door to look at the boxes of goods stacked outside when the door opened and George and Kathy came in. Kathy was wrapped from head to toe in warm clothing with a scarf around her throat.

'Hello! Strange to see you two in Clayhall,' Trixie said.

Kathy spoke first, hesitantly and breathily. 'Come to thank you for the other night. The crowd loved you.' Trixie noticed how difficult it was for the girl to speak. She walked to the back of the counter and came back with a chair.

'Sit on that,' she said. Just then Grandad appeared with two teas and a plate of biscuits on a tray balanced one handed and with difficulty. He looked at them and said, 'Want a cuppa? I'm just making.'

George nodded gratefully and Grandad disappeared again.

'Get on with it, Georgie,' said Kathy.

He looked sheepish and then grinned. 'We've been picked up by an agent.'

'No!' Trixie was happy for them. 'You deserve to do well,' she said. Then she frowned. Why had they come to see her?

'The agent wants you to sing with the band.' The tears in Kathy's eyes were plain to see. 'He doesn't want me because I can't travel and keep up with all the hard work the travelling involves.'

Trixie was reeling under her words.

'Me?'

'Yes, you.'

Trixie took a couple of steps towards Kathy and bent towards her. 'But you're the singer.'

'I *was* the singer. Now I'm a singer who can't sing and this is a business. I'm asking you to give the lads their big chance and do whatever the agent suggests.'

Trixie looked at George. His face was almost as pale as Kathy's. 'This girl loves you, you know,' Trixie said to him.

George put his hand on Kathy's shoulder. 'I told her I wanted no part of it without her but she insisted we come together to ask you.'

'It's his big chance. If he lets it go by, it may not come again.' Trixie could almost touch the love shining from Kathy's eyes on to George. She turned to Trixie. 'Will you give it a go?'

Trixie thought for a moment. If this agent came to her and told her she'd need to spend all her time with the band and possibly travel abroad, could she do it? It would mean leaving Clayhall – not for ever of course. Leaving Jem – but she could write to him. Leaving Joan would be hard, but she could keep in touch by letter and come home as often as she could. And she might even discover Teddy's whereabouts.

'Yes,' Trixie said. 'But I need to talk to this manager or agent, first.' She could see the relief on Kathy's face.

'You'll look after him,' Kathy asked. She turned her head to look up at George.

'Of course. But who is going to look after you?'

Kathy blushed. 'I'm going into a nursing home. It's too late to operate. Every day is a bonus now,' she whispered. 'I've wanted all my life to be a singer with a band and if it's not to be then I want you to take my place.'

Trixie wiped the back of her hand across her eyes. 'You're a brave person,' she said. Just then the rattling cups announced Grandad's presence and as Trixie moved to take the tea tray from him a customer entered.

Before Trixie knew it a management deal had been struck, tour dates arranged and even Eva had come aboard as a dresser.

Joan had given her and the family shelter when they needed it and Trixie would be for ever in her debt. But now Trixie was going to stand on her own two feet. Joan's smile, as Trixie's news unfolded, grew larger until the woman was almost weeping with happiness for her. 'Just you make sure you write often, and telephone. I need to know you're well. And if Teddy turns up, he'll want to know your whereabouts.'

Trixie had Joan's blessing.

'I'm not happy about doing this at the expense of Kathy, though. This was her dream, not mine.' Trixie was adamant.

'If you don't step in, someone else pretty soon will.' Trixie looked at Joan and knew she was telling the truth. 'Besides, you have inside you the hunger to be a success,' Joan said. 'You go for it, girl!'

Teddy moved his satchel of school books further along the train's seat and put his feet up. He wouldn't have done it if he hadn't been alone in the first-class carriage. Galloways had taught him manners, along with many subjects that before he'd met Rafe he never knew existed in the school's curriculum. Teddy had surprised even himself by doing well at the school, even though he hadn't wanted to leave Rafe and their home on the Isle of Wight.

Galloways was a small school, one of the best in the south of England, chosen by Rafe because he himself had spent several years boarding there.

In the beginning Teddy had had to prove himself.

A smile hovered at the corners of his mouth as he remembered the childish pranks played on him. Water poured into his bed. Bigger boys treating him like a servant as he was made to clean their football boots. Running errands for the older boys. All this he stoically stood until the night he'd been trapped in the showers with Fergusson and Manship. He was going to be beaten up and he could do nothing about it. Two against one.

The other boys watching from the door had giggled and urged Manship on, and the blasting water from the shower managed still to spray over them. Manship kept hitting him while the crowd of boys looked on and cheered.

Here, at Galloways, if he didn't stick up for himself Manship would continue to make his school life a misery. But this assault had taken him by surprise. He felt belittled. Afterwards he had fled to his dormitory and lay curled up on the bed, bleeding, bruised and crying. Manship had beaten other even younger boys. Teddy knew he had to put a stop to the bully before he grabbed him again.

Life at the end of the Ryde pier had taught him a few things.

Teddy was streetwise.

Manship's father was not only on the board of governors of the school but the man's money made it possible for special 'treats' for the boys.

236

Holidays, rock-climbing in Scotland, narrow-boating in Wales – and a special few boys were allowed to follow costly hobbies. Manship was passionately fond of the orchids he grew in the greenhouse and which he visited alone each evening after dinner.

Teddy was waiting for him. He didn't need spectators. Just a spectacular potted plant held in his hand that he threatened to throw to the ground unless Manship desisted. A small crowd had gathered outside the greenhouse to see Teddy knocking the plant pot on the side of the wooden shelf and disturbing the roots of the beloved plant, while Manship cried out, 'Don't hurt the orchid, please.'

Teddy said, 'Don't ever mess with me again. And watch out who you do mess with. I'd hate to see these beauties beaten and broken like me.' Again he knocked the plant against the steel tubing of the worktop and more earth fell from the pot to scatter on to the ground. Manship had tears in his eyes. The plants were his passion.

A titter came from the audience of boys. This was weakness in the extreme – Manship crying over a flower!

Teddy left him then. He'd handed the pot plant to Manship, who'd grabbed at it hungrily. Teddy pushed his way through the crowd of boys and went upstairs to finish his homework. He'd found the bully's weakest point and he'd earned respect from his peers. No one need ever know how scared he'd been or that he too admired the fragile blooms so much he'd never have destroyed them. The next morning Manship had gone home for a 'holiday' break.

Teddy excelled at rugby, rowing and football but his passion was art and Galloways excelled with their tutelage. Best of all he liked the open days when parents visited the school. Rafe never let him down. Arriving in his two-seater Alvis, he would park the car, then stride across the grass to greet Teddy. A tall, handsome, pedigreed, slim man who it was rumoured about the school was really Teddy's father. And Teddy didn't dispel the rumours. He was proud of Rafe and his artistic success and longed to be like him.

And now he was going home, as he thought of the island, for the Easter break.

Rafe was waiting at the station. Teddy's heart swelled at the sight of him. He was too old now for hugs and kisses and shook Rafe's hand. In the car they spoke about the proposed holiday to Italy.

'Two days to mess about, then a taxi to the airport.' Rafe smiled at him. 'We might get some painting done if the mood takes us,' he said.

Back at school Teddy had felt guilty about not telling his benefactor about his past. He wanted to unburden himself. Now, looking at the man beside him driving, the wind in his hair, threads of grey hair mingling with the blond, making Rafe look more distinguished than ever, Teddy knew his past life was so far in the past it wasn't worth bothering about. He would never tell Rafe about his life before they met. And then his heart constricted. Trixie ... how was she? How was his mother?

And he knew if he ever set foot again in Clay-hall his uncle would make sure the police arrested him for the murder of his father. Think of the shame that would bring to those two people he loved most. And shame to Rafe as well.

No, he must keep his secret, always.

Chapter Seventeen

'It's the chance of a lifetime and you have to take it.' The words came from his mouth, but only because it wasn't fair to tell her he wanted her to stay near him. He moved the mug of tea in front of her and sat down opposite her at the scrubbed table. He pushed aside the invoices and picked up his pen, tapping it on the table to distract himself from the thought of her imminent departure.

'Will you go and see my aunt to make sure she's all right?' Trixie's eyes were moist, like she'd been crying. Jem reckoned she'd spent a sleepless night deciding she must leave the prefabs and Joan.

'Now she has a job she'll be fine. I've even heard on the grapevine that Jack has got his eye on her. Might even do her good to find she can manage on her own. Certainly she can do without that bastard Sid.'

'You've not answered my question.' She picked up the mug and drank deeply. He pushed the plate of biscuits towards her. She was too thin.

He looked into her eyes. 'Of course I will. Do you doubt me?'

Trixie shook her head. 'I want to give her money, but I'd prefer to send it to you.'

'Frightened she'll drink it?'

'I trust her not to slip back into her old ways, but if Sid comes home he'll take it off her. Despite her saying she'd never take him back, I don't think she'd be able to help herself.'

'That's the trouble with loving someone; you can't turn it off like a tap.' And I should know, he thought. But he said instead, 'I'd do anything for you – you know I would. I'll make sure she's looked after.'

He swept away the memory of Ellen, the woman who was part owner of the Grayfield Nurseries. He'd spent a couple of nights in a London hotel with her. She was married and didn't want the family of her wheelchair-bound husband to know she was taking time out for her own bodily needs, so Knightsbridge had been a one-time haven for the both of them. Ellen loved her husband and her business. She'd made it quite clear he was just a convenient lover. And that had suited him fine.

Trixie stretched up and kissed his cheek, then whispered, 'I've got a lot to thank you for.'

His grip tightened on her. 'I had thought we'd found each other,' he said. Her perfume was inflaming his senses.

'I have to find myself before I settle down,' she said. Her eyes danced and he wanted to crush her tightly, hold her so she couldn't leave him. But he pushed her away; he had to let her go.

So this is what it's all about, is it? Trixie stood behind the stained brown curtain and awaited her turn to walk onto the stage of the grubby room in a beer hall in Hamburg. The smell of cigarettes and drink and a pall of smoggy air in the window-less space made her eyes smart.

The noise from the people the other side of the curtains who had paid ticket money was deaf-ening. So noisy that she doubted very much that when she was introduced and walked out to sing that they would even bother to listen to her. The German girls who had turned up to watch The Tropics had come to feast their eyes on three Eng-lish boys and they were letting everyone know it.

Fourteen hours it had taken in the bus, not counting the ferry crossing to get to this desti-nation. The boys had been excited and even more so after spending time in the bar on the boat.

She and Eva had sipped tea and discussed the dresses Eva had designed and made for her.

'Leave it to me,' Eva had said. 'I'll make you frocks that'll make you look a knockout.' She wouldn't tell Trixie what they were like and knowing Eva's penchant for patchwork Trixie hadn't liked to pursue the matter. But now, standing in the dark red velvet calf-length dress with her waist nipped in and her bosom pert and pointed in the season's new Lovable range bra, she was glad she'd asked Eva to accompany her.

'I'm surprised that after the war we're welcome here,' she said softly.

Eva stopped fiddling with the belt of Trixie's dress and said, 'Bloody Hitler kept his people away from anything he considered non-Aryan, music especially. Now Germany's regaining her financial standing after we bombed her to bits, the people need to express themselves. Recording studios have opened up and jukeboxes are practically a

241

way of life. Frankfurt, Berlin, Munich – those places are opening their arms to the music business.'

'How do you know so much?' Trixie was impressed.

'You didn't think I'd come away without knowing where I was going and what it was like, did you?'

'Comforting to know that you're a bleedin' oracle,' said Trixie. She might not have researched the trip well but she wasn't blind to Eva's blatant pursuit of Eddie. It was almost as if she'd finally realised that Jem would never look upon Eva as anything more than a friend and had turned her attentions elsewhere.

Trixie watched as Eva pulled back the curtain a fraction. 'I reckon the boys look great in their suits,' said Eva. She turned back to Trixie with a smile. 'That's why I thought it would look good for you to be wearing fabulously smart clothing.' Trixie knew Eva had more of a say in the lads' outfits than they had. When they'd played in the Gosport pubs their outfits were whatever was clean in their wardrobes – George had told her that – but now she had to agree that Eva's input had made them look like a proper band. 'Scared?' Eva stared into Trixie's eyes.

'I'm petrified.'

'But you've had loads of practice.'

'Only in the prefab, when Joan wasn't there, because she said the noise gave her a headache. And of course in the pub.'

Eva laughed. 'I don't know what you're going to do when you lot are top of the bill.'

The band, as unknowns, weren't headlining. They were filling the bills at various venues. Mostly doing the ends of the first half or filling in before the headline singer or band came on. Eric Blomberg had explained that that was the way most careers were started in the music business and that they couldn't expect to run before they could walk. It was his job to get venue managers to take a chance on their unknown status. He'd seemed pleased by his achievements, so Trixie didn't worry. Not even when he insisted that she keep her own name as singer, instead of going under the banner of The Tropics.

'What's your name?' he'd asked.

'Trixie True,' she'd replied.

'I couldn't have made up a better name,' he'd gushed.

And now Trixie looked at Eva. 'I know when to come on and go off. I know the boys will follow me because, unlike Kathy, I don't read music. That means there's a sort of silence until I sing and thank God they're such good musicians they can conceal any mistakes I make with the timing. I'll know I'm rubbish, the band'll know I'm rubbish but they'll cover for me and the audience won't know – hopefully,' she added. 'If I'd been singing with them as long as Kathy had it would be entirely different.'

She was tired. The journey hadn't been comfortable and she hadn't prepared herself for the constant closeness of them all in the van and the bickering that erupted and Max dealt with. She hadn't realised that men could be so earthy when they discussed gigs, music or women. But she knew she was the newcomer and, along with Eva, they had to fit in. So she pinched her nose to smelly socks, closed her ears to burps and farts and ignored degrading remarks about the girls who hung about them or that Mo and Eddie sneaked in the van to fuck. They'd done it in Gosport and felt no need to change their ways abroad, especially when groups of girls threw themselves at them.

George was a different sort of bloke. He was quiet and seemed to be seething with anger about the responsibility that had been taken from his shoulders. He was the founder of the group, she discovered, but resented the fact he could take them no further than local gigs and if anyone could get them a recording contract, Eric Blomberg could. But Trixie knew he was worried all the time about Kathy. He phoned home every night.

Trixie meant it when she said she was scared. There were a lot of people out there. The audience were loving the boys and their music. Suppose she spoiled it? Her heart was thumping so hard she was sure that Eva would hear it above the clapping. Oh, God! They were clapping for *her*.

'Bless you,' said Eva as Trixie glanced worriedly at her then strode purposefully out to the centre of the stage, where a microphone had been set up at just the right height for her. The cheering from the already excited audience accelerated.

Trixie smiled at the audience and said quite simply, 'Thank you for inviting me.' The noise stilled and Trixie began singing the opening chorus to Gracie Fields' popular Maori song, 'Now Is The Hour'.

She sang it for Teddy, sweet and clear. Maybe he was sailing across the sea. She wanted him to remember her. Her heart and her voice were breaking. And then Trixie knew she was where she was supposed to be, doing what she was supposed to be doing, singing. The audience was hushed. It didn't seem to matter that she sang in English and her audience were mostly Germans who probably knew not a word of English. As her last notes died away, the clapping and whistling began and she bowed her head to the audience, then left the stage.

Eva wrapped her arms around her. Trixie felt the tears on Eva's cheeks. It was ages before the cheering stopped.

'They want you to go out again.'

Trixie shook her head. 'Not until it's time for me to sing "On A Slow Boat To China".'

'But you're the star of the show.'

Trixie was still shaking her head. 'No, the boys are. They sing and play and I do three songs every show. That's all. I came to fill in for Kathy, not to take the limelight. Now, are you coming with me to help me change for the next number?'

Trixie walked towards the room they'd been given to change in. It was the space where the cleaners kept their materials and brooms and it smelled of disinfectant and bleach. Broken chairs were stacked along one side of the small space.

Eva disappeared to get two cups of tea and Trixie sat down on a chair, put her head in her hands and cried. After a while she stopped sobbing and looked at the blue velvet straight-skirted calf-length dress hanging on the back of the door. Eva had poured her heart into the making of this dress. The blue was almost black and as she ran her fingers over the luxurious material she tried to dispel all thoughts of Teddy from her mind. While on the stage her eyes had scoured the audience. She knew it was improbable, but then you never knew; one day she might just see him.

By the time Eva returned with the teas she'd put on the blue dress and told herself she had to be strong. Touring was tough. She mustn't let herself slip back into the depths of despondency that had caused her breakdown.

'Drink this. I've put sugar in to give you more energy.' Eva passed her the mug of tea.

Trixie mumbled her thanks, then said, 'I absolutely love the dresses.'

'You look lovely. But then I knew you would. And I chose velvet for them all, deep and sensual colours to heighten your blondeness. I like the green one best.'

She got up and touched the sweetheart neckline of the dress.

'The simple lines used with such expensive material draw attention to you. There's no frills or colours to distract the viewers. You open your mouth and your voice holds them.' Trixie watched as Eva turned and smiled at her. 'I thought about it a lot. If you were older I'd have used black velvet. But you're too young and vibrant for a colour that can drain the skin. The songs you sing are simple and heartfelt. I wanted to present you that way and for the lads in their dark suits to be a background.'

Trixie looked at her with a new understanding.

'Jesus,' she said. 'And I thought you just sewed patchwork thingies to sell at the market.'

Trixie's last song was 'Saturday Night Is The Loneliest Night Of The Week'. Successfully sung by Frank Sinatra, it told how alone one could be on the busiest night, when other people had dates. The audience loved Trixie's way of singing it. She left the stage and didn't return at the end of the band's slot in the show.

Instead she gathered up her stage clothes, slipped them in the suitcase, collected her make-up that was in a brown paper bag and walked the short distance back to the cheap hotel that let rooms by the hour. Trixie spent ages trying to get the shower to give out more water than a cool dribble, then she put on a thick nightie and got into one side of the double bed. Singer or not, she was sharing with the wardrobe mistress.

There was a large neon sign outside that flashed continually, but the light left on in the room softened its glare. She looked around. The double bed, chairs either side that doubled as bedside cabinets and a wardrobe with the mirror cracked on the door that hung crookedly. The sheets were clean. The noise from the busy street outside was practically intolerable but she was so tired she knew she would sleep. Trixie wasn't looking forward to the times she would have to sleep in the van with the others.

She'd refused Eva's plea to celebrate. Celebrate meant getting paralytic drunk. Possibly smoking cigarettes that made her head buzz and the room more colourful. It could also mean waking up in someone else's bed. That's what the lads needed, they reckoned. It was the sex part she couldn't handle.

If she was going to have someone make love to her she would like it to be Jem. It would mean something to him and to her.

But whenever his hands touched her she was reminded of Sid and his searching fingers and she wanted to crawl into a corner and hide.

This wasn't how she envisaged it should be when wanting to make love with someone. Because of Sid she was afraid of men and the damage they could do. To be petrified of Jem was pathetic and stupid. But she had no control over her feelings. She wished she could scream the ridiculous feelings away.

Trixie closed her eyes. The pillow was soft and clean and her body smelled of the rose-scented soap she had brought with her.

Each week money was going into a bank account she had opened in her name at Lloyds Bank in Gosport. It was the first bank account she had ever had. Some of that money was transferred to Jem's account so he could look after Joan.

Trixie was going to sing at every venue Eric Blomberg had arranged on this three-month tour. She wouldn't let him down. There were so many venues, so many towns in different European countries. If the band was a success it would make money for them and for Eric Blomberg. He was at this moment arranging a tour of England.

Trixie smiled to herself. Surely while touring England it would be possible to find Teddy? She closed her eyes and let sleep take her.

Chapter Eighteen

'Is that Freddie Mills?' Teddy could hardly contain his excitement.

'Why shouldn't the world's light heavyweight champ be interested in art? Come along and I'll introduce you.' Teddy felt himself being steered through the crowd of people celebrating the reopening of the Tate gallery after the Blitz until he stood within handshaking distance of the curly-haired fighter.

'Freddie, old man, here's a chap who'd like to say hello.' Rafe was totally at ease. Oh, how Teddy wished he had the same aplomb.

'So this is the ward you've been keeping secret until now, is it? I'm pleased to meet you.'

The grip of the boxer was firm. Teddy knew he had to speak, even though he was in awe of the man. 'You beat Lesnevich well, left him no room to manoeuvre.'

'So you follow the fights, do you?'

Teddy nodded. 'I do, but I'm afraid I prefer art.' Oh, dear, he thought, had he offended the man?

'How do you feel about Jackson Pollock's work?'

Teddy never thought he'd have to answer a question like that from Freddie Mills. 'It's different. His radical way of dripping paint with sticks or brushes held above the canvas is innovative. The weaving of colour spatters creates richness and complexity. I believe Abstract Expressionism will sweep the globe.'

'I couldn't have put it better myself,' said Freddie. His wide smile was infectious. 'Myself, I like something that looks like a picture I can relate to, without having bits of glass or bees' wings imbedded in the paint. I like your work.'

Teddy knew he was blushing and couldn't do a thing about it. 'Really?'

'I bought the one entitled *Gates at Midnight*. Portsmouth Hard with the bollards and boats and the cockle barrow.'

'I hope you enjoy it.' Inside his head his brain was reeling. To think someone of Freddie Mills' standing had purchased a painting of *his*. His heart was beating fast.

'Tell me, the cockle barrow, does it have meaning? I daresay if writers write about what they know then artists paint scenes and objects that touch them in some way?'

Teddy had painted the cart because it haunted his dreams. He would always see superimposed on whatever he drew or painted, the barrow that had ferried his dead father to his final resting place. Freddie was looking at him. Waiting for him to speak.

Rafe broke in with, 'That painting was from his first exhibition. The gallery in Wardour Street allowed Teddy to present some of his work in tandem with mine.'

'So talented,' Freddie said, putting his hand on Rafe's shoulder. 'I was going to say, and so young but time passes quickly.' He grinned cheekily at Teddy. 'He's a good-looking young bloke. Watch he doesn't throw his career away for a pretty face

250

and a curvy figure.' He turned to Teddy. 'Have it all, young man, have it all.'

When the talk in the gallery amongst Rafe's friends turned from art to the London Olympic Games, Rafe and Teddy decided to move on.

At a small pavement café in the heart of the city Rafe paused while lifting the coffee cup to his lips and Teddy waited for him to speak.

'You'll be leaving Galloways at the end of the term. I've procured a place in art college.'

Teddy wanted to rise from his seat and throw his arms around Rafe, but he was much too old to cause a scene. Rafe's eyes met his and Teddy realised Rafe knew how excited he'd be.

'You'd pay for me to go to college?'

'Why wouldn't I want to see how far you're willing to go with your love of painting? Mind you, I'll miss you. I'm sending you to Paris.'

Paris! Of course he wanted to learn. His natural style of art was well received but he knew he could be better. And here was Rafe willing to spend money on him to assure him of his dreams.

'I don't know what to say,' he said.

'There's nothing you can say. I've watched you handle yourself amongst my friends and already you're a fine young man so I might as well complete your education.' He put his hand up to signal the waiter to bring more coffee.

Teddy was ebullient. His smile was widening by the moment. He wanted to shout, to run, to cry with the excitement of it all. Instead he got up and left to go to the lavatory, and as he walked inside the building he saw on the table a newspaper opened at a page upon which was printed a picture of his sister!

At first he just stared to make sure it was Trixie. There was no mistake. Trixie True, in Prague. His finger traced the black and white photograph. Then he read on.

The article had used Trixie's success as a peg to hang the news on of the new seven-inch micro groove unbreakable vinylite records expected to take over from the twelve-inch seventy-eight shellac ones.

With shaking hands and his heart beating fast, he read of her success with the band in Prague. She was pictured outside a jazz club. He studied her features. Thinner of face, her eyes were magnificent as she was looking up at the dark-haired girl hand in hand with one of the group's guitarists. His eyes scanned the item. The Tropics had a hit record. 'Last Love' had climbed the hit parade. Well, well, well! Who'd have thought his big sister with her husky voice had shed the shackles of their awful childhood. She deserved every bit of her success. And then his heart fell. Now more than ever he had to make sure he was never in contact with her. If he was found out and accused of murder Trixie could become a figure to be ridiculed. How could he have that on his conscience?

And then he remembered his proposed stay in Paris and was glad he could do Trixie no more harm if he was out of the country.

That evening back at the London hotel, celebrating at the nomination party for the Oscars, at which Sir Laurence Olivier would appear, Teddy watched the proceedings in between dancing with the cream of society and chatting with Rafe's friends.

The girl Teddy was dancing with wore a chiffon dress, and her breasts, plump and inviting crushed against Teddy's jacket. The band was playing 'Some Enchanted Evening' and Teddy could smell the lemon shampoo in her freshly washed hair. Over her shoulder his eyes roved around the room looking for Rafe. When he saw him, Rafe seemed to sense he was being stared at and looked around, meeting Teddy's gaze.

Instantaneously they smiled at each other.

The girl, Esther, snuggled against Teddy. Teddy looked away from Rafe. But it was too late. In that split second Teddy realised the pretty girl in his arms held no fascination whatever for him. He might as well have been dancing with a paintbrush. No, he thought, he would have had some feeling for a paintbrush. He knew then he didn't fancy this girl, wouldn't fancy her in the future and would never fancy any girl, ever.

He wasn't shocked, but he was surprised that his sexual orientation had only just occurred to him. Over her shoulder Teddy perused the men on the dance floor. Each one he studied, then mentally discarded, until he saw the wine waiter staring at him.

Dark silky hair, long enough to be fashionable yet short enough not to draw attention to himself. Shoulders large enough to carry substantial weights. He looked strong as well as sinewy. And those long legs in tapering black trousers. Teddy smiled at the waiter. It was as though through eye-contact he had been drawn into a certain knowledge of himself that others had realised and he had not, until now, known. Momentarily Teddy closed his eyes with the excitement of it all.

He escorted Esther back to her parents and exchanged trivialities with them, then went in search of the waiter.

'Thank God this tour is practically over. I need to get home and away from this crazy life.' Trixie looked out the window of the bar above the Beer Cellar where they were playing, at the majestic sight of Cologne Cathedral. Scaffolding surrounded practically every stone of it. 'We did that,' she said. She heard the disgust in her voice. 'Devastated Cologne.'

'It'll all be rebuilt,' snapped Eva. 'You're in another of your melancholy moods, aren't you?' She glared at Trixie. 'By the end of the 1950's the cathedral will be whole again, as will this magnificent city.'

The air was thick with the smell of beer, cigarettes and the cheap perfume of the girls ready to throw themselves at the boys. The boys were still upstairs. The longer they kept out of sight the less the fans mobbed them. Trixie reckoned she had an inbuilt sensor that switched itself on, proclaiming her coldness towards unwanted men and women who thought she was public property. Eva said she was like Greta Garbo who wanted to be left alone.

'We'll be back home in time for Frank Sinatra's visit to London,' Trixie said. She loved most of his work, especially the songs that were throaty and sung slowly.

'Highest-paid singer in the world,' sang out Eva. She had on her tight Capri pants and a loose top. The day had been warm and Trixie had spent most of it alone in the gardens, reading. The lads had gone to a party the night before and when they eventually resurfaced had practised for a while, but Eva and George had gone sightseeing.

'Life in England's improving all the time. Petrol's off ration.'

'Where d'you get all this information? Trixie held the tankard of beer to her lips. She didn't drink much but sitting in the sun had made her thirsty. She foraged in her handbag for a handkerchief to wipe off the froth that had collected on her top lip. It was then she saw the letter that had caught up with them for George. 'I forgot to give George this.' She passed it to Eva, who took it from her, got up and went upstairs to the rooms they were sharing.

An anguished howl rent the air and for a moment the customers in the beer cellar stopped talking and looked at each other with expectation. Trixie bolted for the wide staircase, taking the steps two at a time. She pushed open the door of the boys' room and stared at George, who was curled on the floor as though he was protecting himself from a beating. Eva was bent over him, smoothing his hair; the letter was screwed up on the floorboards.

'It's Kathy. She died.' Eva looked up at Trixie.

'But she was in remission!' The words flew from Trixie's mouth. She sank to the floor beside Eva. 'Where're the others?' Eva shrugged her shoulders. 'They've got to be around here some-where; go find 'em.' Eva rose and left the room. Trixie put her hands beneath George's shoulders and tugged him into a sitting position. He looked as though he was in a trance. 'Come on, get up. You can't lie here.' She looked around the untidy room. There was a bottle of whisky on the top of a chest of drawers. She left him slumped and went into the bathroom, tossing toothbrushes out into the sink. Within moments she was watching him gulp the whisky down. 'Hang on,' she said. 'You've got a show to do.'

He stared at her. The smell of whisky fumes was sweet. 'Not tonight.'

'Yes,' she said and pulled him to his feet. She took him to the unmade bed and smoothed the wrinkled bedspread then pushed him down. 'We've got to talk.'

Talk? What the hell was she on about? She was near to tears herself and here she was telling this man who loved a woman who had died, that life had to go on. Strangled sounds were coming from him. He put out a hand towards the whisky and she slapped it away.

'After the show you can get paralytic,' she said. 'Not now.'

'Fuck the music.'

She picked up the letter and read the short sentences. Written by Kathy's mother it stated that the funeral would be in two days' time. Kathy had died in her sleep in hospital with the family around her and despite phone calls, they'd not been able to reach George.

'Music is all you have now.'

'Fuck it,' he repeated. He slid his thin legs to the side of the bed and Trixie pushed him back again.

'Where d'you think you're going?'

'Home, back to England.'

She sat down on the side of the bed and held on to his hands. 'You won't get a plane tonight. Tonight you need to play, for her. Make it the best gig we've ever done. The gig in Pulheim the day after tomorrow'll be cancelled and we can all leave ahead of schedule with a legitimate reason for going. We need to stick together. The road manager needs to know. Where's Max?'

She needn't have asked for he burst into the room like a tank with Mo and Eddie behind him. To Max she said, 'Get in touch with Eric, tell him we'll go on tonight but we'll be leaving Germany tomorrow. I'll go on the plane with George.'

Max left and she looked at her watch. 'We've got a couple of hours yet. Let's practise.'

Eddie looked at her then narrowed his eyes. 'You're a hardhearted bitch,' he said. 'Can't you let him grieve?'

'Not now. You know that old saying? The show must go on? Well, it didn't come out of my arse and maybe I've had a lot in my life to get hard-hearted about.'

Mo looked surprised at her words but she was grateful to hear him say, 'She's right. We signed a contract and there are people waiting outside to hear us play. We're professionals, aren't we? The people at Pulheim will get their money back; this lot will make a fuss if we don't give them what they've paid for.'

257

Trixie looked at him and smiled. 'Thanks,' she whispered.

George looked at her. 'Kathy was a professional. She would have wanted us to go on stage.' Trixie breathed a sigh of relief. The sooner they were back in England the better.

A few days later Trixie sat in the armchair in the prefab. She was reading the write-up of Kathy's funeral at St Mary's church at Alverstoke. The picture showed a grief stricken George held upright by Kathy's brother-in-law. No one else in the band had attended. For the family's sake, Eric had said.

Chapter Nineteen

'I'm not paying ninepence for a bleedin' cup of coffee.'

'For God's sake stop moaning, Joan.' Trixie gave her a poke in the ribs. 'Have a bloody cup of tea instead. Anyway, I'm paying, not you.' They'd stopped to rest in the jungle of greenery near the Dome of Discovery. Joan immediately kicked off her shoes and pulled up another chair, upon which she slung her handbag and coat and hoisted up her legs to ease her feet.

'You go and get the teas then, 'cos my feet is killing me. I never thought there'd be so much walking to do.'

Trixie grinned at her, stretched herself then wandered off towards the counter of the café, at which a small queue was gathered. It was a hot day and it seemed that people preferred ice-creams and soft drinks to teas and coffees for she'd seen long queues at kiosks. Twenty-seven acres of bombsites and derelict ground had been transposed into the long-awaited Festival of Britain in London, presided over by the Skylon, an aluminium symbol pointing its cigar-shaped body towards the heavens. She looked about her. People were everywhere and the air smelled of candyfloss and excitement.

And then it was Trixie's turn to be served with two teas and two squares of bread pudding that she hoped might put Joan in a better mood.

'Not as good as *my* pudding.' Joan chomped away on it.

'No it's not, I agree, but it keeps the hunger pains at bay.'

'Big place, this.' Joan spoke thoughtfully through a mouthful of currants. 'Such a lot to see. Thank God it's not far to Waterloo and the trains.'

Trixie brushed crumbs away and set her face towards the sun. It was nice not having to go on stage every night. She liked being back at the prefab. Even working in the Fighting Cocks. She never was one to sit and stagnate. Hence the trip to London before the festival ended in September. She wondered if Teddy had been to see the great exhibition to celebrate the gesture of faith by the government for Britain and her future. She stopped herself from thinking about Teddy just as Joan asked, 'How long you staying home?'

'A while,' she answered. 'After our last record, "My Man", went to the top, we all wanted time to catch our breath. We'd worked so hard, selling ourselves abroad, visiting places like Sweden and Norway to become known so that people would buy our records. People think it's a glamorous life but it's tiring. On the stage we give all we've got. The boys sometimes party it up after gigs but mostly I'm whacked out and just want to sleep. And it's hard living with people you don't like.' She was thinking about Mo. He'd been a tearaway as a lad in Gosport, even been in trouble with the police, but she'd thought having people buy the group's records and girls hanging around him so he could have his pick of them would have been enough for him. And let's face it, she thought, he couldn't be short of money. None of them was fabulously wealthy because their income had to be split so many ways, but not one of them could grumble. Eric Blomberg had promised to look after them and he'd kept that promise. No, Mo was a bad lot. He'd smoked a lot of weed, which was to be expected in the music business, even took a few pills that he seemed to keep under control. Other drugs she didn't want to think about. She had her suspicions but so far his habits hadn't interfered with the success of the band. It wasn't her business what he got up to when he wasn't on stage and she was pretty sure Eric knew what was happening.

'I didn't like living with Sid,' said Joan. Trixie looked at her. Joan's face was screwed up remembering the bad times. Trixie put her hand out and touched Joan's fingers.

'Well, he's not living with you now. Come to think of it, I don't know why you don't move into the pub with Jack. You might just as well; you spend nearly all your time there.'

'Wash your mouth out!' Joan's face was bright red. 'I can't have people talking about me if I live over the brush. I'll get called a harlot.'

Trixie spluttered into her tea. Anyone less like a harlot was Joan!

'It's 1951, you silly woman. People do live together, you know.'

'Not women of my generation,' huffed Joan. 'Anyway, ain't it about time you settled down? You're not getting any younger.'

'I'd love kiddies.' Trixie took a piece of tissue from her handbag and mopped up the mess of tea. Yes, she would love a child of her own to care for and love. But that would mean sleeping with a man who might hurt her or treat her badly or, she shuddered, become indifferent to her. It had happened to Joan, and to her mother. So there was every possibility that when that gorgeous honeymoon feeling of first love had passed, it would happen to her.

'Don't you think Jem's waited long enough for you?'

Trixie looked at her with surprise. 'I've never suggested he wait,' she said. 'And he's a man so I don't for one minute think he's been celibate all these years.'

'To a woman love is all but to a man it's part of life.'

Trixie looked at her. 'You've just made that up!' Joan's cheeky blue hat with its feather at the side wobbled as she started to laugh.

'Of course I bloody did. But if ever there was a man who could love you properly and look after you it's him.'

'I'm waiting.'

'Waiting for what, a bleedin' number nine bus?'

'Somewhere out there is a man who makes my heart sing every time I see him.'

'Life's not like that, Trixie. You have to settle for what you can get.'

Trixie shook her head. 'Then I'll stay as I am.'

'I've read what they call you in the newspapers.'

Trixie sighed. She thought of the men who sent her gifts, which she returned. Of the men who waited outside the theatres and halls where the band played, so they could talk to her or take her for a meal. Of the letters she received from admirers. But she refused them all. Her habit of leaving the stage when she'd sung her songs hadn't helped stop the name 'Miss Ice Cube' becoming her tag either. Some newspapers had even suggested she preferred women to men. She didn't, but she wondered whether women hurt each other even more, knowing which buttons to push.

'Don't believe what you read. I don't,' she said. 'Anyway, have you heard from Sid?'

Joan said, 'No, and I don't want to. With your help, the money you've been sending me, and what I've been earning I don't care if I never see him again. I don't mind not being at his beck and call.'

Trixie began to laugh. Oh, it was nice sitting here in the sun with Joan.

'I see Eva's not back yet?'

'She's still here in London, partying with new friends she's made.'

'She's a tart.'

Trixie tapped her fingers on the table and tutted. 'No she's not, she's enjoying herself.' She thought of Eva and her constant love for Eddie, which sometimes demoralised her. He took her to parties and disappeared with other women, leaving her to get home on her own. He gave her expensive presents then broke promises to her. Constantly his name was linked in the media with long-legged blonde models and always Eva was there in the shadows. In retaliation she drank too much and often ended up in bed with dubious characters. She said she was having a whale of a time. Trixie told her if she couldn't remember who or where she was when she woke up, how exciting a time was that?

'Don't you start on about Eva, she's a good friend to me,' Trixie snapped.

Joan looked at her. 'I know that,' she said. 'I love her as well.'

'Yeah,' said Trixie. 'You're right. She's a lovable tart.' Good humour restored, Joan insisted it was time to do a bit more exploring, ending up with a walk through the fun-fair before they got the train back.

Joan was sitting with her feet in a bowl of hot water and Trixie was stirring the tea in the teapot when the knock on the door startled her.

'All right, all right, don't knock the door down.' She opened the door to find Marie with a letter in her hand and a smile the size of the sun on her face.

'He's on his way back! He's on his way back!' Marie pushed her way inside and in the living room plonked herself down on the sofa next to Joan. All the springs in the sofa seemed to bounce.

'Jesus Christ, watch it, you'll have me water all over me new carpet and I ain't finished paying for it yet. Whatever is it?'

Marie shook the note and read, '"I hope to be with you on Monday." It's my man; he's coming home.' There were tears in her eyes. She looked at Trixie then said, 'I couldn't half do with a cuppa. Only if you're making it, though.'

Trixie bent down and kissed her forehead. 'So,' she said. 'Teas all round, coming up. How long is Dmitri staying?' She was happy for Marie.

'That's just it: for ever, he says. He's got a job lined up an' all.' Marie's eyes were bright. She pulled off her headscarf. 'The government is making a big to-do about getting our shoreline back to normal after the war. There's still a lot of it cordoned off where bombs were planted in case them bloody Germans invaded. He's somehow wangled a job with a firm here specialising in dangerous jobs.'

'I suppose he'll need a work permit?' Trixie didn't like to think of Marie's man being blown to kingdom come. All them lovely red-haired kids would be fatherless.

'All that's sorted, Trixie. It's something called European Volunteer Workers who are coming to England to provide labour to industries for economic recovery after the war. We got to get on our feet again after them Germans thought they could step all over us.' Marie sat back contentedly. 'He also says his family is all sorted out over there and later in the year his brother is coming to England as well.'

'Have you told the kids?'

'They're at school. But wait till they get home, there'll be bedlam in our prefab.'

In the kitchen Trixie tipped biscuits onto a plate then put the mugs on a tray. Long-distance love, she thought. Dmitri still loved Marie, even though he'd been parted from her for years. She wiped a tear that had dared to escape to the corner of her eye. She was so happy for Marie, and happy for Dmitri to be reconciled with his children.

Trixie heard the telephone ring and went into the hall to answer it. It had been an easy decision to have the phone installed in the prefab. It certainly saved her walking up to the phone box in the rain. Have to keep abreast of the times we live in, Trixie thought. The television she'd paid cash for was being delivered on Wednesday and they were going to set it up and have it working on the same day. It was to be a surprise for Joan.

'I'm arranging another tour, England again.' Eric sounded firm.

'I want to stay home a bit longer.' Sharing the bus once more with the lads wasn't something she wanted to do. It was a new bus and bigger but they were still cooped up together like chickens.

'No can do, pretty girl. You all need as much exposure as you can get. There are too many rock 'n' roll singers and rock bands jumping on the bandwagon. That American lad Elvis Presley is ready to make a name for himself. Take a look at the hit parade, sweetie, and you'll realise you'll have to fight to keep selling tickets to the gigs.'

She wasn't stupid. He was telling the truth. Fresh-faced youngsters like Tommy Steele were likely to make it big. 'You talked to the others?'

'They're all for it.'

Trixie groaned.

'Almost all. Have you seen George?'

'That's a funny thing to ask,' she said. 'We don't socialise; you know that. Eva's a mate so it doesn't count with her. Why d'you ask?'

'I haven't been able to get him to answer the phone and he's ignored a letter I wrote. Doesn't he live near you?'

'Okay,' she sighed. 'I get the message. I'll go down tonight and report back as soon as possible.'

As soon as she put the phone down she rang Jem and asked him to drive her to the town. He seemed pleased to do it.

Jem opened the car door for her and Trixie slid inside the Bentley.

'Nice car, this,' she said.

'Don't know why you don't learn to drive,' he said with a grin. 'It's not as though you can't afford to buy a car now.'

'Never thought about it,' she said. 'You know I just might.' She laughed. 'A little sports car would suit me fine.'

He shook his head. He could see by the glitter in her eyes that she was considering learning to drive. He was about to offer her driving lessons when he bit his tongue. Sure, that was one way of seeing more of her but he knew what sort of driver he was and how finicky he got about his car and its gears and engine. One crunch of the gears from her and he might shout at her.

'Forton Driving School are good,' he said. 'They arrange the test and everything, so I've heard.'

She turned and gave him a smile that told him she knew exactly what he was thinking. He coughed and asked, 'Where's George living now?'

'He's got a room above a café in North Street. Not posh, but clean. He said he wanted to be where there were people, but be on his own as well.'

'Have you been there?'

Trixie shook her head. Her hair fell around her face in blonde waves.

'Didn't see the need to. He's a big boy and can look after himself.'

'He took it hard about Kathy. That's why he moved. Couldn't bear to be where everything reminded him of her. They'd been together since school, you know.' He didn't know what he would do if Trixie upped and left Gosport. Jem knew he couldn't help it; he'd never stop loving her. Even if she married someone else and had ten children she'd always be the scruffy girl he'd fallen for at the market in Portchester all those years ago.

He parked the car on a piece of rough ground opposite Bert's café and helped Trixie out. The door of the café was wide open and enticing fried breakfast smells hung in the air. Jem's stomach rumbled, even though he'd eaten.

The noise from the café's jukebox was loud and there were youngsters standing around the large machine talking and laughing. A man was serving teas behind a scrubbed counter and looked up, grinning.

'What can I do you for?'

Jem thought he was a decent sort of bloke who certainly knew how to make a good cuppa, judging by the colour of the teas.

'I'm looking for a mate; his name's George...'

He didn't get any further for the man said, 'First door up the stairs. You can go through there.' He pointed to an open door that Jem now saw was the stairway to rooms. The actual entrance was on the street outside.

'Thank you,' said Trixie.

The man was staring at her. 'Are you Miss Ice Cube?'

Trixie quickly put her finger to her lips in case the boys heard him. She needn't have worried: the jukebox was on too loud for that. Trixie nodded.

'Well, I'm blessed,' he said. 'Got your latest record on there.' He nodded to the music machine.

Trixie smiled at him. 'Thank you,' she said.

'C'mon, Glamour Girl,' said Jem. 'We've got to talk to George.' He took her hand and led her up the stairs and outside the first door he waited, listened, then knocked. After a while he knocked again. 'I don't want to worry you,' Jem said, 'but I've got a funny feeling about this. Go back and ask your fan if he's got a key or can come and open the door.'

Trixie glared at him. Jem smiled back at her.

'I haven't seen him for a couple of days,' said the man. 'I'm Bert, by the way; this place belongs to me. I wasn't particularly worried as the young bloke says he writes music and...' He thumped the side of his head. 'He's that quiet one with the guitar, ain't he?'

Trixie bent her head and nodded. 'He's like me; we don't like a lot of fuss and bother.'

Bert put the key in the lock. 'I don't like intruding,' he said. 'A person's a right to his privacy.'

'Open the door.' Jem didn't mean to sound sharp but the bad feeling inside him had grown.

Bert turned the key in the lock and both men practically fell inside the room. The smell hit him first. George was lying on the floor with mucus in his eyes and vomit stuck to the side of his face and in his hair. A pool of the foul-smelling stuff covered the front of George's shirt and had flies feasting on it.

Jem put his hand to his mouth. Then his brain took over and he stopped himself from gagging. 'Phone for an ambulance, Bert,' he yelled. Luckily the man didn't argue. He left straight away without uttering a word.

Trixie was down on her knees, listening at George's face. 'He's breathing, shallow but it's there,' she said. Then, 'Fuck!'

'What?' Jem knelt on the floor alongside her and saw the spoon, scorched and bent, half-hidden by his clothing. A syringe was where it had fallen on the lino. Jem got up and stared down at George. There was a plastic belt on the floor that he'd obviously used to clarify his vein and Jem saw it wasn't the first time he'd injected himself. There were scabs on his arms and Jem bent down and pulled apart George's toes. There were bloody scabs there too. It was obvious he'd been using heroin for some time. Jem touched George's clammy skin. 'He's overdosed. Where's he getting the stuff from? He's too nice to know scumbags who'd sell him this shit.'

'I know one scumbag,' said Trixie.

Jem looked at her through narrowed eyes. 'You can't make assumptions,' he said. But he thought she was probably right. Mo was a mover and shaker; he probably didn't take anything more than marijuana himself – he was a strong-willed bastard – but he wasn't averse to selling the stuff, any stuff to an unsuspecting person.

'Did you know this was going on?'

Trixie looked up in alarm. 'Of course not. If I'd had even an inkling I'd have shopped him to Eric.' Jem looked at her and frowned; he didn't think she would be a tittle-tattle. 'Eric Blomberg deserves to know what's going on. He made us, and he can break us.' Jem nodded. She was right.

He looked at the unmade bed. There were pieces of hand-written music and pages with writing on lying on the candlewick bedspread. He picked up a sheet and read. 'It's all about Kathy,' he said. '"Kathy's Song".'

The words were haunting. 'He's not over her,' he whispered.

Footsteps filled the room. 'I've closed up, turned the lads out. We don't want anyone knowing about this, do we?' Bert's face was kind. 'The ambulance is on its way. Don't worry, none of this should get out.'

'Thanks, mate,' said Jem. He wondered if Bert would start talking money for keeping quiet. That's what usually happened. But somehow he didn't think so. Bert looked like he was an honest man and after a quiet life himself.

Trixie was crying softly, and he put his arm

around her shoulder. She'd mentioned something about another tour. He reckoned it would be a while before George was mentally fit enough for that.

The sound of a siren stopped outside the empty café. Heavy footsteps clattered on the floorboards and through the open door a man's voice called, 'Anyone there?'

Chapter Twenty

'Elvis Presley dominates the charts.' Trixie turned the pages of *New Musical Express* then set the chart magazine down on the new Formica table with matching yellow stools she'd bought from Blundells in the town. She sighed, '"Heartbreak Hotel" and "Singing the Blues" by Guy Mitchell are the only records I ever hear blaring out from radios if I take a walk through the prefabs.'

'People like rock 'n' roll, Trixie.' Joan pushed back a stray lock of hair that had fallen from her turban. She had on a frilly apron and was in the process of a massive clear-out. She'd got as far as the shed where a lot of Sid's stuff was stored after she'd thrown it out. Trixie knew she was waiting for her to give her a hand, but she couldn't face going through Sid's stuff. Even after all these years the thought of him gave her the creeps.

'But I can't sing those fast songs.' Trixie knew she was moaning but the band was losing money. Gigs had dried up. She didn't want to blame

271

anyone but the replacement guitarist that Eric had hired didn't have the same magic that George had. The public hadn't taken to him and the band's sound wasn't the same. Pete was a nice bloke but he wasn't George. Pete went back to playing the club circuit up North.

She thought back to those dark days when she'd gone on the bus or got Jem to drive her to Knowle Mental Hospital. George had been a basket case. Eric had paid for privileges and aftercare at Knowle when the hospital at Portsmouth released him but he'd had a long slow recovery.

When Jem had found him in that room at Bert's café, apparently he was in the throes of a heart attack, brought on by the drugs he'd taken.

She remembered how she'd sat on a bench with George at her side in Knowle's leafy grounds. There was frost on the earth but George hadn't spoken a word to her about the weather. But then she hadn't expected him to talk because he'd shut down. It was like a lid closing on a box. Bam! George was gone.

He'd sat next to her scratching at his skin like it was crawling with nits and she'd been reminded of Teddy and his blasted nits that no matter how much she'd washed his hair she could never get rid of the critters.

Slowly George came back to being a shell of George but she'd had to endure his fits of depression and his indifference to life. She knew he was on the mend when he started writing music.

'I couldn't face my life without Kathy and I blamed myself for having a career that she too wanted but that her illness took from her.'

As George grew stronger he confided in Trixie. He told her he'd taken a lot of stuff that Mo had procured for him. He banned her from saying anything, telling her he was the weak one and that in their business, as well she knew, drugs were thrown at them from all sides. 'I thought I had it under control but didn't realise it was controlling me,' George had said.

They'd celebrated his return to the band, after his 'severe tropical illness caught on holiday in Africa', that Eric had fed to the media, as a reason for his departure from the band, with a recording of 'Kathy' that went to the charts but didn't stay long.

Jem had gone to the Midlands to buy some land. He wrote regularly for the few weeks he was away then the letters stopped. Trixie was recording a new song, but the music wouldn't gel. When another letter dropped on the front door mat she was glad things were back to normal. She never asked Jem why he'd stopped writing. It was almost as if she knew he'd become entangled with some woman. Trixie knew she had no right to feel aggrieved. If she didn't want him in her bed she had no right to feel jealous that some other woman did. And yet, she needed to know Jem was there for her.

Trixie decided to buy some new furniture and took driving lessons that resulted in her owning a Ford Popular that Jem helped her choose.

'You gonna sit there all afternoon dreaming or are you going to help me?' Joan's voice brought Trixie back to the present.

The shed was damp and spidery. 'I don't like it

in here.' She thought back to the time when Sid had grabbed at her in this shed and she shuddered. She propped open the door of the small Nissen-like concrete building and began dragging out an old bike. 'This can go for a start; look at the state of it,' she said. It was thrown on the grass to be put out later in the hope the dustmen would take a fancy to it.

'I reckon there's a bigger pile for the dustmen than there is to put back in the shed,' said Joan. 'I'm fed up now, I'm going in to make a cup of tea.'

'Bloody typical,' Trixie said and went on hauling out not one but two rusted push-along lawn mowers. Filthy as she was, she was determined to empty the shed, sweep it out, then put back only what she reckoned was necessary.

Brown, damp, paper carrier bags that crumbled contained Sid's clothing. Trixie felt sick touching the stuff but it had to be carried out and thrown away.

'Joan!' Her aunt came to the back door with a half-eaten biscuit in her hand to see what she wanted. 'Find something stronger to stick this in, will you?' said Trixie. 'If you can tear yourself away from that nice cuppa.'

A glare was her answer, but Joan returned with a large cardboard box and Trixie went on throwing his stuff onto the path while Joan sorted through it and stuffed it in the box.

There was a lull in Joan's movements and Trixie stuck her head out of the door. 'You ain't got time to read,' she said.

Joan snapped a small notebook shut and

laughed nervously. 'No, I haven't.'

'What's that?' If it was anything to do with Sid, Trixie really couldn't care less but Joan seemed to find the notebook interesting.

'Nothing.' Joan quickly put the notebook in the box. 'C'mon, the sooner we do this the sooner we can watch Richard Greene in *The Adventures of Robin Hood* on the telly. Now, there's a bit of beefcake.' She licked her lips in a rude gesture and Trixie laughed as she picked up the box containing Sid's clothing and took it into the prefab. 'If it suddenly rains this'll get soggy,' she said from the doorway. 'And you know how fussy the bleedin' dustbin men are.'

When Joan reappeared moments later she stood and looked at the accumulated rubbish. 'No one's gonna want that,' she said. Trixie agreed. She went on sweeping out the shed. 'An' I don't think the dustmen are going to take it.'

'Well, I'm not putting it back in this bleedin' shed,' Trixie said. She thought for a moment then said, 'Go up to Marie's and see if Dmitri'll take it to the tip in Grange Road for us, or if he can't spare the time, ask him if I can borrow his works van to do it myself.'

Joan looked crestfallen.

'It's your bloody rubbish.'

'Won't it go in your car?'

'No, it bloody won't, you silly cow.' Trixie kicked at the lawn mowers.

Ten minutes later the red-haired hunk sounded his horn on the council van and pulled up out-side number nineteen in the lay-by. He vaulted over the wire netting fence and began poking about in the rubbish, examining first the bicycle, then the lawn mowers.

'I take these, make good?'

He has such beautiful brown eyes, thought Trixie. 'Yes, take them,' she said, watching his muscles ripple on his bare tanned arms as he put the stuff he wanted to keep to one side. No wonder Marie has so many kids, she thought. 'How's Marie?'

'She's good. Not sick any more.' He made a face of sympathy for Marie that made Trixie smile.

Even his broken English was good to listen to, she thought, but it was his hair that caught everyone's attention. A marvellous, glossy red the colour of rich, ripe conkers. Marie was pregnant once more but the first three months had come with unequalled morning sickness.

She helped take the rubbish to the van and Dmitri packed it inside. Trixie knew all about men and the way no one, especially not a woman, could stack stuff in vans like they could. Joan went indoors and got the box of unwanted clothing. This involved another rake-through for stuff for Dmitri, but all Sid's clothing was too small for him and where it had been so long in the shed it was damp and mouldy.

Trixie looked at the council van with its Gosport logo on the side. 'You found all them unexploded bombs yet?' It would be nice to one day be able to walk down to the beach without having to go by the road. 'The sea's so near, yet so far,' she stressed.

He stood still in the act of throwing a pile of tied up newspapers. 'Not possible to do quickly.

We started cutting the defence barbed wire at Lee-on-the-Solent. That area must be cleared first because Lee is, what Marie say? Posh, that is it. First, posh Gosport, last Clayhall. You know they want make golfing place?'

'Lee?'

He frowned. 'No, here by Fort Gilkicker.'

Trixie thought for a moment. 'That's for posh people as well,' she said.

'Marie say the same.' He heaved the newspapers in the van and looked at the dwindled rubbish. 'No need for you to come to tip,' Dmitri stressed. 'I take ten minutes to throw this away. Then I go see my brother at Stoke Road.'

Trixie nodded. 'Fine,' she said.

As Dmitri drove away Trixie thought how people at the prefabs pulled together. It was like living in a small community of friends, she thought, the only drawback being there was absolutely no privacy because everyone knew everyone else's business and what they didn't know they made up.

Joan, standing at Trixie's side with her hands on her hips said, 'Well, clearing the shed didn't take me long, did it!'

Sid O'Hara slammed his fist into her ugly face. The surprise in Melanie's eyes made him want to laugh but if he did the silly cow might think he'd forgiven her and there was no way he was going to do that, yet.

'My toof! You've busted it!' Now he could see her tongue working around her top lip and the blood staining the rest of her teeth a pinky-red.

'That's what you get for keepin' back money to

'ave a drink with. I tell you when you can sit on yer arse an' drink.' He advanced towards her again and she shrank back against the wall in terror.

'I was thirsty. I was down the docks all mornin' an' me feet was killin' me.' She pushed back the dirty blonde hair that had come loose from her bun.

'If you was down the docks, you should 'ave made more. Where's my money?' He knew she wouldn't make top whack now. The poor bint was past it. She'd let herself go and had got all floppy and big arsed.

He put out his hand, waiting for her to delve into her sagging bosom and take out the money she'd hidden there.

'Don't hit me.' A few notes appeared held in her nail-bitten fingers. He snatched the money from her. 'There's a good girl,' he said. 'Don't I always treat you right when you bring back all your earnings?'

He saw Melanie was too tired to do more than nod. She'd been selling it since yesterday when he'd run out of fags and he'd sent her out to earn enough to give The Screw a payment on the loan outstanding for that last meat shipment. And some fags, of course. The Screw was called The Screw because that's exactly what he put on you if you didn't pay up. Sid knew how lucky he was to still be alive, especially as meat rationing had ended now. He wondered if it was time to go home to Gosport. Southampton wasn't so hot when everyone wanted a piece of you.

He thought about Trixie. She must be rolling in money now. All that prancing about on the stage.

Not that she'd give him the scratchings off her arse. But she was probably subbing Joan and that one was as easy to twist around his finger as a gold ring.

And now he looked at the few measly notes he held. He put out a hand towards Melanie and she flinched. 'C'mere, girl,' he said. He pulled her against him. 'I promised you years ago I'd look after you, didn't I?' She mumbled, yes. 'Well, how can I do that if you don't help me?'

'I'm pregnant, Eddie,' Eva said. There, she'd managed to get the words out of her mouth at last. He lay against her, naked, slim and his skin slick after their lovemaking. She felt his body go rigid. His limbs, just seconds ago languidly draped across her nakedness, now seemed to be as hard as iron. He slid across the bed and sat on the edge with his back to her.

'I can't be a father.' Eva's heart began to beat furiously. He didn't even have the guts to face her, she thought, but continued talking, almost breathlessly. 'The sales of records are slipping enough as it is. Our redeeming feature is we're available. Lads in the public eye who aren't married sell more records to girls who dream one day they can marry their idols.'

'I'm pregnant.' Her voice was loud and harsh.

Now he turned and looked at her through narrowed eyes. 'Sure it's mine?'

Eva got out of bed and began putting on her clothes, scattered around the room in their haste to get into bed together.

When, finally, she paused to look at him he was

279

back beneath the sheet, facing her, his arms behind his head. 'Don't get huffy, Eva. If this is some kind of trick to get me to marry you, it hasn't worked. You'll get nothing from me for the kid.' He laughed but it was more of a sneer. 'You put it about, then tell me I'm the daddy. How do I know it's the truth?'

Now, fully dressed, Eva turned away. She'd never begged in her life and wasn't going to start now, certainly not with a second-rate guitar player she'd thought she loved. 'You bastard,' she said. 'Fuck you.' Tears blurred her eyes. She picked up her clutch bag, slung her coat over her arm, and opened the door.

'You already did, Eva,' he said with another laugh. 'You already did.'

Eva lay on the table in the kitchen, a pillow beneath her head and with her knees wide apart. The memory of the woman's fingers entering her, prodding her, only moments before, made her feel sick. She turned her head and eyed the dirty cups in the stone sink. A sink tidy was full of foul-smelling scraps of rubbish.

When she'd first knocked on the paint-blistered door of the terraced house in Old Road, she'd been terrified. She'd said a few words, then she'd been ushered into the living room and bade sit on a lumpy sofa while the money was discussed.

'How far gone do you say you are?'

'Four months, maybe a little more.' Eva tried to sound calm.

The woman nodded, as if confirming the size of the foetus. She had the remains of a cold sore on her lip but she looked kindly. 'I suppose you want rid of it, like, yesterday?'

'I've got money. On me, I mean.' Eva drew in her breath waiting for the reply. The woman's eyes glittered in the semi-darkness of the room.

For a wild moment Eva thought maybe the woman wouldn't want to do the abortion. Maybe she wouldn't want to make the baby growing inside her go away?

She shut her ears to the tiny voice in her head saying, 'This is a child, your child.' But notes had exchanged hands and Mrs Simms had put the money in her overall pocket.

Mrs Brenda Simms was good at her job, so Eva had been told; she used to be a midwife until the arthritis in her hands and knees stopped her working for the newly formed National Health Service. Her midwifery skills she now used in a different way.

When Trixie had been raped and Eva had discovered Trixie's pregnancy she'd made it her business to find a way out for her friend. But Trixie had wanted to keep the child. Mrs Simms' business and address had been filed away in Eva's mind.

What would Eva do, alone with a child? How would she live? She wouldn't be able to tour with the band. She wouldn't be able to go back to the markets selling, not with a child in tow.

Eddie had make it quite clear he wasn't prepared to marry her or to accept the child as his own. Getting rid of it was the only sensible option.

'Won't be a moment, dearie.' Mrs Simms was washing her hands. She wiped them on a towel hanging on the back of the kitchen door, then she came over to the table and looked down at Eva's open legs. 'That's it, dearie, keep them legs open wide.' She grinned. 'Only one way in and one way out for the baby. It's going to be painful and you'll have terrible cramps. When it all comes away get rid of the foetus and remember I had nothing to do with this. I never set eyes on you before, understand? I'm not allowed to do this and if I get copped, think of all them young girls who'll have no one else to go to. They might do something silly.' Eva nodded. Why didn't the woman get on with it, instead of chatting away? 'When this is over, get home as quickly as you can. Go to bed, keep warm and drink lots of fluids. Tea's good. In a day or so you'll be fine. Now lie back, relax, and let me get on with it.'

Eva felt something thin and cold slip inside her. She screwed her eyes shut tightly, not wanting to see what was being done to her own body, down there. She felt a sharp, stabbing pain that made her wince and cry out. Then it nipped at her again like an animal with a long, thin, cold nose gnawing at her insides. Eva smelled soap powder, Dreft, and felt water flush inside her at the same time as she experienced the sound of rubber being squeezed. Wetness dripped from the insides of her thighs that were being constantly wiped by the woman.

'Open your eyes, dearie; it's all done,' said Mrs Simms.

Eva saw her throw rubber tubing into the sink. It slithered against one of the cups that clattered as it fell on its side. The woman swept up some strange-looking metal utensils from the table and put them into the sink before going to the dresser and opening a drawer.

'Put this in your knickers.' The woman handed her a sanitary towel. 'Go home and do as I told you.' Mrs Simms went out of the kitchen. Eva heard the wireless in another room and Perry Como singing 'They Say it's Wonderful'.

Eva swung her legs off the table. Standing up, she felt the room shift and she grabbed hold of the table to steady herself. After a while she stepped into her underwear, which she'd left on a nearby chair, patting the sanitary towel into place. Then, curious, she took a look. Already the towel was spotted with bright red blood smears.

Eva realised she hadn't even taken off her coat. She gathered her bag and made her way down the passage, opened the front door and stepped out into the sunlight. She hadn't been aware of how stuffy it was in the house until she breathed in the fresh air. Mrs Simms seemed not to notice she'd gone.

The nearest bus stop was outside the Forum Cinema in Stoke Road and she joined the queue feeling unreal. Almost as though she was watching herself in a film. A dragging sensation low in her stomach made her grit her teeth. She was glad when the bus arrived. Thankfully, she collapsed on to a seat. The pain was worse now, screwing up her stomach as though it needed to be grabbed and thrown out of her body.

Eventually Clayhall and the prefabs came in sight and she grabbed hold of the back of the seat in front, hoisting herself up. The insides of her thighs were wet. A red patch had dampened the seat. She touched it and recoiled in horror at the sticky blood, her blood. Fearful that someone might notice, she gathered her coat around her and stepped as quickly as she could along the aisle and out from the bus. When the bus had turned the corner, she examined her coat but there were no tell tale marks. She was suddenly enormously tired.

Outside her prefab she stood and looked at the pretty curtains, at her freshly polished door knocker. She felt as though they didn't belong to her.

She didn't want to be on her own.

Eva held on the fence post for a moment, then walked on down over the uneven paving stones to number nineteen. She felt relieved because she could hear the wireless. Through the kitchen window she could see Trixie washing her hair at the sink. Eva knocked on the back door, but she needed both hands to make a loud enough sound.

She slapped the door. Her knees buckled and she slithered down the door to sit on the cold stone path. The door opened.

'Oh, my God,' said Joan. 'Whatever's the matter?' There was a pause. Eva felt her clothes being moved aside, and at the same time it was getting dark, which was silly because it was still afternoon. 'Trixie!' yelled Joan. Then louder, 'Trixie!'

Darkness covered everything.

Chapter Twenty-One

'I've no idea why Eva allowed herself to be butchered like that.'

The service hadn't started yet and the coffin, with its simple spray of white lilies, was a lonely island near the font of the Victorian Gothic St Mary's Church, half a mile from the shore at Stokes Bay. Trixie remembered how she'd sat in the back of the ambulance holding Eva's hand. She'd then stayed up all night waiting at Haslar Hospital while the medical staff tried to save her friend. When it looked as though that wasn't going to happen, she'd been allowed to sit beside her in a tiny white-painted room and wait until Eva regained consciousness. Eva had opened her eyes, two points of colour in a grey, wax-like face.

'Eddie didn't want me,' she'd breathed. 'I'm getting what I deserve for not wanting his child.' Trixie looked at her for a long time, not sure how to make the right noises to help her friend leave this world. No one, she thought, should have to go through what Eva had. 'It's right what you said, Trixie,' Eva breathed. 'Life's a crying game.'

In the early hours of the morning, Eva died.

Now Trixie replied, 'She just couldn't have the baby, that's why she got herself cut about. Fuckin' 'ell, I hate Eddie for what he did to her. If only he'd shared some of her burden.'

'That's men for you; they always get off scot-free.' Joan took out a hanky and blew her nose. 'It's decent of you to fork out for the funeral, Trixie. Any idea who messed her insides up?'

Trixie, used to Joan's habit of flitting from one subject to another, shook her head. 'She wasn't in any state to have a proper conversation and anyway, get rid of one back-street abortionist and another takes their place.'

Trixie sighed and looked about her. The church was filling up. It smelled musty, like they'd over-done the incense, and the scent from the flowers was overpowering. Trixie felt for Joan's hand for reassurance. Her other arm was safely entwined with Jem's. Grandad sat at the end of the aisle, looking forlorn. There was a button missing from his suit waistcoat. Trixie knew he had liked Eva and admired her fighting spirit.

'With Eva there, travelling about with the band was just about bearable. I'm not doing it any more.' Jem turned his head and looked at her but didn't speak. Trixie squeezed his hand and asked him, 'I think you met someone while you were away.'

Jem looked down at her. 'Even if I did, I had to weigh up whether I could lose you and leave Grandad. How did you know?'

'Just a guess,' she said. 'But I think I know you very well, Jem.'

'Well,' he said, squeezing her hand back. 'Don't worry about it. It's over. Done and dusted. But that's not the only thing on your mind, is it?'

'No,' Trixie sighed. 'I don't think I can face the lads and the way the girls hang about them when we're on the road. I know if I see Eddie messing

286

about it would make me want to have a go at him.'

'And when will you tell Eric you'll be leaving?' Joan asked. 'I can see you've made up your mind.'

'After the funeral.'

Trixie looked about her. Eric was way back in the middle of the congregation standing next to Max. Trixie turned and he put up a hand in salutation. She stared at him for a moment, at his face – it was narrower. He was growing older; they all were.

The vicar was now in front of the cross bearing the Jesus figure. Trixie wouldn't cry, not now, Eva was safe. No one could hurt her any more.

Afterwards, she would lead the mourners to the Fighting Cocks, where Jack had hired outside caterers and closed the pub to the public for the day.

The church was quiet now and the vicar faced the coffin.

And then the noise started up at the back, the clatter of the heavy oak door opening and then banging against the wall of the church. Two laughing, chattering girls tumbled into the cool interior, adrift from the small crowd surrounding Eddie. Eddie, drunk or drugged, dressed in black leather and wearing dark glasses, stepped into the church as though he was opening a show.

And now, the vicar forgotten, the congregation turned to stare and mumble.

'I can't do this,' said Trixie, slipping from Jem's yielding arm, saying, 'Make sure Joan gets back,' and then she walked swiftly up the side of the church, out of the side door, to the lych gate where her car was parked.

Once inside she fired it up and drove out to Stokes Bay beach, where she parked near the sailing club.

Over the stones the sea crashed against the shore. Trixie wound down the window and let in the sounds of the gulls crying and the rush of the water dragging back the pebbles. Dry eyed she watched the water, thinking of the show Eddie had made of Eva's funeral.

'Let them get on with it,' she said softly. 'Eva, you were a damn good friend to me. I'm going to miss you so much.' The tears came then.

'Do you not feel you shouldn't have run out on Eva at her funeral, Trixie?' Jem's eyes were questioning. He was still wearing the dark suit he'd had on earlier and a blue shirt that complemented his colouring. That infuriating lock of hair hung across his forehead and he ran his fingers through it. A loud rolling noise from outside caused the both of them to look towards the back window of the pub, where Marie's brood were playing tag in the garden. A dustbin had been knocked over. Trixie looked away and thought about Jem's question.

'Better that than cause an even bigger scene, and I imagine the vicar knew how to deal with tiresome people.' Trixie put her glass down on the table.

'He eventually got them to sit quietly at the back, but by the time the service was over they'd filed out,' said Jem.

'Well, thank God for that and it's a blessing that Eddie, so far, has decided not to turn up here.'

The band's manager was pushing through the crowd and moving towards them. 'Eric's not going to like what I'm about to say.' Jem made to stand and move off, but Trixie clutched at him. 'Oh, no, you don't. I need a bit of moral support.'

'Good turn-out, Trixie. Shame about earlier,' said Eric. He was twisting his gold ring round and round nervously. She knew exactly what he meant; the fuss in the church was probably a talking point for everyone. Eric smells of violets, she thought. Always she associated the tiny mauve flower with his cologne.

'Eddie always likes to run the show,' she said quietly. 'I've had enough.'

Jem nodded towards the bar as he raised his glass. Then he left, carrying Eric's glass along with his own and Trixie's, for a refill.

Eric's face was a blank mask. Trixie could see by his flickering eyelids that he was mulling over her words.

Eventually he said, 'Miss Ice Cube wants to melt away?'

'If that's how you want to put it.'

He sighed. There was a dirty mark on the sleeve of Eric's beige suit. Trixie smiled to herself. He obviously wasn't aware of it. He'd fuss if he knew he was less than perfect in company.

'It's how the papers'll write it up.'

'I don't care.' By telling him she felt as though a large weight had been lifted from her shoulders.

Eric stared into her eyes. 'You do know that I've already had this conversation with Mo?'

'He wants *me* out?' Trixie was taken aback at Mo's underhandedness.

Eric slowly nodded.

'How do *you* feel about that?' It seemed important that she know Eric's true feelings.

'Three lads on their own, two with good voices, can't lose. You on a solo career?' He fingered his yellow tie. Trixie suddenly thought how much of a one-off he was, to roll up at a funeral wearing a mix of pale colours. Most people had worn some sort of mourning clothes, and even she had on a black suit.

'I want to do local clubs and pubs with a pianist for back-up.' Her words brought her back to the subject in hand.

'You won't miss travelling?'

Trixie thought of the cities she'd never really had time to explore properly because she had to move on to another grubby hotel, another boarding house. Cologne, Prague, Paris, the list was endless. She shook her head.

There was more sighing before he said, 'You'll be taking a step backwards.'

Trixie knew that most singers wanted what she was throwing away.

'Yes, and my money will fall dramatically; that's the next thing you're going to say to dissuade me, isn't it?'

He put his hand on her shoulder. 'You're not exactly coining it now.'

'Peace of mind means more,' she said. 'You got a lad on your books who plays the piano? My first choice would have been George and his guitar, but he'd never leave Mo and Eddie and he'd be a fool if he did.'

'I'll find someone for you,' he said. 'Let's discuss this when I've thought it over properly.' He laughed then, a throaty sound that shook his body. 'I suppose you know George has found God, or rather the Maharishi Mahesh Yogi?'

Trixie stared at him. 'Whatever are you on about?' Jem had returned with another gin and tonic for Eric, who took it gratefully and sipped at it delicately. His own and Trixie's drinks Jem put down on the table.

'He went on holiday to India,' said Eric, 'and discovered transcendental meditation and now believes in the guru and his preaching of creating world peace.'

'This is George, our George who filled himself so full of heroin he gave himself a heart attack?'

'Yes, Trixie.'

'And I thought he was getting himself well enough to begin playing again.'

'He is, now. There were a few months when he didn't lift his guitar, but now he's playing stronger than ever and there's even an Indian influence in his work.'

'I guess if it helps him then it's the right thing.' She thought for a moment, then said, 'I know the right thing for me is to break with the boys.'

Trixie hauled herself from bed to make the morning tea. She stood watching the kettle, then went back to bed and buried her head in the pillow. Eva's coffin floated inside her head. The smell of the lilies wouldn't go away.

Then Joan was shaking her. It was like watching a television programme and Trixie wondered what would happen next as Joan, her other hand wrapped in a towel, was waving the kettle about.

'You've burned the bleedin' kettle,' she said. Her voice seemed far away. Trixie wondered why Joan's voice was coming from the distance when she was standing right here by the side of the bed. Trixie put the pillow over her head and held on to it but she could still hear Joan shrieking. She heard the kettle drop to the floor then the cold air hit her as the blankets were yanked away.

Joan climbed in behind Trixie and pulled the blankets over the two of them. 'Fuck, fuck, fuck,' Joan was saying over and over again. Then she put her skinny arms around Trixie's body and implored, 'Don't be ill, Trixie. I need to depend on you. How can you look after me if you're in that dark place?'

The heat of Joan's body seeped into her and Trixie felt warmth begin to flood through her, soothing her. She thought of the words Joan had just said and realised she must have got up, gone into the kitchen, lit the gas and put the kettle on. Then she'd returned to bed, forgetting all about the kettle.

She turned round and held Joan in her arms. Joan was right. She mustn't go back into that dark place. She slept.

It was dark when Trixie awoke, alone. She got out of bed and went into the kitchen. A new kettle sat on the stove. On the table was a jam jar filled with Michaelmas daisies, some of Trixie's favourites. She took one of the sprays out of the jam jar and examined its delicate blue petals and smiled. It was all right. She was all right. *She was all right*. Francis Craig's old song 'Near You' entered her head and she began to sing.

The beach at Mykonos was deliciously sandy. Teddy rolled over on the lounger and looked at Rafe, who was in the process of turning a golden brown. Rafe opened one eye and said, 'Want to go for a drink?'

'In a while,' said Teddy. He thought about the cutting from the *Daily Mail* he'd put in the scrap book just before they'd left England which proclaimed his sister was now going solo. She'd looked calm and quite beautiful in the accompanying photograph, he thought. So badly did he want to get in touch with her, though maybe she'd forgotten about him after all these years. He lifted one of his arms and held it against the sun-browned skin of Rafe's.

'You're the wrong colouring to tan as deeply as I do.' Rafe sat up, looked around the busy beach and beyond to the village and said, 'I absolutely love this place with its tiny cube houses and the way nude bathing doesn't seem depraved.'

'Why don't you take all your clothes off then?'

'My dear boy,' Rafe's laugh was infectious, 'my dangly bits are certainly not so pretty as they were once upon a time. You, on the other hand, are the perfect shape to have the young men swooning.'

Teddy smiled at him. It hadn't escaped his notice that the young Greek men eyed Rafe. But wherever Rafe went when he sometimes left him at the hotel in the evenings was his own business. As for him, he liked to look at the Greek men with their incredibly toned bodies. They were beautiful and they knew it. But they were, after all, simply

293

holiday romances on the island of dreams. Mykonos was the gay capital of Greece and the nightly parade of newly tanned and oiled flesh in the labyrinthine streets was overwhelming.

Of course he'd experimented in Paris. It hadn't stopped him working hard. Rafe's generosity had paid off. Teddy's name on a canvas sold it. He had money now and loved taking Rafe away to the sun, in search of adventures, of which Rafe never tired. Sometimes he thought he had everything he'd ever wanted. Sid O'Hara was the only fly in the ointment. He belonged to a life Teddy tried to forget. If only Teddy could see Trixie. But according to the newspapers and media she preferred to live at Clayhall now.

What if Sid was still around Clayhall? He couldn't take the chance that Sid didn't know Teddy's nom-de-plume of Edward Somersby. The rogue could expose him, or blackmail him, and no doubt Trixie would become involved. A crime committed by him in another life, long ago, would bring both his and his sister's careers crashing down. He loved her too much for that to happen.

'What are you thinking?' Rafe was getting up now, taking up his towel and shaking it away from Teddy so the sand wouldn't stick to him.

'Nothing much,' said Teddy. 'Though I think I'll come with you. We could sit in that taverna near the harbour and watch the pelicans.'

Trixie looked at her tea, picked up the spoon and stirred thoughtfully. Again the bleakness enveloped her. It was Friday the thirteenth and Trixie was apprehensive about the new venue in the town, the Star Inn.

As if reading her thoughts, Jem said, 'Did you know that place was once the haunt of thieves and press gangs?'

'That's making me feel better about singing there, Jem.' She sipped her tea and made a face.

'Yes, a nineteenth-century coaching inn,' he said proudly.

'Why don't you move your arse and make me another cup of tea; I've let this one get cold. Please,' she added. Secretly she was proud of the way Jem made sure he vetted new venues himself. Since he now owned many smallholdings on the south coast that were run by employees he could take time out to spend with Trixie. Secretly, she knew he quite liked arranging and checking venues for her. He and Eric worked hard to keep her in the public eye.

She finished outlining her lips with a darker lipstick and blotted them. Then she searched in a velvet case for a pair of pearl earrings and slipped them through her ear lobes. 'I'm nervous as hell, and all you can talk about are thieves.'

'I'm driving you down there and staying while you sing, to give you all the confidence in the world, Miss Tetchy!' he said.

'Go! Tea!' she commanded. Jem began to laugh, a lovely belly laugh that made her smile.

A few more brush strokes from the mascara block and she surveyed herself in the mirror. Slim, blonde and still pretty. She wondered how Teddy fared and how his life was going.

Occasionally she and Jem visited the island and always she watched the crowds of holidaymakers intently. Maybe, just maybe, one day, Teddy would be amongst them. She feared he would have moved on by now, but never would she stop looking for him.

'What are you singing tonight?' Jem put the cup of tea within reach on the dressing-table and gratefully she smiled at him. She didn't know what she'd do without him. Always he was there for her. And she didn't tell him enough how much she cared for him.

'Only Sixteen', 'Smoke Gets in Your Eyes', 'Travellin' Light' and ending with 'Mack the Knife', but I'm doing requests as well and a bit of banter if the audience wants to talk back.'

'And Kenny at the piano?'

She nodded. 'Nice to have an older man playing for me. I like to hear about his family.' Kenny lived at Bridgemary with his wife and three kiddies and two Siamese cats called Samson and Delilah. He had no pretensions and adored his missus and went shopping with her every Saturday.

'You ever miss having a family of your own, Trixie?'

Trixie looked at him but she was thinking of her dead child. 'Sometimes,' she said. 'But you, Gramps and Joan, you're my family.' She picked up the cup and sipped from it.

'You can't be an island all your life,' said Jem. 'But when you think it's time to swim to the shore, I'll be here.'

She went on staring at his reflection in the mirror. What woman in her right mind wouldn't want a man like him who also had a healthy bank balance?

But Trixie didn't care about money and was in no hurry for marriage. Though it would serve her right if another woman came along and he fell head over heels in love with her.

So far it hadn't happened.

It was only by chance that she'd heard Jem had a dark-haired girl he'd visited from time to time over in Southsea. She wasn't shocked. He was a red-blooded man who needed release. Trixie remembered another girl from the Midlands. The woman had refused to believe the affair was over and telephoned him constantly. She'd nearly driven Jem to distraction. Trixie hadn't felt threatened in the slightest. She knew she had only to say she loved him and she'd marry him and he'd settle down.

But the figure of Sid O'Hara loomed large in Trixie's background.

She still woke sweating in the middle of the night, imagining his hands on her body. Sometimes she woke in the mornings smelling his perspiration on her skin. She knew it wasn't possible, but to her it was as real as if he was there. And where was that special spark between her and Jem? The one where if your eyes lighted on them, you knew you couldn't live without that person? Or was this gentle, everlasting love that felt so comfortable, the right kind of loving for her and Jem?

Trixie set down her cup and got up. Now wasn't the time for meditation, not when she had an audience to entertain.

'You're ready?' Jem slipped her coat around her shoulders.

'I'm ready,' Trixie said, picking up her stage outfit. 'Let's go to the Star Inn.'

She could have driven herself to the venue. But Jem wanted to be with her and she was touched by his consideration.

It was a cold, clear night with the possibility of a frost, she thought, sinking into the depths of Jem's leather car seat. Trixie liked working local venues. She never knew how many people would be there and was always thrilled when the places were filled to capacity. It still humbled her to think people would pay to hear her sing.

Kenny was outside in the wide alley nursing a pint and a cigarette when they pulled up.

'It's packed upstairs,' he said. Kenny always arrived for every gig right on time. He told her about the new recipe his wife had discovered and tried out on him for tea: lasagne. 'Greek, she reckons,' he said with a grin. 'Sort of strips of spaghetti stuff and tomato mince. Can't see it catching on. Not like shepherd's pie.' He smoothed back his dark hair and polished his shoes by rubbing the toes of them on the backs of his trouser legs one after the other.

The manager, Roy Adams, greeted her and as she and Jem followed him along a narrow corridor upstairs, Trixie saw the huge people-packed room where she was to sing. She noted the stage, and the hand-held mic already in place on a stand.

Everyone seemed to be in high spirits, sitting at small tables arranged around the outside of the room so there was space in the centre of the hall for her to wander about with the mic, if she wanted.

'Tests done?' She nodded towards the equipment.

'Yes,' the manager said, then he fussed over her and showed her to a small room to use as a dressing area.

'It's a bit different from the Portsmouth Guildhall where you sang a few years back,' Jem said. She saw him looking at paint-scratched surfaces and grubby walls. He hung up her dress behind a screen and shook its protective covering.

'Here's where I'd rather be,' she said, patting her hair into place as she stood before the mirror, then realising she had to get changed so would need to attend to her hair all over again. 'At least afterwards I'm going home to my own bed and Joan and her bloody cocoa and that's got to be much better than making excuses to refuse a drunken brawl of a party where someone's been sick in the lav and couples are copulating on the lawn.'

'Don't be so graphic,' broke in Jem. But Trixie was thinking of some of the drug- and drink-fuelled social gatherings that had ended with drastic results.

She threw her coat on a chair and within moments, behind the screen, had slipped her stage clothes on: a grey velvet dress based on one of Eva's creations but hand sewn by a seamstress from the town. Eva's words were imprinted on her memory – about the importance of sophisticated dresses, plain, simple in design and letting the material speak for itself. Then she headed out of the room towards the rust-coloured velvet drapes at the rear of the stage where she could peek out at the audience without being seen.

'We've got a few high-spirited lads in tonight,' said Roy. 'Call-up boys off tomorrow for their basic training.' She took a sneaky look. 'Some say National Service is a waste of time now the war's over but I reckon it teaches the young blokes discipline,' he sniffed. A loud guffaw of laughter came from an alcove where three young men, complete with giggling girls, were drinking wine.

'Those lads don't look old enough to fight for our country,' Trixie said. Her eyes were immediately drawn to a fair-haired lad with a cheeky grin. She noted that when he wasn't laughing his composed face was classically handsome. He reminded her of Teddy.

'All men living here in England are liable for call-up from the age of eighteen,' Jem said. Trixie knew he had been anxious to go into the Navy but was refused admission due to a hearing impairment. He'd been angry and it had taken him a long time to come to terms with being turned down. He, too, peeked around the curtain and looked towards the noisy booth. 'I see what you mean but it's not unusual for young blokes to lie about their age or even to falsify their birth certificate to get into a branch of the services they feel they're best equipped for.'

'Two years, isn't it?' Trixie asked.

'Yes, unless the bloke decides to make a career out of being in the forces.' A wistful look entered Jem's eyes.

'If you'd been in the Army you'd not have the financial security you have now,' said Trixie. 'Ever thought that that knock-back became the making of you?'

Jem sighed. 'You're probably right,' he said.

More loud laughter interrupted Jem's words. Then came a squeal from one of the girls.

'Who is that blond boy?' Trixie asked, staring as he rubbed at his scalp in exactly the same way Teddy used to. That simple action caused her heart to beat faster. 'Anyone would think he had nits, scratching his head like that.' She was transfixed.

'Actually, I do know the lad. His father owns a rather upmarket restaurant in Fareham. The Incredible Edible it's called. Mind you, the pricey eaterie is only a hobby for Dad; he's something in local government as well.'

Trixie looked at Jem in wonderment. 'How d'you know all that?'

'Because I provide the restaurant with its excellent salad, fruit and vegetables,' Jem said.

'Bit full of yourself, aren't you?' Trixie dug him in the ribs.

'Oi! Bony elbows!'

Trixie was laughing but she stopped long enough to ask, 'What's his name?'

'Mark, Mark Barr.'

'Call him over.'

Jem stared at her. Though she was kind and often talkative to her fans it was rare for her to ask to meet someone. Trixie watched as Jem strolled towards the table and spoke to the revellers. At first it seemed the young man was irritated at being disturbed, but then he grinned at Jem, apologised to his friends, rose and walked towards her. Then her panic set in. Did he think she was about to proposition him? Time after time she'd watched as Eddie or Mo had decided which girls were fuckable and had sent word for the females to be in the dressing-room ready for them when the show ended.

She didn't have time to worry as Jem pulled aside the curtain so the young man could step behind it and away from the peering eyes in the crowded room. He was a whole head and shoulders taller than her and she could smell his tangy aftershave. He smiled and all her fears of being intimidated by him flew away.

'Hello.' She put out her hand as though for a handshake and he gripped it firmly. His nails were cut squarely straight across, his hands uncallused.

'I'm thrilled to meet you,' he said. 'I love your voice and I have some of your records.' His teeth were very white and there was a golden sheen to his skin that spoke of being out in the open air a great deal. She wondered if he played some kind of sport.

Trixie looked into his eyes and immediately felt as though she'd known him for years. 'Thank you,' she said. 'Jem tells me, Mark, you're off to start your National Service?'

'Yes, I'm off to West Kirby for some square bashing but I've signed on for three years and it's possible I might make a career out of the RAF.'

For some unexplained reason Trixie felt a sense of loss settle over her and she asked. 'Where's West Kirby?'

'Somewhere in Cheshire,' he said. Then, 'Was there a special reason you called me over?' A cheeky wave of hair fell across his forehead and he slipped his long fingers through it and shrugged it back in place. Trixie thought it would be a shame that one of his first chores would be a trip to the barber, who would lop off that glorious golden hair.

'Well, you remind me of someone I used to know and then I was told you'll be going away tomorrow, so I wondered if you'd like a special request. I'll buy you and your friends a drink, of course, to send you on your way.'

'That's really nice of you,' Mark said. She could see he was thinking quickly. 'Do you know the Everly Brothers song, "All I Have To Do Is Dream"? It's one of my favourites.'

'It's one of Trixie's favourites, too,' broke in Jem.

'I do know it,' she said, with a laugh to both men.

'When I get back to our table I'm telling my mates you're much prettier close up.'

Trixie knew she was blushing. She rubbed her perspiring hands down the sides of her dress that perfectly matched the colour of her stiletto-heeled shoes and nearly missed the signal from Roy, announcing that he was ready for her to go on.

'Better go now,' Jem said to Mark. Trixie took a look at the piano on the side of the stage. Kenny was sitting up straight, watching her and waiting for the 'off' signal.

Mark turned just once and smiled when she whispered, 'Good luck in the RAF, Mark.' Then he continued on his way back to his friends. Trixie nodded to Kenny and moved down to centre stage behind the curtains. Roy took the microphone and announced her.

The clapping began and stilled when the curtain went back and she walked, smiling, towards the microphone. The piano player cued her in for her first song. A hush descended on the huge room and once more Trixie True became a singer, losing her own identity and taking on that other persona reflected in the mirrored walls and polished floor that gleamed below the crystal chandelier.

At the small table, Mark Barr seemed mesmerised. Trixie moved around the room, touching an arm, a cheek, pausing to make a customer feel as though her soulful voice that she hoped tugged at heartstrings, was singing just for them.

When the show ended to rapturous applause Trixie knew Mark's eyes had never once left her.

She didn't see him leave but felt the loss that he had gone.

Back in the dressing-room the manager fussed and praised her. When she was once more in the dress she'd arrived in and the grey velvet outfit was safely packed away, Jem surprised her by asking, 'Are you going to see that young man again?' He swept her stage make-up back into its box.

Trixie laughed, 'He's a kid!'

'No, he's younger than you. But he's not a kid and he does look old for his age. He's serving his country.'

Trixie stared at him, at the unease in his eyes, at the sharpness of his tone. It wasn't like Jem to be jealous. More that he wouldn't want her to get hurt and find herself thrown into a depression like before.

'He reminded me of Teddy,' she said softly.

Jem turned away.

Trixie could feel an atmosphere between them.

Wordlessly he passed her her coat. It wasn't like Jem to be so quiet.

'Don't be cross,' she said. 'I can't help it if I can't get the loss of my brother out of my mind. Don't forget it was me that brought Mum and him to Gosport. It's always there in my head that it's all my fault that Sid sent him away.'

Trixie turned from Jem so he wouldn't see the tears that were trying to squeeze out of her tightly closed eyes.

'I don't know what else to do to find him,' Jem said, coming up behind her, taking her coat from her hands and slipping it across her shoulders. 'And he must have a good reason for not contacting *you*.'

They hardly spoke a word on the way home.

Joan was at the treadle sewing machine making curtains for a guest bedroom at the Fighting Cocks.

'I don't know why you don't move in with Jack,' said Trixie. 'A blind man can see how that fella dotes on you.' She marvelled at the long lines of straight needlework that was beyond her. Trixie was bending over Joan and could smell the scent of Amami shampoo in her freshly washed hair.

'How many times d'you need telling that all the while Sid's floating about, he'll expect me to be faithful. If I so much as look at another man Sid could find a way of getting him rubbed off the face of the earth. You think I want that to happen to Jack?' Joan examined her work, then pulled it from the machine and snipped the cotton. The curtain seemed to match her expectations.

Trixie sniffed. 'Suppose you're right,' she said.

Chapter Twenty-Two

'Don't you just wish this bleedin' train would get there?'

Blue jeans with the colour practically wrung out of them and a leather jacket that even though he was sitting down, looked too big on him, gave the man a scruffy appearance.

Mark stared at the skinny man with the big ears who had just spoken to him. 'Can't be long now; we're already in Cheshire. My name's Mark Barr.' He put out a hand and shook the proffered one. It was the kit-bag the man gripped between his knees that showed he was possibly going to the same place as Mark himself.

'Eli, Eli Watson. Sorry, I had a late night last night and although sleep makes the journey pass quicker it's made me feel as though me guts are gonna spill out.'

Almost as he'd finished speaking the train, with a great deal of noise and smoke belching from it, halted at a small station and from nowhere a corporal banged on the outside carriage window. 'Get out quick, you dozy lot and get fell in.' Even through the glass of the window his voice was extremely loud. Mark looked at the man and made a face.

'There's your answer, mate. We're here. Jesus, these kit-bags are awkward.'

With much pulling and pushing his heavy bag

was hauled down from the overhead luggage rack and Mark led the way out of the train's corridor and caught up with the corporal.

'Where do we go?'

'To fuckin' 'ell you talk to me like that again! Where do we go, *please sir!*'

Mark, chastened, repeated his request and eventually found himself sitting in a three-ton lorry on a slatted seat that had never been made for a human form.

There seemed to be too few lorries and too many men in the field next to the station. Soon the wagon Mark was in was bursting out of its canvas seams as men stood, sat and generally sagged against one another until the lorries finished winding through country lanes to eventually pass through the high wired gates and barbed wire fencing that surrounded huts and hangars all painted green. RAF West Kirby.

The shouting began again and confusion reigned once more as names were called, lines were formed and unformed, and the many different callers arranged men into divisions.

Now Mark found himself being shouted at by a drill sergeant named Grant and forced to run, carrying his kit-bag, along concrete paths that all looked exactly the same until they arrived at Hut 429 and were informed, 'This is your home for the next bleedin' eight weeks.'

It was a Nissen hut that felt as cold as charity inside and was filled with twenty unmade iron beds and the smell of disinfectant.

He was surprised to find Eli Watson in the bed next to him. It was obvious to Mark that they were going to become mates.

The end of that first day saw them sorting out their bedding and trying to determine the use of the strange equipment given to them and for which they'd signed.

Eli waved his hand about the hut. 'I dunno how I'm goin' to sleep with this lot round me.' Eli had his own bedroom in his mum's London council flat.

'You get used to it.'

'I'm surprised you didn't have a room of your own, you bein' posh like, and living in a big 'ouse.'

Mark didn't like to confuse Eli by explaining he was used to sleeping in a dormitory of boys from the public school he'd attended when younger. The two men were as different as chalk and cheese yet somehow understood the nature of each other perfectly.

'Me girlfriend'll go mad about me losin' me Tony Curtis.' Eli ran his hand over his shorn locks. 'Still, I don't look as bleedin' bald as you do, mate.'

Mark sighed. Being blond it looked as though they'd given him a Yul Brynner. His wave of hair no longer fell across his forehead, it didn't fall anywhere because it just wasn't there. He foraged in his kit-bag and came out with a couple of photographs.

'Cor! 'Ere, I seen her somewhere. She's, or she was, the lead singer with that group The Tropics. You must fancy her.'

'I'm going to marry her.'

Eli looked at him, then raised one eyebrow. 'In yer dreams, mate, in yer dreams.'

Mark slept.

Reveille at six fifteen was no surprise, for Mark was awake long before that. The first item on the agenda after washing, shaving and breakfast was inoculations and more aptitude and intelligence tests. Mark was also given another medical. He knew the physical training in the RAF was especially strenuous. The basic training would be arduous but he was looking forward to the map reading, fieldcraft, lectures and learning to shoot on the rifle range.

A taster of that came in the afternoon when he and Eli went to the range for fixing and unfixing bayonets. Not real bayonets, but metal spikes that were used instead of the short knives. For Mark it involved holding his rifle between his knees and reaching around and replacing the bayonet in its scabbard. Not easy at the best of times, he decided. Time after time he was remarkably slow until, nervous, he was being watched by the corporal, who said, 'I pity your girlfriend if you can't get it in quicker than that!' Mark knew he was in big trouble if he laughed, so he left that to the other men. He merely said, 'Thank you, sir.' He saw the corporal stifle a laugh and felt better. He knew there was a lot to learn, but he was enthusiastic about it.

He thought about Trixie. He was eager to see her again but had decided he wouldn't enter her life until he'd made something of his own. He wanted to fly, to travel the world. To travel under his own steam, not to be taken on holidays paid for by his parents.

He stared at Trixie's photograph and she gazed

back with her wide-eyed, hypnotic smile.

She was a self-made woman who had built her future on her voice. He admired her for that. His grandmother had left him some money and his maternal grandfather had left him land in Scotland. But he needed to prove to himself that if she'd have him, he'd be able to provide well for her by his own means.

He promised himself he would achieve his ambitions by the time he was twenty. All of them.

The bitch had done it again. He peered through the frosted, patterned glass of the Navy Arms window and watched the woman, *his woman*, sitting with Dicky Summers and laughing her stupid bloody head off. Like she had all the time in the world to fritter away throwing drink down her skinny neck instead of being out earning. And now she was about to make him look a fuckin' fool in front of his mate for interrupting the couple.

Dicky Summers looked up as the door opened. Waves of fag smoke swept over Sid O'Hara. He scowled at Melanie, who had so many of her buttons undone on her blouse he could very nearly see her fanny.

'Watcher, Dicky.' He scowled some more at Melanie. The bitch wasn't worth wasting his breath on. She looked scared and it made him want to laugh. He slid his legs around a chair and sat down.

'Want a drink?' Sid nodded at Dicky's offer.

'Don't mind taking one off a mate,' he said. Dicky got up and went to the bar.

'Taking a few minutes off work to park your

arse, are you, girl?'

'I ... I didn't like to refuse Dicky's offer, him bein' your mate an' all.' Sid waved her to be quiet.

'When he gets back you wait until I've drunk up, then we'll go out together.'

She bit her lip and nodded. All the sparkle had gone from her face, like she feared yet expected a few slaps. Well, he'd just have to give her what she expected, wouldn't he?

Dicky reached the table and handed Sid a double whisky. Well, thought Sid, a single would have been another insult, wouldn't it? Dicky fingered his red tie. Every day the old boy sported a different coloured bow tie. Said he wore the colour to match his moods. Red. What fuckin' mood did that signify? wondered Sid.

'Look, Sid, me an' Melanie was talkin' about that Marilyn Monroe.'

'Oh, yeah,' interrupted Sid. He couldn't give a fuck what they was talkin' about. 'Look, Dicky, I got a bit of business so I'll return the drink tonight.'

He got up, closely followed by Melanie.

'Right then, see you both tonight,' said Dicky, looking like he had all the worries of the world on his shoulders.

Once outside and round the back in the alley where the dustbins were lined up like soldiers Sid pinned Melanie against the wall.

"Where is it?'

'Where's what?' She could hardly get the words out, for Sid's arm was cutting off the air supply at her neck. He brought up his other hand and gave her a slap.

'Where's my fuckin' money?'

'I got nothin',' she croaked.

Another slap sent her head sideways.

'You been out since eight this mornin' 'n' it's now twelve. He looked her full in the face. Her jowls were slack and a missing front tooth made her face misshapen. He hated himself for being her pimp and hated her for her ugliness and for letting him knock her about. He drew his fist back.

'Don't hit me no more.' That pathetic voice made him sick to his stomach. He let go his fist and heard her nose shatter, but instead of satisfaction he felt even more hate and pulled back his arm, repeating the punch a second, third, fourth, a fifth time until she hung unconscious, only his grip holding her up. He let her fall and she slid to the concrete to lie amongst the rubbish from the overflowing bins.

He kicked her. 'Fuckin' get up.'

Her leg, where he'd kicked her, was the only part of her to move. She was a bit too still for his liking.

'I said, get up, you fuckin' cow.' Her body was curved round so he kicked her in the stomach. Hard enough for her body to rise off the paving stones and then fall back limply, like she was a big, floppy doll.

Was she dead? He bent down to feel for a pulse, careful of the blood and gore that seemed to have altered the shape of her face. He touched her neck. He couldn't feel a thing. His fast-beating heart was disguising it, that's what it was. Or had the silly bint croaked on him?

Fuck it! The bloody coppers would soon be

312

nosing about in this godforsaken hole.

They'd come looking for him. That fucker Dicky would tell 'em he left the Navy Arms with her.

With a bit of luck he could slip away out of sight if he went now. It was time to go home to Gosport. To Joan.

The young man's slim fingers plucked at the many strings of the kora. Rafe took a sip of his whisky and sighed as he set the glass back on the long wooden table. The kora player stopped singing.

'Most unusual instrument, Teddy. I believe the African people used to listen to that instrument and the tales told in its music, much the same as we listened to our wandering minstrels and town criers.'

Teddy smiled back at Rafe. 'I could go on listening to you for ever,' he said. 'You've taught me so much.' He glanced at the remains of his excellent meal then towards the creek, which was below the restaurant built upon stilts over the black mud of the mangrove swamp. 'This place is certainly romantic.' A couple of lovers were sitting at a nearby table gazing into each other's eyes. The air smelled of jasmine and the soft jungle sounds were muted.

'Then it's spoilt for you by sitting with an old queen like me,' said Rafe.

Teddy stared at him. 'If I'm supposed to laugh at that then you've lost your sense of humour.'

'I merely meant...'

'I know exactly what you intended and it hurts me that you feel yourself so unlovable.'

'Teddy, I have worshipped at your feet from the first time I saw you scratching your head that was full of those blasted nits.' Rafe paused. 'I now feel that I have been well and truly chastised. And don't come out with some flippant remark about my choice of word there,' he finished.

After a moment's silence they both began to laugh.

The kora player began again and the music floated into the African sky.

Teddy refilled Rafe's glass. 'Now you know I'm in love with you, what are you going to do about it?'

Rafe sat back on the bamboo chair. At the edge of the forest baboons played, the young tumbling about each other with the sheer enjoyment of being alive. 'I've only ever looked upon you, Teddy, as the son I never had. I took you into my home and heart because I could see you needed love and I was prepared to give it unconditionally.'

Teddy broke in with, 'But I lied to you all those years ago. Too scared to reveal the truth, I told you what I thought was best you should know.' Teddy thought about the village of Ashampton in Suffolk where Rafe's family had lived the life of gentility for generations in their manor house. That family had accepted him but it was far removed from his own, true humble origins.

'I don't care about your past, Teddy.' Rafe waited until the waiter had collected the utensils and plates. 'Remember how we worked on the biography that accompanies your paintings? All artists doctor their biogs to give the fans what they want or what will help in the sale of their work.'

'But I want *you* to know the truth.'

Rafe gazed at him. 'Then it's time you told me,' he said.

Teddy threw back his drink and began talking. He didn't look anywhere except at his empty glass, his eyes never leaving the tiny amount of alcohol contained as dregs. When, eventually, the tale was told Teddy admitted, 'I have a scrapbook back home on the island with all my sister's triumphs recorded. I'd like to show it to you.'

Rafe leaned across the table. 'I'd be honoured,' he said. 'I'm glad I know the truth about you, but it changes nothing. For me our lives began the day I ran you down in my car.'

Teddy wondered how he could have been so lucky to have this wonderful man in his life. He saw that the kora player had changed position on his cushions and now sat cross-legged. His voice was pure and clear. For the first time Teddy realised the player was hardly more than a boy.

Rafe touched Teddy's hand. 'You must contact Trixie. She must know you are safe.'

'Not while Sid O'Hara lives. Imagine how it would damage her career if it came out she'd shielded me for killing our father.'

Rafe stroked Teddy's hand. 'We'll see it through together. There's always the possibility Sid O'Hara is no longer with us. We'll make enquiries.' His face grew serious. 'How will your sister feel about us? Our unconventional lifestyle?'

'Trixie works in a medium known for unconventional lifestyles. And who knows? Maybe one day the world will change its views and accept homosexuality.'

Rafe left his chair and went round to the other side of the table and pulled Teddy up into his arms. Teddy's heart soared.

Chapter Twenty-Three

As Trixie heard the chords fall away she looked towards the back of the stage, where Jem stood waiting with Joan at his side. Joan? What on earth was Joan doing here in the town at the Star Inn?

The applause was long and Trixie felt grateful that so many of her fans had turned up on such a filthy night to hear her sing. She considered herself a very lucky woman indeed. Eventually she was allowed to leave the stage and once she was in the dressing-room, Joan had turned up at the door with her news. Trixie had been stunned. She scrubbed at her lips with kitchen roll lathered in Pond's cream. Its delicate smell soothed her frazzled nerves after her outburst.

'What d'you mean Sid's come back to you? I can't live in the same house as the man that raped me. You don't know how relieved I was that he left again after my baby was born.'

Joan had flung at her, 'He was the first man I ever loved, Trixie, and I haven't got over him. He's changed.'

Trixie had come to think of the prefab as *her* home. But it was Joan's name on the rent book.

She stared in the mirror at the reflection of Joan's face, grey with misery. How could Trixie ever forgive Sid when memories clung to her like grapes on a vine? Why, it even hurt her every time she had to pass by Eva's prefab. There was another woman and her small child living in there now. The woman had dark hair and was similar in looks to Eva. The first time Trixie had spied her she'd nearly had a heart attack, thinking it was Eva.

'I can't believe Sid O'Hara could knock on the door after all this time and you'd ignore all the pain and heartache he's put you through and let him back into your life!'

'I love him. You can't understand that, Trixie, can you? I hoped you could forgive.'

'I understand that when he left after raping me he'd already turned you into an alcoholic.'

'He needs me.'

Jem stepped in then, calling in the manager. 'Look, mate, could you take Joan downstairs for a drink in the bar? I want to talk to Trixie.'

Trixie didn't say a word until Joan had gone, then she rounded on Jem. 'Ever the bloody peacemaker, eh? I don't want to be hurt by Sid any more.'

Jem pulled her from the chair until she was in his arms. 'When you told me what had happened with Sid, my first impulse was to kill him. But what good would that have done? He's worse than an animal because animals care about their young and he cared nothing for you or Teddy. But Sid O'Hara is the only person who knows the true whereabouts of your brother. Give Joan your blessing and come and live with me.'

Trixie took in every word he'd spoken. She stepped away from him and sat down in front of the mirror again. Then she scooped more cream from the pot and in a circular motion began removing the rest of her make-up.

In the mirror she stared into Jem's eyes. 'You're bloody marvellous, aren't you?'

He looked confused.

Trixie continued, 'I have to go on living with Joan because that way I can find out the truth of what happened to Teddy.'

She could see Jem didn't like that idea. He opened his mouth to speak.

'It's the only way, Jem.' She paused. 'Besides, if I'm at number nineteen I'll be there for her when Sid hurts Joan again. And without a doubt, he will.'

'But what if–'

'I'll make sure I lock my bedroom door.' Again he protested but she said, 'My mind's made up. One way or another I'm going to find my brother.' She threw the tissue into the rubbish bin and with a face devoid of make-up got up and opened the door.

Joan was sitting at a table drinking tea and looking miserable. Trixie went over and put her hand on her shoulder. 'Pour me out a cuppa, will you? I'll just have time to drink it before it gets cold. I'll be with you in a minute; mustn't keep you away from your fella waiting at home for you, must I?'

'Are you being sarcastic?'

'No,' said Trixie. Joan looked at her in surprise, then she rose and threw her arms around Trixie.

318

Half crying and half sniffing, Joan said, 'You don't know what it means to me to have your blessing. He's a changed man, Trixie, he really is.'

Trixie didn't like to say a leopard doesn't change its spots.

Jem's face was tight with anger but, ever the gentleman, he offered Joan a lift back with them. In the car, Joan prattled on like a monkey, telling them about Sid's appearance at the prefab.

'I made him promise never to lie to me again, Trixie, and I told him if he so much as sniffs at another woman's skirts, he'll be out that door quicker than a cat with a scalded tail.'

Trixie squeezed Joan's hand. 'I hope you mean that, Joan,' she said. 'You deserve better than Sid.'

It was quiet then in the car and Trixie knew Joan was thinking about Jack and his kindness towards her. But then, if Joan loved Sid, no one else could take his place.

The car drew up outside number nineteen but Trixie stayed put.

'You not coming in?'

She stared at Joan. 'You know I get hyped up after doing a show. I'm going round to see Grandad. Anyway, you got a reunion to go to inside with Sid.'

Joan shook her head. 'Nah, Sid didn't have any money, so I gave him a few bob to go and meet his mates.'

From the car Trixie watched Joan turn the key in the prefab's door. Jem started up the engine again. She could see by the thin straight line that was Jem's mouth that he was still unhappy. She knew he'd never trust Sid O'Hara again and neither, for that matter, would she.

How would she cope with him in the prefab?

She remembered the touch of his hands on her skin and she shuddered. She would never get the stink of him out of her nostrils. How Joan was able to put all the bad things in a box and throw away the key Trixie would never understand.

It wasn't long before Jem drew the car to a halt outside the smallholding that always gave Trixie a feeling of security. The little house at the back of the buildings had a fairytale quality to it. It was as if it had been caught in a time warp, simply waiting for the right person to claim it and live there.

Grandad was asleep in the kitchen in his chair.

'Wake up, we've got a visitor.' Jem made a great deal of noise filling the kettle with water and setting it on the stove. The old man opened his eyes, and when he saw Trixie he gave a welcoming smile.

'I wasn't asleep,' he said. 'I was just resting my eyes.'

Trixie kissed him on the forehead then began making the tea, finishing the job started by Jem. She could see Jem slowly thawing out. His face was less grey and angry-looking and once or twice he even smiled. She knew he wouldn't stay cross for long.

She poured tea for herself and the men. Gramps and Jem talked about Sid and Trixie knew sooner or later Jem would confront Sid. He'd be unable to help himself. She just hoped it wasn't before she'd managed to find out more about where Teddy had been sent all those years ago.

And then the telephone rang.

Jem listened intently without speaking, except at the end when he said goodbye to the caller. He turned and faced Trixie. His voice was quiet and his face grave.

'That was your manager. Eric tried to reach you earlier. Mo and Eddie were killed today.'

Trixie gasped.

'They were coming home in the early hours in an open-top sports car after a gig. Both were high and had been drinking and a lorry in front of them braked unexpectedly. Its load was telegraph poles and the chains holding them cut loose. The two never stood a chance.'

Trixie sat down heavily on a chair.

'They didn't deserve to go like that,' she said, covering her face with her hands. The vision of the accident was too much for her to bear.

Jem came over and knelt down in front of her.

'Karma sorts everything out, Trixie. What goes around, comes around.' She traced his face with her fingers and stared into his eyes.

'I'm glad I wasn't alone when that call came,' she said.

It was late when Trixie finally went home to the prefab. The place was in darkness and as silent as the grave. On the table was a letter addressed to her. Mark Barr was coming home on leave and he'd like her to spend a day with him.

'I'm beginning to think I've made a mistake in agreeing to go out with Mark.'

'Why?' Joan seemed to look younger these days, thought Trixie; maybe it was because she was now back with the man she loved. Not that Trixie saw much of Sid.

He seemed to be at the prefab only when she was out singing, and when she was home he was out with his many mates from the local pubs. 'If it's because he's younger than you, I shouldn't worry about that,' said Joan.

She wondered if Jem would be hurt knowing she'd spent the day with Mark. She'd tossed and turned all night worrying, but had finally decided that a day out wasn't such a big deal.

She was still looking out of the prefab's window when the blue Mercedes two-seater convertible came round the corner and stopped in the parking area.

Trixie felt her heart leap as Mark climbed from the car and began walking towards the prefab. She'd wondered whether he would wear his uniform but he had on jeans and a brown leather jacket that looked expensive. She thought he looked out of place in her scruffy neighbourhood. He kept looking about him as though expecting something to happen.

'Do you think I look all right?' she asked Joan. She'd spent ages backcombing her hair. Trixie's cream shoes and jacket matched the colour of her pedal-pusher trousers and a black jumper made a good colour contrast.

'You look lovely,' Joan said. 'Go to the door; don't keep him waiting.'

She practically fell into his arms. Mark hugged her, then arm in arm they made their way down the path and out onto the paving stones. Trixie was excited, wondering where they were going.

He was opening the passenger door for her when a female voice shouted, 'Hello, Trixie.'

Recognising the voice, she turned and waved to Marie and Dmitri who were hand in hand with a gaggle of their children dancing around them. 'My friends,' she said proudly to Mark. It pleased her when Mark, so handsome, in his costly clothes, waved also.

He started the car and it threaded its way through the prefabs and on to the main road.

'Where are we going?' she asked.

'The New Forest.' He turned and looked at her, waiting for a reaction. She didn't care where she went as she felt easy in his company. So easy that there didn't seem to be any need for idle chit-chat as they drove out of Gosport and towards Southampton, the gateway to the forest.

Trixie marvelled that she hadn't panicked at being alone with him. Normally shy and used to her own company, it was only when she was on the stage that her alter ego took over and she became the chatty woman who smiled and sang and was totally outgoing. When she got home it was like taking off that outer skin and drawing back into herself again. She was quiet, shy and terrified of life and men, except for Jem, who understood her and acted as a buffer between her and the real world.

With Mark, as with Jem, Trixie felt no need to pretend. Strangely, she felt it was the quiet person in her he liked, and not the outgoing stage character.

The light wind blew her hair back from her face and she marvelled at the different colour greens of the trees. There were still leaves clinging on branches despite the sudden, sharp frosts they'd had lately. The air was sweet-smelling, making her feel glad to be alive on such a sunny day.

Because she didn't feel pressured Trixie enjoyed the drive through Fareham, Titchfield and Southampton. At Lyndhurst Mark parked in the car park near the church and together they strolled the cobbled streets, peering in tiny shops selling gifts and sweets. He left her standing on the pavement while he rushed into one such shop, only to re-emerge a moment later with a bag containing a stick of rock.

'We're on holiday, today,' he said. 'You have to have a stick of New Forest rock.'

'You're mad,' laughed Trixie. All the same she thought it was a nice thing for him to say and do.

'Shall we have tea and cakes?' Without waiting for a reply from her, Mark led Trixie into a pretty tea shop with frilled net curtains at the windows and a lady dressed in black with a white apron, waiting to take their order and write it down in a notebook. In the background a medley of Bing Crosby songs softly played and it seemed just the right background for them to talk and sample the tall cake tray of delicacies the waitress set on the table.

'I think we must be on holiday,' said Trixie. She was enjoying herself and softly singing along with the music.

'I told you so,' Mark said. He told her tales of his settling-in days at the camp, making her laugh with some of the exploits the lads got up to. In return she regaled him with stories of gigs in

Germany and France. She looked at the clock, shaped like a tea-kettle on the wall of the tea shop, and realised they had been talking away non-stop for hours and there still seemed lots to say.

'Tell me about your family,' she insisted.

'Oh, they're going to love you. Dad has a finger in local government and many other pies besides. And Mum helps him all she can. They both play golf. Do you play?' He told her there was a golf course and clubhouse being built near Fort Gilkicker. His dad had been extremely keen to get that passed by the council.

He might just as well have asked her if she flew to the moon as play golf. Trixie shook her head, for panic had set in. 'I don't think I'm ready to meet your parents. I've only just met you.' She felt life was moving just a little too fast.

'Mum was a showgirl.'

Now that was a surprise.

'Dad met her, took her away from that life and gave her a different one.' The way he emphasised the words made Trixie think Mark's father hadn't thought much of his new wife's past occupation. It sounded, thought Trixie, as though Mark's mum didn't have much of a choice.

'Brothers? Sisters?'

'I have a pampered, spoilt sister. She hates me because she won't inherit and I will. But I'll make sure there's enough money set aside so she can go on being pampered and spoilt. But that's enough about me, I want to hear all about you.'

Trixie gave him the sanitised press release biography. Only to Jem was she scrupulously honest. It wasn't as though she didn't want Mark to know all about her, she did, but not yet.

When they left the tea shop he took her for a walk in the woods. Trixie realised it had been a long time since she had been so close to nature. Birds sang in the trees, the grass was vibrantly green beneath her feet and a little brook they found gurgling alongside the path almost sang as its waters tumbled over rocks and stones.

They walked until Trixie saw they had come upon a clearing that had probably once been a small hamlet. Amongst the ruins only one house seemed inhabited.

'This is where I wanted to bring you,' Mark said. He smiled down at her.

The house lay inside an overgrown garden. Tangled briars grew over the path to the front door almost as if defying visitors to enter. Smoke curled lazily from the tall chimney. A movement in the undergrowth and a scraggy yellow cat disappeared deeper into the bushes.

Mark went before her, clearing a way, and knocked loudly on the door.

'Granny Tillotson,' he called. When there was no reply he shouted again. The front door, Trixie noticed, was slightly ajar. Another yellow cat slid through the opening and began twining itself around Mark's legs. He bent down and petted the animal, then pushed open the door, saying to her, 'Follow me.'

Inside the cottage it was bright and cheerful. A fire spluttered in the leaded grate, sending flames of yellow and orange up the chimney. A black and white cat lay on the rag rug warming itself in front of the fire.

A bundle of clothes in a chair next to the fire turned into a wizened woman with skin so paper-thin Trixie was sure if she touched her she would fall apart. But when the woman took her hand, it felt satisfyingly warm and strong.

'Hello, Granny.' Mark bent and kissed the woman, who, in a small clear voice, asked him about his life in the RAF and his parents' welfare.

Trixie was bidden to sit on a small stool and she heard the woman ask why Mark's father hadn't bought him a commission. The orange cat now made a fuss of Trixie and she heard Mark reply, 'I don't want to be cosseted any more, Granny. I need to make my own way in life.'

'That's good, my boy,' she said. 'It will stand you in good stead when...' And there her voice tailed off and she turned to Trixie, picking up her hand once more and smoothing the skin with her ringless fingers.

'You've travelled well, my dear, but it will end soon.' Then she tightened her grip on Trixie's hand and said, 'You're looking for something and someone. You will find both but you won't be able to hold on to one. One you will lose for ever. My dear, you will also lose your childhood that you've clung to all these years. Let it go; you are a woman now.'

Trixie felt a cold chill steal over her. She could suddenly smell geraniums. Their strong, bitter scent filled the room and then just as quickly as it had come the aroma vanished. Trixie looked about her to see the room was devoid of flowers.

The woman said, 'Go, I can tell you no more but that you are a fool not to listen to the one who cares for you.'

Then she let Trixie's hand drop and settled back in the chair to be almost swallowed in its depths. Her eyes closed.

Mark said, "We'd better leave now; she's tired.'

Trixie pushed the cat away, which now seemed to have made a nest on her lap, and stood up. 'Is she all right?' She stared at the sleeping woman.

'Take my hand,' Mark said. He led her out of the cottage and round to the back, where the grass was shorter and a middle-aged woman was pegging incredibly white washing onto a low line. As they approached the woman asked, 'Is Granny all right?'

'She gave a reading.'

The woman stared at Trixie. 'To you?'

Trixie, unsure of the right response said, 'I think so.'

'This is Margaret, Trixie.'

The two women smiled at each other. Mark took out his wallet and slipped some notes into the wicker washing basket.

'It's not often she feels moved to read for any-one. You must have touched a chord somewhere,' Margaret said, and picked out the money and held it back towards Mark. 'You know very well she don't ask for money.'

'It's a gift. It's not payment.'

'Always was difficult, you,' she said, smiling again at him.

Margaret asked if they wanted a cup of tea. Trixie immediately refused. They'd just left a tea shop and she wanted to be away from the cottage. The old woman had disturbed her.

Once safely back inside the car Trixie said, 'Well, that was quite an experience.'

'I hope it was one that didn't frighten you. I never expected her to see into your future.'

'What is she, some kind of witch?' Trixie thought of all the cats in the house. Weren't cats witches' familiars?

'Not really a witch; she's an animist. All objects have souls.'

Trixie sat thinking. The old woman hadn't frightened her. What had terrified the living daylights out of Trixie was that she understood the woman's warning.

She shook away her thoughts and turned to Mark.

'I really do want to leave it a while before I meet your family,' she said.

'We don't have to formally meet them to get married, you know.'

Trixie sat forward in the front of the car. 'Marry? Who said anything about marriage?'

Mark leaned towards her and stroked her hair. 'You can't fight it. It will happen.'

Chapter Twenty-Four

'So you enjoyed yourself out with Mark Barr?'

'Nothing gets past you, does it, Joan?' Trixie stifled a yawn. Joan realised she was dead on her feet after an afternoon gig at the Green Dragon in Gosport. Joan hoped her tiredness wasn't going to affect the outcome of Jem's proposed chat with Sid, who was sprawled in front of the television watching *Coronation Street*. Joan knew he liked Elsie Tanner. Joan also knew Trixie had a right to be tired. She'd had three shows in as many days and Joan hadn't had time to talk to her since her outing with Mark. Joan had also, just quite by accident, found out about the deaths of the two band members, Eddie and Mo. Trixie had refused to go to the funerals, saying she didn't want to be a hypocrite. She blamed Eddie for Eva's death. She also knew that, should she appear at the church, it might cause disruptions with fans asking for her autograph.

Trixie answered the front door and Jem's voice floated to Joan, 'He can hardly say he's too busy to talk, can he?'

Earlier Sid had shown Joan a piece in the paper about a woman who'd been found battered to death near some dustbins in Southampton. 'Poor bitch,' he'd said, appalled. Joan thought it was funny he should comment on a newspaper article. He didn't usually do things like that. Sid had come back from Southampton, hadn't he? Did he know that woman? Were the police looking for him?

Jem took off his coat and put it over the back of a chair. He refused a drink.

'Let's get down to brass tacks, shall we? When you took Teddy down to the ferry did you know where he was going, Sid?'

'Sure,' said Sid, his eyes still on the television. Trixie got up and switched it off, ignoring the hard look he gave her. 'He was going to a farm on the coast.'

'You had proof of that?'

'As much proof as anyone had in those days of evacuees going off to the Isle of Wight. I gave Joan's sister, your mother,' he nodded towards Trixie, 'the address.'

Joan nodded, confirming his words.

'The address was false,' Jem said.

'I can't be held responsible for that,' he said lazily.

'I don't know, Sid, but it seems to me your answers are just a little bit contrived.'

'Really? Well, think about the facts. The kid, your brother,' he emphasised to Trixie, 'had killed his father, accidentally, so it was claimed.' Trixie could hardly keep her temper. Joan could see it in her face that she was likely to boil over any minute. 'Anyway,' Sid continued, 'I got the boy away from here because it was too dangerous for him to stay. If now he stays away because he has a life of his own, you reckon I got anything to do with that?'

Sid was waiting for someone to challenge him.

He didn't have long to wait. Jem sprang forward. 'You lying bastard.'

Trixie managed to restrain him just as Joan shouted, 'It's the truth!'

Taken aback, Trixie looked at Joan. 'He's telling the truth,' Joan repeated to them all. Then she stared at Sid and thought of how much she loved him, had loved him, would always love him.

And she thought about the small diary in her drawer, found the day she and Trixie were clearing out the shed. The diary Sid never knew she had. In the book was an address for Teddy, different from the one given to Bess. By the side of the address was the amount of money Sid O'Hara had been paid to deliver the boy. The small book held so many secrets – not that Joan had read it properly; she wasn't much of a one for reading.

Many years had passed since Teddy had been sold. But surely by now he had his freedom? And if that was so, why hadn't he got in touch with Trixie? She wasn't hard to find, not with her name in the papers and on posters advertising her gigs. So, Joan reasoned, if Teddy hadn't got in touch with Trixie it was because he couldn't or didn't want to. *And that wasn't her Sid's fault, was it?*

No good would come of her dredging up the past and showing that little book to anyone. Not when Sid had turned over a new leaf and she and him were looking forward to a bright new future together.

Sid was her love, her life, her happiness. Convinced she was right, Joan said, 'I'm making a pot of tea, who wants a cup?'

Jem looked down at her. Then he took off his coat and slipped it around her shoulders. It was chilly standing on the concrete path that divided the prefabs and led to the road.

'That was a waste of time,' he said.

'Joan seemed to think he was telling the truth, but I don't,' said Trixie. 'I won't give up searching for him. Joan loves that bastard. He could tell her the moon was made of green cheese and she'd believe him. I don't blame her. Love makes us do funny things.'

He looked at her and began to smile. 'So you've

finally realised that, have you?'

Trixie leaned towards him. 'You are a sod. You know I care for you, but I'm not ready to settle down.'

'Jesus, Trixie.' He was blushing! Actually blushing. 'When will you be ready for marriage? You know I love you.'

Trixie traced her fingers over his chest. 'If it hadn't been for Sid O'Hara, I daresay things would be different.'

'He hasn't tried...' It was as if the mention of his name stirred things up again.

'No, he keeps away from me and that's the way I like it.'

'He doesn't keep far enough away from you that he refuses to take money from Joan to spend gambling and on women.'

'Women?'

'Oh, for God's sake don't say anything to Joan – it'll break her heart – but he was spotted in town–'

'Stop! I don't want to hear it.' Trixie knew they were on dangerous ground here.

'There is something you can tell Joan if she hasn't already heard. A man lost a foot the other day walking out near the golf course. He was looking for a ball in the long grass on the other side of Fort Gilkicker. Dmitri told me about it. The poor bloke trod on a mine. Just because the war's over doesn't mean it's safe out there. Dmitri said they are clearing the land but it's not something that can be hurried. And I'm telling you because I know Joan likes to walk along the shore there. Oh, I also heard from Dmitri you were out with Mark what's-his-name. Did you have a good time?'

'His name is Mark Barr, as well you know.' Jem was staring at her. 'Yes, I had a *nice* time.'

'How do you feel about him?'

'The same as the last time you asked me: he's a child.'

But as the words left her mouth, Trixie wasn't so sure it was true.

Mark Barr was being drafted to Hong Kong.

'You jammy bastard,' said Smudger Smith, throwing a pillow at him.

'You could throw something at Eli; he's got a posting there as well.' Mark had dodged, picked up the pillow and Smudger was being killed with it.

'Just think about all them luscious women,' said Eli.

'They'll still put bromide in the tea,' said Smudger. 'Always trying to lower our sex drives.'

'Don't worry, one look at our uniforms and the girls'll fall at our feet,' Eli said.

'I heard there was this girl at Kai Tek who was obsessed with RAF blokes, couldn't get enough of 'em. She'd fuck anything in a blue uniform, she would.' Smudger's eyes were sparkling. 'The men used to smuggle her in at weekends and she'd move from bed to bed in the billet like she was on a conveyer belt. Then she got pregnant and she still came in. No one really knew who the father was. Anyway when she had the kiddie, everyone chipped in with money an' stuff to keep it. As far as I know, the boy's three and he's still got more dads than any other kiddie!'

Mark didn't think it was funny but he laughed because it was expected of him.

'I heard you got to be careful of the brothels out there – women are poxed up to the eyeballs.'

'So, you're refusing a plum posting?' Eli asked.

'On yer bike, mate, on yer bike!' said Mark and hit him full on with the pillow.

'I'm going to ask Trixie to marry me when I come home on leave.'

In the vast kitchen of The Incredible Edible the busy chefs were preparing for the evening meal.

'You hardly know the woman.' His father's face was red with the heat, showing up the blue veins on his nose, caused by drink. He slammed down the menu card on the chopping board. A startled washer-up looked over and then quickly looked away. 'Why don't you set her up in a nice little flat or house somewhere? Bit drastic, eh, marriage?'

Sometimes Mark barely understood his father.

'Whether you like it or not, I'll marry her.' The noise in the kitchen drowned his words.

'Does she know?'

Mark shook his head. His father shrugged. 'You're of age,' he said. 'It doesn't mean your mother and I will agree about your choice. I hope you're not going to do anything silly like leave the Air Force?'

Mark shook his head. He was looking forward to Hong Kong and Kai Tek. 'Wouldn't dream of it.'

He thought his news had gone down well.

Mark missed the balmy air of Hong Kong. He parked his car near the top of Bemister's Lane and walked along the cobbles to the market. A market was a market in any country, except he was used to street vendors selling fried insects and meat and fish of an indeterminable nature that smelled quite delicious and tasted like nectar.

But it was good to be back in Gosport, watching the vendors in the High Street. Smells attacked his senses: fish and flowers, cakes and curtain material and the vibrant colours of the armful of flowers that he'd bought gave him great satisfaction. They were to be a surprise for Trixie.

Back at the car they filled the space behind the two seats, giving off a subtle perfume. He patted the small box hidden in his breast pocket. It wouldn't do to lose the ring he had bought for her. He went in search of Trixie.

She was performing at a special party for an elderly lady who had a birthday today.

For once Trixie was alone, except for her pianist. Chatting to the staff at the Green Dragon he discovered the pub manager had set up the equipment for her and the show had gone well. Jem, who usually attended small functions with her, so he was told, was at Titchfield finalising a strawberry deal with other growers from the area. The pianist had left earlier.

Trixie nearly bumped into Mark as she opened the heavy door to leave the building. 'Hello!' she said. 'This is a surprise. I thought you were still abroad. I never expected to see you today.'

'Do you have to go straight home?' He took her case and make-up bag. She seemed pleased to see him. He noticed the shadows beneath her eyes. She seemed quiet and withdrawn, not at all her usual bubbly self. He led her towards the car and opened the door.

'Oh, Mark!'

'For you, madame,' he gushed.

One look at the flowers and she swung round on tiptoe to kiss him on the cheek.

'It's mademoiselle; I'm not married,' she corrected.

'I hope to change all that,' he said. Her quizzical smile gave him hope. He was glad the flowers had brought a smile to her face – he so wanted to please her. But would she say yes, when he asked her to marry him?

Mark thought about the man who'd always been there for her, Jem. How would he take it if Trixie consented to be his wife? After all, they'd been friends for years. And Mark was sure that's all they'd been, friends. If Jem genuinely wanted Trixie to be happy he wouldn't stand in her way.

In Hong Kong Mark was on a special training mission. All he had been told was that as the base at Kai Tek housed flying boats as well as jets, his training was important and secret. The RAF was never very forthcoming where information was concerned. So far the forces had been good to him and for him.

And he'd been extremely lucky to have found a woman like Trixie.

Now he needed to take her somewhere quiet and propose. And he knew just the place. France.

'Do you fancy coming away with me for a few days?'

'Where?'

'France.'

Her answer was a squeal of excitement. He guessed it meant she'd agreed! He'd make the weekend perfect so they'd always remember it.

She began to chatter away about the show, about the elderly woman and how excited she'd been to find Trixie singing her favourite songs that reminded her of her youth.

Then he felt her stiffen beside him.

'Stop the car!' It was a command, not a request. Nevertheless he pulled over and without another word she opened the door and fled into the crowded street, leaving only her perfume on the air. He caught a glimpse of her face and it was set white as wax.

Trixie was sure it was Rosa, the barmaid from Nelson's – the public house in Portsmouth where her father used to drink all those years ago just along the road from where they used to live.

Okay, it was years since she had seen the woman or even spoken to her, but she had to find out if she knew anything at all about Teddy.

Trixie ran through the crowded High Street. Shoppers slid to one side to allow her to pass and her eyes scoured the stalls, the pavements, the people. Then she saw her gazing into the window of Bishop's, the shoe shop.

Breathlessly Trixie touched her arm. The woman turned. She seemed hardly to have changed at all. The same blonde hair, falling in wisps around her plump face.

'Rosa?' Her eyes were blank until realisation

dawned and she clasped Trixie to her heavy bosom.

'How are you, my love? My, you do look bonny.'

'So do you!' Trixie was half laughing, half crying. Rosa had always been kind to her and she was remembering those kindnesses now.

'You've grown, Trixie. Why, your dad was only talking about you last–'

Trixie stepped away from her. It was as if the High Street shoppers had magically gone quiet and the town had turned into a dream sequence.

'Did you say, my dad?' Surely Trixie must have misheard Rosa.

'Yes, he was only saying the other night, that you had certainly made a success of your life.'

'I don't understand.' The pavement was beginning to sway beneath her feet.

'Your dad was thinking back to the war when he came into Nelson's one night with a terrible hangover. Said he'd found himself out all night, but when he got back to the house there wasn't no sign of you. He had a cut on his head the size of Cheddar Gorge.' Rosa paused and looked into Trixie's eyes, 'You all right?'

Trixie nodded.

'I took the poor bugger in.'

Here she stopped again, and looked a little sheepish. Trixie knew exactly what she meant by those words. Rosa had always had a soft spot for her dad. 'He had no idea what had happened.'

Suddenly, Trixie wanted to run, to think, especially to think about the conversation with this woman that had made a mockery of her life and Teddy's life.

Trixie realised Rosa knew nothing of Teddy. If she had, she would have let it slip.

'I must go.'

She ran then, back through the crowds and into Bemister's Lane, where she found Mark parked and waiting.

'What's the matter?'

'Nothing. I'm fine. I just need to be home.' More than anything she wanted Jem. But he was at Titchfield.

When the car reached the prefabs, Trixie tumbled out. 'I'll explain later.' Only there wasn't anything she wanted to explain to Mark. It was Jem she needed.

Finally she managed to fit her key into the lock and open the front door. Sid stood in the living room. His braces were hanging about his waist and he had no slippers or socks on. Trixie ran for the safety of her bedroom.

'You all right? Can I do anything?' he called.

'You've done enough,' she spat and slammed the door, locking it. Then she climbed into bed fully dressed.

Chapter Twenty-Five

The ferocious banging on Jem's kitchen door made him lose concentration. The figures he was adding up were abandoned and the notebook slammed shut. He put a smile he didn't particularly feel on his face before opening the door, then dropped it when he saw Joan's worried expression.

'It's Trixie. She's in her bedroom with the door locked and I can't get her to come out.'

'Oh, my God, it's not anything to do with Sid, is it?' Jem'd not long come back from a meeting at Titchfield that hadn't worked out as well for him as he'd hoped, so he was ready for Sid if the bugger had been up to his old tricks again.

'He's not to blame for everything.' Joan gave him a haughty look and stalked off down the garden path towards the road. He could feel her anger lingering in the air. 'Though he thinks he is. He's pushed off in a mood.'

Jem caught her up at the roadside. 'Didn't Trixie go to Gosport to sing at a party?' She didn't immediately answer but stomped along the paving stone path through the prefabs towards number nineteen.

'Whatever's knocked her over the edge has happened since then.' Joan put the key in the lock of the door.

He went straight in and tried the bedroom door. It was as Joan had said: Trixie's bedroom door was locked.

'Let me in, Trixie.'

After a while Trixie said dramatically, 'I want to die.'

'You can't do that – Joan can't afford a wreath,' said Jem. He was trying for a little light relief. Joan stifled a giggle. 'Now open this bloody door.' He heard Trixie laugh and he breathed more easily.

The bolt went back. She stood there, small, her eyes red with crying, then she went to the bed and climbed back in.

341

Jem went and sat down on the side of the bed and stroked her hair. 'Want to talk about it?' he asked.

'It's my dad,' she said. 'Teddy never killed him.'

Jem frowned. 'What do you mean?' he asked. Joan hovered in the doorway, waiting to find out what was happening. The air was charged with electricity.

'It means Dad's alive. We've been living a lie for years, me, Mum and Teddy.'

'How do you know this?' Joan came in and stood next to Jem. Her face was white, as though all the blood had been drained from it.

'I met the woman he's been living with. Rosa from Nelson's.'

Jem's heart had almost ceased beating. Could it be true that her father *was* still alive? Stunned, he sat quietly thinking, then he said, 'But this is good. It means your brother can't be tried for murder.'

'It means we ran away from Portsmouth for nothing and I blame myself for losing Teddy.'

Trixie was crying. If she didn't snap out of this, she'd make herself ill again, thought Jem. She was always poised on the edge, was Trixie. If there was any truth in this revelation then they had to continue looking for Teddy. If he didn't already know the true facts, then he must be told at once.

'Tell you what,' he said. 'Why don't we go over to the island on Sunday and see if we can find him.'

'I can't, I'm going away for the weekend with Mark.'

The silence could be cut with a knife. 'And

you'd rather go with Mark?' Jem couldn't understand her reasoning. Her one aim in life had been to find her brother and now she was making out a young man she'd not long known was more important. This could only mean one thing. She loved Mark.

'To France, yes.' She dabbed at her eyes with a corner of the sheet. 'Besides, we know Teddy's not on the island.'

'Then you must do whatever you think is best,' he said. The one thing he didn't want was for her to have a repeat of the breakdown that she'd suffered early on in their relationship. He could see the news had thrown her completely. But he also loved her so much all he wanted was her happiness and wellbeing. What if she didn't know what she was doing and her reasoning was off kilter? He gave her a long cool look, got up and went out of the bedroom.

'Joan!' She came out into the kitchen to join him. 'Why don't you make Trixie a nice cup of tea? She could do with a bit of coddling and I'm sure she's longing to talk to you.'

He knew he was leaving Joan to sort things out, but he had to get away, back to his own house. Trixie didn't realise how much he was hurting inside. Of course he was jealous that she wanted to go off with Mark. Well, he'd go back home and get on with some work, that's if he could concentrate. Damn woman!

'I'm off then, love. Don't wait up for me.'

Joan, in the kitchen, stirred the tea for Trixie but didn't shout goodbye to Sid. She heard the door close behind him and breathed a sigh of relief. They'd sat together watching the television, he quite content, smoking and drinking a few bottles of beer.

Inside she was seething, waiting for him to explain himself, but he'd merely sat, every so often grinning at her like he was the cat that'd got the cream. She hadn't told him about Trixie meeting Rosa. He hadn't asked why Trixie was still in bed.

Trixie was huddled up in the covers. Joan put the mug on the bedside table and pulled a chair up so she could sit with her.

'You've got to pull yourself through this, Trixie. We all have lives that deal us bloody great blows occasionally. Think of all you've accomplished since you've lived here with me in this prefab.' She put her hand on Trixie's hair and smoothed its softness. 'You've got a career. You're loved and you have friends. Some people don't even get a sniff of those luxuries.'

Trixie sat up and leaned into Joan's arms. 'But I should have waited. All those years ago I should have waited until me dad came round. We'd still be living in Portsmouth and Teddy would be with me.'

'Would he though? How do you know your dad wouldn't have kicked ten bales of shit out of him for wounding him? You'd have no singing career. And I shudder to think of the life Bess would have had, had she gone on living, if you hadn't had the strength to get away from that bastard.'

'But I should have known better.'

'*You was a kid!* For Christ's sake, you acted far beyond your years in getting away from the bully.

344

One day, quite out of the blue, you're going to discover what's become of Teddy.'

'Do you really think so?' Trixie wiped her hand across her tear-stained face.

'Not think, I know so.' Joan leaned across and lifted the mug and pressed it into Trixie's hands. 'Drink this; you'll feel better. A cuppa always works wonders.'

There was silence in the room while Trixie sipped, then Joan said, 'He's playing up again.'

'Who? Sid?'

Joan nodded, Trixie looked so sad for her.

'He promised if I took him back he wouldn't so much as speak to another woman. Well, he's been takin' shopping in to that young bit of stuff as lives in Eva's prefab.'

'Perhaps he's just being neighbourly.'

'Neighbourly my arse. Sid don't do nothin' unless there's something in it for him.'

'Don't be upset about a bit of gossip.' Trixie downed the last of her tea. She'd got a bit of colour in her face now, thought Joan. She took the mug off her and set it on the bedside table, then went and stood looking out of the window at the weed-filled garden. It was a relief to talk to Trixie, even though Joan knew she shouldn't be bothering her with more misery. But perhaps thinking about someone else's problems might help to take her mind off her own. She took a deep breath and began talking.

'When the pubs turned out and he didn't come home I went down and peeked in her window. You know what these places are like if you don't draw the curtains; it's like livin' in a bleedin' goldfish bowl.'

'Was he there?'

'Oh, yes, looking like he owned the place, sprawled on the sofa with her kiddie lolling all over him.'

'But he's old, Joan. And she's what, half his age? What's a young piece want with him?'

When Sid was dressed up, he was still quite presentable and his cheeky charm? Well, he could lay it on with a trowel when he wanted to, thought Joan. Though he'd stopped trying to impress her.

'If you ain't got no money and an' old man comes along giving you a few bob, are you goin' to turn him away?' Tears sprang to Joan's eyes. She hadn't meant to cry. 'It hurts me, Trixie. It bloody hurts me.'

Joan thought of all she'd given up to take Sid back. Her job at the pub, and the laughs with the customers. And she missed the cheery banter with Jack, who was a king amongst men. Joan could feel herself sliding down into a pit of filth with Sid. Look at how she'd hidden the things about Teddy that had been written in that little book. Not to mention the other terrible secret gnawing at her conscience. It was all to save Sid's skin.

Trixie had got out of bed and was tying the belt of her dressing-gown around her.

'Let's go in the kitchen and I'll make the tea this time.' She led Joan into the kitchen and started busying herself with the kettle.

Sometimes, Joan thought, they bloody lived on cups of tea!

'Have you tackled Sid about it?'

'What's the point? He'd lie and wriggle out of

346

it.' Joan stared at Trixie. 'There's something else bothering me – besides Sid, that is. This Mark bloke, do you love him?'

'He makes me laugh. Makes me feel young, and that's what I need right now. I feel as though I know everything about him, which is silly, as it's not possible. He keeps on about marriage. I'm being swept along like a bit of driftwood on the waves and I can't quite work out what the right thing to do is, as my head's in a permanent daze. As to loving him, I've watched you loving Sid and sometimes I know you're so unhappy. If that's what loving someone does, I don't want to find out. I feel unhappy enough as it is. I wish I knew what had really happened to my brother.'

Joan stared at Trixie. Trixie had never once let her down. Maybe she could help her find Teddy. That would make Trixie well and happy again.

Mark left Chartres and headed towards Orléans. He was a good driver and was at ease with the French roads.

'We turn off at Vierzon, Trixie,' he said. 'Bruniquel is about six hours away. We'll stop for coffee if you want.'

Trixie shook her head as Mark turned towards her. He was an extremely good-looking man, she thought. He lacked the serious qualities that Jem had and was more 'one of the lads' than Jem had ever been. But he was funny and tactile. She'd had to get used to his hand searching for hers as they strolled down the street, and the way when they met he threw his arms around her, holding her as though he didn't want to let her escape from him.

'It's lovely watching the tiny villages and the green fields as we pass through them,' she said. Her eyes lit on a field full of blue flowers. 'What are they?'

'Flax,' he said. Their scent wafted towards her and surrounded her in the two-seater car. 'This flat countryside is ideal for crops.'

She and Mark had chatted about inconsequential things. She wondered if she should tell him about meeting Rosa and how Rosa's news had weighed so heavily on her mind that she could barely function properly.

But wouldn't the explanation of her attitude cause him to ask questions? Then she'd feel pressured to unfold the story of her life to Mark. She didn't want to do that, did she? Damn, it was all so confusing.

She felt mean at refusing Jem's offer to look again for Teddy. Whatever must he think of her? But it wasn't so much to be with Mark that she'd come to France. More that she wanted to get away from Gosport, to get away from thinking about her father being alive. But that was impossible, wasn't it? Trixie was all mixed up and she knew it.

She gazed at the scenery, its beauty stretching for miles. She dozed.

As Mark drove through a small, quiet village she saw a large turreted house in spacious grounds and was surprised when Mark passed through the open iron gates. He drove along the pebbled road to pull up at the bottom of a steep flight of steps that led to the front door. He stopped and came around to her side to open the door for her.

'When you said, "cottage in the country" I didn't

expect a mansion,' Trixie said. Before she'd finished speaking the door had opened and a middle-aged woman stood at the top of the steps waiting to welcome them.

'Meet the housekeeper – Mrs Jennings. She's English; her husband looks after the grounds.' The woman, dressed in a grey skirt and long grey cardigan, smiled warmly at her.

'Hello,' Trixie said nervously. She was beginning to see there was a great rift between her life and Mark's life. 'Is this your place?' She turned to Mark.

'My paternal gran left it to me.'

The hall was chandeliered and had a marble floor so shiny it reminded her of a mirror. Marble busts on plinths were glistening as though they'd been polished frequently. Surely with a place this size there was more staff than just a housekeeper, thought Trixie.

After Trixie had been shown to her room – a red velvet-curtained bedchamber at the back of the house overlooking the lawned gardens – she freshened up in the en suite bathroom and then went in search of Mark.

Her first visit was to the sitting room where a fire burned brightly. Already the light had faded from the sky. It had been an early start. The morning seemed such a long time ago, and she was tired. Trixie sat down on a gold satin-fringed chair that probably cost more, she thought, than all the furniture in Joan's prefab put together. A chandelier glittered from the high ceiling, its drops creating tiny rainbows on the cream wallpaper.

Mark came in from the garden. 'Oh, here you

are. Come and see what I've arranged for you outside.'

He had changed into a dark suit and he looked just a little unsure of himself. He took her hand and led her outside. She saw champagne in a cooler on the wooden table, and tiny candles in glass holders covering every available surface like small spears of glittering light in the inky darkness. Jasmine and other scented flowers gave her a light-headed feeling of unreality.

He made her sit down on one of only two chairs set at the table, then he took from his pocket a small box and opened it.

Sparkling as brightly as the candlelight was the most beautiful ring Trixie had ever seen. A wide band of white gold embedded with white diamonds.

'Oh, it's lovely,' she cried. He didn't wait for her to speak but picked up her hand and slipped the ring on her finger.

'I want you to marry me,' Mark said.

Marrying Mark would change her life. If she refused him, she would lose him, just as Teddy was lost to her. And Mark was something different. Trixie felt as though she had known him in another life.

And then he was kissing her, the taste of his lips an aphrodisiac. He kissed her nose, her eyes, her mouth, his lips as light as an angel's touch.

Trixie felt her body loosen. Pleasure filled her as he gently began pulling away her clothing, dropping first one garment then another on to the ground. She felt the shift in his mood as his clothes too, were released and cushions were thrown to the grass and she was lowered to lie on them.

And then she froze.

Sid's fingers were groping at her. Sid's tongue was licking at that special place at the base of her throat.

Trixie rolled away, grabbed at her clothes and amidst tears, said, 'I'm sorry.'

Thoughts of Jem entered her mind, and she pushed them out of her head, the feeling of guilt too strong for her even to stay near this man who'd brought back such strong memories of Sid O'Hara and his filthy, filthy invasion of her body.

She pulled her clothes about her and scrambled up and ran, stumbling, across the grass. Trixie only once looked back at Mark and at the anguished look on his face, incomprehension in his eyes.

Trixie ran through the kitchen and up the stairs to her bedroom. Throwing herself on the bed, she cried as though her heart would break. Would she never be free of Sid and his legacy? Why couldn't she give herself to this man who evoked such strong feelings in her? And why was it always Jem's face that seemed to imprint itself whenever she looked upon a man as a possible lover?

After a while, a single knock on the door stopped her tears. She realised she was being overly dramatic now and needed to apologise to Mark, who must be feeling as though he was some kind of pariah. She got up and opened the door to find the housekeeper standing with a small tray, upon which was a single cup of tea and a cut-glass vase complete with a red rose.

'I've been asked to tell you to come down to the drawing room.' The woman stepped inside the bedroom and set the tray down next to the bed. 'I had a feeling you'd prefer a proper cup of tea, not the scented variety.' Trixie gave her a watery smile and nodded a thank you. Quietly, the woman left.

Trixie sipped the tea. It was exactly how she liked it, strong and bracing. Going into the bathroom she tidied herself then went downstairs. Apologising would be simple. Explaining about the rape, which would then involve telling Mark about her breakdown, and her fear of men, would be harder.

Already her head was swimming, her thoughts in turmoil as she walked into the drawing room.

'You don't need to say anything.' Mark had risen from the long velvet sofa to greet her. 'It's my fault for pushing you. I should have realised that your career, thrust on you at such an early age, meant you've not had time for serious involvements with men.'

He put his arm around her shoulder and led her to the sofa.

'But–'

'It's all right. I don't usually have a girl run naked from me.' He tipped her chin so he could look into her eyes. 'It makes a change from the women who have nothing on their minds except the pound signs because they've found out my family's quite well off. I've never met a woman like you,' he added. Then, 'Are you all right?'

Trixie sat down in the plush depths. No, she wasn't all right. Mark was a sweet man, understanding and kind. But he was ready to brush her behaviour under the carpet and out of sight as though it didn't matter. And, if she was to have a happy marriage with him it meant sharing secrets. Much as she didn't want to tell him about her past she knew she owed it to him. Trixie was glad she was sitting down; she felt most peculiar. Rather like she was on the outside looking in at a film and yet she was the main character.

'I make my own money.'

'That, too, makes you unique,' he said, interrupting her. 'Look, I know I'm younger than you but I can take a knock back once in a while. And if you want to wait until our wedding night,' his eyes searched hers, 'it's fine. It'll be a new beginning for both of us.' He took one of her hands in his. 'I can wait, Trixie,' he said.

'But it's not–' Trixie found her lips covered by Mark's fingers.

'Shhh! You don't have to explain. Let's forget about it. We'll go in to eat,' he said.

In the dining room, the table was set for the two of them. Candles flared in glass containers and a centrepiece of roses dominated the table.

Trixie sat facing Mark. She'd barely tasted the soup. Now the meat was choking her. It was like chewing on cardboard, she thought, even though she could see the meal of beef and young fresh vegetables was temptingly and beautifully cooked.

Every time she tried to explain to Mark why she couldn't bear to think about his hands on her flesh, it was as though the very words themselves grew large in her mouth and threatened to fall out in an unhindered, insensible mess. And all the time Mark was talking about his mother and the wedding.

353

'I'll plan everything darling. You won't have to worry about a thing. Mother'll love to help. Mothers always have a way of forgiving when there's a wedding to be planned.'

At last, after refusing dessert, Trixie got up from the table of what she felt had been the meal from hell. Did people really still live like this? She looked around at the highly polished antique furniture and at Mark's smiling face. She was being suffocated by kindness. She couldn't think straight. And then, horror of horrors, she felt tears prickle at her eyelids. In a tiny voice she asked, 'May I go to bed?'

She didn't wait for an answer but walked swiftly out of the room and up the stairs again to the haven of her bedroom. Once inside she shut the door and leaned against it and allowed the tears to fall.

What was the matter with her? All she needed to do was to tell him she'd been raped by her uncle and that it had traumatised her so much she was terrified of another man's touch. Inside her head it was so simple; all she had to do was speak. But she couldn't. And then suddenly she felt so lonely. She wished Jem were there, with her.

After a while the tears gave way to a melody she'd sung as a child, and then she slept.

Trixie sat in bed eating breakfast off a tray. Another lone rosebud stood in a tall cut-glass vase. Mark was sitting on the side of the bed and talking about the wedding. Trixie wondered why she didn't feel excited. Still, Mark showed enough happiness for the both of them.

354

'St Mary's Church at Alverstoke, I think. After-wards I'll take you to a pretty little hotel in the country where we can be alone before I leave for Hong Kong. Wouldn't it be great if you could come with me? I must look into the availability of married quarters.'

Chapter Twenty-Six

Trixie knew she had to tell Jem before he heard the news of her wedding elsewhere.

He was cutting the grass in the orchard of the small house at the back of his home. He left the mower and walked across to meet her, a smile lighting up his face. Taking her by the elbow, he guided her into the kitchen of the house. Trixie admired the light, airy room.

'I've never been inside here before,' she said, looking at all the white kitchen paraphernalia.

'Not many people have. You know how Grandad feels about this place. He'd sooner keep it empty than have someone living here who didn't under-stand about his feelings and what this house means to him.' He pulled out a kitchen chair that squeaked on the stone floor and she sat down at the table. 'It's good to see you, but you look agi-tated. What's the matter?'

'Mark's asked me to marry him.'

There, she thought. It was better that she came straight out with it. But if she could have bitten her tongue off for the pain she could see her words had caused, she would have. He turned away.

'Is it what you want?'

'Seems to be.'

The silence went on for ever, until he walked to the window and began fiddling with the fitting to the blinds.

'Why are you telling me?' he snapped, turning and confronting her. There was indifference on his face that a moment ago held the tan of the sun and was now white and wax-like.

Now she was confused. Ever since Mark had been talking about the wedding and the arrangements Trixie had been worrying about how Jem would take it. Now it seemed as if he didn't care.

'What... What do you mean?'

'Stop being stupid, Trixie. If you've said you'll marry the bloke, what d'you want from me?'

Actually, Trixie didn't remember saying she'd marry Mark, but everything had happened so fast. And she didn't like it that Jem was angry with her. Her heart began thumping against her ribs and she felt as though this whole scenario wasn't really taking place now, but was a sequence in a dream. She pinched the flesh at her thigh to make sure she really was awake. 'Congratulations might be nice.' Trixie's tongue began to run away with her. 'The wedding is the week after next at St Mary's, Alverstoke.' She got up and turned to walk away, angry now because he hadn't made it easy for her to tell him. He grabbed her arm and swung her around to face him.

'Are *you* happy about this?' he demanded. She'd never seen Jem as cross as this before.

'Yes.'

He stood looking down at her, unblinking, as though he was thinking what to do next. Then he let go of her arm and tried a half-hearted smile that didn't reach his eyes.

'I want you to be happy. That's all I've ever wanted, Trixie. And I'm happy that after what happened with Sid you've found someone you feel able to trust yourself to love.' He looked away, then his gaze returned to her. 'I only wish it could have been me.'

And Trixie felt like crying, like she shouldn't have hurt him, because without a doubt he was hurt. He couldn't conceal his pain. Her head was buzzing. What if he wouldn't come to the church? What if she'd upset him so much he refused to come to her wedding?

'You will be at the church?'

'I'll be there.' His voice was filled with weariness. He sighed and after a while he put out his hand, and his fingers traced down her cheek with a feather-like touch.

Trixie's satin shift dress skimmed her hips and bust, the oyster colour exactly matching her heeled pumps. Even Joan had had to admit that Mark's mother, Belle, had exquisite taste. A short veil held in place by a tiny pearl tiara over her bouffant hair made Trixie look both innocent and demure.

She'd arrived much too early; she blamed it on her habit of being early for gigs, in case anything went wrong. She had decided to wait in the darkened area between the oak front door of the church and the inner door. Here she could see but not be seen.

The air between Mark's parents and her was for some reason cool, but she'd refused to let any sort of rift spoil the day. And though she had set eyes on Jem only once since the day in the small house, she had been bright and cheerful with him and he had been cordial to her.

She knew very few of the people who had been invited to see her and Mark married. But she had to agree Belle had made a grand job of decorating the foliage-bedecked church. Belle had also planned the service and the forthcoming reception down to the finest detail. Mark seemed happy about this and since no one had asked her opinion on any matter at all, Trixie decided it would be best if she simply went along with all the arrangements.

'It's strange just turning up at my own wedding,' she confessed to Joan who looked a treat in a silky blue outfit with a matching blue hat and veil. Joan had allowed Trixie to make up her face and it had taken years off Joan's true age. Nevertheless, instead of being happy, Joan was on edge and with a permanent frown on her face. Whenever Trixie spoke to her she either barked back at her or ignored her altogether. Trixie tried to remember if she'd done something to upset her but she didn't think so.

Trixie had refused to be 'given away'.

Belle had remonstrated with her but Trixie said, 'I've been earning my own living since I was fifteen and I won't be *given* to anyone.'

Instead she requested that Joan accompany her down the aisle and stand with her. Joan seemed pleased by this turn of events. Or was until today, when the silly woman decided to be the grumpiest woman alive.

A choir straddled both sides of the aisles, though the hymns that had been chosen meant nothing to her.

Sid, sitting in the front row near Jem, looked dapper in a dark suit. But it was Jem who caught her eye, dressed in a new suit with a single cream rosebud in his buttonhole. He looked stiff and unyielding, even as now when he leaned across to say something to Grandad.

Her heart went out to Jem. And for a single moment she remembered the night in Greece when she was trying to hold herself together and had found such comfort in climbing into bed beside him, feeling safe as his arms encircled her. But that was then and this was now and today she was marrying a sweet boy who adored her and had told her he was willing to wait for as long as it took for her to love him physically.

And that would be never. If she couldn't make love with Jem, how on earth could she ever believe she could find happiness with Mark?

In the row behind, Marie and Dmitri were fighting a losing battle to keep their brood under control and Trixie smiled as Dmitri slipped the fingers of one hand to the back of Marie's neck and caressed the fine hairs there. Not only a sign of love but one of passion. His other hand was wrapped around the white knitted bundle inside which his latest child, a little girl, slept peacefully.

Mark stood talking quietly to his father. It was difficult for Trixie to imagine she would spend the rest of her life with him. Whether she wanted to or not it was too late now to do anything about it.

Again her eyes sought Jem. As if on cue he looked at her. Why, oh, why wasn't she marrying him? How did she get into this mess?

The sadness in his eyes was too much for her to bear, so she looked quickly away.

Eventually the church was full to bursting point, the vicar was waiting and the doors of St Mary's were closed.

Trixie took a deep breath and squeezed Joan's hand. 'I can't go through with this,' she said, exactly at the same time as Joan whispered, 'I love you, you do know that, don't you?' Trixie leaned across and kissed her on her cheek. It was a strange thing for her aunt to say, but Trixie put it down to nerves and with her arm tucked in Joan's began walking down the aisle to the sound of the organ music.

'I wish Teddy could have been here,' Trixie whispered. It seemed as though Joan hadn't heard her before so she said, more loudly this time, 'It's not right that Teddy isn't here.'

When Trixie reached Mark he smiled at her.

Jem looked away from Trixie. How was he supposed to feel happy for her when he hated every moment of being here and watching this farce? He was sure the news that her father was still alive had sent her into a downward spiral. But, on the other hand, if she truly loved Mark, all he could do would be to wish her happiness.

The silence, punctuated only by coughs and sneezes, was broken by the vicar explaining his duties, and then the service began. It was like watching a film in which she was the central character, Trixie thought, and why didn't Joan listen when she said she couldn't go through with this wedding? Why was she marrying Mark? If she was going to marry any man it should be Jem.

'Repeat after me,' advised the vicar. Trixie repeated words and listened to Mark and there was no mistaking his happiness. Trixie shook her head. It was all going terribly wrong. Why didn't Jem do something? She could feel his eyes upon her and she stared across first at Grandad's serious face, then at Jem, whose eyes pierced into her heart. He must see I don't want this, she thought.

Then came the vows and Trixie was asked to say, 'I do solemnly declare that I know not of any lawful impediment why—'

Joan stepped forward and in a loud voice said, 'You can't marry Mark Barr.' There was a huge intake of breath, as the congregation, as one, gasped. Then Joan said loudly. 'He's your son!'

At first there was a hush, then Joan shouted again, 'I have the information here.' She waved the small diary high in the air. Then she looked at Sid and said, 'You betrayed me once too often; I'm fed up sticking up for you.' To the congregation she shouted, 'He told this young woman her baby was dead, then he sold that child, Mark.' Again silence reigned as her words were taken in by everyone, then began the shouting. Everyone was talking animatedly at once. Joan's anger boiled over and she flew at Sid, scratching him, tearing at his hair, while he tried to fight her off. 'Bastard, bastard!' she was screeching.

Jem heard Trixie ask Mark, 'Did you know you

were adopted?' He saw the bewildered young man shake his head. Trixie seemed to shrivel as she stepped back and held on to the pew for support. Marie stepped forward to tend to her, just as Jem rushed towards Trixie.

Pandemonium reigned in the church.

Sid, managing to push Joan away, hit out at her and she fell against the stone font, then to the floor. Then he ran along the aisle nearest the wall to the rear of the church. Jem moved too, chasing after him, brushing away the seething congregation as though they didn't exist.

Sid, agile as a cat, jumped the wall leading into Church Road and Jem followed. 'I'll kill the bastard,' Jem cried.

Hot in pursuit was Dmitri. The three men ran through the sleepy Alverstoke village, knocking aside shoppers and tripping across pushchairs and bicycles.

Sid, still ahead, looked back as he ran down Ashburton Road and out onto the bay from an overgrown alley.

'We cannot let him go,' shouted Dmitri, his face red with the effort of running.

Sid, whose age should have slowed him down, was wiry as a cat as he disappeared into the horse field near The Crescent.

'Fuck!' Dmitri skidded to a halt. He put out a hand to stay Jem, and puffing and panting said, 'He has gone into the wired area.'

'What d'you mean?' Jem's eyes raked the bushes and he pushed Dmitri's hands away and made to step forward.

'No! He has gone to the area we have not

cleared of unexploded bombs!'

'I have to catch him. I should have killed the bastard years ago.'

'There he is!'

Jem saw Sid, in the distance, crawl into the undergrowth near the disused Fort Gilkicker. Brambles and thorns tore through Jem's suit trousers as he pushed through the overgrown brambles.

A flash of white knocked Jem to his knees. Dmitri seemed to fly off his feet and tumble next to him on the thorny ground.

Orange, red and blue smoke rose in the air and the noise of the explosion followed. Drifts of grey obscured the blue of the sky, then absolute silence followed.

Jem rolled away from Dmitri. 'You all right, mate?'

Dmitri opened his eyes and stared at Jem. He blinked. 'I think I have been better,' he said. 'And I'm better than him.'

A large, shallow hole had appeared in the stones near the beach. An object that could only be the remains of Sid lay near.

'What a way to go,' said Dmitri. He wiped a hand across his sweat-stained face. 'Look, go back to the church, and get the police out here. I'll stay until they come and you help Trixie. Though I am sure my Marie's taken charge of her by now. She'll need friends.'

'If you're sure?'

'Go,' said Dmitri. 'Before I change my mind. You need to get this diary as well; the police will be wanting that.'

When he got back to the church the vicar had made tea in the vestry and as Dmitri had prophesied, Marie had taken charge. Her children were playing amongst the gravestones but the vicar simply smiled and said, 'Where else to sort things out but in the house of God?'

Joan had recovered from Sid's blows and had taken it upon herself to guard Trixie from nosy people, not that Trixie was in any state to talk to anyone. She had been crying and was sullenly huddled in a blanket. One look at her blank expression told Jem he needed to get her home as soon as possible.

'Thank you for allowing the bride to stay here,' Jem said.

'She wasn't in any state to go home,' the vicar said.

Jem took Joan to one side and told her about Sid's death. 'We'll get a visit from the police,' he said. 'I reckon that little book you've got will clear up a few mysteries.'

'All this is my fault,' she said. 'I wanted to get back at him for hurting me.'

Jem put his arms around her. 'No, he brought it on himself.'

'Trouble was I really loved that bad bugger.' Joan dabbed at her eyes. She looked thoughtful then said as brightly as she could, 'There's an address where Teddy was sent. I doubt he'd still be there now.' She took the book from her pocket and gave it to him. 'For the police,' she said.

'It's a start,' said Jem, flicking through the pages. 'If there's one thing that will bring Trixie back to her senses it will be to find out where her brother is.' He looked about him. 'I see Mark did a disappearing act.'

'He was sobbing like a baby when his parents took him away. I believe he really cared for Trixie. His parents obviously thought that what had happened years ago when they bought the baby from Sid was all in the past. I doubt they would have been told about his true parentage. It must have been a terrible shock for them as well.'

Jem looked into Joan's eyes. 'But Sid must have known Mark was Trixie's son.'

'He couldn't let on without incriminating himself, could he?' Joan's face hardened. 'He really was a piece of work, wasn't he? And now I've spoiled Trixie's life.'

'Don't blame yourself. You couldn't have let this wedding go on. Trixie'll understand when she comes to her senses.' He looked at Trixie, and at Marie trying to get her to take sips of tea. 'I'm taking her home.' Joan opened her mouth to speak, but Jem hushed her. 'Not to the prefab. No doubt there'll be a few newspaper people sniffing around and that's the last thing she needs. I'm taking her back to my place.' He looked across the room to where Grandad was threading a piece of wool around his fingers, playing cat's cradle with Marie's youngest girl. The new baby was at his feet asleep in a Moses basket. 'It's time that little house was lived in.'

'Won't Grandad mind me being here?'

'He's already said he thinks this is the best place for you. You're going to be looked after by me, and

Dr Dillinger, so we don't have a repetition of ... of...'

'You can say it, Jem. It's an illness, not a dirty word. I had a breakdown and I'm certainly not in command of my senses now, am I?'

He shook his head.

Trixie looked around the chintz-covered bedroom. Everything looked clean and welcoming. The iron bedstead with the brass scrolls was topped with a thick patchwork quilt that looked so inviting Trixie wanted to climb inside the bed and hide away until she felt well again. For a fleeting moment she wondered if Eva had made the quilt. If she had it would add to the safe feeling that was stealing over her. Trixie knew she couldn't cope with life at the moment and she also realised how lucky she was to have someone who loved her, really loved her, as Jem loved her.

'Can I go to bed?'

'Of course.'

She thought of Mark and how shocked he must be. What would happen to her son now? *For he was her son*, there was no doubt at all in her mind. No wonder she had felt close to him. The bond between them would last for ever, wherever he went and whatever he did with the rest of his life.

A great feeling of calm descended over her. All those years ago when she'd been told her baby was stillborn, she'd known deep in her heart that it wasn't so.

The consolation was that Mark had been happy growing up. It was easy to believe that his parents – for the Barrs were his parents, maybe not his *birth* parents but still his mother and father – had loved him and given him a good life, and she was thankful for that. As to the future it was impossible to say what would happen. She could never enter his life as his mother any more than she could as the woman who had almost become his wife.

But from the bottom of her heart she wished him a future filled with love and happiness.

She prayed he would be able to rise above the gossip provided by the media. The newspapers were going to have a field day with this story. She shuddered. So, too, people would point their fingers at her. They would never let her live a normal life. Jem knew this and had brought her to this little house to escape. Well, she would hide here, for ever, if need be.

Someone was singing a very sad song. Its words cut through her heart like a knife through warm butter. Trixie put her hand to her face and realised she was crying and the singing came from her.

'Jem, will you stay with me until I sleep?'

'Just try and stop me,' he said.

Chapter Twenty-Seven

Jem took the ferry to the Isle of Wight. He saw the young boys at the end of the pier and watched as they accosted lone men. How had he never been aware of this practice before? A great feeling of sadness swept over him that in all probability Teddy had been forced to do this. He was even more sad that years had passed and although the boys had changed, the Meatrack still flourished.

At the tea kiosk he asked the man serving teas about the boys and drew a blank until the man realised he wasn't a copper.

'That bloke over there sitting on the steps, reading a newspaper – he's been with the boys for years. If he doesn't know anything you ain't going to find out sod all.'

There was a light breeze ruffling the pages of the newspaper and Jem waited until there were few people about before he went over and asked, 'Your name Mel?'

'Who wants to know?'

Jem took a few rolled up banknotes from his pocket and pressed them into the older man's hand. 'Don't worry, I'm not the law, but I'm trying to trace this lad.'

He took from his wallet the photo of Teddy that had been shown everywhere and put it in front of the man's face. 'I believe he worked here around the end of the war.'

'Little bleeder,' the bloke said. Recognition flooded his eyes.

'You know him?'

Mel laughed, showing brown-stained teeth. 'That little sod nearly cost me my job. He kicked the shit out of one of me best clients. Then he disappeared. Just as well he was never found. I'd have killed him, if I'd got 'old of him.'

So Teddy had escaped the Meatrack.

And disappeared.

When Jem got back late that night he found Dr Dillinger and Grandad sitting in the kitchen drinking whisky and talking about old times.

'Sleep's good for Trixie,' Dillinger said. 'It's a buffer between her and the terrible thing that's happened. But sooner or later you've got to get her interacting with the outside world again.'

'That's the trouble,' Grandad said. 'She said she ain't going out from that house ever again.'

Jem hurried down Stoke Road. It had just started to rain, it was market day and he was on his way to have a word with Bill Sansome at the plant stall about some bulbs that were being shipped over from Holland. He hoped Bill hadn't decided to stay at home like most customers when it rained.

The painting caught his eye as he hurried, head down, collar up, shielding himself from the blustery weather.

It depicted a gull hovering above a barrow and in the background the Dockyard Gates. Jem halted outside Frank Fisher's emporium and stared, mesmerised. Didn't Trixie own a similar print? The clean lines and the hovering bird with the sea close to the cart made him think of days gone by. The barrow was empty, tied to a bollard, but the whole picture seemed to call to him.

He opened the door, a bell chimed, and he stepped inside where the smell of turpentine, paint, and cleaning fluids greeted him. A small man stood beside a large desk examining another watercolour.

'There's a painting in your window, the gull. Could I have a closer look?'

Without a word the man drew back the curtain at the back of the window's showplace and brought it out, taking it to Jem.

Again, Jem couldn't explain why, but the picture held him in its thrall. He peered at the signature. Edward Somersby. The name meant nothing to him.

'The artist has found fame over the past ten years. This is only the third piece of his work that I've taken, but no sooner does a piece goes in the window than it's taken. He comes from the Isle of Wight and his work is always a variation on the same theme you see there. A cockle barrow, the Hard at Portsmouth, near the Dockyard Gates. This piece is called *Freedom*.'

Jem knew he had to buy the painting for Trixie.

'How much?'

Jem whistled when he heard the price but continued. 'I can give you a cheque. I appreciate you'd like a twenty-four-hour clearance on the money?'

The man nodded.

'Tomorrow evening then, could you deliver the painting?'

'That's not a problem, and thank you, sir.'

Jem wrote down his address, then shook the man's hand.

Outside, despite the rain, he felt elated. He was sure that the artist who had painted *Freedom* was Teddy. *Teddy was alive and living on the Isle of Wight.*

It was obvious now his previous searches had ended in failure because he'd looked in the wrong places. Teddy had made something of his life. It was time to start searching again.

Jem watched her face as she tore at the paper covering the picture. When it was free of its wrapping and she stood it in front of her her hands began to shake. Tears spilled fresh from her eyes.

'Is this some kind of cruel joke?'

Alarm flashed through Jem's mind. Of course, Trixie had no idea, any more than he himself had, that Teddy had made a career out of his childhood love of art.

'Is it a fake? I don't think so. It's very like the sketch you have.'

Her eyes met his. 'My brother's been missing so long I'm sure he must be dead.'

Jem took her in his arms. 'No, Trixie. If this is genuine, your brother is alive. The man I bought this from knows of the artist and of his success.'

She looked up at him. 'Can this really be my brother's work?'

'You have to tell me that.'

A tear spilled down her cheek. 'Somersby is a family name and the cart painted here means something that only I can know. I have a feeling this is genuine and that Teddy is alive and trying either to tell me something or to use the composition of the painting as a salve to his conscience. I've read that writers scratch the surface of their own skins to set down on the paper words that will reach out and touch the readers. Surely painters use their brushes to do the same?'

'It makes sense,' he said. 'You said he always sketched that part of Portsmouth.'

She was animated now. 'It's the winkle cart. This is the barrow we used to transport our father's body. It's not part of the scene and was never at any time left standing there. It's almost as if his work is making a statement about the death of our dad. Do you really believe Teddy's alive?'

'Apparently so. He's made a name for himself in the art world. And tomorrow you and I are going to find him.'

She seemed to shrink away from him. 'No, I can't leave this house.'

'Of course you can.'

She shook her head. 'No. You don't know what I feel like inside. Can you even begin to imagine my shame?'

He put his hands on her shoulders. 'Nothing that happened was your fault. And you'll only draw attention to yourself if you stay cooped up in here. We've all had to get through this as best we can.' He thought of Joan and Jack, open now about their friendship and growing love. The gossips had crowded the pub to get a look at the wife of Sid O'Hara, the man who had sold babies. Joan had straightened her back and stood tall, refusing to bow down beneath their gaze. She'd even suggested to Jack that the extra profits she'd provided should be used for them to take a holiday! But Trixie wasn't able to shrug life off like a wet overcoat. 'Now is the perfect time to leave, to make a new start. To find Teddy,' he begged.

'But...'

Jem swung away from her. 'Either you come with me tomorrow morning – I'll call for you at eight – or you forget you have a brother.' His voice was harsh and he hated himself for talking to her like that. But this state of affairs couldn't continue. Then he did the hardest thing he had ever done in his life. Despite his great love for her, he left her, crying as though her heart would break in two, and walked away.

'It's been a while since we travelled this road.' Trixie looked out of the car's window at the rolling fields one side and at the sea with choppy white-tipped waves on the other side.

'So you're speaking to me after my harsh words last night?'

'You *were* horrible,' said Trixie. 'But it was for my own good. I cried myself to sleep trying to convince myself the first step away from the safety of the house would be my salvation.'

Jem took a hand from the steering wheel and laid it across her arm. She could feel the warmth seeping through her. 'I've only ever wanted what was best for you,' he said. Trixie looked across and smiled at him. She realised now what a dear, dear man he was.

The small town at the edge of the sea was bathed in sunshine. White buildings hung over the edge of the cliff, their colour set off with tubs of red pelargoniums.

'I reckon we walk from here,' Jem said. He drew the car to a halt and helped her from the front seat. He'd told her he'd spent the evening before telephoning to find exactly where the artist, Edward Somersby, lived. He wanted to clarify that Edward Somersby and Teddy were one and the same person. And that Teddy was eager to meet his sister again. For Teddy to refuse to meet Trixie would have crucified her.

'I've got butterflies in my stomach,' she said. She could see a sandy beach below them and a house set apart with hanging baskets and tubs of flowers. She pulled her grey skirt straight to her suit and then bent and rubbed smudges of dust from her high-heeled shoes. How would Teddy be? Would he remember her? Was he feeling as nervous as she was right now?

'Is this really the house where he lives?' They'd walked through the gate facing the sea. A grey cat lay in the shade asleep and barely noted their presence. 'It's a dream of a house,' Trixie said.

Jem rang the doorbell and after what seemed an eternity yet she knew was only seconds the door opened and Teddy stood there.

His blond hair was faded, yet flicked across his forehead much as it had always done. He was tall and slim, and oh, how like their mother he was, with her gentle eyes and ready-to-smile mouth.

'Come in and welcome,' he said. Then he moved aside to let them pass, but it was as if he suddenly changed his mind and he turned and grabbed hold of Trixie and hugged her until she almost begged for breath. 'You don't know how often I've wanted to hold my sister,' he said. 'I thought I'd never see you again.' He released her and shook Jem's hand, pumping his arm energetically. 'Thank you for reuniting us. Good to see you again,' he said.

Trixie was unable to stop her tears. 'I thought you were dead.'

Jem turned back to the open door and stepped outside, but Teddy pulled him back. 'And where d'you think you're off to?'

'You two have years to catch up on and I don't want to be in the way. I'll go for a walk and if I may, return later?'

'Of course,' said Teddy. This time he let Jem pass.

'All these years,' whispered Trixie. 'Why didn't you get in touch with me?'

'I knew you were making a name for yourself, singing, and the last thing you needed was to be embroiled in a court case about your brother killing your father. I couldn't run the risk of Sid O'Hara turning nasty and I had no idea of his whereabouts or even whether he was dead or alive.'

He led her into a sitting room, light and airy with paintings covering the walls – his work. The furniture was expensive and comfortable. He began talking. He sat her down in an easy chair and gradually, little by little, they shared their life stories. When she told him their father was still alive, his shocked face was almost too much for her to bear.

'How would you feel about seeing him, Teddy?' Trixie asked.

'Having believed he was dead, and now finding out he's not it's a lot to take in. I think I really need to think long and hard about that,' said Teddy.

'I feel exactly the same,' said Trixie.

'All these years we've lived a lie,' Teddy said. 'But I always knew where you were and what you were doing.' He got up from his chair and went into another room, only to come back moments later with a large book that he put on her lap. She opened it and turned the pages to find it was a scrapbook, chronicling all the gigs she'd ever done. Cuttings from newspapers tumbled to the floor. Trixie had never felt so humbled.

'You kept these because of me?' Her voice was little more than a whisper.

'Oh, Trixie, I've been so proud of you. I've followed your career and it was almost like being with you.' His eyes were downcast, but already Trixie had caught the glitter of tears in them. Teddy went from the room to find tissues and Trixie looked about her. On the top of a grand piano were photographs of a man. A fine chiselled chin and honest eyes stared back at her. From the way the photos were given pride of place, Trixie could see the man was well loved.

'Who's that?' She took the tissues Teddy held out towards her.

She saw the tears spring to his eyes again. 'That's the man I loved.' His voice was proud, yet gentle and held so much emotion. He sat down again next to her. She took hold of his hands. 'He died earlier this year,' Teddy said. 'If it hadn't been for Rafe I'd have died long ago,' he whispered, sadly. 'The Meatrack would have killed me.' He grew silent and Trixie decided she wouldn't push him, she'd let him talk about Rafe in his own time.

'And where does Jem fit in to all this?' Teddy asked.

Trixie began talking and she thought she'd never stop. 'That man has been a tower of strength to me,' she said, realising at last the truth of her words. 'He found your painting and helped me interpret it. By making a reoccurring theme of the winkle cart in your work you were working

376

through your own traumas from that night, weren't you?' Trixie looked at him, for the first time seeing the man and not the child.

'Whether you did it intentionally or not, I daresay it helped you to come to terms with the past. I simply fell to bits. Depression claimed me.'

'But your lovely voice,' he said. 'Didn't your success with your singing show that you could pour your emotions about Dad into your work?'

She sighed, 'I don't think I'm as strong or as clever as you. All I know is that I've taken Jem for granted all these years and it's about time I realised how fortunate I am to have a man like that loving me.' Then she smiled at her brother. 'It's taken a long time for us to find each other, Teddy. Please say we'll never be parted again. I couldn't bear to lose you after all we've been through.' She was quiet for a moment, then gripped his hand. 'I have good friends in Gosport.' She thought of Marie and Dmitri and Joan and Grandad. 'You must meet them. Auntie Joan turned out to be a real gem. And you're invited to a wedding, if you'd like to come,' she said. 'Marie and Dmitri are planning on getting married.' Trixie thought of her friends and how lucky she was to have them care about her.

A gentle tapping on the window caused her to look round and she saw Jem smiling at Teddy. The grey cat was happily lying in Jem's arms, looking as though it was determined to be part of the reconciliation.

'I've a feeling you have something to talk to Jem about.'

Trixie knew she was blushing.

'I'll put the kettle on and set the table for a meal, unless you'd like something stronger than tea?' Teddy had raised his eyebrows.

Trixie shook her head. 'Tea's fine.' She went out to greet Jem and slipped her arm through his – the one not holding the cat, who was now purring so loudly it was almost drowning out the gentle sound of the sea tumbling upon the shore. The scent of the geraniums was overpowering and she was reminded of Granny Tillotson, the animist who lived in the New Forest, and her wise words that Trixie would lose someone close to her and find someone. Well, it had certainly come true. She'd lost her son, the son she never knew she had, but time would tell whether they'd ever be reunited. And she'd found her brother and at last true love with Jem.

'Everything all right?' Jem asked. The cat jumped to the wall and sat washing itself in the sun.

'Not really,' Trixie said. She saw his eyes darken and a frown gather on his face. 'Do you realise that all these years you've cared about me and I've never thanked you?'

'I care because I love you. I always have and always will.'

'Can we be married?'

He looked at her as though she had made him the happiest man on the island. 'Only if you tell me you love me, Trixie True.'

He bent his head down and she tasted the slightly salty taste of his lips. His fingers tousled her hair, and she smelled his cologne, sweet and safe. As safe as she knew Jem would always keep her. Tears, born of passion and pleasure, spilled down her cheeks. 'I love you, Jem. Oh, how I love you.'

Acknowledgements

A big thank you to my agent, Juliet Burton, and to Laura Gerrard, my editor, and to everyone at Orion for their unfailing support.

The publishers hope that this book has given you enjoyable reading. Large Print Books are especially designed to be as easy to see and hold as possible. If you wish a complete list of our books please ask at your local library or write directly to:

Magna Large Print Books
Magna House, Long Preston,
Skipton, North Yorkshire.
BD23 4ND

This Large Print Book for the partially sighted, who cannot read normal print, is published under the auspices of

THE ULVERSCROFT FOUNDATION

THE ULVERSCROFT FOUNDATION

... we hope that you have enjoyed this Large Print Book. Please think for a moment about those people who have worse eyesight problems than you ... and are unable to even read or enjoy Large Print, without great difficulty.

You can help them by sending a donation, large or small to:

**The Ulverscroft Foundation,
1, The Green, Bradgate Road,
Anstey, Leicestershire, LE7 7FU,
England.**
or request a copy of our brochure for more details.

The Foundation will use all your help to assist those people who are handicapped by various sight problems and need special attention.

Thank you very much for your help.